I0736839

Division One:
Head Games

by Stephanie Osborn

Chromosphere Press

Huntsville, AL

Head Games
© 2019 Stephanie Osborn
ISBN 978-1-947530-09-6 (print)
ISBN 978-1-947530-08-9 (ebook)
Cover art © 2019 Darrell Osborn
Fiction

First electronic edition 2019

This is a work of fiction. All concepts, characters and events portrayed in this book are used fictitiously and any resemblance to real people or events is purely coincidental.

Chromosphere Press
POBox 252
56 Hughes Road
Madison, AL 35758
www.chromospherepress.com

Table of Contents

Chapter 1

When the Alpha One team finally arrived back at PGLEIA Division One Headquarters from their successful assignment, they smiled at each other, weary but satisfied and happy, and by unspoken consent headed immediately for the living quarters, bypassing the Alpha Line Room. It was very late, well past the end of their shift; they were tired, and they were ready to crash soon. Debriefs and reports could wait until the morning; the mission had not been difficult, but the travel time was long.

As they walked, no word was said. But the tall, dark-haired, experienced male Agent glanced, with warm dark eyes in which was a hint of a smile, at his colleague, a trim, athletic platinum blonde in a French braid. In turn, she flashed him a smile with eyes that glowed like sapphires. They continued on their silent way.

Upon reaching their adjacent quarters, however, the man bypassed his own door and accompanied his companion into her apartment. He closed the door behind them. Then he turned to her, and the smile spread from his eyes to his mouth as he stepped forward, reaching for her.

"They're here," an authoritative voice suddenly announced, and the two Agents were abruptly besieged.

"Echo, m' man!" exclaimed a handsome young black man, "what'd th' pretty lady say? She said yes, right?"

"Where is it? Let me see," insisted a beautiful Afro-Asian woman with striking amber eyes.

"Son, did it go the way we hoped?" a tall Apache woman in black scrubs and with a long, sleek black braid wondered, even as a brunette attired in identical black scrubs stepped forward, smiling eagerly.

"So tell me, Echo, Omega," the Director remarked, putting an arm around the brunette for a moment, "do I need to change the status of Alpha One?"

"Calm down, everybody," Echo said, raising his hands for silence. "Meg?"

The lovely blonde in the black Suit, who stood beside him, held out her left hand. A glimmering bauble on her ring finger sparkled in the light.

"Is this what y'all wanted to see?" Omega asked in a soft Southern drawl, a gentle smile lighting her features.

"Oh, Meg, it's beautiful!" India breathed, staring at the star-shaped hyperdiamond solitaire, and taking her friend's hand in her fingers, turning it from side to side to watch as the facets of the stone caught the light. "Congratulations, girlfriend!" The two women embraced.

"Way ta go, Echo, bro!" The black man clapped his ex-partner on the shoulder. "You got good taste, man!"

"I thought so, Romeo," Echo deadpanned, and raised an eyebrow. "I take it you and India approve?"

"Damn straight!" Romeo grinned, moving to join the women in a group hug. The Apache woman eased closer to Echo, taking his elbow in her hands with affection. Echo glanced down at her, and she smiled. He returned the expression, then gave his attention to the Director.

"What about you, Fox?" Echo asked his superior quietly. "Do you...approve? Meg IS my partner, after all..."

"Echo," Fox replied with a smile, "after all this time? Of course I approve, zun! I've never seen you or Omega happier. I know you fought this for a long time, old friend, and I understand why. Working so long for Chase, only to have her turn to another man, then both of 'em be killed by your old enemy...I don't blame you for being leery of another relationship. And I know that things kind of took a while to get off the ground once you finally quit fighting it, because the two of you kept talking past each other! I know, because I watched it happen! But I'm very pleased to see you both so happy now." Fox paused thoughtfully. "As far as the blend of business life and personal life—you know as well as I do, Echo, Division One person-nel—on Earth, at least—wouldn't have a personal life otherwise. Witness Zebra and myself!" He smiled at the brunette in scrubs, who leaned into him with loving appreciation. "And it took me a couple of decades to find HER! After all, the general population isn't supposed to know about us until they're ready to be made aware of the larger galactic community...we found THAT out the hard way, during the Klydonian invasion a few years back. But I do think it'll be rather interesting to see how your teamwork is affected by your private relationship. You already work more closely together than just about any other team we've got, and I can't think but what it's only going to get better. I'll upgrade your status to 'life partnership' first thing tomorrow. Or, well, as soon as I come up for air, I guess; it's almost time for the monthly division leads meeting, I'm afraid, and Bravo and Lima have me up to my eyeballs with prepping for it."

"Yeah, I get it. That works. I assume this," he waved his hand at the gathered agents, "is your doing, Fox? Or is it Ma's? The two of you were, I THOUGHT, the only ones who knew I was gonna do this..."

"It was mine, son," Dihl, the Apache medtech and Echo's birth mother, confessed in a quiet voice. "I hope you are not offended."

"No, Ma," Echo said with the ghost of a smile. He shot a quick glance at Omega, who reflected his expression, then added, "...Neither of us is offended. We just..."

"Didn't expect a welcoming committee!" Omega finished for him with a laugh.

"Well, Dihl came to me and we discussed it," Fox admitted. "And we got to thinking that, what with everything that's been happening lately," here he shot a meaningful look at Omega, who nodded understanding and tucked her head, flushing slightly, "maybe it warranted 'the family' making a big deal out of it, to make sure you BOTH understood how pleased we are about it. So she gave Alpha Two a heads-up, and I told Zebra, and..."

"Here we are," Zebra concluded. "We care, guys. I know—

WE know—the two of you are really reserved, and we're not trying to embarrass you, I swear we're not. And we haven't told anybody else, 'cause that's YOUR business. We just wanted you both to know that we're happy for you, we love you, and we want the best for you."

"The truth is, we were also kinda worried," India pointed out. "After everything Meg's been through lately, we were afraid she might have...said no."

"In all honesty?" Omega murmured. "If it hadn't been for Echo's solution of using Zz'r'p as my counselor, and last night Zz'r'p removing the telepathic programming module that Tt'l'k inserted who knows when...well, um, I might have. I, I, well," she flushed, even as a flash of pain crossed Echo's face, "let's just say it had me convinced that, that I wasn't...wanted. Like, anywhere. By anybody."

"Which couldn't be farther from the truth, baby," Echo told her in a low voice.

"I know that...now," she asserted, laying her hand on his forearm in a gentle, soothing fashion. "At least...well, I'm... still struggling with some of it. But that's what the counseling is for."

"Right," Zebra agreed. "And that starts tomorrow. Try to be open and willing to consider things from other viewpoints, honey, and I think you'll start to develop a new perspective on...everything."

"I will," Omega averred.

"So Mr. an' Ms. Badass done gone an' got engaged," Romeo said with a wide grin. "That is some FINE news, guys. I can't tell ya how happy we are for ya, India an' me."

"It shows, Junior. And thanks; Meg and I both appreciate it. What's the word on convening the Sydys Concordat council?" Echo asked then. "To get something a little more...formal...on our record?"

"Pressing forward, Echo," Fox responded. "I submitted the request, and appended the rationale, along with the three of us," he indicated himself, Romeo and Echo, "as principal petitioners. Well, I added all six of us, if the truth be known—because together, we comprise the Director, the Assistant Chief of Medical, the Alpha Line Chief, the Alpha Line Assistant Chief, the Alpha Line backup lead, and the Alpha Line medic! None of us are exactly slouches, or personnel to be taken lightly. And that adds a lot of weight to the petition, weight which I can already tell you has been noticed...at the highest levels. So. With a little luck, we'll have the Division One charter for Earth amended within a few months, and Alpha One—and Alpha Two, if they want—can walk down the aisle together. Along with Zebra and myself." He put an arm around the dark-haired physician, who was his own life partner.

"Sounds good, Fox," a soft, feminine voice remarked behind the two men, and they turned. Omega stood there, smiling at both men, but with eyes only for Echo. "We can't really set a date until the charter is amended, anyway." She looked at Fox, and blushed slightly. "Fox...can I ask a favor?"

"Of course, Omega."

"Um...when Echo and I do 'tie the knot'...will you give me away?"

A startled Fox paused and abruptly dropped his gaze, staring at the floor. Echo watched his oldest friend, and grinned slightly: He had never seen Fox completely speechless before. The room was silent, in deference to the Director's uncharacteristically emotional response. Finally Fox looked up.

"...I'd be honored, Omega, tekhter." He offered her a slight smile, more than a hint of pride in it.

"Good." Omega beamed. "That's settled, then. I've already asked India to be my maid of honor. Echo? Did you—?"

"Not yet, Meg," Echo answered. "Ma? I know this is kinda unusual, but Meg and I talked about it on the way home a bit ago, and...well, just like Fox is gonna walk her down the aisle, I was hoping you'd walk with me up to the altar, too." He shrugged. "What with you joining the Agency medlab a couple months ago, we sorta got each other back after all these years, and I'd really like you to be part of the ceremony."

"Oh, my brave Apache warrior, I would be delighted," Dihl, the newest Headquarters—and, of late, the Ranch—medtech, murmured, and hugged her son.

"Good," Echo said with a wide smile, turning to Romeo. "That's settled, then. Junior? Let's you and me talk for a minute..."

* * *

At last the friends and colleagues—the adoptive family, as well as some legitimate family such as Echo's mother, which Omega had gathered about herself—prepared to depart. A smirking Romeo nudged Echo, off to the side.

"Guess it's time we got th' hell out, huh?"

"Well, it's been a long, busy day, hot shot," Echo commented with a slight, tired smile.

"An' looks like bein' a busy night," Romeo grinned slyly. "Betcha gonna get a special look at that little blue silk number India an' I gave th' pretty lady for her birthday."

Echo's face suddenly resumed its customary expressionless mask.

* * *

"Romeo," he said firmly, "let's get something straight. Meg is an old-fashioned, Southern lady. And I like to think I'm an old-fashioned gentleman. And I put a hyperdiamond ring on her finger tonight. If it's any of your business, what does that tell you?"

Romeo stared blankly at Echo; the older Agent could see realization dawning in his gaze.

* * *

"Thaaat...it's gonna be a while before ya see th' little blue number?" Romeo tried then, feeling sheepish.

Echo raised his eyebrows as Romeo felt a sharp tap on his shoulder. He glanced behind himself.

"Go home, Romeo," Omega said pointedly, if good-naturedly. "You handle your relationship with India. Echo and I will see to our own."

"C'mon, Romeo." A mildly-embarrassed India—if the tawny flush in her deep buff skin was anything to go by—grabbed her partner's arm. "Let's go. Echo and Meg probably want to TALK anyway." She emphasized the word.

A thoroughly-chastised Romeo allowed himself to be towed toward the front door.

* * *

"Don't forget, Meg has her first counseling session with Zz'r'p in the morning," Zebra reminded, as she and Fox headed for the front door, Alpha Two right behind. Dihl had already slipped through the 'back door' between Omega's and Echo's quarters, to access the classified 'warp escape tunnels' via Echo's closet, in order to keep secret her relationship to Echo—Omega had already been targeted by Echo's old enemies; no one wanted his mother in the same situation.

"Right," Echo recalled. "Meg?"

"I haven't forgotten. I'd already planned for it, Ace," Omega averred. "I already did the paperwork to let Zz'r'p have files pertinent to...everything."

"Oh, was that what you were doing on my tablet during the trip down?" Echo wondered.

"Bingo," she replied.

"Well, good, then," he decided.

"VERY good," Fox said, opening the door. "I cannot tell you how glad I am to hear that, and personally even more than professionally. Your family has been worried about you, tekhter. And once more...congratulations to you both."

The addendum was echoed by the others.

And they were gone.

As the front door of Omega's quarters closed, Echo turned to his partner, pulling her close.

"Finally," Echo remarked.

Omega merely smiled.

* * *

"Ace, um, I mean Echo...no, I think this needs to be... Alex," Omega decided as she addressed her partner and fiancé a bit later, when they came up for air, "Alex, I think it's time

7

for me to...I mean, there's something I've been meaning to do, except I didn't know how to do it, and it was never the right time, only now..." A distracted and decidedly uncertain Omega ran a hand over her face and up into her hair, dislodging several strands from the braid. "Oh, just come in here a sec..."

"What is it, baby?" a puzzled Echo wondered, following her as she rose from the sofa and headed toward her bedroom. "Is everything okay? Do you want to tell me something, or need me to do something?"

"Everything's fine, and neither," Omega said, offering him a slight smile as she moved to her dresser and knelt. She pulled open the bottom right drawer and reached into the back corner, extracting a small rosewood box. "I just...I need to give you something." She stood and turned toward him.

"I...don't get it," he said in puzzlement, watching her.

"You will, in a minute," she told him. "See, this is...well, I'm not sure how far back this goes," she admitted. "I know it goes back at least to Grandma and Grandpa, but it might go back a good bit farther. It's hard to tell for sure, Mom didn't know, and I've never had it appraised..."

Omega opened the little rosewood box, and a silver pendant on a chain lay there on an antiqued, slightly faded blue velvet lining. It was a simple cross with some engraved scroll-work on the ends—made of obviously antique silver, as it was fairly hefty, and considerably worn to a soft, satiny finish—on a heavy curb chain. She reached into the box and lifted it out carefully.

"This is a family heirloom," she said. "Best I had it to understand, Grandma got it from her parents and gave it to Grandpa when they got engaged. Mom got it from them and gave it to Dad when THEY got engaged. Daddy was wearing it when their car crashed...or, more likely, was dropped...and the police gave it to me in his effects. I found this box in their stuff at the house, and the cross fits in it perfectly, so I think it all went together. So I had the necklace cleaned, and kept it in here. I dunno how many generations it goes back, but I sorta suspect it might date from as far back as sometime kinda early in the Victorian era, based on the style of the cross and the scrollwork. I've been wanting to give this to you for a year now, I just...I didn't...I was afraid you'd...that you'd..."

"You didn't know how," Echo realized. "It has a traditional, romantic significance for your family, and until the last few weeks, we didn't have that kind of relationship."

"Right," Omega said, in obvious relief that he understood. "I mean, I knew I loved you, and I knew there was never gonna be anybody else, not really, and...see, I wanted it to get passed on somehow, even if we didn't develop THIS kinda relationship, but, but I mean, only...well, I didn't know how you'd... take it." She bit her lip and looked up at him.

"And now you do," Echo said softly, watching her with a smile. "I'm...more honored than I can say, sweetheart."

They had already divested holsters, jackets, and ties some time earlier, unbuttoning collars for comfort, and now Echo undid the top several buttons of his shirt, pulling it open, then knelt before his partner, enabling her to easily slip the chain over his head without having to unfasten the clasp. The cross rested lightly against his upper sternum, in the cleft between his well-defined pectoral muscles, and she smiled.

"There," she murmured, patting it lightly with her fingertips. "That's perfect. I knew it would look...right...there."

Echo adjusted his shirt as he stood, then took her into his arms.

"And now *I* am a member of YOUR family," he breathed into her ear.

"You always were, I think," Omega declared, right before he kissed her.

* * *

Omega was intensely nervous when she got up the next morning; it was time for her first counseling session after the stalking and attempted rape by the other 'augmented human' which Echo's old enemy, Slug, had created. It had been bad enough, she considered, when she discovered that she had been extensively modified in a highly cruel fashion by the psychopathic gastropoid who became known as Slug—the alien criminal had performed wholesale reconstruction surgery on her pre-teen body, essentially from crown to sole, without the use of any anesthesia or means of pain relief...among other forms of modification. Then he had used his innate telepathy to brainwash the young Megan McAllister into forgetting...until the trigger that had unleashed an assassin program, buried deep in her mind. Echo was still alive only because she had fought desperately against the programming until Alpha Two could arrive and disable said programming. Zz'r'p, the Deltiri ambassador from the Arcturus system—the Deltiri were natural telepaths as much as the gastropoid Snails—had subsequently deprogrammed her, unleashing her memories of the torture in the process.

But when Mark Wright—the man Slug had chosen for her mate whether either of them wanted it or not—had shown up mere weeks earlier and tried to rape her under the influence of his own telepathic programming, it had been the last straw. More than a year of discovering the ramifications to those modifications came to a head as a result. Rather severe posttraumatic stress had manifested, and Omega found herself in a steep downward mental and emotional spiral.

Fortunately, Echo had realized that Zz'r'p, the same telepathic Deltiri who had deprogrammed her, a close friend—as well as the entity who had trained Omega in her budding mental abilities, brought about by those same 'enhancements'—was himself a certified counselor. More, he already knew much of Omega's personal, private history—partly as a result of training her, and partly from having to deprogram her. This knowledge obviated the need for her to explain all of the painful details to a complete stranger.

This had proven an acceptable option to Omega's pained and humiliated heart and mind, and only two days before, she had agreed to meet with the ambassador—to the considerable relief of those close to her, who had begun to fear where her rapid emotional deterioration might lead.

The fact that a mentally-ill Deltiri had inserted telepathic programing while she slept, designed to exacerbate that deterioration, had not helped matters in the least. However, Zz'r'p had suspected precisely that, and was able, with Omega's permission, to 'delete' the programming...which had improved her mental outlook immensely.

But Zz'r'p did not yet know all—no living being other than Omega did, as yet, though Echo knew more than anyone else—and the counseling would require that Zz'r'p learn everything. In fact, she had had to give him access to her medical records, in lieu of telling him some of it herself. It was the easiest way for her to do it, she considered, as she would neither have to vocalize it nor depict it telepathically. However, it also meant she was going into the counseling session blind as regarded Zz'r'p's reaction to that information. This produced no little trepidation in the female Agent while she prepared for her day.

"Aw, c'mon, baby," Echo encouraged over breakfast, at which Omega only picked despite her best efforts. "It's Zz'r'p. He's your buddy, your mental-skills mentor. He KNOWS you. It'll be okay."

"I know, Echo," she said, subdued. "And I'm...pretty sure... you're right, and it really WILL be okay. I'm just not looking forward to it, that's all. It's bad enough to have it all in the back of my mind. It's worse to have to actively remember it. Never mind discuss it with somebody else."

"Well, lemme throw the dishes in the dishwasher, then we'll grab our weapons and our jackets, and I'll walk you to his office before I head for ours. Will that at least help a little?"

"Yeah, Ace, that'd be nice," Omega admitted, throwing him a slight smile.

* * *

Echo waited with Omega as she knocked on the door of Zz'r'p's personal office inside the Arcturan embassy, on one of the middle floors of Headquarters. "Come in," the Deltiri's muffled voice said, and Omega glanced up at her partner and fiancé.

"Here we go," she murmured.

"Unlax, baby," Echo soothed. "I think it won't be as bad as you're afraid it will be."

"Probably not," Omega agreed, and leaned up to meet his kiss as he bent his head to deliver it. "I'll see you in a bit, in the Alpha Line Room."

"Roger that," and Echo was gone.

A grim Omega turned and entered Zz'r'p's office.

* * *

"There you are, my friend," Zz'r'p said, getting up from his desk chair and coming around to meet her. "You are nervous?"

"Well, yeah," Omega confessed as the tall, blue, fishlike alien led her to a small cluster of comfortable armchairs in the corner. "All things considered, I can't help it. I guess...let's go ahead and broach the main thing, and get it over with, if you don't mind..."

"Go ahead, then."

"Okay. Have you had a chance to look at my medical records?"

"I have. I have studied them in some detail." Zz'r'p watched her, and she knew he was surface-reading her reactions. "And this is what frightens you most."

"Um, yeah." Omega bent her head and made a business of sitting in the chair Zz'r'p offered, adjusting her trousers and jacket as he moved to take his own seat. "The, uh, the genetic augmentation?"

"Yes, I have seen it."

"And?"

"So?"

"Do you understand the implications?" Omega wondered. "What it means Slug was trying to do?"

"I discussed it with Zebra, and with Dihl," Zz'r'p noted, and Omega winced. "I know what they believe. What I should like to know now is what YOU believe."

"Well, it isn't really what I believe," Omega said, stifling a sigh. "It's what I now KNOW to be the case."

"Is this something that Zebra knows, that Dihl knows?"

"No. Or, well, I doubt it. Because it took me a while to dredge it all out, and some of it, I only discovered in Mark Wright's mind. It...sorta filled in some puzzle pieces for me. I'd suspected for a long time, but didn't quite understand, and that...confirmed it."

"Tell me, if you can."

Omega drew a deep breath.

"So, Slug...he wanted a highly-intelligent...animal," Omega said, voice low. She chose a point on the floor and stared at it with fixed, unfocused, unseeing gaze, unwilling to meet the Deltiri's eyes, afraid of what she might see there. "He specifically did NOT want a 'real' human. He wanted a custom-built creature BASED ON a human template that he could control, that was smart enough and capable of doing enough, to pass as a human. So, after obtaining certain, um...classic fantasy literature from Earth—though I'm still not sure how a being with no eyes could 'read' it—he had the idea to take a live human... and, and corrupt it, degrade it, debase it, while simultaneously making it stronger, faster, smarter, more cunning, more capable...until he could make it do anything he wanted it to do, and still give the appearance of being human. More, of being an EXCEPTIONAL human. All while still being a monstrous, depraved...beast." She paused. "I'm sure you saw the suspected origins of the various genetic material he used."

"Yes..."

"Then you know that he chose to use some of the most disgusting creatures in the galaxy, at least from a humanoid perspective," Omega pointed out. "And he located the specific genes he wanted expressed, extracted them, put them into me, and forced their expression."

She finally looked up at the alien telepath. Her normally-expressive, bright blue eyes were subdued, the light in them gone, dull in a pale, almost gray face.

"I'm that monstrous creature, Zz'r'p," she confessed. This

time she met his gaze, straightforward, if intensely pained. "Look into my memories. You can see it. You can see when I began to realize it, back when Zebra first showed me the genetic studies. And you can see when I started to suspect the full extent not that long afterward, and then when I found the missing puzzle pieces in Wright's mind, in his memories."

She waited and watched as the Deltiri's large eyes defocused, and she felt the gentle touch of his mind in hers. Finally his eyes focused on her face again, and he nodded.

"Yes, Omega, my child," he murmured. "I see it, and I see the steps in your logic, and I cannot fault it. You are most likely correct."

Omega sighed.

"I'm waiting," she said.

"For what?"

"Doesn't it...disgust you?"

* * *

"I suppose that depends on what you reference," Zz'r'p said, leaning back in his chair and considering. "And since I can see that in your mind, I know that you are really referencing yourself. So let me answer you: no...and yes."

Omega blinked, patently confused.

"Explain, please," she requested. "I'm...I don't understand. How can it be yes AND no?"

"I find what Azeln—Slug—did to be disgusting, abhorrent," Zz'r'p admitted with distaste. "Even insane as he was, mad with grief and the neural feedback from the death of his symbiote wife and unborn children, there is still NO excuse for such atrocities. There can BE no excuse. However," the telepath continued, "he failed."

"Huh? What do you mean, 'he failed'? I'm here," Omega said, tilting her head and staring at him, narrow-eyed.

"Precisely. You ARE here, and so is Echo," Zz'r'p pointed out. "Through no less than three known plans—one primary, and at least two backup—which Slug laid down. As well as who knows how many variants he may have laid out to spin off from those three, in order to accommodate any variables introduced. You and Echo are HERE. Because you fought, and successfully overcame, ALL of his planning, all of his work. Yes, you had help...from the people who came to care about you, those who now consider you family. More, you are not only still accepted throughout the galaxy as a Division One agent, you are an Alpha Line Agent, known AND RESPECT-ED across that galaxy. And not merely AN Agent, but the assistant chief of that department, and in all likelihood, its future chief. You, my dear child, are the number two Agent on the entire planet, and likely in the entire Division, second only to your partner, who has many years more experience. You are fierce in your defense of the right; temperate, rational, and compassionate in your pursuit of law. No law-abiding being need have any fear of you...ever. Why? Because you and your partner will always ferret out the truth. Even those who have wronged you personally receive compassion and mercy at your hands—as Alpha Seven and Eight have reason to know. You are beloved in the Agency—your birthday party only days ago demonstrated that—you are revered on several worlds and admired on many more. You are, as you and Echo so like to term it, a badass Agent...but with a gentle, loving heart, and a sense of overall RIGHT, of morality, which is every bit an equal to those you love best." Zz'r'p cocked his head. "So please explain to me how this makes you a depraved, debased beast."

Omega stared at him, eyes wide.

"Holy shit," she said blankly.

Zz'r'p grinned.

* * *

Omega arrived in the Alpha Line Room a little while later with a thoughtful expression on her face, Echo concluded, watching her enter in silence and sit in her desk chair in the front of the room, to the left of the large Division One and Alpha Line logos, opposite his own desk to the right.

She seems relaxed, at least, he decided. *I guess it must have gone well. She looks like she's thinking things over, though. I*

15

won't ask her how it went; she'll tell me when she's ready. Let her ponder it on her own; ultimately, she's gotta resolve everything in her own mind. And while I can and will help support her, I can't help her with THAT.

So he gave her a few minutes to settle in, then turned in his desk chair.

"New batch of Alpha Line applications here," he said, patting a stack of paperwork. "Go ahead and make a cup of coffee," he nodded at the pod brewer on the credenza along the front wall, "and let's have a look, what do you say?"

"Sounds good to me, Ace," Omega said, throwing him a smile and reaching for her mug.

* * *

The *Hsshthh*, or as other species knew it, the *Winged Serpent*, flagship of Galactic Coalition President Pulgey Entiyti, slid smoothly into its berth in the orbital dockyard over his home planet of Emdali, also known as Draigon. The Draconan lord had returned home, as he did every year, in order to observe an ancient and very special holiday on Emdali: the anniversary of the day several millennia before, when the planet's two sentient races, the Draconan and the Reptoids, made a permanent peace between their peoples. It had been the beginning of the planet's rise to the galactic community, a rise which some said culminated in its most famous nobleman being made Coalition President, not just once, but twice. It could not be denied that Lord Entiyti was much loved, not only on Emdali, but on most of the worlds of the Galactic Coalition.

More, Lord Entiyti was meeting an old and dear friend on Emdali, a Reptoid, one Suud Guurn, who had once upon a time been his chief bodyguard, succeeding the only human ever to have filled that position, Franz Levy of Earth—an even older friend of the galactic president.

Entiyti smiled as he debarked with only a small guard contingent. He was glad that the days when he felt he needed such a heavy guard unit were behind him.

Better yet, the Draconan thought, *I shall be able to stretch my wings for a change, perhaps even spend a day or three at the glide park, simply enjoying the wind over my scales. That will feel marvelous; I do get so tired, some days, of the confinement of governmental buildings and spacecraft. I never get to flex my wings.* The leathery 'cloak' hanging from his shoulders arched slightly at the thought, as he strode across the gangway and into the concourse of the orbiting spaceport, a wide and cheerful smile gracing his flat, broad face.

In his eagerness to return to his homeworld, Entiyti moved out at some considerable speed, headed for the private shuttle area that would take him and his small entourage of three guards down to the planet's surface. The guard unit, a mix of several species—one Reptoid, Uussa Cuuseer by name, and future daughter-in-law to the being Entiyti planned to visit; one Lambda Andromedan, Goobop Ogoobah; and one Wintourn, called Sigrund Dalgaard, currently Entiyti's chief bodyguard—scurried to keep up.

"This way," he called to the guards, as he turned the corner into the smaller corridor that led to the shuttle berths. "My personal shuttlecraft will be waiting."

"Milord! Slow down!" the Wintourn exclaimed. "Let us lead!"

"Ah, there is no need," Entiyti said, and laughed. "I am HOME, my friends! I am in no danger!"

But he was wrong.

* * *

The sudden roar and blast of heat took them all by surprise. Lord Entiyti, the Wintourn guard, and the Reptoid guard, both of whom were trying to flank Entiyti, were thrown across the concourse, slamming into the far wall; the Lambda Andromedan bodyguard, who had been guarding the rear, was knocked down. The Reptoid lay where she fell, her head canted at an odd angle relative to her body. Lord Entiyti sprawled awkwardly in a growing pool of cerise-tinted blood, moaning softly. The Wintourn, one arm dangling at an unnatural angle, rose to a crouch and drew his weapon in his good hand with a suppressed grunt of pain, even as the Lambda Andromedan picked himself up from the floor and ran to join his fellow.

"Goobop, check Uussa," guard chief Dalgaard growled, scanning the area for hostiles. The Lambda Andromedan diverted for a quick check of their downed comrade, then shook his head.

"She is dead, Sigrund," Goobop replied. "It looks like her neck broke."

"Uskit'r," Sigrund cursed. "Lord Entiyti?"

"He is still alive, but he is hurt badly. One wing is shredded, and it is nearly ripped off anyway. How bad are you?"

"Ugh," Dalgaard grunted. "I'll live. I may need some cybernetic work after this, though. See if you can stanch the bleeding on milord's wing until we can obtain help. And call the *Hsshthh*; tell them to send reinforce—"

Just then, a projectile slammed into the bulkhead between Goobop and Dalgaard, only inches above Entiyti's prone body. Both bodyguards instinctively ducked, but spun and brought their weapons to bear.

Suddenly the entire corridor—which had been oddly empty when they entered, and what few other beings had been there had run in fear at the explosion—erupted in a storm of projectiles and energy beams. Goobop reached out with one tentacle and grabbed Dalgaard, yanking him down, even as the Lambda Andromedan's other two 'arms' gathered Entiyti and pulled the downed leader's body under his own, shielding it. Then the Lambda Andromedan used those long, strong, flexible arms to grab anything within reach and pull it in front of them for cover; this included a large planter with a dead plant, a bench, a waste disposal container, and a metal table, which he upended.

"There," Goobop noted. "That will help...a little."

"Yeah. It won't shield us much, but at least it breaks up our outlines."

"The planter should be good, however; it is that heavy lime amalgam with a steel casing."

"Stay low and behind it, then, and keep Lord Entiyti behind you."

"As you say, sir."

Dalgaard opened fire with his weapon, one-armed, but still deadly accurate, as he traced the energy beams back to their sources and began picking off assassins as soon as he could take a good shot. Behind him, he could hear Goobop on his comm device.

"Emergency! EMERGENCY! This is Lieutenant Goobop! Assassination attempt on Lord Entiyti in the private-shuttle concourse! Entiyti is down, repeat, Entiyti is down! We have lost Uussa; Commander Dalgaard is wounded! Send reinforcements immediately!"

Then no less than three more weapons opened up beside Dalgaard, as Goobop triple-wielded his blasters.

* * *

Goobop focused on the firefight, trying hard to protect his employer—and friend; Entiyti had a penchant for getting to know those who worked for him, and this had usually resulted in fast friendships, trustworthy relationships that extended over decades—and as a result, several would-be assassins fell, and did not rise again.

"Where the helvete are the spaceport security guards?" Dalgaard growled. He had somehow managed to get his second weapon into his other hand, Goobop noted; while he had no ability to raise the arm—given a substantial part of his shoulder was missing, and raw meat and bone showed through the jagged hole in his uniform—he could still fire it to relatively good effect, once he managed to position it, at least. With a painful effort, the Wintourn used his good arm to lift the wounded arm and brace it along the edge of the overturned table; it was then only a matter of shifting his body position a bit to aim the blaster in hand. That meant they now had five weapons in action, protecting Entiyti.

And it does not appear that the assassin squad members are sufficiently well-trained to fire more than one weapon at a time, Goobop decided. *Which is fortunate for us. There are still considerably more of them than we have weapons in action. I count...at least a dozen different locations from which fire has been originating, maybe more.*

"I do not know, Sigrund," he replied, targeting a being hidden behind a waste disposal can. "Either they were bribed...or diverted...to be elsewhere..." The squat gray being behind the trash can fell, a pool of blue forming around it. "...Or perhaps they were taken out before we arrived."

* * *

Goobop's communications device jangled, and he extracted it from a uniform pocket with one tentacle, while firing with the other two.

"Goobop. No, we are still under heavy fire. Energy beam AND projectile. And it began with a bomb of some sort. Oh, gloob a floop. All right; hurry."

"What's wrong?" Dalgaard wondered as Goobop replaced the device and resumed firing with all three weapons.

"The emergency bulkheads deployed, they think as a result of the blast, though it could have been sabotage," Goobop told him. "The ones that section off the station in the event of a rupture. The deployed area is between us and the *Hsshthh.* They are trying to recircuit or cut through, but we are alone, meanwhile."

"Meinfretr bacraut!" Dalgaard cursed. "Now what?"

* * *

Just then, Goobop felt something touch one of his three legs from behind, and he glanced down, startled, to see a white-scaled, clawed hand grasping at his uniform trousers and trying to tug at them.

"Lord Entiyti!" Goobop exclaimed, crouching. "Just lie there and try to rest, milord. We are in the midst of a firefight."

"I...know," Entiyti panted. "And cut off. I heard. Call...call Suud. Suud Guurn. Was meeting...he's waiting. He can...can fly up. He will have...help..."

And Entiyti collapsed, lapsing into unconsciousness once

more. Goobop and Dalgaard exchanged glances.

"Do it," Dalgaard ordered. "If we can't get help from one direction, maybe we can get it from another. Otherwise, we're all dead."

Goobop reached for his communications device.

* * *

Upon receipt of the emergency summons, Suud Guurn, one of the three best chief bodyguards Pulgey Entiyti had ever employed, managed to cram five more bodies into his two-person personal shuttle than it was designed to hold, complete with as many weapons and equipment as they—and the shuttle—could carry, and made for the transfer station as fast as he could. The little shuttle's manufacturer-spec mass/weight capacity was exceeded by nearly an order of magnitude, but Suud's mentor had taught him to 'hot rod' his vehicles, and it would manage.

Upon arrival in the emergency berth which Emdali Station Control reserved for him, he exited the gate into the concourse and set his six friends in position with a few hand gestures. Then they moved down the narrow concourse in a grim, determined phalanx, sweeping away any opposition with blasters, stun-guns, and gas grenades. Four assassins went down almost immediately. In short order they had neared Entiyti's position, clearing the assassins before them, taking out three more.

* * *

The orange warning lights on the two bodyguards' weapons had lit; they were about to lose power.

"And then we join Uussa," Dalgaard muttered.

"Indeed," Goobop averred. "I am sorry to have failed Lord Entiyti. I wonder what this will mean for the Coalition."

"No idea. I only hope things don't dra til helvete med jaevel."

"Yes, my friend. I hope so, as well. It...has been good to work with you."

"And y—"

Suddenly a new set of beam weapons inserted themselves into the battle; they came from down the concourse, toward the gate, and targeted the assassins. Dalgaard dared to peep around the upended table.

"Mikill Skaperen!" he cried. "Guurn has arrived—with reinforcements!"

"Thank Maker," a relieved Goobop agreed. "Look, Sigrund—the assassins are fleeing."

"Not if I can help it," Dalgaard growled. "Keep firing, Goobop! We'll overload the batteries and fling our blasters like grenades before we let those damned terrorists get away!"

* * *

"What the nether world?!" Suud exclaimed, looking around. "How many WERE there?!"

"There were at least fifteen by my count, possibly twenty," Dalgaard murmured, finally letting the dead blaster fall from his bad hand and sinking to the deck in pain and exhaustion. "By my estimate, we took out three or four before you arrived...maybe as many as six. Maybe." The retired military medic friend that Suud had brought with him bent over Dalgaard, beginning a swift triage and bandage of the wound; full treatment would have to wait until they were out of harm's way—the main firefight was currently around the corner, but that didn't mean they were out of danger.

"And Pulgey?"

"Is in bad shape, sir," Goobop noted, allowing the reinforcements to take over and sweep the area. "I have bandaged him as best I could, around keeping the assassins from gunning us all down, and with what I had to hand. But he has lost a good deal of blood, and his wing may have to be amputated."

"Goobop, correct?"

"Yes sir."

"Are you injured?"

"I took two projectile grazes, and one slight blaster burn, as well as a few scratches from bomb shrapnel, but I am relatively unharmed," Goobop averred. "Sigrund needs assistance far more than I."

"Any other wounded?"

"No sir, I fear not. The bomb blast threw Uussa into the bulkhead; her neck broke, and she died within moments. I...am sorry, sir. I know she was about to become...family."

"Mm. I am very sorry, as well. My eldest son loved her deeply, and she was a good woman; I liked her and looked forward to having her in my clan. I will not enjoy passing on the news to him that his intended has been lost. We must see to it that her body receives proper treatment. Can you carry Lord Entiyti?"

"I can, sir."

"Good. Then do you and Sigrund take Pulgey and head for Gate A23," Suud ordered, issuing additional orders via hand gestures. "The medic and one of my armed friends will go with you; Gord, make sure you sweep the area and our ship before you let them enter, just in case. I will stay here long enough to ensure that my people are likewise doing a proper sweep of the concourse, and take anyone into custody that we find...though by the sound of things, they are now fleeing; between us, we have taken out at least half their number already, and my people are fresh, with backup weapons." He shook his head, then gave a toothy, if wry, grin. "I will be along very soon, and will take you down to Emdali, while my unit 'mops up,' as Franz used to call it. If I can, I plan to meet with station security before I go, though I will not delay getting Pulgey to medical care to do it. Now go."

* * *

Suud was as good as his word. Within moments, both bodyguards—with Goobop carrying Entiyti—and the medic accompanied Entiyti aboard the *Rsssus*, Suud's private shuttle. The medic stabilized Entiyti as much as he could in the cramped quarters, placing the galactic leader on an antigrav stretcher and strapping him down, and scant minutes later, Suud arrived.

That worthy called Transfer Control, declaring an additional emergency, and immediately departed the facility, himself piloting the craft down to Slliith City, the capital of Emdali, outside which was the Entiyti hereditary estate.

But as the craft neared the landing center, the galactic leader regained consciousness.

"S-suud?" he murmured. "Suud? Did I hear...? Is...is that you, old f-friend?"

"Hush, Pulgey," Suud said, looking over his shoulder. "Try to relax, as much as you can. I am here, and you are safe. We are taking you to the emergency medical facility in Slliith City. I am about to signal approach to their hoverpad on the roof."

"NO," Entiyti declared. "Medical...facility...my manor h-house. Con...conspir-acy."

"Ah, of course," Suud noted, changing course and heading for the Entiyti family estate some distance beyond the suburbs. "I am not thinking! If they infiltrated the transfer station, where else have they couched themselves? But I did not know you had installed a medical facility in your home, old friend."

"Ye-yes," Entiyti whispered. "Planned...ahead...when I was...reinstated. Just...in case. Not as...as young as...once was. Suud...call Franz. Have him...Zebra...they will...will help..."

"Yes, that is an excellent idea. I will do that at once. Meanwhile my personal physician will attend you until Franz can arrive with his physician-mate—I have already notified her, and she has notified your personal physician as well; I will let them know of the change of destination momentarily, and they can meet us at your house. Is there anything else?"

"Lydhuu," Entiyti breathed. "Call..."

"I will. Rest, now, old friend."

And Entiyti slumped in the stretcher as the *Rsssus* approached the estate.

Chapter 2

"Okay, so we have the latest batch of finalists?" Echo asked Omega, and she nodded.

"These are only the candidates that passed our criteria on the testing—obstacle course, range, and hypercube. I think they look pretty good, Ace."

"I do, too, though there's a few I'm not as sure of, but the interview oughta tell me whether to keep 'em or not. Call 'em in. I think I wanna stick to the practice of interviewing each team individually and personally. That way, I get a better feel for attitudes an' shit, and whether or not they can work with the department as a whole, or think this is a promotion they're owed. You know, like that team last fall."

"Yeah, I remember. Never mind how Alpha Seven and half of Eight got in."

"Bingo. Although, in the end, Monkey's done great, and I think Alpha Seven is gonna come back with a better attitude, probably in just a few months; I talked to Yankee before he went on 'probation,' and he was already looking at you different. But at least now we've got a pretty decent feel for what questions to ask, before it gets that far."

"Yup. And I think that's been working pretty well, too," Omega agreed. "Do you want me with you, or do you wanna do it one-on-one this time? I know that both of us seriously intimidated the team outta the Gaborone Office, last time. I hated that, so bad."

"I know. I fully intended to add 'em, too. And then they pulled out, 'cause they decided they couldn't cut it."

"Yeah. Um, I did something a little bit ago, where they're concerned...like, half an hour ago..."

"What?" Echo shot a curious glance at his partner and department second.

"I emailed 'em," she confessed. "I apologized for us intimidating 'em—I guess I'm still only just realizing what kinda reputation I have, let alone what the two of us together have got, especially after some stuff Zz'r'p said this morning—and told 'em we really liked them, individually and as a team, and that they'd actually made the cut, but decided to pull out of the selection process before we could announce it."

"All true, baby."

"Yeah. And then I told 'em I thought they should reapply, like, for the next batch of applicants. It won't be THIS batch, of course, but..." she broke off and shrugged. "If they do it soon, then they don't have to re-test."

"Also true. And we can then go ahead and immediately accept their applications, as being it got put on hold while they worked out something at their home Office—never mind the something was dealing with the intimidation factor—and now their application is reinstated and pre-approved."

"Exactly! Oh, I knew you'd get it, Ace!"

"When it's you? Of course, Meg." Echo smiled at her. "I think that was terrifically done, and it gets us a really good team in the department, with some excellent skill sets, one that I wanted. I suppose we'll need to maybe boost their confidence for a bit, until they get comfortable in the department, but we've had to do that with one or two other teams, so no big deal. But today, I think I want you here, doing the interviews with me. I didn't see anybody that appeared THAT intimidated by us. And they'll need to get to know us, and work with us, anyway." He thumbed through the final group of applications. "Are all of these guys still at Headquarters?"

"That's an affirm, Ace. I added that to the process a while back, only to be superseded by an emergency summons out of their home Office, and nobody's gotten a summons, so they're all here."

"Good. Set up a roster, one team every quarter-hour, and call 'em in. We'll make one last cut, based on how they do. If they all do great, they all go into the department. But this gives us one last chance to weed out the 'tudes."

"All over it."

* * *

The interviews—and their aftermath—took a good chunk of the rest of the day, as matters went. Only one team turned out to have a problem, and they were an older team that had been recruited straight out of the military only a few years prior. Unfortunately, that team completely misread the entire situation, including the abilities and competence of the department leads, given neither Echo nor Omega especially looked their ages...and a happy, content Echo looked even younger than usual, after establishing Omega as his soon-to-be mate.

"Son, I really think you don't have the right idea 'bout this whole shit," Kappa declared to Echo. "This department needs to be run more like a Green Beret unit. Ditch that sissy 3-D puzzle shit! Add some physical fitness testing in there, double the length of the damn obstacle course, and make PT mandatory, every damn day! And aren't you really too young to be leadin' this squad? Ya can't have been doin' this agent job more 'n, what, five years? Hell, I was a master sergeant for that long! Me 'n Nun, here, we prob'ly got more time in th' military than you've been alive, son! Either one of us could do this job ten times better. You really need to get with it, son, or else step aside an' let somebody better qualified do it—an' frankly, I'd recommend th' latter. This ain't gonna cut it. You'll get somebody killed! I mean, I get th' whole idea of cannon fodder, but if ya want an elite unit, ya need to try ta keep 'em alive so's they get th' experience ta BE an elite unit."

Echo's face remained expressionless; he turned to Nun.

"What was your background before the Agency recruited you, Nun?"

"I was Master Sergeant Ba-uh, I was Kappa's staff sergeant, Echo," Nun replied, not bothering with honorifics to the Alpha Line chief.

"For how long?"

"Um, lessee; 'bout a year, maybe? Not quite."

"Didn't miss it much," Kappa noted.

"Mm-hm. I see," Echo said, dispassionate. "And you feel this background makes you both suited to Alpha Line?"

"Damn straight," Kappa declared.

"Absolutely," Nun averred.

"All right," Echo said, scanning their records, "according to your files, Kappa, you started college but didn't complete the degree. You left the university at 21, went through eight jobs in the next five years, then enlisted in the Army at...26?" He glanced up, and a slightly red-faced Kappa nodded, but for a wonder, said nothing. "Given you weren't much short of your degree...why didn't you finish?"

"It was boring as hell, sitting in a classroom all day, every day," Kappa declared, blunt. "Only reason I was there was my dad insisted. I wanted something more interesting. Soon's he died, I dumped it."

"Okay. So you enlisted as a specialist, given your education, and moved up through the ranks at a reasonable rate, taking ten years to reach master sergeant."

"Right. An' I was master sergeant for five years, 'til your people approached me."

"And you've been in the Agency for about two years now."

"Yup, sure have, son. Field work outta the Dallas office."

"You're currently 43 years old, maintain your Agency weapons certs, and still perform all the physical workouts you did in the military."

"Yup. Ya don't stay in shape, ya end up dead."

"Good. Nun?"

"Yes?"

"Your file says you have an associates in applied science, with a focus in network security. But when you graduated with your associates, you couldn't find a job..."

"Yeah. The job market in that field tanked along about then," Nun explained. "An' it stayed bad for a while, there."

"Yes, I remember that. It was shortly after we signed the trade agreement with the Delzantians; nobody expected either their systems or their immigrants to create that kind of situation in our own markets." Echo shrugged. "So you also enlisted in the Army as a specialist."

"That's correct."

"You saw combat in the Mideast on two separate tours of duty, picked up a field promotion to E-5, then moved up to E-6, and had been working with Kappa as his staff sergeant for not quite a year when the two of you were recruited into the Agency in one recruiting run."

"Yeah," Nun said with a grin.

"Your recruiters know good people when they see 'em, son," Kappa decreed. "He and I have been with the Agency for about two years now. We came in at the same time and made sure we got partnered, so's we could work together like we did in the Army."

"Nun, you're—what? 32?"

"Thirty-three, back in the spring," Nun corrected. "Early May."

Echo flipped back several pages, scanning for Nun's birth date. "Ah. Right."

"Well, he can read decent," Kappa chuckled. "Arithmetic, maybe not so much."

Echo raised a displeased eyebrow; Nun sat back in his seat, eyes growing wide at the expression on Echo's face, but Kappa seemed oblivious.

* * *

Omega sat through this exchange beside Echo, taking notes with a stylus on her tablet, gritting her teeth and saying nothing; a brief—and completely unnoticed, by their interviewees—series of coded exchanges with Echo had told him that she was concerned about saying too much if she said anything at all. Just then, Kappa leaned over and tapped her on the knee.

"Hey, honey," he said, "when ya get done taking notes for your boss, here, make me a cuppa coffee, wouldja?"

Both members of Alpha One froze...then began to scowl. And as a general rule, when perps saw Alpha One scowling, they tended to get worried.

"Honey, didja hear me?" Kappa tried again, squeezing her knee, before rubbing it suggestively. "I need you to get me a cuppa coffee, sweetheart. Cream, two sugars. Oh, and your phone number would be nice, too."

"Take. Your hand. OFF. My partner's. Knee," Echo growled.

"Partner?" Kappa said, blinking. "Oh, you mean this is your girlfriend, not just your 'executive assistant,'" he smirked, finally removing his hand. "Back when I started, we still called 'em secretaries. I gotta say, you have good taste, son."

* * *

"All right, let's get a few things straight, here," Echo said, maintaining his cool with an effort; Omega was still scowling, and he could fairly feel the raw fury radiating from her. *And that ain't good,* he thought, *so soon after all the other shit she's been through.* "First off, AGENT Omega is not only NOT my secretary, she is my partner, the other half of the Alpha One team. Second, she is the Alpha Line Assistant Chief—"

"Oh, now that just won't do a-tall," Kappa decreed. "Ain't no way a purty young thing like that is gonna be—"

"Shut. Up," Echo ordered.

"Son, you need to settle down and—"

"The Man said, SHUT UP," Omega snarled, standing and seeming to expand in size. Both candidates blinked, then grinned.

"She thinks she's hot stuff, huh?" Nun said to Kappa.

"Looks like it," Kappa agreed, reaching for her arm. "Now look, sugar, you sit back down and beha—"

Before either man could blink, Kappa found his wrist caught, and the visitor chair spun around a full one-hundred-eighty degrees...and it was not a swivel chair. His arm was twisted behind his back, hand pinned between his shoulder blades.

"What the hell?!" Kappa exclaimed, struggling to free his hand and finding it locked in an iron grip.

"Let go of him! Now!" Nun cried, jumping up.

"Sit down," Echo ordered in a deep, commanding voice, towering over the smaller man as he stood to bring into play his full six-foot, three-and-a-half-inch height—plus stacked cowboy-boot heels; he was wearing the boots Omega gave him for his birthday, and those put him nearly six and a half feet tall. Nun only stood about five-foot eight. "I will not say it again."

Nun sat abruptly.

"Meg, turn him back around, please, but hang on to that wrist for a few more moments; I want him to actually listen, this time," Echo said, letting his voice drop in intensity a bit—ONLY a bit. Omega complied, and Echo moved to loom over the seated Kappa...who was taller than Nun, but not by a lot, and was a couple inches shy of six feet. "Now, let's try this again. Agent Omega is my partner. Yes, we have a personal relationship, as of the last...eh, 'bout three weeks...out of nearly TWO YEARS of partnering together. She is not my secretary and never has been. She IS the assistant chief of this department, duly promoted to that position after behavior that went FAR above and beyond her duty requirements, and has commanded multiple departments simultaneously in joint operations. Despite her youthful appearance, she is older than Nun, and has no less than four degrees in six different science and engineering fields, including at least one Ph.D., and was an astronaut when we recruited her, with over a decade of NASA experience. She is an associate professor of astronomy and physics at Division One University—essentially founding the astronomy department—and has been requested to teach at some of the other division universities. She is also an enhanced human—"

"Enhanced? What the hell does THAT mean?" Kappa wanted to know.

"It means," Omega leaned forward to snap in his ear, "that my genetics were tweaked, and my systems reworked, to put me in the top fraction of a percentile of the human race, according to the Medical department."

"It means you don't want to badger or harass her, because

you will not win," Echo added, "and together she and I still hold the records for every Alpha Line test you just went through. As for me, 'dad,'" he delivered the word with derision, "appearance notwithstanding, I have been in the Agency for nearly two decades, so the TWO of you put together exceed my time in active duty by only a couple of years, if that. Omega and I together are pretty much an equal of the two of you, at least for time in the job. As for ability, I am probably not exaggerating when I say that either one of us could take down both of you; entry into Alpha Line is NOT the culmination of your Agency career, it is the beginning of a whole new journey—I expect the Agents in my department to work to increase their abilities by at least an order of magnitude. I am the Alpha Line department chief, and I am the Ennead-approved Assistant Director and successor to Director Fox...who has been doing this, and related jobs, for well more than half a century, HIS apparent age notwithstanding...and who was, and is, my mentor." He glared at the two agents, who were gaping in shock. "Agent Omega and I are EACH qualified to fly every craft in the Division One fleet; wield every weapon in our arsenal, including tandem; together have taken out more interstellar terrorists than you have fingers; been in several space dogfights; and handled some half a dozen first contacts—and that's JUST since Omega came into the Agency nearly two years ago."

The pair's eyes grew wider.

"Go ahead and let him go, Meg," Echo gave permission, "but if he puts a hand on you again, feel free to lay him out. You can decide whether or not he keeps the hand; we'll just ship him down to the medlab if we have to."

Kappa blinked.

"Wait just a damn minute, now," he began, annoyed. "Quit this bluffin' shit an—"

"Bluffing? No," Omega interrupted, releasing him and stepping around to stand in front of the pair. "YOU wait, and you listen up. You come in here, knowing nothing about Alpha One and precious little about Alpha Line, and sit there telling us what YOU think it should be, and implying that YOU should be in charge, because you think you're older and more experienced. When we've seen your files! The truth of the matter is, the two of you were at the BOTTOM of our list of finalist candidates for this application term! Do you get that?! All the other finalists scored HIGHER than EITHER of you. YOU... BARELY...MADE...THE...CUT."

Speechless, Nun and Kappa looked from Omega to Echo, expressions expectant.

"She's telling it straight," Echo affirmed. "This was your chance to impress us, to convince us why you would make good Alpha Line Agents. Alpha Line doesn't have a physical fitness test, gentlemen, because if you aren't in shape, you won't even survive the obstacle course test to get IN. If you don't STAY in shape, of your own volition, you won't survive, period."

"We are the special forces department for the entire Division," Omega tag-teamed.

"But there's only—what?—fifty of you?" Nun expostulated. "That's not nearly enough for—!"

"One riot, one team," Echo paraphrased, letting his native Texan dialect out to play. "You're used to battalions. We don't HAVE battalions! Given what the Agency does, and the secrecy under which we operate, we can't AFFORD to have battalions—they're too big and draw too much attention. We work with what we've got. Each one of us has to be the equivalent of a squad, or at least each partnership has to be." He stared at them, and after several seconds, both men dropped their gazes in chagrin. "Now...do you think you two have what it takes to be an entire squad, just the two of you?"

Nun and Kappa turned to look at each other, shocked.

"I..." Nun began, then silenced at the expression on Echo's face.

"What say we take 'em on, you and me, in the training room simulator?" Omega suggested. "I'm tired of being constantly challenged like this. This time, let's show 'em firsthand what it takes to be Alpha Line."

"What?" Kappa said, voice flat.

"We could," Echo decided. "We'd have to issue stun guns, and get Fox's approval for it, but I think we could swing that. Maybe they need to see what we can do when we open up."

* * *

"...You mean, fight against each other?" Fox said, surprised, from behind his desk, as Alpha One stood before it. Nun and Kappa remained silent, uncertain, in chairs near the door. "No, no, I don't think so, zun, tekhter. I understand why you're asking, and that you're thirteen and a half kinds of annoyed, and a brokh! I have to admit, it's tempting. But that's more apt to leave them resentful, don't you think? I believe what we need to do is simpler than that."

"We're listening, Fox," Echo said. "We'll take all the ideas we can get. We're tired of this shit." Omega nodded.

"Let me set up a scenario for you in the training room, and the two of you go in with your normal weaponry and equipment, and your candidates—all of 'em, not just these two—can watch," Fox recommended. "And we record it on vid. That way, whenever anyone wants to know why Alpha Line has such a high standard, or thinks they're better than you...which seems to happen more often than we'd like, since neither of you looks your age, especially in the last few days...we can pull out the recording and SHOW them."

"Which ain't a half-bad idea, there," Omega decided. "Plus, it lets us get in a training session, Ace."

"Yeah. Which we postponed on account of your, um, appointment this morning," Echo tap-danced around the counseling session; he didn't want Kappa or Nun asking too many questions, and they were still sitting in the corner of Fox's office, still dumbfounded, still listening.

"Give me five minutes to wind up what I was doing, and we'll head down there," Fox decreed. "Meanwhile, contact all the candidates and have 'em meet me in the observation room."

* * *

"All right, kinder," Fox said to Alpha One as he stood at the control panel in the training room, setting up the scenario; a recent series of upgrades as a result of the new trade agreement with the Ganotians had made the training facility nearly as good as any such construct to be found in science fiction—comic, novel, television or film. "This isn't going to be like anything you've ever done before, but I have no doubt you can handle it. You do have an audience watching the live video in the observing room, and that includes not only all of your current batch of candidates who've made it through the selection process, but several Alpha Line teams that were available, as well as a few of the field teams who want to try to learn a few things from you." Fox threw them a smile. "I thought it might make a good training seminar for the others, so try not to knock out the hovercam tailing you." He pressed a button on the console, and the tiny device emerged from a recessed panel in the console, spun around, then zeroed in on Alpha One.

"That's fine, Boss," Echo noted. "You good with it, Meg?"

"Yeah, Ace, I think so," she said, scrunching her face for a moment. "If, uh, if some of the things that were said in my, um, meeting this morning hadn't already been said, I might not be, so much. But," she added, subtly inching closer to him, "we're a damn fine team, and this'll be good."

"You got all your usual equipment, baby?"

"Yup. I won't even bother asking the Boy Scout Who Wasn't."

"Of course."

"All right," Fox decided, surveying the console settings, "I think that's got it. I'm going to take the remote and step just outside, use the intercom to give you a countdown, then initiate the scenario."

"Go for it," Echo agreed, rolling his shoulders to adjust his Suit jacket, as Omega reached over her head and stretched briefly.

"Oh, one last thing," Fox said. "Omega, you might recognize a little of this, based on some...conversations...we've had of late. Don't worry, and don't hold back; they wouldn't want you to."

Omega knit her brows in confusion. "Oh-kaaaay," she drawled.

"What the hell did THAT mean?" Echo demanded to know.

"You'll find out," Fox said, slipping out and closing the door. Then his voice came over the speaker, "...In three...two...one...GO!"

* * *

The room around them abruptly seemed to fade, to be replaced by a semi-urban landscape in shades of brown and gray; the only real color was found in the faded brick which comprised a handful of the buildings. But the buildings were old, and poorly maintained; the red brick structures were two- and three-story, and a couple were a kind of yellowish-gray stucco, but most were crude wooden structures, long and low and barnlike. The few brick structures had a vaguely Teutonic style, but the wooden buildings were more reminiscent of an American frontier board-and-batten, or occasionally, post-and-plank construction...although sometimes the battens were left off. And to judge by the scant foliage and the air temperature, wherever they were, it was winter.

In the far distance was what might have been a railroad track, though it was hard to tell; abundantly strung here and there were literal miles of barbed wire, sectioning off the area into many smaller partitions. Tall guard shacks, of the same board-and-batten construction, lined the periphery, which was also framed with a double row of barbed-wire fencing. In the near distance, a tall, square, brick smokestack belched black smoke high into the air.

There was no living being to be seen.

"Huh," Echo murmured, as he and Omega turned in a circle, surveying the singularly unpleasant vista. "What the hell is this...?" Just then, he spotted an identifier—the statue of a stylized eagle with outspread wings perched on a circular shield of some sort, over the doorway of the main building, which stood

36

along the railroad tracks. "Uh-oh..."

* * *

Omega turned at that, and followed his fixed gaze, then pressed her lips together, becoming grim of face.

"Oh no, Fox, tell me you didn't..." she murmured.

"Didn't what?" Echo asked. "You know where we are, of course."

"Yeah. In his nightmare."

"Nightma—? Oh boy."

"Hell yeah. Operative word being hell," Omega added.

"He's told you about this?"

"A little. We, uh, were starting to talk about...about stuff like that, you know, after...everything, lately," she tiptoed around the matter, aware of other agents watching, as the faint hum of the drone hovercam behind her reached her ears.

"Do you know what's going down here, then?"

"No, but given where we are, it ain't gonna be good."

"Well, I figured THAT..." Echo said, and shrugged.

* * *

"Where IS that?" Nun wondered. "Kappa?"

"No idea," Kappa said. Monkey turned and glared at them.

"You're kidding," the Alpha Line Agent said, shaking his head.

"Nope," Kappa averred. "You got any ideas?"

"Yeah," Monkey declared. "Majdanek."

"What the hell is a May-dah-neck?" Kappa wanted to know.

"See if these mean anything to you, idiot," the Alpha Line Agent practically spat in disgust, as the other agents nearby listened. He ticked off fingers. "Auschwitz-Birkenau. Bergen-Belsen. Buchenwald. Dachau. Ravensbrück."

"Ohmigaw. Those are..." Nun began, shocked.

"What?" Kappa asked.

"Nazi concentration camps," Nun whispered.

"You're kidding," Kappa said in disbelief. "But that's...I mean, how did...?"

"Everybody shut up and pay attention," Golf growled, di-

37

recting the comment at Kappa and Nun, who silenced.

* * *

"I guess we can stand here and wait for something to happen, or we can go looking," Omega decided.

"Yeah, looks that way," Echo agreed. He pulled both blasters, and Omega followed suit. "Let's explore a deserted concentration camp, baby."

"Right beside ya, Ace."

"Just where you're supposed to be."

"Permanently."

"You got it, baby. Don't go far; we don't want to get separated."

"Nope."

The pair moved forward, silent, cautious, and watchful, dropping into their unspoken codes to communicate when necessary. Edging to the end of the nearest inmate barracks, they flanked the closed door; Omega produced a small device and scanned it, then nodded. So Echo tapped the doorknob. Finding it safe to the touch, he tried it; it was unlocked. In one smooth move, he turned the knob and pushed open the door; Omega, weapons at the ready, rushed in and to the opposite side of the door; Echo followed suit.

There was no one within. Rank upon rank of rickety, multi-tiered wooden bunks, with little but a rude blanket and a straw-tick mattress on each, filled the huge, barnlike building. Narrow aisles ran between the long rows.

Where is everybody? Echo coded to his partner. *This place should be jam-packed with prisoners.*

No idea, but I have a bad feeling about it, she responded in kind.

* * *

The small hovercam, following close in the wake of Alpha One, projected a realistic image onto the blank wall of the observing room, along with audio from the stereo speakers, enabling everyone watching to follow what was transpiring, even when the pair entered one of the buildings. So the varied assortment of agents paid close attention, each one tense and expectant, as Omega and Echo eased their way down the long barracks, occasionally using the tip of a blaster to nose about the scant bedding, and finding nothing...except the occasional nest of bedbugs.

"They really got a hot thing goin' there, don't they?" Kappa snickered then, distracting the other agents again in a particularly jarring fashion, given the tenseness of what was transpiring in the training room onscreen. "He can't even stop with the bedroom talk when they're in a training session."

"What, calling her 'baby'?" Easy wondered.

"Oh, hell yeah." Kappa snorted, amused.

"He's been doing that from pretty much the first of their partnership," Berta remarked. "It doesn't mean what you think it does. There's no sexual connotation to it, not the way they use it. It was originally just a shortened version of the common reference to a rookie as a 'baby agent.' He had been teasing her about her rookie status when she got too serious over something, trying to get her to lighten up, and it became a nickname. They both like it; she told me once, it reminded her of home."

"Yes indeed; I was present during the 'something' she was serious about, so I can confirm the matter," Madrid added. "And it was VERY early on in her career as an Agent, scant weeks into it—not even a month. She calls him 'Ace' in the same way, ever since he taught her to fly our specialized aircraft." He had heard about the training session and showed up to watch his friends, and only discovered the reason for the open session after arriving.

"Now, will you SHUT the hell UP," Easy added, annoyed at Kappa. "SOME of us are trying to learn something."

Kappa threw the Alpha Line Agent a dirty look, but silenced.

* * *

That's it, Meg, Echo coded, as they reached the far end of the barracks. *Not one thing, and not one body. Living or dead or otherwise. What the HELL is going on?*

39

I dunno, Ace, Omega responded. *I guess we keep looking until we figure it out. It's what we'd do on a real mission. But this isn't what I expected Fox to set up, given what we were trying to accomplish with Kappa and Nun.*

No, but it would illustrate why problem-solving is part of the testing, he pointed out. *So it'll make a good training video, I guess. Provided we don't hose it up.*

True. Well, let's head back out and keep looking. We'll figure it out sooner or later. Hopefully sooner.

Roger that.

They headed for the solitary door at the far end of the long, low ramshackle building, trying to ignore the chill winds that whipped through the cracks and crevices.

* * *

"What are they doing?" Nun wondered in a low tone, to avoid annoying the other agents.

"Vhat?" Kako, Monkey's partner from the Moscow Office, said in his soft Russian accent. "Vhat do you mean?"

"They look like they're talking, but they're not saying anything, just making a few little hand gestures an' shit," Nun elaborated.

"Oh, that," Monkey said. "Those two have signals an' codes an' stuff for when they need to be stealthy. They're really good at 'em, too. If they don't want you to know they're communicating, it's real hard to tell—impossible, depending on circumstances. Kako and I have been working on doing that sort of thing ourselves. We're trying to develop some subtle codes, and practicing 'em."

"Good, zun," came a familiar, deep voice nearby, and Fox moved away from the door of the darkened observing room. "I'm glad to hear it. And they will be, too. They have developed their own little 'tricks of the trade,' you might say, but in general, they're happy to share tips and suggestions with any of the other field agents, whether in Alpha Line or not. Ultimately, we are all one big team, after all, trying to keep everyone safe and progress the planet to being a full participant in the Galactic Coalition." Fox waved a hand at the images being transmitted. "You lot only saw maybe one or two gestures, but they just carried on an entire conversation."

"Wait. You mean you know what they said?" Kappa wondered.

"Yes; I taught Echo a few of the codes I used when I worked as bodyguard for Pulgey Entiyti, back in the day," Fox explained, "and he's developed more of his own, taught them to Omega, and they developed still MORE, between them. I gather that around one night a week, they tend to devote to practice by ONLY communicating like that. But I can generally extrapolate reasonably well, based on what he and I used to do."

"What did they say, then?" Kappa challenged, with a sly smirk. Fox frowned at the arrogance of the other man.

"They're puzzled because they haven't found anything yet, and don't understand why there aren't any inhabitants in the barracks."

"So they ain't the hot shit they want us to believe," Kappa snorted.

"On the contrary," Fox corrected. "I expressly programmed this section of the scenario as a problem-solving puzzle, to depict why puzzle-solving is an essential part of the testing program for the Alpha Line department. And by the way, 'that little 3-D puzzle' you disparaged during your interview with them... isn't. It's actually four-dimensional, it's called a hypercube, it's one of the hardest test sequences in all of PGLEIA—across all divisions—and the two people in that training simulator at the moment have the two fastest times in the Agency on it."

"Hmph," Kappa grunted. "Fastest time? I didn't figure him for being that smart."

"Echo has the SECOND fastest time," Fox corrected. "Echo did it in...let me see. I think it was fifty-eight minutes and a few seconds—just shy of an hour, which is about thirty or forty minutes faster than anyone else has managed, so far. But OMEGA finished it in under twenty minutes. Short of gray matter, they are NOT."

Kappa gaped.

* * *

The Alpha One team headed back toward the only door. About two-thirds of the way there, and without any communication, both abruptly halted.

"Oh, shit," Omega murmured in realization.

"Yeah," Echo opined. "One door..."

"...No windows," Omega continued. "It's a trap."

"And we walked right into it, dammit," Echo cursed. "We really need to rein in our natural curiosity a little better, Meg."

"I know," Omega sighed. "But I think I've figured out a little of it, anyway..."

"Oh? Do tell."

"No prisoners; no guards; no officers," Omega pointed out. "That means that the prisoners..."

"Have been turned," Echo realized. "They don't need the guards any more, because the prisoners are working with them. Which also means..."

"The prisoners have somehow been made to work against their will," Omega filled in. "How is what we'll have to figure out, and then determine if it's possible to free them."

"Damn. Fox came up with a doozy," Echo decided.

"Didn't he, though?" Omega agreed. "Okay, the first thing we gotta do is not walk into a trap. THEN we can figure out what happened, and what to do about it."

"Okay, that's easy enough," Echo said, turning and heading back to the far end of the barracks, Omega on his heels. Then he reached into his pocket and pulled out his hurgir.

"Ooo, I'd almost forgotten about that little thing," Omega breathed. "And you and I worked out how to use the small, portable ones to make larger excavations, right?"

"Yeah, and I figured out how to put it into stealth mode," Echo agreed, keeping his voice quiet. "First off, though, I'm gonna have it make us a peephole. It won't help to sneak out the back if they have the building surrounded."

He adjusted the settings on the instrument face of the device, then hooked it onto the back wall of the barracks. Spindly six-inch metallic legs emerged and grabbed onto the rough wood surface, as the device 'hunkered down,' as Omega thought of it; the instrument's design was rather crab-like. A tiny orange light on the instrumentation blinked for a couple of seconds, then became continuous, and when it went out, Echo removed the hurgir from the wall. A little hole, not much more than three-quarters of an inch in diameter, was revealed.

"Meg? Be my guest," Echo whispered, waving at the peephole.

Omega stepped up to the wall and peered out through the hole, twisting her head this way and that to try to get the widest field of view she could. Then she turned to her partner and shook her head in the negative, giving him a thumbs-up.

So Echo made more adjustments to the hurgir's settings, then placed it back on the ramshackle wooden wall. It scuttled a few inches, then latched on with its little claw-legs, and the orange light began to blink again. But this time, instead of hunkering down, the hurgir began a slow, crab-like creep across the wall, gradually sketching out a large, vertical rectangle. In its wake, the wood disappeared.

Omega and Echo grabbed hold of the panel being freed as the hurgir neared completion of its circuit. It cut through the last of the wood and let go of the central panel, dangling from the wall by half of its legs, as Echo and Omega lifted free the panel it had cut, quietly setting it aside. Then Echo caught up the hurgir and hit the 'purge' button. It promptly shat a large pile of fine sawdust onto the floor from an orifice along one end, whereupon he deactivated it and replaced it in a warp pocket.

"Weapons back out," he breathed, extracting both blasters from his shoulder holsters, then led the way out of the barracks.

* * *

Alpha One slipped over to the corner of the building, and from one of her warp pockets, Omega produced a tiny hovercam of her own design. This particular device was extremely miniaturized and possessed a sophisticated passive cloaking system, as well as a remote control. Omega activated and cloaked the hovercam with the remote, then piloted it along the side of the building toward the far end. The view from the camera showed on a small screen on the remote.

"Oh, shit," Echo murmured, as the view at the far end of the barracks came into view.

There were some five dozen Nazi soldiers and 'prisoners' waiting.

"Well, we ain't goin' that way," Omega observed, recalling the little drone.

* * *

By this time, Alpha One had realized exactly where they were: Majdanek, the Nazi concentration camp known during the Polish occupation as Konzentrationslager Lublin—it had been where an early-teenage Franz Levy had somehow managed to survive World War II as an inmate, when the rest of his family had been killed.

They also knew, by the look of the sky and the air temperature, which was growing bitterly cold as the day waned, that it was winter, likely around January if the sun's southerly position was taken into account, and it was now midafternoon... which meant, in that part of Europe, the sun was getting very low in the sky.

So the pair made use of the fact, ignoring the cold, slipping from shadow to building to shadow in their black Suits, gradually flanking the force that had been set to capture them.

Meanwhile they began searching for what had happened to the prisoners.

* * *

As soon as they were far enough away from any sign of people to risk speech, Echo turned to his partner.

"Historical records don't say Majdanek was where the human experimentation went on," Echo noted to Omega.

"It wasn't one of the centers for such," Omega informed

him. "It was mostly just an extermination camp. But according to Fox, some experimentation went on just the same; it wasn't like there was anybody who was gonna stop it. Granted, I think the majority of that went on at Auschwitz and Dachau, Buchenwald...but there was a lot of it, at most of the camps, from the research I've done. It's possible that the main experimentation for...whatever's happened...happened elsewhere and orders came down to extend the experimentation here, for a bigger database."

"Did Fox tell you any of...this," Echo waved a hand around, "actually happened?"

"No," Omega replied. "Like I said earlier, I think this is one of his...nightmares. Which may mean there IS no information on what happened to them, because it never really happened."

"Literal nightmare?"

"I...dunno. I don't THINK so," Omega decided. "At the time, I thought he meant it was something he feared happening, you know, back then. Now...I'm not as sure."

"Do you know where in the camp it might have happened, if it did?"

"Either in the workshops, or in the SS headquarters, I guess," Omega decided. "But based on what Fox showed me of the layout of this place, they're more or less on opposite ends of the camp. And it's a big camp."

"Of course they would be," Echo sighed. "Which are we closest to now?"

"The workshops."

"Then let's check that out first."

* * *

But there was nothing there of any interest, any more than there had been in the prisoner barracks, merely wood-and-metal-working equipment, much used but currently abandoned.

By this time, the sun had set, and the western horizon, while still painted with reds and oranges, was fading to purples and blues. So Alpha One took advantage of the darkening evening to slink more rapidly back in the direction they had come, aiming for SS headquarters.

Unfortunately, they found there was a tall double fence comprised of yet more barbed wire, followed by a considerable open space without cover, between their location and said SS headquarters. More, since there were insulators along one of the fences, accompanied by a faint humming sound, the barbed wire appeared to be electrified.

"And by the look of the insulators, there's some oomph behind it," Omega concluded.

"Okay, we'll have to cut our way through the fence," Echo decided, focusing on the problem at hand. "We have to be careful, though, because the particle beam from the blasters can cause arcing, and you don't want the whole thing to ground out through the gun and you..."

"Echo..." Omega said, glancing over her shoulder.

"I'm thinking we should use a Winchester & Tesla, but its hum is kinda louder than the blaster, and we don't want to attract any more attention than we can help..."

"Oh, that won't be an issue," Omega noted, turning to face away from the fence, blasters up and ready. "We already got plenty of that."

Suddenly a spotlight snapped on, focused on Alpha One.

"Huh?" Echo said, surprised, and spun.

They were surrounded by a crowd of at least a hundred former prisoners, standing some twenty yards away from the Alpha Line team, each one of which had a crude electronic device wrapped around a shaved head. These were backed by a dozen or more smirking Nazi officers.

"Tear them apart!" one of the officers ordered.

The camp inmates began to shuffle toward Alpha One.

* * *

"Lovely," Omega grumbled, backing up a bit. "Nazis with brainwashed victims in front of us, a high-power zappy fence behind. THIS is gonna be a fun day. If we could take out the control devices without hurting the prisoners, we might actually have this."

"I dunno, baby," Echo decided, as the Nazi officers goaded the prisoners forward with prods. "I'm not sure we need to..."

"Why not?"

"Look at their skin."

Omega studied the controlled prisoners intently, all while wondering which of the Nazi officers was the commander, and whether or not she could manage a tight-beam kill shot to his cranium. Abruptly it hit her.

"Oh shit," she murmured. "Their skin—even the Nazis—they're gray. They're..."

"Dead already," Echo completed her statement for her. "That one's about to lose an ear, and THAT one doesn't have a mandible. I'd lay odds the same controller devices are on the Nazis under their uniform caps."

"But then who's controlling 'em?"

"Get ready, Meg," Echo murmured, retreating before the shambling army. "They're gonna charge any second. And remember what you told me? This is 'Fox's nightmare.' There may not BE anybody controlling them, as such. It's only an imaginary subset of the regime."

"Oooh," Omega said, suddenly understanding. "And remember what FOX said, just before starting the scenario?"

"What?"

"He said, 'Don't worry, and don't hold back; they wouldn't want you to.'"

"Because they're already dead, and wouldn't want their bodies used as unwilling soldiers," Echo murmured, grasping where she was headed. "We're in the middle of a damn Nazi zombie apocalypse."

...And the 'zombies' charged.

* * *

The crowd of agents from various departments, watching in the observation room, uniformly dropped jaws as they watched the ensuing battle—the Alpha Line chief and assistant chief, against over a hundred mind-controlled, techno-zombie slaves.

Echo and Omega went back to back and opened up with

47

both blasters each in an astonishing display of gun-fu; Echo briefly swapped out one blaster for his Winchester & Tesla, in order to punch a large hole in the double perimeter fencing, and take down the circuit powering the electric fence.

His next blaster shot targeted the spotlight, situated in a guard tower; it went dark instantly, and the two black-dressed Agents gained a significant advantage in the gloom of the deepening twilight. A third shot, wide-beam and carefully angled, took out two of the tower's legs, and it toppled to the ground in a loud, splintering crash.

* * *

"There!" Echo called. "That'll give us some room to work, baby! Head through the fence!"

"Got it! Oh SHIT! WATCH OUT!" Omega screamed, even as one of the officers pulled a shoulder-slung Mauser MG 42 and began firing bursts at the pair of Agents. She dropped to the ground to avoid the machine-gun fire, rolling onto her back and firing upward, into the throng of zombies trying to dogpile her, then leaped up, flinging no-longer-moving dead body parts hither and yon.

"On it!" Echo cried, even as spattered dirt and wood splinters flew past him. He ducked behind a tall fence post for cover—mostly to break up his outline and make it harder to see him in the near-dark—and took careful aim with his primary blaster. Seconds later, the officer's body fell, sans head.

Several other officers who had already drawn various weapons met the same fate seconds later, from the same weapon. Meanwhile Omega kept the zombie 'prisoners' from flanking Echo.

"Good shooting!" she called.

"Thanks! GET THROUGH THE FENCE, MEG! I'll cover you!"

"I'm there! Hey! Alpha-Red Omega twenty-four, Ace!" Omega responded, even as she lunged through the opening, rolling over her shoulder and coming up on her feet, still firing.

"It's a plan! Cover me through!"

"All over it!"

Echo followed his partner, darting through the opening in the fence, diving, and rolling, as she laid down cover fire. As soon as they both made it to the open space on the other side, they set up the maneuver—a scything, continuous-fire cross-beam sweep with all four blasters, positioning themselves at an angle relative to each other, to avoid inadvertent friendly fire.

In seconds, every member of their opposition was lying on the ground in pieces, along with the tattered remains of that section of fencing.

"END SIMULATION!" Echo called.

The concentration camp faded away, to be replaced by the training room, as if nothing had ever happened.

* * *

The observation room was eerily silent. Every face held astonishment—save one; many mouths hung agape.

"Holy shit," someone whispered. "They just took out..."

"Over a hundred zombies," someone else finished in a low voice. "In seconds."

"One hundred twenty-two, to be exact," Fox said, moving to the front of the room. "A hundred twenty-seven, if we count the guards in the tower...who were about to open fire as well." His hazel gaze swept the room. "And THAT is why they are Alpha Line, ladies and gentlemen. That is why they are the Alpha Line LEADS."

No one said anything to that.

Chapter 3

"No, I think they both got the message," Fox said to his Alpha Line leads, back in his office. "So did quite a few other people, I think. But I thought Madrid was going to pop some buttons, watching. To be honest, I was kvelling more than a bit, myself. That was excellent work, kinder."

"Thanks, Fox," Omega murmured with a smile, then she dropped her head, embarrassed. "It...feels good to know that our friends...well.. after everything, lately..."

"It's nice to know we're appreciated," Echo finished for her, easing an arm around her shoulders.

"And then some," Fox agreed, offering them both a smile of his own. "I do wish you could have seen the reaction in the room, however, Omega; I think it would have done your self-esteem a world of good, my poor tekhter. I may see if the security cameras caught anything. I'd like for you to see it, if we can arrange it. At any rate, I'll be handling Nun and Kappa from this point out. I take it, you do NOT want 'em for Alpha Line..."

"Damn straight," Echo agreed.

"Nope nope nope," Omega averred.

"Good. Just as between us, I intend to break up that particular partnership; I had the impression that Nun, being younger, might be redeemable, if he were out from under Kappa's influence. As it is, though, they're self-reinforcing. You might even find Nun eventually reapplying for Alpha Line—and maybe making it, next time. Kappa is another story, however. He even had the temerity to challenge me, during the training run."

"You're kidding," Omega said, voice flat in disbelief.

"No, I wish I were," Fox confirmed. "I intend to issue a formal reprimand, a black mark which will be permanently on his record. He will be yanked from field work and placed...mm, I haven't really decided yet where I intend to place him. Perhaps as a basic security guard for the Lemurian Local Station, or... oh! Maybe I'll send him to McMurdo Office to play security guard there at one of the perimeter outposts; it would be not unlike a punishment meted in one of my favorite science fiction series, which notion amuses me. Though I hate to unload him on the McMurdo people. Or," Fox considered, "I could send him to the Lunar Farside Drydocks, to work an outpost..."

"A dead-end job in an unpleasant field station, in other words," Echo noted.

"Exactly, zun. Drill sergeants are one thing, and I understand them. But his arrogance simply will not do in a field agent. It will get someone killed."

"Works for me." Omega shrugged. "After he got done fondling my knee in the Alpha Line Room, I was ready to take his hand off, anyway."

"HE DID WHAT?!" Fox all but roared. "That amoretz momzer!"

"Yup," Echo corroborated. "And if he'd left his hand there two seconds longer, Meg wouldn't have had to, because *I* would have."

"Oh, that will NOT do! They BOTH get remedial training in proper behavior befitting an agent, and THEN I'll reassign them!" Fox waved a hand at the door. "Back to work, both of you. You have finalists to consider. I'll take care of those two. And good job, impressing the hell out of your colleagues. Never mind backing up your professional reputations."

"Thanks, Boss," Echo said, as Alpha One headed out the door.

* * *

Fox watched them go, rising and moving to the bay window in his office.

"That truly was some excellent work," he decided, as he saw them enter the Alpha Line Room together, Echo gallantly holding the door for his partner. "And if anything, I think their relationship is making it even better. Ach! I haven't filed their life partnership paperwork yet! Well, it will have to wait; this

51

mess with Kappa has to be straightened out first. I'll do it as soon as I ream him and Nun new ones, I suppose." He reached over to the desk and hit the intercom to his assistants' office.

"Lima here, Boss," came the answer.

"Lima, contact Kappa and Nun and have them sent to my office at once, please."

"All over it, Fox," Lima responded. "We heard about that from some of the Alpha Line guys who watched the—"

"Yes, I'll ensure you get to see the video, both of you," Fox anticipated with a chuckle. "And yes, it was a thing of beauty to watch. Now get Nun and Kappa up here, please."

"We expected that," Bravo's voice noted. "We'll have 'em there in, like, five."

"Good. Fox out."

"Lima an' Bravo out."

* * *

But by the time Fox got done with Kappa and Nun—neither of whom was happy about the reprimand, and Fox had to get stern when he told them he was breaking up the partnership, nearly having to call in security—another urgent matter had deposited itself on his plate.

"Fox, Bravo," came the comm annunciation into his all-too-briefly-quiet office.

"Go, Bravo," Fox said, hitting the mic button and stifling a sigh.

"Urgent incoming communication from Emdali on the secure line, sir," Bravo said. "Code Emdali Black One."

"Oh, farkakte," Fox breathed, as his gut abruptly tied itself in knots. "Pipe it in to my wall screen five minutes ago, zun." He quickly opaqued the bay window.

* * *

"No, Franz, it is not good," a worried Suud said on the vid comm, as he gazed at Fox's image on the screen. "Pulgey is severely injured. He has lost a great deal of blood, and it is highly probable that one wing will have to be amputated into the bargain, according to my personal physician. Pulgey's own physician is en route at his best possible speed. But..." he shrugged, concerned. "We are not certain he will survive."

"Oh, HaShem help us," Fox whispered, paling. "What's the word on the assassins?"

"We are still unsure how many there were," Suud admitted. "They had sophisticated personal cloaking systems and solid holograms. Some nine or ten were killed—I am still waiting for confirmation on body count, because there was still fighting going on when I evacuated Pulgey—four were captured, and an unknown number escaped into the tourists and commuters."

"Get some Deltiri interroga—"

"Already on it, my friend," Suud said, baring his teeth, a formidable expression, and one he used to use to intimidate those who posed a threat to Entiyti. "With instructions that they do not have to be particularly gentle...though chances are, you will arrive before they do. But Franz?"

"Yes?"

"Of the four we captured thanks to the use of the somniferous grenades, two were Zargothian, one was Teludal...and one was Reptoid."

* * *

"Damnation. There may have been inside help," Fox realized. "Which means the threat may not be over."

"Exactly. How fast can you and your mate get here?"

"I can be there within hours, Suud. I'll bring Zebra, all her medical gear, and if I can, I'll even bring Zarnix. The Division is quiet for the time; I think it will be all right."

"That leaves some rather large holes in your hierarchy."

"No; Whiskey is the third in charge in Medical, and he's here and he's good. And I'll bump Echo from Assistant Director up to Acting Director while I'm gone. Omega is his assistant department chief, so he can bump her up in turn, and she can run Alpha Line for the time being, and with his help. Hell, she's done a fine job of it several times already, when he was out of pocket. Those three can pull this off."

"That...is excellent. Come as soon as you can; I cannot be

53

sure he will last the night, Franz."

"I'm on my way, Suud."

And the screen went dark, as Fox deactivated the comm link.

Then he reached for his cell phone, putting it in high-level cipher mode, and called—in order—his assistants, the head of Diplomacy, and his life partner, Zebra, the assistant chief of staff of Medical.

* * *

"No, bubeleh, we don't have time," Fox noted to the video image of his mate on his cell phone, all while struggling to maintain his cool; Pulgey Entiyti was his oldest living friend, as close as family, and though he would have refused to admit to it, his gut was churning in anxiety, nigh unto fear, that that dear friend and family member might not survive. "Grab the bug-out bags we had prepared for emergencies, grab all the medical gear you can, and be ready to go when I get home."

"You want me to see if Zarnix can accompany?" Zebra wondered, and Fox noted that she was, herself, pale.

My bubeleh has grown attached to meyn fremd bruder, I believe, Fox thought. *And that is a very good thing. Though perhaps not in this instance; it very nearly undid her to work on Echo's mother. How much the more someone she already knows, and considers family? But Zarnix may help matters in this respect.*

"Yes, meyn gelibte, I think that would be a very good idea. IF he is willing and able to come."

"I already know that he had no particular plans, Fox," Zebra averred. "And this is a quiet time of year for the medlab. No general epidemics this time of year, and no significant influx of visitors."

"Excellent. Make sure you use the ciphered comm, though, tei-yerinkeh."

"Got it. You've already told Lima and Bravo?"

"I have. And gotten a temporary-duty-handover order started with Sugar; I thought, in the circumstances, it behooved us to make sure everything was diplomatically worded, but I simply don't have time to do it myself..."

"Right. Good plan. You're gonna notify Alpha One while I ping Zarnix, right?"

"Within moments after we end our call. Probably while en route."

"Okay. You do that, and I'll call Zarnix, then grab our stuff, and be ready to go when you get here."

"Vunderlekh." Then he sighed despite himself. "A brokh! Eizeh farshtinkener balegan."

"What a stinkin' rotten mess? It sure sounds like it, honey," Zebra agreed. "All right, you go do what needs doing on your end, and I'll take care of things here."

"Gone, bubeleh. See you soon."

* * *

Alpha One had just finished their evening meal, which Echo had prepared; it was a decadent three-course concoction that started with crepes wrapped around a mixture of ricotta, sautéed morels, balsamic vinegar, and honey-roasted walnuts. This was followed by savory herb-cheese-stuffed tortellini drizzled in truffle oil, and culminated with a frozen dessert that Echo said his mother called 'xocolatl ice cream,' a mildly-spicy Aztec-style variant on chocolate ice cream, garnished with cinnamon-sugar-dusted, fried tortilla strips. An off-duty Echo pulled out all the stops—he'd actually started preparation before breakfast that morning, unbeknownst to Omega—and laid out a very private, elegant candlelight dinner for his partner and newly-minted fiancée. Now they sat on his sofa in the den with the last of their glasses of Dulce Lambrusco, lights still dimmed, discussing possible plans for the evening.

"That was lovely, hon," Omega murmured, patting her belly as she took his empty glass along with her own and set it aside on the end table. "Utterly delish. I can't believe you did all that cooking, just for me."

"Well, I kinda wanted to do something special to celebrate, just you an' me," Echo admitted, leaning over to kiss her. "I

55

mean, your birthday, and us getting engaged, and all that. And we didn't get a chance yesterday, ON your birthday, all things considered."

"Well, but you threw me a birthday party, night before last."

"Yeah, but that was, like, EVERYBODY. And India did way more of the planning than I did; I mostly just had the job of ensuring you got there! I wanted US to do something special. JUST us."

"So you made me the most romantic dinner you knew how to make?"

"Um, yeah." Echo flushed. "I...guess so. You liked it?"

"I loved it, hon. And I swear I'll help you clean up later."

"Nah, it won't be that bad. I got it. I already had most of it in the dishwasher by the time I got things plated, anyway, just to get it outta the way."

"Aw. In case I haven't told you lately: You are a very special guy." She leaned up to kiss him. "And now, you're MY very special guy."

"Yup." He grinned at her. "And I have no problems at all with being 'possessed' in that way. 'Cause, frankly, you're my special gal, too. So. What do you want to do now? We've got the rest of the evening to ourselves." He glanced at his wrist chronometer. "I suppose we could always go out dancing, if you wanted."

"Nah, after that nummy meal, I'm a little too lethargic for that!" Omega replied, and they both laughed. Omega stretched up to kiss him again. "A movie, maybe?"

"Aw, I dunno. There's nothing out there that I'm interested in seeing—at least, not that we haven't already seen at least once."

"As busy as we've been lately, you'd think there'd be something out there that we missed getting to see. I mean, between dodging Wright, and then the Broadway thing..."

"You'd think, wouldn't ya?" Echo shook his head. "Down time outta Hollywood, I suppose. This is sorta one of the slack times of the year for film releases. Plus, they DID have that little earthquake out there while you were back in Alabama, after all—which triggered that big wildfire when a transformer blew an' some live power lines went down in the brush. The whole ball o' shit combined did some serious damage, and I saw in Juliet's report outta the L.A. Office where that had kinda thrown a lotta schedules off. And not just the studios' schedules."

"Ooo, I bet. Well, we could always pop a movie in the player, I guess," Omega suggested, as Echo pulled her closer.

"Orrr..." he began, considering.

"Or?" she echoed.

"I kinda like this," he admitted, nuzzling her cheek. "It isn't like we GOTTA do ANYthing, really..."

"Ha! Good point," Omega agreed, blushing in shyness, yet turning her face to catch his mouth with hers. "It IS kinda nice, just like this."

"Okay, decision made," Echo declared, leaning to one side, lifting his legs, and pulling his partner into his arms as he reclined on the couch. "We spend the evening making out."

"That'll work..."

* * *

Alpha One had been on Echo's sofa, kissing and cuddling and occasionally murmuring together, making plans for their future, for just over an hour when Echo's cell phone went off. Instinctively, he slapped at his trousers pocket, then reached in and grabbed the thing, activating it and holding it to his ear in one motion.

"Echo."

"Zun, it's Fox. Where are you and Omega? Are you out on a date? If so, I need you two to get back right away. I'm terribly sorry to interrupt your evening, but it's extremely urgent."

"No, Fox," Echo said, gesturing to Omega, who sat up and helped him sit up as well, "we're in our quarters. Well, in MY quarters—our joint quarters, I guess you could say...or it will be, eventually. We just finished dinner a bit ago, and we were sitting on my sofa and, um, talking." Omega desperately stifled

57

a snort, clapping both hands to her mouth and nose to muffle the noise. Echo rolled his eyes, then dropped into their unspoken codes and told her, *Well, we were.*

Sort of. Not much, though. What's up? Omega responded.

Dunno yet.

Lemme hear. Unless it's classified.

Don't think so. Might be, but he asked about BOTH of us.

So Echo held the phone where Omega could listen in on the conversation, hitting a button to activate the external speaker, then made to continue the audible portion...except Fox interjected before he could speak.

"Zun? Are you there?" Fox asked then. "Something clicked. Is this connection...?"

"It's okay, Fox, I'm here. So is Meg now, if that's okay—she was just asking what was up, so I put the phone in speaker mode. That's probably what you heard click."

"Ah. Yes, it's fine; in fact, it's good. I need both of you right now."

"What's wrong, Fox?" Echo wondered. "Something's obviously not okay..."

"You got that right, zun. In YOUR quarters, you said?" Fox verified.

"Yeah..."

"Vunderlekh! Don't go anywhere, either of you. I'll be there inside five; I'm already on the way. I have to swing by my own quarters anyway to pack and meet Zebra..."

"Pack!? Fox, what's going on?"

"A kappore. Not on the phone—yours isn't in cipher mode. Tell you in two."

The line went dead.

"That did NOT sound good," Omega declared.

"No, it didn't," Echo said, worried. "Something's bad wrong for Fox to sound upset."

* * *

Fox emerged from the elevator on Alpha One's floor of the housing section of Headquarters at a dead run, shoving his just-deactivated cell phone back into a pocket. He skidded around a corner, sprinted another hundred yards down the corridor, and stopped in front of a door.

The sole identifying marker on the wall beside it was a capital letter E on the nameplate—as the very first recipient of the codename corresponding to the letter, the designation belonged to Echo, and would for as long as he remained with the Agency.

Fox raised a fist.

* * *

Scant moments later, Alpha One heard a banging on Echo's front door.

"Zun?" came the familiar voice from the other side over the tiny intercom. "It's me."

"Whoa, that WAS fast," Echo murmured. "He musta already been halfway here by the time the call connected."

He leaped to his feet, Omega right behind him, and hurried to the door, both trying to straighten rumpled, displaced clothing as they went. Since both of them still wore their Suit trousers and shirts—though they had ditched jackets and ties in respective bedroom closets as soon as they had arrived home— they were only mildly successful.

Echo jerked the door open, and a slightly pale Director Fox entered.

* * *

"I'm sorry to bother the two of you like this," he began, his speech as rapid-fire as he knew how to make it, and still keep it understandable. A cursory scan of his two top Agents took in their rumpled appearance and mussed hair—as well as a slight reddening around Omega's mouth, likely induced in her fair, sensitive skin by Echo's beard stubble, despite evidence that the male Agent had recently shaved in deference to same—told him all he needed to know about what he had interrupted; he hid a wince. "...I know you were enjoying some private time together in your off hours, and all things considered, it's about time, but a brokh! Things have gone keyn farkakte! I'm afraid

I need your help, meyn kinder."

"Come on in, Boss, and tell us what's happened," Echo noted, as Omega took the older man's arm and gently tugged, while Echo closed the door. Fox moved a little farther into the room, but held up a hand.

"I don't have time to visit," he explained, "and I can't take long to explain, either. Just stop and pay attention, both of you."

Omega and Echo both stopped dead and focused their entire attention on the Agency Director. He nodded, pleased at their immediate response.

"Good. Now listen closely. There's been an assassination attempt on Pulgey."

* * *

"Oh, no," Omega whispered. She and Echo exchanged horrified glances.

Given that Lord Pulgey Entiyti was the current duly-elected chairbeing of the Ennead, the core committee of the Galactic Coalition, he was the effective presidential leader of the entire Milky Way Galaxy...as well as assorted adjuncts and affiliates from the nearest of the several satellite galaxies of the Milky Way, most of whom participated in the Coalition in some fashion. He was, in addition, one of the hereditary leaders on his homeworld of Emdali, also known as Draigon. As such, he was one of the most powerful beings—probably THE most powerful—in the entire galaxy.

And he was a dear, trusted, and old friend of the trio currently assembled in Echo's foyer.

"How bad?" Echo demanded, scowling. "They didn't get him, did they?"

"I don't know yet, and yes," Fox admitted. "I got the call from Suud..." he checked his wrist chronometer, "less than half an hour ago; say twenty-two, twenty-four minutes, and I've been hopping since then. What I DO know is that, yes, they did get him—Suud thinks it was a bomb, though there was gunfire as well, and he doesn't know exactly WHAT happened, not yet, not until the physicians figure it out and he gets some after-action reports, I suppose. Two bodyguards are injured, one critically, and Suud's son's fiancée, the third bodyguard, is...dead."

"Oh no," Omega whispered again, shocked.

"...But whatever, Pul is injured, probably severely—possibly fatally," Fox's voice cracked slightly, and he broke off abruptly.

Pulgey Entiyti was also Fox's oldest living non-human friend as well as a former employer—in his previous life as former Mossad agent Franz Levy, Fox had been the best chief bodyguard Entiyti had ever employed, and the two runners-up-slash-successors, Suud Guurn and Lydhuu Raiit, had been Levy's protégés—and Levy and Entiyti had saved each other's lives several times over, in the decades since they had met by accident in Earth's war-torn Middle East. Some thought—privately, for both males had a badass reputation, and neither took bullshit in the least quantity, nor did they openly express sentiment readily—that they considered each other non-species brothers of a sort; Echo and Omega, who had discussed it between themselves, were two of those who held that opinion. More, since a heretofore-lonely and isolated Omega had assembled a kind of non-genetic family about herself in the Agency, with Fox the patriarch of same, this made Entiyti a beloved 'friend of the family,' at the very least—or, as Echo considered, a doting, if intimidating, uncle.

Omega took Fox's arm again, in a very gentle hold this time, rubbing her fingers against his forearm through his Suit jacket and shirt, a gesture intended to soothe her adoptive father-figure; the rattled and deeply upset Director threw her a grateful glance before continuing.

"...And I'm one of the people Pul called for," he continued, "before he lost consciousness. I'm taking Zebra and Zarnix, and heading for his estate on Emdali to see if we can help. And hope we get there before...well, before Mlakh Samael does."

"Mlakh...what?" Omega murmured.

"The angel Samael," Fox explained. "In Jewish writings,

he's known as the angel of death, among other equally unpleasant things."

"Oh..." Omega put her other hand to her mouth in distress.

"Oh shit," Echo breathed. "Let us know if there's anything we can do, Fox. We can be ready to go by the time you can get back to your quarters, Meg and me."

"Will do, Echo, but for now, what you two can do for me—for us—is to fill in," Fox pointed out. "That means as my successor and deputy, until further notice, you're the Acting Director, zun. And Omega, that leaves you in charge of Alpha Line, tekhter. Whiskey will be running the medlab for you until we get back. I've already issued orders to that effect; it's official—or it will be, once the formal announcement goes out—and that's something you'll have to be careful about, too. Because news of the assassination attempt will tend to unsettle the Coalition—insofar as I can tell, word hasn't made it out yet, but it's only a matter of time, and things will go to Sheol in the proverbial handbasket if we're not damn careful. So be aware, because until I make it back, you're running the show, kinder."

Fox spun on his heel, grabbed the doorknob, and was gone.

Echo and Omega stared at each other in shock.

"Ohhhh, shit," Omega breathed, distressed and dismayed.

"That, right there," a concerned Echo agreed.

* * *

Zebra was waiting in the den when Fox burst into their joint quarters, only moments after leaving Echo's quarters.

"Okay, honey, I got everything together," she said, pointing to several bags filling the sofa. "Both bug-out bags, your regular travel kit, my regular travel kit, and a full-up portable medikit. Zarnix is bringing the special medlab kit along with his stuff, and he got a volunteer medtech to come along, too."

"Ah, well—" Fox began.

"No sweat, Fox; it's Yorker," Zebra said with a grin, holding up a forestalling hand.

"Oh, he's the one with the high security clearance to work

on diplomats?"

"The same. Oh, and they're coming by with an antigrav cart for all the kits. What craft are we taking?"

"We'll hit Grand Central out to Penn Station, then take the *Exodus* up to the *Genesis*," Fox explained, double-checking his personal kit for a couple of incidental items he had forgotten to tell her to include, and pleased to find them already packed. "I've already sent out an emergency alert for a skeleton crew for the *Genesis*, and we're good...except for the pilot and navigator. So I'll be handling piloting and celestial navigation myself."

"Oh!" Zebra said, eyes widening in surprise.

"Not afraid of my driving, are you, bubeleh?" Fox said with a smirk.

"No, I've just never seen you fly anything quite THAT big before," Zebra admitted. Just then, there was a knock at the door, coupled with a *ding!* on Zebra's cell phone. "That'll be Zarnix and Yorker with the antigrav cart," she said, double-checking her phone. "Yeah. C'mon, grab some of this shit and let's haul tokhes, honey."

"Right behind your tokhes, meyn gelibte. And, by way of some much-needed frivolity right now, let me note that it is a very cute tokhes."

Zebra snorted.

"You should know," she observed.

* * *

Zarnix and Yorker were waiting in the corridor outside their front door, their own gear already strapped to the cart; they grabbed the bags from Fox and Zebra, adding them, as Fox went back for the rest of it.

Moments later, they were sprinting for the emergency elevators, and Grand Central Station.

* * *

A scant seven minutes after that saw them aboard the *Exodus*, a powerful interstellar shuttle which was already prepped, with a priority launch window. The shuttle's captain, a Glu'g'ik named Du'ven'de, met them at the hatch, helping them to load their gear—including the antigrav cart, which they would need on the other end of the trip—into the small-but-swift ship's minuscule stowage.

"Strap in," she told them then.

Ninety seconds later, they were cloaked and going exo, toward the *Genesis'* dry dock on the lunar far side.

* * *

Upon boarding the *Genesis*, Zebra, Zarnix, and Yorker headed straight for sickbay, while Fox made for the bridge. There, he found a skeleton bridge crew awaiting him.

"Admiral Director on the bridge!" the security chief, Zero, announced, and the others snapped to attention.

"Stand down, stand down, we don't have time for that formal nonsense," Fox declared, waving a hand at them as he moved toward the helm. "So Übermut and Cast definitely couldn't make it?"

"No sir," Sail, the comm officer, affirmed. "I got definitive word not two minutes ago. They wish us Godspeed and sent their deepest apologies, but they were on shore leave, visiting family, in eastern Europe and the Sudan, respectively, and couldn't get to an Office or Station in time to reach us before departure—they both gave it their best efforts, but failed—so you are without helm and navigation. We assume you'll be handling that yourself?"

"You assume correctly," Fox declared, sitting at the helm console and quickly rerouting all command and navigation control to it. "Is Uncle in the engine room?"

"She said to tell you everything's humming, and ready for departure at your word, sir," Sail averred with a grin.

"Very good, then. I brought along some medical staff, as you might expect," Fox said, bringing up the navigation function and laying in a course for Emdali—first ensuring the oversized *Genesis*, the flagship of the Division One fleet, would get out of Sol system undetected by standard observers, before dropping into interstellar warp. It was possessed of several different forms of cloaking, and Fox intended to use them all, but accidents still occurred. "Get me a line to the sick bay, Sail."

"Line open, sir."

"This is Fox. Who've I got?"

"Zarnix, Fox. Give us about ten seconds...there! Everything is safely stowed. You may fire when ready, my friend."

"Copy that," Fox murmured. "Get yourselves strapped in; I'm not going slow. That goes for the bridge staff, too," he said, glancing around the ship's control center. "Fox out."

Sail was already at his designated station, so he simply strapped in; Boy moved to the weapons console, down from Fox, and likewise took her assigned seat, buckling the five-point harness across her body, as Zero took his little-used seat along the aft bulkhead. Once he was strapped down, he glanced at Sail and Boy, who nodded.

"All bridge crew...except yourself...at stations and restrained, sir," Zero said.

"Oh, good point," Fox muttered, reaching for his own restraint harness. "Sail, get me the engine room."

"Engine room waiting, sir."

"Uncle, this is Fox. How are you doing, old girl?"

"I'm good, Fox, and so are our engines. I assume you'll be hitting emergency cruising?"

"You assume correctly, as usual, mcyn khaverte."

"All right, I waited until the last moment to adjust the gain...there. The *Genesis* is ready at your command, sir."

"Forward view on screen. Hail dry dock," Fox ordered, bringing up the large viewing screen, but not bothering with the tank systems. Sail nodded.

"This is Lunar Farside Drydocks Control. Admiral Director?"

"Affirmative, Control. Take her out of dry dock, if you please."

"Tractor beams locking on, sir."

"Docking clamps disengaged," Fox made the call even as he released the clamps, "now."

"Copy that. Locking beams...now."

There was a slight shifting of the deck beneath them, but otherwise there was no evidence of the tractor beam lock until the dry dock's structure began to slip past the viewing screen. Fox alternated between watching his instrument readouts and the viewscreen, as the huge saucer moved farther and farther away from the docking superstructure.

"Drydocks Control to *Genesis*."

"*Genesis* here," Fox replied.

"You are clear, sir, and ready for interplanetary drive. All other traffic has been halted until you depart. Intended course has been received via secure channels, and entered into the appropriate database; still, I would recommend travel with max shields."

"Roger that; I'd planned on it, as well as a full stealth cloak."

"Excellent plan, sir. You may engage interplanetary engines at your discretion. Godspeed, and here's hoping you find things aren't as bad as we fear when you arrive, and that Lord Entiyti is much better than initial reports make it."

"Amein," Fox murmured in response. "From your lips to Adonai's ears. Engaging interplanetary drive...now."

And the *Genesis* began to move at speed.

* * *

Alpha One got dressed in full Suits again and headed straight for the Core. There, they found Lima and Bravo both awaiting them outside the Alpha Line Room.

"Hey, guys," Bravo said, subdued. "We kinda expected you'd be along any minute."

"Hey," Echo murmured, jabbing a finger toward the door. "Let's go in here, rather than having a briefing like this in the middle of the Core. What's up? I figured for one of you two to head out with Fox."

"We discussed it with him," Lima confessed, as they all followed Echo into the departmental conference room, Omega closing the door behind them, "and we were both willing, but we all three kinda reached the conclusion that, with Zebra and Zarnix and several members of Security with him—the security guards went ahead as soon as they got their orders, and joined Fox at the ship—well, we figured he'd be fine, but YOU might need US to ensure a smooth transition."

"This sounds like you don't think he's coming back," Omega noted, perturbed. She grabbed one of the small desks, intended for Alpha Line members during a team meeting, and spun it around, then sat. The others followed suit, arranging the little desks in a loose circle.

"Oh, he's planning on coming back," Bravo averred, "he just doesn't know when. He might have to play guard dog for a while, he said. It seems that Lord Entiyti never retained a proper bodyguard unit after coming back from retirement last winter. He only had a handful, Fox said, like MAYBE a third what he needed."

"Even after being reinstated as the full chairbeing, not just interim," Lima added. "But Bravo and I both know that Fox tried to convince him to do so, 'cause we were there when Fox called and bugged him about it. Like, four times."

"Entiyti just didn't think it was necessary," Bravo said, and shrugged.

"Aw shit," Echo grumbled. "No wonder somebody tried to off him. And nearly got away with it."

"Might still," Lima said, subdued.

"And no wonder the first two beings he sent for were Suud Guurn and Fox," Omega pointed out. "His two main chief bodyguards, from back in the day."

"Well, there was the lady Ergisol, too," Echo reminded her. "Her name escapes me..."

"Lydhuu Raiit," Bravo filled in. "From what Fox let slip, I think Lord Entiyti called for her too, but while she's going to meet Fox and the others on Emdali, she can't stay; she's teaching at the University on Aleancë, and it's mid-term, and she's pretty much the head of the department these days. If it comes to it, though, and Fox and Guurn think they need her, she's already said she'll hand her classes over to a colleague and come at once. AND if needed, she'll then command the same fleet she did during the Battle of Orion, to try to help ensure the Coalition stays...sane."

"Ooo," Omega murmured, wincing. "Good point. This could all go to hell in a really big handbasket."

"Yep. Okay," Echo sighed. "So I'm in charge of the whole damn Division, never mind the Agency, and Meg is running Alpha Line. What do we need to know...?"

* * *

Fox chose the most direct route out of the solar system, keeping the Moon between the *Genesis* and Earth; fortunately, the majority of the outer planets were in a different quadrant of the system, and he could take a fairly direct line outbound, at least until the point where he had to leave the ecliptic and enter the galactic plane proper, which was some sixty degrees inclined to the plane of the solar system. For an ordinary space-craft, that point might have been somewhere on the other side of the asteroid belt, or even the Kuiper Belt, but the *Genesis* was anything but ordinary. In a matter of some twenty minutes, she was far enough away from the Lunar Farside Drydocks— hence the Moon itself, the closest celestial body of any im-port—to safely engage the Alcubierre drive.

"Full cloaking on," Fox announced, fingers dancing across the console. "Sensor scrambler...on. Sail, shipwide speakers, please."

Sail hit a couple of switches. "Go, Fox."

"Fox to *Genesis* crew. By now, you know we are on an emergency mission with a skeleton crew, and you know why. I thank you deeply for coming when called, but I'm not going to spend a lot of time with details or niceties, people; Pulgey Entiyti is not only Galactic Chair, he is my oldest living friend. All stations prepare for emergency warp." His hands sought the correct controls. "In three...two...one..."

Abruptly, at Fox's command, the big dreadnought enfolded itself in a warp bubble and fairly leaped out of the solar system, as the warp's wave function accelerated toward Emdali at several thousand times lightspeed.

* * *

"Well, that doesn't sound too bad," Omega decided, after the two Director's Assistants finished briefing them. "Looks like nothing big is lined up any time soon, at least that's been sent down the pipeline."

"Yeah, we lucked out on that one, baby," Echo agreed, busy sending an official missive on his phone. "There; approval away. Yeah, we lucked out. Shit can happen, though, so don't let your guard down. What about an announcement about the temporary change of command? Fox said that would be going out soon."

"Fox already has Sugar working out the wording," Lima said. "Once Sugar finishes wordsmithing it, he'll pop it to you for approval; he already has Fox's official go-forth on it, so there won't be any problems. And it'll also note that Omega is filling in as head of Alpha Line, and Whiskey as head of Medical. That way, it's all covered, and people know who to report to."

"Yeah, it should go out not later than in the morning," Bravo said. "Though you might well get it in the next few hours, on your phone, for approval before it's officially released; Sugar was working hard to get it out A.S.A.P. As soon as you buy off on it, it goes out to the full distribution."

* * *

Just then, a loud *BA-DEEP!* sounded on both Lima's and Bravo's cell phones. Bravo yanked his from a pocket.

"They're off-planet?" Lima wondered.

"Yup," Bravo confirmed, reading a text message. "Out of system, it looks like. Fox is piloting, personally. And guys?" Bravo looked up from his phone. "He took the *Genesis*. With crew. Skeleton crew, but still."

"Ooo," Lima murmured.

"Which means he's going armed for Aurigan were-bear," Echo observed.

69

"Exactly," Bravo agreed. "So. As of this moment, Acting Director Echo, you are in charge, sir."

"All right, that'll have to work," Echo decided. "First things first. What do YOU need from US at the moment?"

"Tap this with your cell phones, guys," Bravo said, holding out a device. "This'll set up all the electronic relays necessary for alerts and add the two of you on the emergency alert network in the place of Fox."

"Both of us?" Omega wondered. "But Echo, were you ever on that?"

"Not yet, but Fox was getting ready to add me," Echo noted. "He felt that, as head of Alpha Line and Assistant Director, I needed to be on the network. And that means you do, too."

"Right. Besides, we, um, we heard about the, uh..." Bravo tried, then glanced at the slightly older Lima for help.

"Fox told us you two are engaged now, and congratulations," Lima said point-blank, with a grin.

"Oh," Echo said, and he and Omega both offered slightly sheepish smiles, flushing. "Well, um, thank y'all."

"Hey, we're thrilled for ya," Lima added. "Bravo and I'd had a couple conversations...oh, maybe six months ago, ish... it wasn't long after the whole Cortian shit...about how we thought you two would make a great couple, in more ways than just work. I mentioned that to Fox when he told us about your engagement, and he said we were dead right. Anyway, when the alert thing came up, we pointed out to him that one of you is as likely as the other to hear the alert, and he agreed."

"Especially at night," Bravo said with a slight smirk. Omega flushed a deep crimson.

* * *

"Hold on, guys," a perturbed Echo said, noting his partner's intense blush. "I assume he also told you that we're waiting for the Agency's charter amendment?"

"Yeah," Lima began. "So, I mean, what—"

"OH!" Bravo exclaimed, eyes going wide. "You thought we meant—no, no, no! We know you two better than that.

70

You're both reserved and kinda old-fashioned, which is one of the things that makes you both such excellent peeps, *I* think. You know what you want, you know what's the RIGHT thing to do, and you're not afraid to stand for it. Any of it."

"Ooo. I get it now. Oh damn, that DID come out all wrong! Yeah, Echo, Omega, it's cool—an' so are you guys," Lima agreed. "And yes, he told us. What we meant—an' yeah, I guess neither one of us said THAT quite right—was that we know you both work long, hard hours and probably sleep like the dead, once you finally get to crash. So we figured if we put BOTH of you on the alert network, then we had double the chance of ONE of you waking up to actually HEAR the alert, and whoever heard it would tell the other one right away. Um, sorry for the misunderstanding."

"Yeah, the grin was about the two of you being asleep an' slap out of it—which is NOT your normal, waking state—not, um, the other thing," Bravo admitted, his own face flushing.

Echo snorted, and Omega chuckled, her face returning to a semblance of its usual color. Alpha One extracted their phones and tapped them to the device, and the screens of both phones lit a dark red for a moment; visible through the one-way observing window, the flooring of the Core just outside the Alpha Line Room flashed the same shade between the tiles. Then both grew dark.

"All right, that's taken care of," Bravo noted. "And Fox said to try to keep you on your normal shifts unless shit hits the fan, which it isn't, so head on back home and come in at your usual time in the morning."

"Well, they maybe need to come in a little early tomorrow, remember?" Lima pointed out.

"Oh, yeah. Damn. I almost forgot. If you can cut your sleep cycle short by about six hours, guys, it would help," Bravo said. "Well, Echo needs to, anyhow. There's an unexpected communiqué from the Ganotian potentate about the trade agreement; came in about ten minutes after Fox left his office. She wants to verify some details."

"But isn't that Sugar's bailiwick?" Echo wondered, as they put away their phones. "Or whoever he has assigned to it, at least?"

"Yes, and he has Gamma working it, especially while he's on the announcement wording," Lima confirmed. "But the potentate wants the Director there, too."

"Okay," Echo sighed. "Early wake-up call tomorrow. I guess it's a good thing that we're on 24 and off 24. Meg, you can sleep in, if you want to."

"Hell no," Omega averred. "I'm part of all this; I'll get up and help, some kinda way."

"All right, baby." Echo offered her a slight smile. "I appreciate it."

"Okay, so Alpha One shows up six hours early," Bravo noted on his tablet.

"Only Echo goes to the Director's Office, right?" Omega wondered. "And I come here?"

"Well, that's up to him, I guess," Bravo admitted. "Given you're just across the way, we can always re-route things to the Alpha Line Room if you'd rather. But there's gonna be certain things that you'll have to come to the Director's Office to do, like the monthly Division meetings an' stuff. 'Cause one of those is coming up, later in the week."

"And the Ganotian thing probably needs to be there," Lima pointed out. "She's gonna be thrown off enough as it is, seeing Echo there instead of Fox."

"True," Bravo sighed.

"I'll do my best to ease her mind, guys," Echo told them. "After all, when you get right down to it, I was the first human to make contact with 'em, anyway. She should at least know my code name."

"Yeah. We can make it work, between all of us," Lima averred. "If you wouldn't mind swinging by there first thing in the morning, though, we can take care of that routing right off, get the 'consultation' over and done with, and then let you know when you need to go there for other things."

"That'll work," Echo agreed. "You good with that, Meg?"

"Yeah, I think so, Ace," she confirmed. "And I think that, given Fox is still nominal Director, it'll show proper respect for him, too, if you don't immediately, like, move in to the Director's Office."

"Good point," Echo noted. "One I hadn't thought of yet, too. And a prime example of exactly why having you for a partner is a VERY good thing. Okay, baby, unless the guys here have anything else for us..." He paused, and Bravo and Lima shook their heads, "then let's you and me go back home and discuss this small wrinkle a little bit before it's time to crash. Maybe we can make a few contingency plans in case any excrement does hit some rotating air movers."

"Roger that, Ace."

The four headed out the door. As the Director's Assistants headed for their office, Alpha One turned and headed for the elevators to the agents' quarters.

* * *

The pair entered Echo's front door, and sighed in unison.

"How come I don't think this is gonna be fun at all?" Omega wondered.

"Aw, baby, don't worry. It shouldn't be TOO bad, with nothing major going down. It'll give us a chance to ease into it, since we're gonna have these jobs eventually anyway," Echo pointed out.

"I know, I know, I just..."

"Please don't tell me you have a bad feeling about this."

"All right, I won't tell you."

"Well, shit," Echo grumbled. "One of THOSE bad feelings?"

"Maybe," Omega admitted. "I've been trying to figure that out for the last half-hour. I'm...not sure."

"Any more 'crossover' imagery like before the Cortian contact?"

"Nnooooo..."

"That's something, I suppose," Echo noted in relief. "Now,

you'll let me know immediately if you get anything specific, right, baby? I swear I'll listen, and I'll act on it. AND I'll be in a POSITION to act on it."

"Yeah, hon, I will," Omega confirmed. "Right now it's just a bad feeling. It's kinda like it was then, but this time it's not so intense, and I don't have specifics at all. I guess...I guess it's more like a, 'heads up—trouble coming,' than an all-out emergency alert kinda thing." She drew a deep breath. "I'll keep on it, and see if I can't, sorta, MAKE something float up, if you know what I mean. I'd like to have a little more advance warning this time, if something's gonna go down."

"You and me both."

"Damn, we've been busy; lookit the clock. It's way past time to crash already, especially with the early wake-up. Want a bedtime snack?"

"Fresh shortbread, by any chance?"

"No, I haven't had a good chance to do any baking," Omega offered sheepishly. "Between everything going on, and what Tt'l'k did to my emotions with that little telepathic programming module..." She sighed.

"Aw." Echo came to her side and put his arms around her, pulling her close and cradling her against his body. In response, she rested her head against his chest. "It's gonna be okay, baby. You said your first counseling session this morning with Zz'r'p went well, right?"

"Yeah. It took me about, oh, MAYBE five minutes to show him the last bits of EVERYTHING, and since I'd already signed off for him to see my medical records, by that point he pretty much had all of it. And he really gave me some things to think about. I, um, I wasn't sure how he was gonna react, but...he accepted everything without question, and without..." Omega paused and raised her head, looking for words. "What I'm tryin' to say is that he didn't reject me, an' he didn't look down on me, an' he pretty much just accepted everything at face value. Actually, he gave me some serious ego-boo by way of something to think about."

"Which, if he's willing to do that, how much more do you think I would be, sweetheart?"

"I know. I'm just..."

"Not ready yet. I know. I'm not trying to pressure you. I get it, and I'm being patient. I just wanted to make sure you thought about that aspect of things."

"I have been," Omega admitted. "It's why I ever even admitted to you that there was something you didn't already know, up at your beach house. I...I kinda think, now, that you'd accept. I'm just...scared."

"Because it bothers YOU."

"Right."

"Baby, let ME tell YOU something."

"Okay."

"If you don't want to, you NEVER have to tell me what it is," Echo declared. "It won't affect our relationship at all, either way. I'll still love you."

"I know, but...but it isn't really an option any more, I don't think," Omega decided, pressing her face into his chest. "At least, not to me, it isn't. If we're eventually gonna get married, I think it's only fair to you that you know...ALL of it."

"If you say so," Echo said with a shrug. "It doesn't bother me, whichever."

"But you're curious."

"Well, of course I'm curious," he confessed. "You tell me there's something I don't know about the woman I'm crazy in love with, I'm gonna be curious about what that is. But I respect the hell outta you, honey. And I respect your boundaries, the same way you've always respected—and protected—mine, even the telepathic ones. I'm not gonna go digging out something you don't want known. Never," he added for good measure. "Would you dig out something on me?"

"No."

"Okay, then. Same difference on this end. You'll tell me if and when you're ready. And if you do, I'll listen, and I'll take it seriously because YOU do, and I'll say that's fine because it will be, and we'll go on. But if you're never ready, or never able to, that's okay too. And that's the end of that. Now what did you have in mind for a bedtime snack?"

"Zebra sent over a cheesecake—one of her nummy home-made ones—this morning, by way of congratulating me for my first counseling session, I think. Maybe a little encouragement and motivation, too."

"SCORE!" Echo cried, and they laughed as they headed through the 'back door' into Omega's quarters, en route to her kitchen.

Chapter 4

The next morning after a short night, Alpha One headed straight for the Core. Omega had pinged Zz'r'p before breakfast, to let him know, in strict Division confidence, what was going down—the draft of the announcement had come to Echo late the previous evening, and he'd had some tweaks to it, so Sugar had not yet released it—and ask if it was all right to reschedule her second counseling session. That worthy had immediately become concerned and agreed to adjust his own schedule to accommodate the emergency staffing and hierarchy change. Omega would still come in to see him that morning, but at a different time, allowing her the flexibility to handle departmental matters around the appointment, given Echo would not be available for Alpha Line activities while she was gone.

"Okay, baby, you see about arranging for a department meeting to make the announcement, and I'm gonna run by the Director's office to meet Bravo an' Lima and get things worked out," Echo told Omega, once they'd arrived in the Alpha Line Room. "Never mind working with Sugar, and the consult with the Ganotian leader. It all might take a while, so do what you need to, including going to your counseling session, and running the Alpha Line meeting. Whatever you do, don't wait on me, because I have no idea how long I'll be."

"Roger that," Omega agreed. "Did you reroute your email so that I get cc'ed on everything?"

"Oh, shit! Yeah, hang on a sec," Echo said, waking his desk computer, going into the email and doing as she asked, all without bothering to sit down. "There. That should take care of matters. Not only will it forward everything from this point, it'll forward everything currently in my inbox. I think I'm gonna leave it like that, too. I need you copied on this shit, as my permanent alternate. And you've got the backup password, right?"

"Yup. Okay, off with ya, then," she said with a grin. "You worry about keeping the Agency running. I got this."

"I'm glad to hear it, honey," Echo murmured, straightening and turning toward her. "When you started wanting me to relieve you of duty for a bit there the last couple of weeks, I admit I was worried, bad."

"Yeah, I know," Omega admitted, hanging her head. "I'm... sorry. Between everything that had happened, and then that little 'let's make Omega even MORE depressed' telepathic programming Tt'l'k stuck in there," she tapped her temple, "I've been...a wreck. You'd be amazed how much just getting that telepathic program 'deleted' really helped my mental and emotional outlook. And...well, the very first session with Zz'r'p yesterday—if it wasn't at the front of my thoughts, it hasn't been too far down, ever since."

"And it helped?"

"Oh, good grief, did it. I'm still...well, there's a lotta work to be done," Omega confessed. "But I've been doing THIS job for a while now, and I think I've mostly got my confidence back about IT, at least."

"That's terrific," an enthused Echo said with a wide smile. "Okay, lemme get outta here and see about making sure the Agency doesn't disintegrate while Fox is gone."

"Right." Omega shot a glance around the empty room, hit the switch that toggled the window into the Core to one-way, then offered her face for a brief, chaste kiss, which Echo gave without hesitation. Then he was off.

Omega pulled up the email and quickly reviewed the departmental situation, making sure everything would be handled in a timely fashion, given she was the only one who could see to matters for the foreseeable future.

* * *

An hour later, she was sitting in a comfortable armchair in the conversation corner of Zz'r'p's office in the Deltiri embassy.

78

"How are you today, my dear?" the benevolent ambassador asked. "Especially given what apparently transpired last night?"

"Surprisingly good, Zz'r'p," Omega told him. "Oh, well, to be honest, I got a bad feeling about it, but—"

"Wait," Zz'r'p interrupted, dismayed. "What kind of a bad feeling?"

"Echo asked the same thing," she replied, rueful. "Yeah, kinda sorta one of THOSE bad feelings...like I had before the Cortians got here. But nothing to go on. No visions, no dreams...nothing. Just...a bad feeling. Like..." she broke off. "Well, I told Echo last night it was sorta like, 'heads up, something's coming,' without being the five-alarm fire the Cortian shit was. You know what I mean?"

"Yes, I believe so. May I...'look'?"

"Sure, go for it."

The pair were quiet, as Zz'r'p gently inspected Omega's mind, looking for any sign of the precognition that had manifested the previous winter...but which had remained largely dormant in the months since.

"I do not perceive anything...definite," he decided after several moments.

"No, neither have I," Omega agreed. "And believe me, after last time, I've been looking hard. I just got the feeling, but no advance warning."

"And you yourself? Outside the foreboding, how do you feel about the situation?"

"I'm worried about Pulgey," she confessed. "I hope he's okay. He's like...like a friend of the family, or maybe even an uncle, kinda."

"And your temporary promotion?"

"Oh, that. It's like I told Echo this morning," she said. "Yeah, I'm nervous, because I'm gonna be RUNNING the department. But...I've been the assistant chief for most of this year already—the Cortian incident went down in January, and I was basically running all of Alpha Line and a significant chunk of Diplomacy for the departure 'ceremony' even then—and damn, when it's Alpha Line, two months is like a year of experience, you know? Besides, I've had to run it with him out of pocket or undercover several times already. So, with the little 'subroutine' outta my head, and for the umpteenth time thank you for that, my confidence is back—in my ability to do the job, at least."

"It should be," Zz'r'p said with a laugh. "I saw the video of Alpha One's training session yesterday. The fact that the two of you already had a battle plan capable of doing what you did, as quickly as you did it, and that you executed it in perfect unison without hesitation or error or more than a minimum of coordination...never mind the problem-solving you both did, to arrive at that point from being dropped blindly into the scenario...my dear friend, that was impressive."

"Heh. Thanks," Omega chuckled, flushing in embarrassment, but pleased.

"And I noted you were the one to choose the battle plan," Zz'r'p noted. "Is that unusual with Alpha One, given Echo is the senior partner, or is it a case of, 'we have all these plans developed, one of us needs to choose one and run with it'?"

"That," Omega averred. "Whoever comes up with a workable plan, the other goes with the flow."

"How many plans do you have?"

"Well, I guess it depends on your definition," Omega considered. "See, there's full-on fight plans, like what we did yesterday; and there's smaller segments we can put together, kind of modular, and build a battle plan out of 'em; then there's individual maneuvers either of us can do to get out of a temporary bad sitch." She shrugged. "We try all kinds of stuff to see what works, in the training simulator AND the gym, then add it to our repertoire by assigning it a code and practicing the hell out of it."

"I see...so with a modular approach, your plans are basically infinite in number..."

* * *

The second counseling session went as well as the first, and soon a relatively cheerful, if somewhat thoughtful Omega was back in the Alpha Line Room at her desk, pondering the things Zz'r'p had given her to think about, while she worked her way through compiling the daily report.

About the time she submitted the report to 'the Boys,' as Fox sometimes referred to his assistants, the first few Alpha Line teams began to arrive for the departmental meeting scheduled at the top of the hour. As usual, they crowded around the pod brewer, making fresh cups of coffee and chatting congenially with each other and Omega before finding seats in the rows of college-classroom-style desks that filled most of the room for this purpose. Moments later, a message came in from Alpha Two informing her that they were running a few minutes late for the meeting consequent to a report of a possible problem by an 'import' over in Manhattan, and she acknowledged the message, approving the delay.

She surveyed the room for a moment, noting how many of the desks were filled. *Huh,* she decided. *We're gonna have to ask Fox to put a space warp and more desks in here, at this rate. We have a DEPARTMENT. Well, I better get with it, here.*

Omega moved to Echo's desk briefly, sitting in his chair to pull up his file of 'To Discuss' items for the next team meeting, running over it in her mind and making sure she understood what needed emphasis, then she turned to the department membership—who had already seated themselves in the ranks of desks—and smiled.

"Hi, y'all! Let's get started," she said blithely, and several familiar faces returned the smile and greeting.

Not all, however.

"Who the hell are you?" a strange Agent demanded, even as her partner scowled. "Where's Romeo?"

"Excuse me?" Omega asked, raising an eyebrow. "And you are...?"

"None of your damn business," the Agent's partner retorted. "Where's the department chief?"

"Echo is in Fox's office at the moment—" Omega began. The other Agents in the room stirred in surprise and discomfort.

"Get off it," the first Agent snapped. "Where the hell is Romeo?"

"Alpha Two will be reporting in late," Omega responded, crisp. "They are winding up a previous mission—"

"I dunno who the hell this Alpha Two is," the second agent declared, "but we wait for Chief Romeo to arrive before we start. And get the hell out of his chair! You're not even Alpha Line!"

"Dude," Monkey said, turning in his seat, "who the hell are you two, anyhow?"

"We're Alpha Twenty-Four," the male noted, arch. "I'm Adam, and my partner is Torino."

"And who exactly do you think is in charge of Alpha Line?" Uniform followed up.

"Man, Romeo has been running it from the time we signed on," Torino answered. "Who else?"

"I think there's been a misunderstanding, then," Omega tried. "Alpha One has been on...extended assignment...for most of the last month or so, and Alpha Two has filled in for us a good bit. I'm Omega, the junior partner of Alpha One, and Echo is the senior member of Alpha One. Right now, he's in Fox's office handling some stuff, and I'm going to be running the department meeting today."

"The hell you say," Adam expostulated. "Are the rest of you guys gonna sit there and let her usurp Romeo's role?"

"Yeah, you are," came a voice from the door, "because she ain't usurpin' nothin'. It ain't my role, it's hers an' Echo's, like th' pretty lady said."

Everyone turned. Alpha Two stood there, scowling. Adam and Torino paled.

* * *

"I do get really tired of it," Omega grumbled after the meeting. "I just KNOW the whole 'dumb blonde' stereotype factors into it somehow! I think I'd try to dye my hair black if I thought Echo would let me get away with it again."

"Nah, from th' story Dihl told, you'd just get another duckin', girl," Romeo chuckled. "She said y'all 'uz both drippin', even after ya ate an' rode back t' th' house."

"Yeah, he did NOT like it," India agreed. "We could all tell THAT. But I don't think that was the problem today, honey. Remember, we needed a specific skill set on that Asian mission, while you and Echo were, um, gone because of Wright, and we looked through the applications and brought those two in."

"Yeah, they didn't see anybody runnin' th' department 'cept me an' India, an' they musta got the exact wrong idea," Romeo decided. "I'll haveta be more careful about shit like that. I spent a lotta th' time in Echo's chair, at his desk, tryin' ta keep up with shit an' all; I guess I shoulda routed it t' my tablet or somethin'. It's mostly my fault, I guess."

"No, no," Omega said, waving a dismissive hand. "I mean, I get that there was a mini-cycle of applications that Echo and I missed, what with running around the planet trying to get away from Wright, and then going undercover at the theater, and me being...on light duty. And I could see them mistaking y'all for us. But those two didn't even know who Echo and I ARE?! That's just ridiculous."

"They're young," India soothed. "Half the new, young recruits barely read the application packets."

"You'd still think they'd'a heard 'bout th' two most bad-ass-est Agents in th' whole damn place," Romeo griped.

"That's not even a word!" India stifled a laugh.

"It is if I say it is," he declared, as she coaxed a grin out of him. "I mean, damn! That's like twice in as many days Meg done got challenged 'bout her position in the department. An' Echo got th' same treatment yesterday, an' woulda, today, if he'd been here."

"Pretty much," Omega sighed. "It's getting old."

"Don't worry," Romeo offered. "Soon's I explained as how

India an' me ain't th' actual department leads, we just fill in f'r y'all now an' then, I saw 'em start coming around. Torino turned 'bout fourteen shades o' red when she realized what they'd done. They's good Agents. It'll come out inna wash."

"I know," Omega said with a nod. "It still gets old, though. At least I have the consolation of knowing Echo woulda got the same treatment, I guess. If you can call it consolation, when he IS the most badass Agent in the place." She shook her head in mingled disgust and discouragement.

"Where is Echo, anyway?" India wondered, glancing around. "You said he was in Fox's office? And that Fox was away?"

"Right," Omega verified. "There must still be problems with the wording on the announcement, but as of last night, Fox was headed to Emdali as fast as he could get there." She paused, glanced around to make sure the door was closed and no one was about to enter the room, then added, "This is classified until the announcement comes out, guys..."

"That don't sound good," Romeo decided.

"No, it doesn't," India agreed.

"It isn't," Omega averred. "Yesterday, there was an assassination attempt on Pulgey Entiyti. We're still waiting to hear if it succeeded or not."

"DAYUM!" Romeo cried, shocked.

"Shit!" India exclaimed, equally worried.

"Exactly," Omega said, unhappy. "So Fox grabbed Zebra and Zarnix and some security guards and headed out as fast as he could go...and took the *Genesis*."

"Uh-oh," Romeo groaned.

"What? Why is that important?" India wondered.

"'Cuz, hon, th' *Genesis* is 'bout the biggest ship in th' whole Division Fleet, short of a damn ship carrier. An' it packs some serious weaponry, offensive AN' defensive," Romeo, the former SEAL team member, explained. "Which means Fox is expectin' trouble, an' he's goin' prepared."

"Right," Omega confirmed. "He left Echo in charge of the

Division, me in charge of Alpha Line, and Whiskey in charge of the medlab."

"Well, at least everybody was all lined up to handle those jobs already," India concluded.

"Yeah, but...well, I haven't talked to Whiskey yet, but I know neither me nor Echo are especially happy about it," Omega admitted. "It—"

Just then, the entire Core lit up, as the crevices between the tiles and wall panels glowed a dull red, and all of their cell phones bleeped in the URGENT INCOMING MESSAGE tone. Messages began scrolling across the wall panel displays in the Core. They all pulled their phones and checked them.

"Well, there goes the announcement," Omega noted, pulling a face. "Aaaand it's official. I'm in charge of the damn department."

"Don't sweat it, pretty lady," Romeo soothed. "Me an' India gotcher back."

"Thanks, guys," Omega said, grateful. "I really hope all I gotta worry about is newbies that don't know my reputation already."

"Lotsa that," India agreed.

* * *

Unsurprisingly, given the pilot, the *Genesis* arrived at Emdali in record time; the orbital transfer station, aware of its imminent arrival from the classified trajectory sent through PGLEIA auspices, had already coordinated with the appropriate personnel, both on the station and in Slliith City. So as soon as the craft dropped the warp bubble and cloaking inside system boundaries, the transfer station hailed her with permission to land directly on the Entiyti estate.

"Not that that's...quite...what we'll be doing," Fox noted, raising an eyebrow.

"What do you mean, sir?" Sail queried, puzzled; the rest of the skeleton bridge crew exchanged curious glances, as well.

"I mean I intend to use the *Genesis* to best advantage," Fox said, dropping the spacecraft's velocity substantially as it

85

approached atmospheric interface; due to its size, the *Genesis* did not usually enter atmosphere, and the shock wave caused by a too-rapid entry could wreak havoc when it made landfall. "It's going to be a bugbear to get her back out of the gravity well, and while we're there, Uncle will have to stay on top of things...literally...to keep the gravitic field around the ship stable for everyone else, but I think it will be the best way, given what I know of the situation, and Pulgey's home."

"You've been there, sir?" Boy wondered.

"Oh, many times, my girl, many times," Fox murmured, concentrating on ensuring the bow shock was kept to a minimum—even at a speed slow enough to avoid ground damage, any aircraft or spacecraft in the immediate vicinity of the planetfalling dreadnought's wake was apt to be in big trouble otherwise. "His is an ancient family, and he and I are old, old friends."

"There's more to you than meets the eye, isn't there, sir?" Zero noted. Fox threw a very brief, very tight grin over his shoulder at the security chief.

"Of course, Zero. That's true for all of us in the Agency, of course, but for some of us more than others." He chuckled. "Sail, open a comm to the Division Five Slliith City Office, please."

"Communiqué channel established, sir."

"*D1 Genesis* to Division Five Director."

A few moments went by while the call was routed appropriately. Finally an answer returned.

"*Genesis*, this is Director Taassass Siisshiiss. Fox, is that you?"

"It is, Taas. You know what's going down?"

"I do. Sorry for the delay responding, but I am actually en route to the estate as we speak. Along with nearly an octet of my top agents, and some of my high-clearance security staff."

"Excellent. The *Genesis* is in atmosphere, on approach. I'm planning to perform a maneuver that Pulgey and I once worked out for an emergency situation. I called it our 'tabernacle maneuver.' Ever heard of it?"

"I...think I heard Lord Entiyti tell the story once..."

"Good. Hurry and get yourself and your people to the main house, then let me know as soon as you've arrived."

"Affirmative; will comply."

"Fox out."

"Siisshiiss out."

* * *

Soon, the *Genesis* was hovering at high altitude just outside a large city, the capital of Emdali—pronounced 'Emmdaalii' by the natives; it was an ancient name, and its rare lack of sibilants was a mark of reverence—known to outsiders as Emdali City, or more properly, Slliith City, and to natives as Slliith Kiissh. Fox and Boy worked in coordination with the chief engineer to ensure that the spacecraft's mass did not cause any localized gravitational anomalies apt to cause problems for the planet's inhabitants, while they waited for a certain message. Moments later, the dreadnought was hailed.

"Siisshiiss to *Genesis* for Fox."

"This is Fox. Go, Taas."

"We are inside the foyer, Fox. Suud Guurn has just met us. He says you are go for this...'tabernacle maneuver.' And that it is an excellent idea."

"Copy that, Taas. We are go for maneuver. Make sure you parked close to the house."

"We did."

His fingers tapping across the console at significant speed, Fox brought the spacecraft into the airspace directly over the estate, finally halting as the *Genesis* hovered with its belly some hundred meters above the main house. Its shadow enveloped the surrounding grounds all the way out to the main gate, shading several additional support structures, including the gatehouse, a greenhouse, and several guest houses.

"Boy?" he queried without looking up from his controls.

"Yes sir?"

"Did you see the force field and gravitics plan I popped to

your console while we were en route?"

"I did, sir."

"Can you handle...?"

"I can, sir. Now?"

"Now."

Abruptly a yellow glow flickered into being between the *Genesis* and the Entiyti estate's grounds, arching up and over the *Genesis* itself. The glow wavered for a moment, then deepened in two distinct steps, becoming a brilliant gold.

"Excellent," Fox declared, satisfied.

"Fox," Zero said in dumbfoundment, "what did you DO? Is that really a...?"

"A hard, triple-layered, force field dome," Fox confirmed. "Over the *Genesis* and the entire central part of the estate. NObody is getting in or out of that house, unless we say so. And 'we' means you and me, Zero."

"Um...yes sir," Zero replied, mild concern obvious, "that order is understood. But..."

"But?"

"That means we have to hover, and that means someone really needs to stay at the helm, but you're..."

"Taken care of," a voice said as the door to the bridge opened. Two men stood there.

"Ah, meyn khbrim!" Fox exclaimed. "So you were able to rendezvous with us, after all?"

"Not until the *Genesis* had reached Emdali," the taller of the two said. "Didn't the hangar deck notify you?"

"I took it," Boy said. "Since it was part of the flight plan that we were to take on a shuttle, and Fox was busy getting ready for atmospheric entry, I noted, logged, and approved it."

"Good, tekhter," Fox approved. "And thank you. Lady and gentlemen, this is Dog and his friend Padova. Dog is from Alpha Line—"

"Which was part of the hold-up," Dog, the taller, admitted. "I had to ping Echo and get approval, and he was evidently in the middle of getting briefed on being Director from Bravo and

Lima, so I pinged Lima to grab his attention, and..."

"Right," Fox said, nodding and smearing his hand across his face. "Of course. Sorry about that. But by the time you volunteered, I was already in Grand Central, the lot of us moving at a sprint..."

"Not a problem, boss," Padova noted. "It gave me time to re-pack my kit, which had gotten a little disorganized after my last run, given that damn renegade Cortian pirate interfering..."

"And we knew we weren't gonna make it to the *Genesis* before you headed out, anyway," Dog added. "So we were playing catch-up regardless. We grabbed the *Sneak* and came on to Emdali."

"Which puts two interstellar shuttles in the bay," Padova added.

"Indeed. Which is good. But thank you both for answering my emergency request for volunteers; our usual helm officers were on vacation, off-planet, and couldn't possibly have gotten to us in time—here, OR at Earth. As I was saying, lady and gentlemen, Dog is with Alpha Line, and Padova is part of the courier squad for the Diplomatic corps. And they are both excellent pilots. They'll take shifts at the helm of the *Genesis* while I'm busy with other matters, ensuring she stays stable and steady and protecting the lot of us from anybody who might be after Pulgey."

"Oh, nice job," Zero averred. "So...you and the medical team are headed down to the main house?"

"We are," Fox asserted. "Sail, please notify Medical that we have arrived, and ask them to meet me in the shuttle bay WITH equipment, and alert Captain Prrt or Du'ven'de, whichever one is on duty now. We'll be taking the *Exodus* down to the front lawn."

"Yes, sir," Sail noted, already hitting the intercom to Medical.

* * *

"...And that is all I really know, Franz," Suud said, as he led Fox, Zebra, Zarnix and Yorker deep into the Draconan-style

89

manor house; the layout was similar to an old European aristocratic house, save that it tended to be more rustic in the human aesthetic, with more use of stone, soil, and similar materials, in deference to the history of the reptilian peoples of Emdali. "He got ahead of his bodyguards in his eagerness, then all abyss broke out. The initial explosion killed Uussa Cuusseer...about which I have yet to tell my son, who was betrothed to her, and I dread it...and it seriously injured Pulgey."

"How bad?" Fox, Zarnix, and Zebra asked in unintentional unison.

"Bad," Suud sighed. "One wing—what was left of it; it was shredded—was nearly ripped off, and his back is..." he shrugged, "fairly cut to ribbons, scales and all. There has been a great deal of blood loss. Evidently the explosive tool was rigged as an anti-personnel device..."

"With what Echo would call a shit-ton of shrapnel, by the sound," Zebra observed.

"Yes."

"Damn," Yorker murmured.

"Exactly," Zarnix agreed. "Especially if it got through his scales."

"AND light body armor. As Franz used to say, 'hot knife and butter,'" Suud averred. "The explosive had punch, and the projectiles were sharpened on all edges."

The Division One personnel all winced.

"What about the other two bodyguards?" Fox wondered.

"Sigrund Dalgaard, from Wintou, was also badly injured, though his injuries are not life-threatening," Suud noted. "He took a direct hit to his shoulder, a good deal of which is outrightly missing now, but he did not lose consciousness until later. Once the adrenaline surge left, he said, the pain hit and he collapsed, though that did not occur until after he arrived here and realized they were finally safe. He is conscious again, and his wounds are being tended, though there is some concern about retaining full use of the arm...well, of retaining the arm, period, though there is more hope of it than of Pul's wing.

Goobop Ogoobah, of what you call Lambda Andromedae III, was more fortunate; he had one of the large concrete-and-steel planters between him and the blast, and was the rearguard. He is relatively unharmed, save for a few cuts and mild burns."

"Sigrund is Pul's current chief bodyguard, isn't he?" Fox pressed.

"He is...or was," Suud confirmed. "His degree of healing will determine whether he is able to keep the position."

"Well, let us get to it," Zarnix said. "Lord Guurn, may we please meet the physicians in charge?"

"That would be you, sir," came a voice from behind Suud. They all turned, to find a dark-red-scaled Draconan standing there. "Please forgive my presumption; I had news that you had arrived, Lord Levy, with your entourage, and that you were bringing your very experienced team of physicians. I am Werfer Eretigen, Lord Entiyti's personal physician, and I will be happy to work with all of you...but I do not have the kind of experience required for dealing with...with this."

"Nor does my family physician," Suud added, "and she is here as well—Ssyy Hissheth."

"We are what you on Earth would term, 'family practice,'" Dr. Eretigen noted. "Dr. Hissheth and I are doing our best, and we have managed to remove the projectiles and stanch the worst of the bleeding, but..." he shook his head. "I did part of my apprenticeship in an emergency facility, but still, I have not seen the like before."

"Let's go, then," Zebra decreed, and she, Zarnix, and Yorker headed after Dr. Eretigen as he turned and headed deeper into the manor house, toward the hospital wing.

"And that leaves the two of us, for the moment," Suud said, watching them go. "Lydhuu is on her way, but she is the department chair at the University now, with some octet of classes in session, and was scrambling to find a substitute. I doubt she will be able to stay long, unless...things do not go well here."

"Tell me straight, Suud—how bad is he?" Fox wondered, as the pair wandered in the physicians' wake, toward the tiny hospital wing. Suud drew a deep breath.

"It is not good, Franz," the Reptoid confessed. "It has been, as you would say, 'touch and go' with him from the time my contingent and I fought our way to him on the transfer station."

"Is he conscious?"

"Hard to say. He may be, or he may not. He has been in and out."

"May I see him?"

"That is where we are headed now. He left express instructions for you and Lydhuu to be brought straight to him, whether he was conscious or no. But steel yourself, my old friend and teacher. He looks like a Draconan warrior of old, preparing himself for death."

Fox winced.

"Then let's hurry," he determined, "while I still have a chance to see him. And," he added, fierce, "if he doesn't...survive, by HaShem, I WILL see him avenged!"

"And I shall be right beside you," Suud averred.

* * *

Suud took Fox to the door of the hospital room where Entiyti had been placed, and left him there. The physicians were not yet in the room; Zebra and Zarnix were being briefed by the Emdalian physicians, and would be there soon, but for now, Entiyti was alone—albeit with plenty of monitor equipment to notify the medics if anything went wrong. Fox opened the door and slipped inside.

The big Draconan somehow did not look nearly as tall or as broad as normal, Fox thought, and the usually-gleaming silver-white scales that made him so striking in appearance—the Entiyti dynasty possessed one of the rarer scale colorings among Draconans—had become dull and gray, badly spattered and stained by the deep-burgundy blood of the Draconan species, where he had bled so profusely. He lay largely on his belly, to permit access to his badly-injured back and wing, and to minimize pressure on the injuries. As Fox studied those injuries, he winced; his old friend had managed to get himself nastily sliced up this time, he considered.

He moved forward, but his concern for his oldest friend caused him to be somewhat less careful than was customary for him, and his foot landed heavier than normal.

Entiyti startled badly, trying to come out of the bed as he groggily cried, "Wha?! Who's there??"

"Hush, Pul, hush; everything is all right. It's me, it's Fox-er, Franz," he corrected himself, stooping enough to let the other male look him in the face for a moment and ascertain all was well for himself. "Lie back down there and don't hurt yourself worse, meyn khaver. I got your call and came at once."

"Franz," Entiyti sighed, easing back to the bed. "It is good... to see you. I...I fear I am a, a bit jumpy, brother."

"I know. I would be, too, in your position," Fox agreed, moving to the bedside. "But Suud and I are here, and I brought Zebra and Zarnix to help tend you, and Lydhuu is on the way. Not to mention an entire contingent of Division Five agents, led by their director. You are at home, you are under considerable armed guard, and the *Genesis* is overhead, in a 'tabernacle maneuver.' You are as safe as we know how to make you, alter khaver."

"Thank you, my dear, dear friend and brother," Entiyti murmured, seeming very weak, "but I fear...it may be...a moot point."

"Hush that," Fox rebuked gently. "I won't hear it, Pul. I brought two of the three best physicians I know in the universe to work on you; they'll patch you back up. I can't promise you'll walk away the same as you walked into it, Pul, because..."

"I know. I can, can feel it," Entiyti admitted, stifling a groan with difficulty. "I have...'done a number...on myself,' as you might say. Is...is the wing even still there...? Everything hurts...it is hard to tell..."

"It's still there," Fox said, soothing, deciding not to mention that the descriptor phrase should be 'just barely.' *Because damn,* he thought, hiding another wince, *it's only hanging on by a few strips of flesh. The bone looks to be nearly shattered, right there at the base.*

"Perhaps not for long, by the feel," Entiyti sighed, and Fox realized he had a much better grasp of his condition than the Division One Director would have wished. "I had so been looking forward...to a few days at...at the glide park. Now, it seems likely that...one way or...another...I never shall, again."

"Will you just shush that?" Fox ordered, keeping his voice gentle, almost as if talking to a child. "We are going to do everything we can to ensure you pull out of this as near to normal as possible. I swear this to you, Pul, on the blood of brothers."

Entiyti appeared to consider this for a moment, then nodded.

"Still and all," he managed to get out, "there are...things that want saying...right now, Franz. And for that, I...would look you...face to face. Help...help me turn on my side."

"I really think you..." Fox began, but Entiyti started struggling to roll onto his side, and the human male had little choice but to help him, lest he hurt himself worse. "There. No, don't go any farther, Pul. It wouldn't feel good at all if you did."

"No," he panted, "this will...will d-do, for now, at least." He drew a limp hand across his eyes, then blinked several times, trying to focus on Fox's face.

Hmm, Fox noted, observing the behavior. *I'd best get bubeleh to check for a concussion into the bargain.*

"Ah, finally," Entiyti said then. "Franz."

"Pul."

"You know...you know the...the oath we took, you, and I, and Suud. And you recall why."

"Yes, Pul. But there's no need to talk about that now."

"There IS, Franz. I made you legal...b-brothers so that...I m-might have heirs! I never mated; the only one I...w-would have chosen...d-died when we were s-still...little more than yuh-younglings. I have n-no offspring. Whoever...whoever-r tried this...they nearly succeeded. They may HAVE succeeded." The orange eyes, usually like living flames, seemed pale, as if the fire within was nearly extinguished. "You kn-know it, and I...know it." He paused to pant. "It HURTS, Franz. In so many ways...not just...just physical. And I...am so tired of... dear Maker." Entiyti blinked, and his eyes grew wide, as he broke off what he had been about to say.

"What?!" Fox exclaimed, suddenly afraid that the end had come for his friend. But Entiyti was evidently more alert than that, for he read Fox's face.

"No, no, not...not that," Entiyti said with a chuckle that broke off midway, as he winced in pain at the reaction. "No, I was, was remembering Omega, when she...she was so wound-ed...the Cortians, you know...and you said she was so tired of f-fighting. I...I suddenly...understood. The pain...it wears, you see..."

"Ah," Fox said, grasping Entiyti's reaction then. "Then you know that, just as she had to keep fighting, you do, too."

"Do I, Franz?" The orange gaze met the hazel gaze. "Why?"

"Because you have friends and family counting on you, Pul, if for no other reason," Fox declared, steadfast. "And that, the most important reason, though there are others...like a gal-axy depending on you to lead it."

Entiyti drew a deep breath, let it out in a huff, and seemed to sink in on himself.

"It is easier to let go, you know."

"I know. I've been there a few times myself."

"Yes, I remember." Entiyti rested the side of his head against the pillow Fox drew into position for him. "Very well; I will...will do m-my best. You know, though, if something hap-pens...if this proves worse than...th-than they think, or-r if the assassins come again..." He paused to pant. "The estate g-goes t-to my cousin, but...but the rest...it goes to you a-and Suud, my legal brothers."

"What about Lydhuu?"

"I...I would like her to...to have a part, as well, I think," Entiyti decided. "But I...I have not added that yet. I needed to know... Do you mind?"

"Not in the least. I don't lust after your wealth or possessions, old friend, and never have. I would much rather have you beside me, a staunch friend and ally, than all the possessions in the universe. The only reason I agreed to this plan, long ago, was to see you done right by, when there was a faction of your clan opposing you." Fox shook his head. "I was more than glad to see THAT little matter resolved."

"And Suud? Will he...?"

"She was his protégé, more than she was mine. What do you think?"

"Ah, point. And...and Lydhuu...?"

"I think she would be delighted to be one of your heirs—not in losing you, but rather, that you cared enough to make such provision for her."

"Will...will you talk to Suud...and, and see it...is done?"

"If it becomes necessary, I will," Fox averred. "Do you want her to have an equal share?"

"No, not...not quite. You and, and Suud, s-still my oldest..." he tried, and Fox realized he was rapidly depleting his strength. "But...a nice share. You know. And, and something...to remember me..."

"Ah. Do you still have the memorabilia room?"

"Y-yes."

"Then I will see she gets some appropriate items from it, and Suud and I will also ensure Lydhuu has the kind of inheritance I think you mean. Perhaps a quarter-share for Lydhuu, and three-eighths each for myself and Suud? It is not quite an even, three-way split, so you honor Suud and myself as your oldest and closest living friends and brothers in all but blood, but also honor Lydhuu as family...perhaps a beloved niece..." *Oh by HaShem, what a meshuginah family I have,* Fox thought for the umpteenth time, trying not to laugh at the incongruity of the thought in the solemn setting.

"Th-that...yes...is good," Entiyti gasped. "Help me...need... lie down..."

Fox had just eased Entiyti back into a prone position on his belly when there came a light knock at the door.

"Franz?" Suud's soft voice came from without. "Lydhuu is here; is he awake?"

"Come in, my friends," Fox called, keeping his voice low. "He is awake, but in pain, and very tired."

The door opened, and Lydhuu Raiit entered, followed by Suud. Suddenly Zebra appeared at the door, slipping in behind Suud and closing the door. When Fox gave her a querying look, she shrugged.

"We were going to come in and check Pulgey," she explained, "but then the others saw Suud and Lydhuu coming in, with you nowhere to be seen but them talking to SOMEbody in here, and they thought maybe family was better, for now. Especially when the, um, the 'sister in law' is one of the doctors, I guess."

"Good thought," Fox agreed.

"Indeed," Suud added, and Lydhuu, an Ergisol—which to humans looked like a six-foot-tall, more or less bipedal June bug—clacked her mandibles in agreement. Entiyti pushed up far enough to see the new arrivals.

"Ah," he murmured, offering them a weak smile. "My family is indeed...all here. Thank...thank you for...for coming."

The Draconan held out a hand, careful to curl his claws into his palm, and grasped Lydhuu's claw for a moment, followed by Zebra's hand, then Fox's, then Suud's. "There," he said then. "It is done. I wanted..." he broke off, gasping, and Zebra carefully checked the vital signs monitors.

"You've worn yourself out, talking to Fox, haven't you?" she asked with a gentle but stern bedside manner.

"Yes, he has," Fox tattled on the galactic leader. "I tried to get him to take it easy, but he insisted. Oh, and bubeleh, he may have a concussion; you might want..."

"Done did, and yes," Zebra murmured. "Surprise, surprise, after a big bada-boom like that. Pulgey, can you tell us what you wanted, dear? But once you do that, you need to rest, hon. And if you won't do it on your own, I'll give you something to make you rest."

"Vitals?" Fox breathed, and Zebra nodded; he knew that she was aware of the danger, and was mostly bluffing, though he needed pain medication to get him through what they would have to do to stabilize and heal him.

"I wanted," Entiyti tried again. "Franz...could you tell them? What we just...Zebra is right; I need to...to..."

His head slumped to the pillow as his eyes closed.

"Ohhh, farkakte," Fox said, alarmed, as Zebra yanked her medscanner and ran it over the inert form. Suud and Raiit stepped forward, anxious.

"It's okay," Zebra said then, holding up a calming hand. "He wore himself out and passed out. I know Lydhuu just got here, but maybe you three should sneak out and let me see to him. If things...if you should need to...say goodbye, I promise I'll send for all of you, right away. But meantime, we need to work to make that unnecessary. Fox, if you could notify Zarnix that it's okay for the other docs to come in, it would be good."

"'All over it,' as Romeo might say, meyn teyere."

They slipped out as Zebra began trying to stabilize her patient.

* * *

After Fox explained Entiyti's desire for Raiit to share in any inheritance, and Suud approved the notion, a grateful, deeply-touched Raiit headed into Entiyti's office to call the university on Aleancë and ensure her rushed handover had been success-ful.

"I do not think she really needed to call the university," Suud noted, after she was well out of earshot. "She told me earlier that she had made all necessary arrangements, and ex-pected to have at least a day free."

"No, I don't think so either," Fox agreed. "I think she just needed to get somewhere private for a few minutes."

"Yes."

With that, Suud and Fox wandered into the great hall and studied the familiar furnishings, some antique, some outright ancient, for the hundredth time. They said little, content to be together after so many years. Finally Suud broke the silence.

"Do you think they can save him?"

"I don't know," Fox answered, as honest as he knew how to be. "But if anyone can, those two can. I think—" Abruptly he was interrupted.

"Pater!" a younger adult Reptoid called, sprinting into the huge room. "I just heard about Uncle Pulgey, and I came at once! What happened? Where was Uussa?! Why didn't she get him out of the way??"

"Oh, by the Name," Fox said in shock, "Suud, is this Duuniiss?"

"It is," Suud said, proud. "This is my eldest." Then he sobered, and diverted his son's attention, if only briefly. "Duuniiss, do you recognize your Uncle Franz? It has been many years."

Duuniiss studied the human for long moments, then a look of recognition flashed into his eyes.

"Uncle!" he cried, and opened his arms to the human male; they embraced, and Fox found himself the recipient of an enthused Reptoid hug—secretly hoping he had intact ribs left when it was over. "Oh, it has been years indeed! I was not even adolescent when last I saw you! And you..."

"Gave you a piggy-back ride, as we say on Earth," Fox said with a wry grin. "Then had to have someone adjust my back! You have always been solid muscle, young one." He shook his head ruefully. "And now I DO feel old, Suud, for the first time in...a very long time."

"Oh, it is good to see you, Uncle Franz!" Duuniiss exclaimed again. "But now tell me about Uncle Pulgey. What HAPPENED?"

"Shall I leave the two of you to talk, Suud?" Fox wondered.

Suud shot Fox a pained glance, and Fox understood the other male wanted him to stay, to offer the moral support of family in the difficult conversation that was about to take place. Reptoids, like most reptile species on Earth, were incapable of weeping. But that did not mean they did not hurt as badly as those who wept. Fox gave Suud the subtlest of nods, and Suud drew a deep breath, leading them into the next room.

"Come here and sit down, son," he said, gesturing to a cluster of chairs in the corner of the family sitting room, which was considerably smaller than the great hall. The furnishings had been arranged with an eye to conversation among groups of various sizes, and Fox noted Suud had chosen the most intimate setting there.

"Pater," Duuniiss repeated in frustration. "TELL me what has happened! And where is Uussa?"

"Son, there was a planned attack on your Uncle Pulgey, on the transfer station," Suud explained. "There were at least two octets of assassins, possibly three. The assassins led their gambit with a hidden anti-personnel explosive. It caught Pulgey and two of his three bodyguards in the blast. Commander Dalgaard was injured and may lose the use of his arm—could lose it entirely. Your Uncle Pulgey was badly hurt and lies at death's threshold; Uncle Franz brought his mate and her supervisor along to try to save him. And Uussa..."

Suud broke off, swallowing hard. Duuniiss stared at him with wide eyes, and Fox suspected that the young male already comprehended what his father was about to say but did not want to believe it. Fox decided to assist his old friend.

"Duuniiss, Uussa didn't make it," he said gently. "She bravely gave her life to try to save your other uncle, the being most know as Lord Entiyti, the beloved galactic leader, the President of the Coalition. I'm...sorry, zun. I know you loved her deeply and dearly, even as I love my own mate. But she was very brave, and Zebra—my mate, who is a physician—says it was a quick death."

"Wha-what...?" Duuniiss said, blinking in disbelief. "Uussa...didn't...? She...she's d-dead? But...but she and I were...I loved...the wedding was in two moon cycles..."

"I know, son," Suud said, in the softest tone Fox had ever heard him use. It was also unusually hoarse, betraying the elder

Reptoid's emotion. "I know. It...was completely unexpected. We still do not know exactly what happened, or why, or who was responsible. We do know that there was apparently a significant attack force aboard the transfer station, for after the explosion, they opened fire to ensure Pulgey and all his guards were killed. More, the concourse where it happened was apparently cleared of virtually all...we will call them noncombatants, innocent bystanders...before any of it happened, evidently to prevent eyewitnesses; the few station personnel who were left fled at the explosion, in fear of an atmosphere breach, and thus were not themselves eyewitnesses to much, either. Which," Suud added, turning to Fox, "does not make sense. Normally, such a thing would be planned to maximize death and destruction."

"I know," Fox agreed. "I noticed that little point. Someone was VERY afraid of extraneous witnesses. And that...is curious. But Duuniiss, I am very sorry for your loss, meyn kind. I...have had losses of my own, and...I know how it feels." He turned to Suud. "Does he know about the concentration...?" Suud nodded. "Good," Fox said, gruff despite his best efforts. "Then you know I speak the truth, zun. I DO understand. If there is anything I can do, any way to help ease your pain, you have but to ask."

The younger Reptoid was silent for long moments, eyes narrowed, pupils the merest slits, as his sire and his adoptive uncle watched, aching for him. Finally he spoke, and his voice was harsh, rough with emotion and, Fox suspected, the analogue to the tears his species could not shed.

"But you do not know who did this?" the young male ground out.

"Not yet, no," Fox averred. "But we intend to find out."

The three fell silent again. Fox would have sworn the young Guurn's body was growing, expanding before his eyes, in a kind of righteous anger.

"Then thiss I sswear, on my own heartss' blood," Duuniiss fairly hissed then. "I will assisst you in finding thesse ssllitthhssshhtt, if it meanss my liffe! And then they sshall know my wrattth! No retribution iss too great for thiss! They took my heartss ffrom me, and they sshall pay!"

He spun on his heel and, with slow, measured tread, left the room.

"And thus it begins," Suud sighed.

Chapter 5

The entire medical team save Dr. Hissheth was gowned and scrubbed in the treatment room of the manor house's medical facility. Their primary patient, Lord Pulgey Entiyti, lay face down on the table before them, nude, lower body draped in a sheet for modesty, as they examined him. Dr. Hissheth had taken her own medtech to fetch the large medikit she had brought in her ground vehicle.

"All right," Zarnix decided. "Let us get these deep lacerations in his back stitched up properly. Then we can hit them with some concentrated Rejuvic and start the healing process."

"But as deep as they are, even with the Rejuvic, it's gonna take a while, Zar," Zebra pointed out.

"I know," Zarnix sighed.

"Basting mode?" Yorker wondered.

"What is 'basting mode'?" Dr. Eretigen asked, puzzled.

"Um," Yorker said, flushing. "It, uh, well..."

"It means we will have to periodically swab the area with the Rejuvic, to ensure healing remains as accelerated as possible," Zarnix filled in smoothly. "It is actually a term that derives from cuisine preparation on Earth. A particularly meticulous chef will stay with a roasting cut of meat, 'basting' or swabbing it with seasonings mixed into a liquid, such as fruit juice or vinegar, ensuring that it is saturated throughout. We will do the same thing with Lord Entiyti's back as regards our topical healing medication."

"Ah, I see," Eretigen noted. "A borrowed term. But why did your medtech turn so red? That is usually a sign of emotional distress in humans, is it not?"

"I...was afraid you might take offense," Yorker admitted, looking down in embarrassment. "I wasn't calling Lord Entiyti a slab of meat, I swear...but it coulda sounded like it..."

"Oh, pssht." Eretigen waved a clawed hand. "I may not have the wide-ranging skill of you Division One medical people, but I have worked in an emergency facility. So I understand how the terminology can...colloquialize, is perhaps a word? And yes, I am afraid that old Pulgey here looks like a very bad butcher has been trying to slice him into luncheon meat..."

"You...you could...be a b-bit more...delicate about it, Werf," Entiyti murmured then. "I h-had not felt...like dis-disgorging, b-but...I do, now."

"Hush, Pulgey, just relax," Zebra murmured, stooping beside the Draconan's head as he lay on his belly for the examination and prep, so he could see her. "Ignore what's being said. He was only teasing our medtech, anyway. We all thought you were still unconscious."

"It...c-comes and goes..."

"Yes, about like Omega did after the Cortians got done with her," Zarnix recollected.

"Yep," Zebra agreed. "But we do need to give him a little something for the pain, without lowering his vitals too much. You've lost a lot of blood, Pul," she added to the patient. "And given you have that rare Draconan blood type, we're not quite sure..."

"I know," he replied. "Werf, di-did you remem-ber the blood st-stores?"

"Agh!" Eretigen exclaimed, slapping his palm to his flat face. "No, Pulgey, the thing is too new to me yet! I have had all I could do to find my way around your new medical wing! But I remember NOW!" He ran to the special stasis storage. "Here!"

"You mean we have blood for transfusions?" Zebra said, surprised and delighted. "Blood that matches his?"

"Blood that IS his!" Eretigen averred. "Giissht rare blood type and all!"

"Took-took a large...bag," Entiyti explained, gasping, "then...then cloned..."

"In bulk, months ago," Eretigen declared, opening the special stasis unit to reveal container after container of deep-burgundy Draconan blood, all in perfectly preserved condition.

"Then do you set up an intravenous drip," Zarnix ordered Eretigen, "while...Yorker, you had that certification as an anesthetist, did you not?"

"I did, sir, for just such situations as this," the medtech confirmed.

"Then get with Dr. Eretigen and determine what to use on Lord Entiyti to ease his pain and let him relax while we clean these wounds and get him patched up a bit."

"I-I think," Entiyti decided, "that is...an ex-excellent... idea."

"I have—" Hissheth said, as she and her medtech lugged in the massive case, containing as much equipment as they had been able to cram into it, upon receiving Suud's emergency call. "Oh! Lord Entiyti! You are awake!"

"For the mo-moment," Entiyti agreed. "Th-though I think this l-lot has...other ideas."

"We're getting ready to do something about this back of his," Zebra explained, as she and Zarnix prepped the surgical implements. "Eretigen and Yorker are preparing to give him a transfusion and some pain medication via intravenous."

"Oh, very good," Hissheth murmured. "We have a blood supply, then."

"I cannot believe I forgot the hiigiissht thing," Eretigen grumbled. "But Pulgey had me draw the initial sample container, then clone it, and only after he had properly stored it here, did he even show me where it was, and that once, three months ago!"

"Yes, yes," Entiyti grumbled. "Bl-blame it on your...p-patient."

"Hush, you," Zebra teased the injured male, "or I'll whack this back and hush you the hard way."

"No!" Entiyti exclaimed. "No, I had r-rather...have Franz' peanut b-butter...than that."

"And now we'll take care of 'that,'" Yorker said, bringing over a stand with the prepped IV bags. "In the neck, guys?"

"That'd be my take," Zebra agreed. "Zarnix, Eretigen? You two are more expert in Draconan physiology."

"That was where I had planned," Eretigen said.

"Then that is good enough for us," Zarnix decreed.

"All right, Lord Entiyti," Yorker murmured, prepping the special micropore noninvasive cannula and swabbing a patch on the Draconan's throat to sterilize it, "this won't hurt, but it may feel cool. And you might get a little giddy. Just relax and kinda float through it. We're only putting you under just enough to keep you from hurting or getting distressed at sensations. A light doze, as it were."

"G-good," he fretted. "Ti-tired of-of hurting."

"I can imagine, honey," Zebra soothed, rubbing the back of Entiyti's hand as Yorker seated the cannula and taped it in place. "Now, Pul, start counting back from one hundred for me."

"I-in English, or Dra-draconan?" he retorted, impish despite his injuries.

"Either one," Zebra said, cheerful, "because it ain't about my hearing the numbers, it's about my NOT hearing 'em, once you go out."

"R-right. One hundred...ninety-nine...n-ninety-eight... nine-ty seven...ohhh, there we go..."

"You can feel it kicking in?" Yorker asked.

"Oh, great Maker, yes, what a r-relief," Entiyti responded with a gratified sigh. "Um, lessee, where was I...?" he added, the words already beginning to slur.

"You got to ninety-seven," a tolerant Zarnix said, eyes twinkling in gentle amusement, and Entiyti resumed counting as Dr. Hissheth and her medtech, Ooossi Duurg, unpacked the big kit, producing instruments specialized for the Draconan and Reptoid anatomy and physiology. All were enclosed in sterile wraps.

"And that looks really good," Zebra murmured to Zarnix,

watching the unpacking as Entiyti continued counting.

"It does," Zarnix agreed. "We needed more instruments than what we have here."

"These were intended for here," Hissheth noted. "I had connections that Werf did not, so milord ordered them through me, on Werf's recommendation. The shipment had only just come in days ago, and I had already made arrangements to deliver them while milord was in residence." She sighed. "I never dreamed I'd do it...like THIS."

"...Ninety-one...ninety," Entiyti said, then paused. "Um... ninety, uh, oh, eighty-ni-nine...eighty, um...ei..." Then he fell silent, and his body went completely limp.

"And that did it," Zarnix declared, beginning to prep Entiyti's back with a sterilizing solution, prior to cleaning out the wounds. "Dr. Hissheth—"

"Call me Ssyy, if you would," the Reptoid physician invited. "We are going to work closely together; it is only right."

"And I am Werf to my friends," Eretigen noted, wielding an irrigation cannula and suction nozzle at Zarnix's finger-point direction. "We already know your code names ARE your names, because of Earth's," he shrugged, "not really knowing about the rest of us."

"Well, my full name is Zarnix Chifejuz," the Chesharilzi pointed out, "but effectively my code name is Zarnix, so...yes."

"And your colleague sometimes shortens that to Zar, correct?" Eretigen observed.

"Now and then," Zebra acknowledged. "It's a nickname; I've known him ever since he arrived on Earth years ago. Generally we call him Zarnix, though, just out of respect. He's our chief of staff."

"And I can understand that," Hissheth agreed.

"Very good," Zarnix said, as he and Zebra beamed. "Ssyy, you and Medtech Duurg go ahead and scrub up; Yorker, you keep an eye on the anesthesia. Werf, you lay out the appropriate instruments with Zebra's help, and you will stand beside me and make sure I do not err in my assessment and handling of reptilian surgical technique."

"Very good," Eretigen agreed.

"What will you want me and Ooossi to do?" Hissheth asked.

"And please call me Ooossi," the big Reptoid medtech offered; the others smiled.

"Ooossi, you and Ssyy help Zebra finish laying out the equipment, once Werf leaves off with it," Zarnix explained. "I plan to start closing as soon as I can, and I will need Werf with me. Then Zebra will start cleaning and closing wounds on Entiyti's left side with Ssyy's assistance, while Werf and I will work on his right. Ooossi can swing to whichever side needs extra hands."

"Excellent," Hissheth decided. "Two teams should have him stabilized very quickly."

"I already like his vitals more," Yorker averred. "The IV with the transfusion is helping."

"Even better," Zarnix said.

* * *

Raiit, Fox, and Suud sat in the tiny waiting room for several hours, while the medical team worked on Entiyti. Occasionally one or the other would get up to pace, and they carried on a sporadic conversation as Suud gave Fox and Raiit more details about what he had seen on the transfer station, but in general, they said little.

About an hour into the wait, another Reptoid showed up at the door of the waiting room, and all three beings looked up.

"Fox?" the strange Reptoid queried, glancing between Fox and Suud. "Lord Guurn, is this Director Fox?"

"Taas?" Fox asked, before Suud could answer. "You're Division Five Director Taassass Siisshiiss, aren't you? I recognize your voice."

"Ah! Indeed, it IS you, Fox!" Siisshiiss exclaimed, coming forward to take his hand and shake it, careful to curl his fingers into his own palm to avoid accidentally scratching Fox with his claws. "We have never talked except over the audio comm during the division chiefs' meetings! It is good at last to meet you face to face."

"Yes, it is," Fox averred, shaking his hand with vigor. "I hope they finally get the complexities of that many vid comm channels set up for that meeting sometime SOON. And you're heading the investigation?"

"I am, and I brought along several of my top agents, as I think I mentioned when your ship was still on approach." Siisshiiss glanced at the Ergisol. "And who might this be?"

"Ah," Suud said, "this is Lydhuu Raiit, my protégé and successor as Lord Entiyti's chief bodyguard."

"I am pleased to meet you, Director Siisshiiss," Raiit said, rising from her specialized seat in the corner and coming to meet the Division Five chief.

"And I, likewise," Siisshiiss agreed, shaking her claw. "This is an impressive collection of beings, here."

"We have no less than three 'generations' of chief body-guards in this room," Fox noted, "with a fourth in the hospital wing, undergoing treatment for the grievous wounds he incurred in this incident."

"And the three of you fleet admirals and one division director now, as well. One thing for which I have always admired Lord Entiyti is his ability to select and retain good people to work for him." Siisshiiss glanced at the door into the operating room. "How is he?"

"We don't know yet, Taas," Fox said with a sigh.

"The physicians and medtechs are in there now, working on him," Suud explained. "They planned to try to close up the worst of the wounds in his back, and...I do not know about that wing..."

"Thank you for allowing me to see him earlier," Siisshiiss told Suud. "I hated to do it, but I needed SOME sort of 'official statement' from him, even if it was only, 'Find them.'"

"Is that what he told you?" Fox asked.

"Yes," Suud averred. "He had little energy at that point to say more."

"It was all I needed, anyway," Siisshiiss pointed out. "I had to verify that it was indeed a criminal act, from the principal surviving victim. Commander Dalgaard's statement went a long way in that direction, as well."

"Is there anything I can do to help?" Fox asked.

"No, not right now," Siisshiiss murmured. "You three have your hands full at the moment." He nodded meaningfully at the door to the operating suite.

"Well, but we're here, if you need us," Fox pressed.

"Of course, and if I do, I shall come at once." Siisshiiss declared. "I mostly wanted to come by and get word on Lord Entiyti."

"I will send a messenger from the household staff to inform you when once we know something," Suud determined.

"Very good, then," Siisshiiss agreed. "Then let me get out of your way for now."

He slipped out the door and was gone.

The three returned to their pacing.

* * *

It took a long time, but as the larger wounds were closed, the bleeding reduced to seepage, and the intravenous blood and saline continued to boost his blood volume, Entiyti's vital signs began to stabilize. When the worst of the lacerations were stitched closed, Yorker reduced the amount of anesthetic in the IV to just what was required to keep Entiyti in a light sleep—thereby keeping him out of pain a while longer, as healing began—and extracted a large bottle of Rejuvic and a huge supply of sterile swabs from the equipment stores brought from Earth.

"Shoo," he told the physicians. "Go get cleaned up and rest. Ooossi and I've got this part. I can baste with the best of 'em," he declared. They all grinned, then the tired doctors agreed, and headed for the exit.

"Call us if anything happens," Zebra reminded.

"Of course," Yorker averred, and Duurg nodded agreement. "Now git."

They got.

* * *

Fox, Suud, and Raiit were still waiting when they came out.

"Oh dear, that is a lot of blood on you," Raiit observed in concern.

"That's okay, we were pumping it back in him faster than he could lose it," Zebra declared. "And the saline the medic put in him on his arrival kept him going until we could cork him and refill him."

"We found three more pieces of shrapnel, buried deep, and removed them, too," Zarnix observed. "All that is gone now."

"And the worst wounds are closed," Eretigen averred. "We have but to determine what to do with that wing, and even that is packed and bandaged."

"Pul's going to live?" Fox dared ask.

"Yes, honey, barring something completely unexpected happening, he's gonna live," Zebra confirmed, and all three of Entiyti's former chief bodyguards visibly relaxed. "Now what we need to do is see to the injured bodyguards."

"Yorker took care of Ogoobah's minor wounds right away," Suud informed her, "while you and Zarnix were evaluating Pulgey. And he has Commander Dalgaard stable and out of pain, for the moment, and he is resting. They will wait. You—"

"We are sorry," Hissheth broke in, sad.

"Indeed," Eretigen agreed, downhearted.

"About what?" Zarnix wondered, surprised.

"We have little familiarity with their species," Hissheth explained. "We did not know how to help them without possibly causing harm...so we discussed it and thought, since they were not in danger of their lives, perhaps it would be safer to wait until you arrived..." She put her face in her hands; Eretigen laid a hand on her shoulder. "We did what we could, what we knew to do."

"Oh, that," Zebra said, patting them both on their shoulders. "Not a problem, dear. I'd have done the same thing in your shoes, and be feeling about like you are now. But it sounds like everything is good."

"Yes, and that was a wise decision," Zarnix agreed. "Given the Wintourns have a high percentage of elementals in their population...though not all Wintourns, by any means, and some stronger than others...the biochemistry can get complicated. Never mind the fact that Lambda Andromedan biochemistry is not like ANY bipedal race, anywhere."

"Very good," Suud tried again. "They are stable and pain-free, and you four are tired and in need of food, drink, and clean clothing."

"And we've been arranging for all of that," Raiit said. "We talked to the...what is the word, Suud?"

"The Division One folk would know him as the house steward, I think," Suud said.

"The steward has rooms for all of you," Raiit informed them, "and Franz and I have placed your kits in appropriate rooms. Dr. Hissheth, Dr. Eretigen, we will have to, ah, 'scrounge' for a change of clothing for you—that is how Franz put it—but the steward says there are spare scrubs in the manor hospital. He will have the waiting staff fetch some once he has ascertained your correct sizing."

"And after you change and get cleaned up, the cook will have a bit of a hot meal laid in the main dining hall," Fox added. "Then you can look at your other patients."

"Sounds good, hon," Zebra concluded.

"That," Zarnix averred. "All of it."

"Indeed," Eretigen said.

"I shall not argue," Hissheth agreed.

* * *

Forty-five minutes later, the medical staff was clean, dressed in fresh scrubs, and fed. Zebra and Zarnix tended Ogoobah and Dalgaard, while Eretigen and Hissheth checked on Entiyti.

Half an hour later, they all met back in the sitting room outside Entiyti's office.

"I think we are good," Eretigen decided. "Milord Pulgey is resting, free of pain, with good vitals. The lacerations on his back are closing slowly, even the deep ones. How are the bodyguards?"

"They will be all right," Zarnix noted. "We hit the Lambda Andromedan with some Rejuvic and he is already almost healed. The Wintourn is stable and comfortable while we determine the best way to deal with his shoulder...what is left of it."

"But that's gonna take some brainstorming," Zebra added.

"Which I think is perhaps something that should wait, by the look of you," Suud suggested.

"Yeah. I gotta admit, I'm wiped," Zebra said, rubbing the heels of her hands into her eyes.

"It stands to reason, bubeleh," Fox observed. "You had just gotten off shift, and I was about to, when Suud called with word of this...shtik drek."

"And you, Zarnix?" Suud wondered.

"Zebra and I usually stagger shifts with Whiskey and Rglfrz," Zarnix admitted. "I had gone off duty some hours earlier, and Whiskey came on duty as I went off. Rglfrz was due to come on in a couple of hours, I think...or perhaps he was coming on about the time Zebra got off; I forget now. At any rate, that way, you see, there are always two experienced medicos on staff at any given time."

"Which means you were asleep, in the middle of your sleep cycle," Fox said, raking a hand up into his salt-and-pepper hair. "Forgive me, meyn khaver."

"They are both worn out," Suud decided.

"Indeed they are," Fox agreed.

"And so are you," Suud added. Fox grumbled unintelligibly but did not deny it; Zebra was giving him the stink-eye already, and would have protested loudly had he tried...and he knew it. More, he knew he needed the rest, to ensure he remained alert and able to keep his oldest living friend well-protected, so he decided not to demur.

"What about your medtech? Yorker?" Raiit wondered.

"I think he was just coming on duty," Zarnix remembered.

"He should be all right for a few hours, yet."

"It is still some time until normal retiring, here," Hissheth noted. "Though it is late, almost sunset. It was early morning when you arrived; we have been at this some few hours! As things stand now, I think Werf and I can look after matters, while the three of you get some sleep. Should things go badly, we can notify Suud, who can summon you. Then we can retire late, and rest during our night, and you can stand shift while we do."

"That...might not be a bad idea," Zebra averred. "I could use some sleep, and Zar, you're starting to look like you're sleepwalking, and I didn't even know Chesharilzi did that."

"We have been known to," Zarnix revealed, "though not often. I think this is a good plan. At some point, we are going to have to make a joint decision on how to handle that wing, and I would like to have my wits in full function when that happens."

"Then go rest now," Eretigen ordered. "Now that you have cared for the offworlder bodyguards, Ssyy and I have this, for the time."

"'Off we go, into the wild blue yonder...'" Zebra sang, then snickered. "Meg would like that."

"Go," Fox said, swatting in the general direction of his mate's posterior. "Before you get all loopy, as Echo puts it."

"Too late!" she said, and they all laughed.

Then the Division One agents headed for the stairway to the bedrooms.

* * *

It was several hours past sunset before a refreshed Zarnix, Zebra, and Fox came downstairs; they had not been summoned in the meanwhile, so they assumed that all was going as well as could be expected with their three patients.

Upon arriving on the ground floor, Suud came to meet them.

"Very good! You all look nicely rested. There is a...what was it you used to call it, Franz?" he broke off to wonder. "The sideboard in the dining room has pastries, cooked morning meats, and the like, in a stasis field, ready for you to break your fast."

"Ah, a continental breakfast buffet," Fox filled in the terminology.

"That is it," Suud said, with a tired effort at a smile. "We thought you would like something when you rose, but no one wanted to wake you to find out what or when, so Lydhuu and I discussed it with cook. He determined this would be a good idea, as it would keep until whenever you woke, and the rest of us can stop by and grab something as we have time. It is not dinner, though it is past time for that, but it will do."

"I'm not very hungry yet," Zebra admitted. "My schedule is kinda off, after all this, I expect. I think I'll cobble together a sandwich of some sort, snarf it down, and go see about Pulgey. I can come back and eat a bit more later."

"Provided you actually do," Fox noted, "else I WILL come and get you, bubeleh."

"I will, I will," she protested.

"I think that is an excellent idea, Zebra," Zarnix agreed, as Suud led the way into the dining room and they all grabbed plates. "And yes, I promise, as well, Fox, and we appreciate your effort at caring for us, the caregivers. But I want to see how that wing did while we were unconscious, ourselves. And I have an idea about how we might heal Lord Entiyti AND Commander Dalgaard."

"Pity we didn't bring the regen pod with us," Zebra noted, around a mouthful of something that reasonably approximated a bacon and egg croissant in both look and taste.

"Ah, I see I am not the only one to be thinking along those lines. Did you notice the very large, airtight shipping container in the storage room, however?"

"Ooo," Zebra noted, dabbing a napkin to her mouth. "I did, now you mention it. That might work. And we have all the necessary constituents of the fluid."

"Off with you, then," Fox said, sitting down with Suud for

a slightly more sedate meal. Lydhuu Raiit wandered in as the two physicians headed for the house hospital wing, intently discussing the possibilities of converting a shipping container into a regen pod.

"Do they never make you jealous, Franz?" Lydhuu wondered, watching them go.

"What, Zebra and Zarnix? No," Fox said, tying into the eggs and 'bacon'—which he already knew from long experience was kosher—with a vengeance; he had missed more than one meal in the last Division day, what with normal hectic fires coupled with the emergency summons. "Because I already know they have a relationship more like siblings than lovers. In fact, early on in our own relationship, Zebra told me that Zarnix would drive her crazy if she ever had to live with him. They are good friends, and excellent colleagues, but that kind of chemistry just isn't there."

"Which is good for you, I suppose," Suud decided. Fox glanced up to see the slightest hint of a smirk on the teasing Reptoid's face, then snorted in amusement.

"Which is good for me," he agreed. "How are things going? Did anything happen while we were asleep? Have you heard back from Director Siisshiiss?"

"No, although I did have to give approval to *Genesis* for him and one of his agents to leave the house and go up to the transfer station," Suud informed his former mentor, "so I suppose the investigation is proceeding. They have set up a kind of substitute office and detention area in the old gatehouse of the property, and requested *Genesis* provide a separate force field for it, as well. Unfortunately, they have told me nothing of the investigation. I should have preferred they involve us more."

"Patience, Suud," Fox advised. "When Taas returns, I'll tag up with him as a fellow division director and involved party, and find out what's going on. Then we can put our oars in, if need be."

"Very well," Suud sighed, tucking into his own meal, as Raiit nosed about the buffet, selecting a pastry for herself. "I suppose it will have to do, for now."

* * *

"I don't like the looks of that wing, Zarnix," Zebra murmured, as the four doctors gathered on the sofas and armchairs in the consulting room off the exam room. "It's getting downright nasty. And it's OOZING. Green shit."

"Indeed, necrosis is setting in rather sooner than I would have expected," Zarnix agreed. "Especially given Yorker added an appropriate antibiotic to the IV. Ssyy? Werf? Is this unusual for Draconans, or normal?"

"I see nothing particularly abnormal in it," Eretigen decided. "Undoubtedly the deck of the transfer station concourse was not the cleanest in the universe, I am certain the miscreants did not go to extremes to clean their shrapnel, and as much damage as Pulgey sustained..." He shrugged. "Ssyy? Do you concur?"

"...I think so, Werf," Hissheth said, after a moment to consider.

"Zebra," Zarnix said, "stick your head in and see if Yorker could come by for a moment, would you? I'd like to know what he and Ooossi observed while tending our critical patient."

"Wilco," Zebra said, hopping up and heading for the hospital room in which Entiyti lay resting.

* * *

"...No," Yorker said, shoulders slumping. "You're right. I watched it get worse by the hour, I swear I did. And Ooossi agreed." He looked at them all. "I kept trying to think of what I could do, and I even tried a bit of Rejuvic on the wingtip, where that particularly nasty tear is, but it didn't really help. I dunno if I didn't use enough, or if there's just that much infection and necrosis, but..." He shook his head. "I was starting to worry he was gonna lose it, or worse, develop sepsis."

"Did Ooossi agree with that assessment?" Zebra wondered.

"Um, yeah. We talked about it, or, well, we tried to make sure that Lord Entiyti was asleep or, you know, unconscious, first; we didn't want to upset or frighten him. And he was going in and out a little bit, even with the anesthesia, because I didn't have it too heavy. But yeah, Ooossi said it's lookin' bad."

"I think we have little choice," Eretigen said, shoulders slumping. "The wing must come off, or we risk losing him again."

"Zarnix, did you get Commander Dalgaard into our kluged-up regen pod?" Zebra wondered.

"I did, rather readily," Zarnix confirmed. "The container was designed to be used as emergency life support once its shipment had been removed, so it proved fairly easy to make the modifications, especially with Yorker and Duurg—uh, Ooossi; he asked us to call him Ooossi—to assist with lifting. And Dalgaard was happy at the prospect of NOT having to have a cybernetic prosthesis."

"I think the technology for your 'regen pod' is amazing," Hissheth said, enthused. "I should love to learn how to do it."

"Likewise," Eretigen agreed.

"That's good, because we might want your help," Zebra said. "And it isn't 'ours,' particularly; Doron of Edeptis developed the procedure and system, then showed us how to use it earlier this year, when one of our top Agents was badly injured. Zarnix, how long will it take on Dalgaard?"

"Not that long; Wintourns tend to heal quite quickly under the regen procedure," Zarnix concluded after a moment to think. "I suspect that within a day, day and a half at most, we can decant him. And that is local time," he added.

"That's good, the timing's good," Zebra murmured, thinking hard. "Zar, do you have clue one how to set up the regen fluid for a reptilian? Specifically a Draconan?"

"Ooo. No, I do not," Zarnix replied, "but it is a good idea, and I think I know just the expert who would. After all, is not that one reason Lord Entiyti knows Doron?"

"Yup," Zebra practically sang. "Let's go put in a call to Edeptis and see what we can find out."

"You are considering regrowing Pulgey's wing in this regeneration pod?" Eretigen asked, surprised but delighted. "It can do that?"

"It has the potential, if we can figure out how," Zebra said. "C'mon, guys, let's go find a phone!"

* * *

"Hello there, Minister Teknon," Zarnix said to the image on the small video monitor.

"Greetings, Doctor...Zarnix, is it not?" Teknon replied. "Of the Division One Agency?"

"That is correct."

"How are you today? Are Agents Echo and Omega well?"

"They are doing fine, though I could not tell you what they are doing; we are not currently on Earth. And Dr. Zebra and I are also doing well."

"I assume you need to speak with Doron, then?"

"That's a good assumption," Zebra said with a smile. "Might we have a chat with him? We're working on an old patient and friend of his, someone kind of important, and need his advice and experience on how to set the chemistry of the regeneration process for that species."

"Yes, we've not had to work with this species in the proce-dure before," Zarnix added.

"Oh dear," Teknon murmured, frowning.

"That isn't the answer I was hoping for," Zebra said, with foreboding.

"No, and I am sorry," Teknon said, distressed. "When I re-alized who was calling, I knew this would likely be a problem."

"Why? What is wrong?" Zarnix asked.

"Doron is not even on Edeptis, and I do not know where he is," Teknon explained. "He was called offworld not quite two hands of days ago. It seems there is a system elsewhere in the Coalition that is experiencing a system-wide pandemic, and he was recommended to help stem the outbreak." The alien minister threw up his hands and gazed at them with his yellow eyes. "I have no idea how to reach him, at this point. And I have already tried for several of his Edeptan patients who have asked for consultations."

"Well...SHIT," Zebra said, with feeling.

* * *

"...I'm sorry, sweetheart," Echo told Omega over their cell phones. "I dunno when I'm gonna get done up here. The more I do, the more the Boys find for me TO do, and there's a crap-ton of paperwork to work through, and..." Omega heard him sigh. "I don't see how Fox manages to do all this shit, and still even get any sleep, let alone spend any time with Zebra."

"You don't even know when you'll get off duty?"

"No, baby, I don't," Echo replied. "I thought we had it bad for paperwork with running Alpha Line, but that's nothing compared to what's coming through this office up here."

"But I thought Lima and Bravo were gonna reroute it all to your desk down here," she protested. "You haven't been down here ALL DAY."

"I know. I thought so too, and they're trying, but we've hit a snag with the security. It seems that a good bit of the Director-level stuff canNOT be routed elsewhere except to one of his specific devices, because it's assumed that no other of-fice is as secure as the Director's office. And I'll grant you, there's a shit-ton of security on this office! We've tried a couple of workarounds, but so far, they've failed. The Boys have a request in to Software to see if we can't gin up some modifica-tions to the system, or set up a password or SOMEthing, but we have no idea when, or even if, that's gonna go through, because of the security issues. Still and all, I'm digging through stuff as fast as I can."

"Is any of it, like, you know, emergency stuff? I could come up and help, if you wanted."

"No, it isn't, and you can't, because of that security crap. Well, you probably could, but first, we'd have to do even MORE paperwork to get you approved to do it! It's all just routine shit, but it's got layers on layers of classification on it because of the risk to intelligence operatives, undercover operations, stuff like that. Stop and think about the amount of paperwork we do as the Alpha Line chief and assistant chief for a sec."

"Okay..."

"Now add the equivalent amount of paper—well, electronic; you know what I mean—for Medical, Sciences, Security, Software, Diplomacy, Weapons Development and Testing, Engineering, Facilities..."

"Ugh," Omega grunted in distaste, wrinkling her nose.

"NOW figure you have all of those, for Headquarters, the Atlanta Office, the Chicago Office, the L.A. Office, Dallas, Toronto, McMurdo, London, Geneva, Moscow, Delhi, Hong Kong, Tokyo, Sydney, Rio, Dubai..." Echo broke off and sighed. "THEN add the offworld Division reports."

"Oh my gosh," Omega gasped. "Are you buried yet?"

"Not far off." Echo's voice had a rueful chuckle in it. "I got my nose above water, but that's about all. Damn bureaucracies, anyway. Like I said, I dunno how Fox even manages to sleep."

"It's past end of shift..."

"I know. Over an hour and a half past, pushing hard on two. And I've seen you sitting in the Alpha Line Room, patiently waiting for me this whole time, but I have no clue when I'll be done, Meg. That's why I called. Don't keep waiting on me. I know you're starved, 'cause of that hypercharged metabolism of yours. Go home and grab something to eat, before you keel over."

"What about you?" Omega worried. "I can run down to the deli and get takeout and bring it back."

"Don't worry about it, Meg. Bravo evidently has two hollow legs—it's his norm, Lima says—and he headed out to do that very thing, about five minutes ago."

"Oh."

"I'm sorry, honey," Echo sighed. "I dunno what I was expecting, but this sure ain't it."

"Well, I guess we'd better get used to it," she decided, echoing his sigh. "I'll see you later."

"Sometime, yeah. 'Bye, baby."

"Bye, Ace."

Omega deactivated her cell phone and replaced it in her

pocket, then stood, put the computers to sleep, ensured all printed paperwork was stowed in secure vaults, and headed out of the Alpha Line Room en route to her quarters, waving at the lone figure in the bay window overlooking the Core as she left.

* * *

"Franz, Lydhuu, come here, quickly!" Suud called from the small sitting room outside Entiyti's home office, and Fox ran to his old colleague's side, Raiit scuttling close behind. "Look!" The Reptoid pointed at the news broadcast.

"...And word has it that the attack, which took place on Emdali, or possibly on the rendezvous station in orbit around it, did indeed catch Coalition President Pulgey Entiyti and his entourage. Entiyti is believed dead, along with the rest of his entourage, as well as numerous tourists and commuters passing through that part of the facility. The total number of fatalities has yet to be determined," the announcer declared. "Repeating our breaking news: Coalition President Pulgey Entiyti of Emdali has been assassinated."

"Farkakte, shit, merde, gronk, and abdab," Fox cursed. "Where the hell did Taas get to? This has to be countered at once!"

"And swiftly," Raiit added.

"Indeed," Suud agreed, as Taassass Siisshiiss, the Division Five chief, ran up. "Did you hear, Taas?"

"I heard," Siisshiiss confirmed. "Baseless rumor and innuendo."

"No, it wasn't, meyn khaver," Fox corrected. "That was a deliberate statement, most likely released by whoever was behind the attack, in an effort to destabilize the Coalition."

"Sssht," Suud cursed. "I had not thought of that! You are right, of course."

"It would be an excellent strategy," Raiit decided, mulling the matter, "if a coup is planned in addition to an assassination. Decapitate the head, and divide the remainder, so that the government collapses due to infighting borne of distrust and doubt, then the prepared leader steps in to take over and 'unite the Coalition once more,' or some such drivel."

"Exactly," Fox said, nodding.

"Mm," Siisshiiss hummed, pondering. "You make excellent points, Fox, Dr. Raiit. All right. I will notify my people to get on it at once and see if we can ascertain who leaked that to the media. Meanwhile, if I might request it, could the three of you work on a proper press release? Something that informs the public that Lord Entiyti is indeed alive, but does not reveal too much? Fox, you founded your Division's diplomatic corps; that should be well within your abilities and skills."

"It is, Taas, and we will," Fox agreed immediately; Suud nodded, and Lydhuu clacked her mandibles in affirmation. "And we should get on it right away."

"Yes," Raiit conceded, as Siisshiiss headed out to see about investigating the news item. "We must get it out there as swiftly as possible, before panic can set in."

"Pulgey's desk is over here," Suud noted, leading them through the door to that large, blocky, but efficient piece of furniture at one end of the study-cum-office. "Franz, as Taas says, you are best equipped for this task..."

"All right, let me dig out my tablet, and the two of you, be prepared to review wording with me," Fox agreed, sitting in the large chair that normally held a huge, muscular Draconan, and trying not to feel intimidated by the fact that he could have fit himself and Zebra in the chair with room to spare...and he was not adjudged a particularly small man. He patted down his pockets. "Oh, don't tell me I managed to leave the dratted thing on my desk at home..."

"Here," Suud said, opening a drawer and fishing out a large notepad and writing implement. "It is old-fashioned, but it always works." He laid them on the desk before Fox, and Fox picked up the pen and began scribbling.

* * *

"...Yes, Franz, that is correct," the green-skinned woman on the comm screen declared. "I stepped into the role, effective about six hours ago, a scant five minutes after we received

123

word of the attempt on Pulgey. As the vice-chair, I'll be acting chairbeing until Pulgey gets well, or..." she broke off and glanced away as a glittering teardrop spilled over. Lady Teela Krimnet, the Ennead member from Kor, angrily dashed away the sign of emotion. "So you may put that in your 'press release' as well. Much as we all hate to admit it, such things are a fact of life in these positions we hold, and we always plan for them. There will be a smooth transition of power, regardless of what happens to Pulgey. Don't worry about me, either—we are running with maximum emergency security in the Council facilities. And I have bodyguards and to spare around the clock, and I'm trying not to trip over them." She paused, then added, "Also, thank you for taking the lead on this media release. Since receiving the word about Pulgey, I am afraid I have been scrambling, and I had not heard about this dreadful false report."

"Suud just happened to be watching," Fox explained, "looking to see if he could spot any clues to a destabilization or the like, anything to give us an idea who is behind this. He spotted it and called Lydhuu and me quickly enough that we saw most of it, too. And Taas was watching elsewhere and joined us within minutes."

"Very good, then." Just then a loud *bedeep!* sounded behind Lady Teela. She turned and glanced at something just out of range of the viewscreen, then nodded. "And there is the notice from my people about this potentially-disastrous little announcement. I'll let them know you're already on it, Fox, and we'll add to it once we see what you put out. I know the lot of you are working with Division Five to investigate the whole..." she broke off, searching for a suitable word.

"Mess," Fox supplied. "Though normally I would apply a much stronger term."

"Exactly," Lady Teela agreed with a wry, tired excuse for a smile. "Keep me informed."

"As best we can, Teela."

"Good. And thank you, Franz. Please pass that on to your

colleagues, Suud and Lydhuu, as well as Chief Siisshiiss."

"I will. Fox out."

"Krimnet out."

* * *

"Franz," Raiit noted, watching news reports, "there is already unrest developing in the Coalition. We need to hurry."

"I know, Lydhuu," Fox replied, never looking up from the missive he composed. "I've almost got it. Give me five more minutes, then I'll read it to you both and see what you think. If you approve, I'll pass it to Taas to send through channels."

"That should do," Suud decided.

* * *

"...And the OFFICIAL word from the PGLEIA Division One Director—who is an old friend and colleague of Lord Entiyti, and currently assisting in the investigation—as verified by both the Division Five Director's Office and the Ennead," the same news announcer said some fifteen minutes later, "does indeed confirm that Lord Entiyti was targeted by an assassination attempt. Of his security detail, chief bodyguard Commander Sigrund Dalgaard was seriously wounded, but will survive. Sadly, bodyguard Uussa Cuusseer was an unfortunate casualty; other guards survived with only minor injuries. The only other fatalities were among the attackers; there were no civilian deaths. Entiyti himself is gravely injured, but he has a multi-species team of crack physicians and healers from Emdali and several other planets working on him in seclusion, and he is expected to survive. Repeating the top news: It has been confirmed that an assassination attempt was made on Coalition President Pulgey Entiyti of Emdali, who is injured, but IS expected to survive. Meanwhile, the well-respected Vice-Chairbeing Teela Krimnet has moved into position as Acting Chairbeing for the duration of Entiyti's recovery, and the Ennead and all other Coalition interests have transitioned smoothly to the new, and as Krimnet has indicated, hopefully very temporary leadership..."

"That's a helluva lot better," Fox decided with a sigh.

"It is," Lydhuu agreed.

"But is he really expected to survive?" Suud worried.

"At this point, yes," Fox averred. "I didn't lie about it, alter khaver. I double-checked with Zebra first; we have our little private communications channels, my mate and I." Fox broke off and shook his head. "I will be glad when I can legitimately call her my wife. Anyway, the physicians have him well-stabilized now, and his blood volume is almost back to normal, minus the oozing that is still going on as wounds heal. What kind of condition he'll be in, when all this is said and done, she couldn't tell me." He met the concerned gazes of the Reptoid and the Ergisol. "I'm really afraid he's going to lose that wing, and he may not be in any shape to go back to chairing the Ennead, physically or mentally. But they're more than ninety-nine percent certain he's going to live to find out."

"Which is better than not," Raiit decided, pragmatic as ever.

"It is," Suud concluded as well. "Though to lose the wing will trouble him. He was looking forward to some recreation in the glide park over the holidays."

"I know, but what is, is," Fox said with a sigh. "At least this," he waved at the media screen, "ought to prevent any outright meltdowns in the Coalition."

"It should," Raiit agreed, "though there are probably going to be a few riots here and there, regardless."

"True enough," Fox noted. "But we have those anyway, because there's always SOMEbody unhappy with the current status quo."

"Word," Yorker said, stepping just inside the open door and knocking on the frame. "Sorry to interrupt, Fox and everybody, and I swear I wasn't eavesdropping; I just heard that last comment, is all. But Zarnix and Zebra both wanted you to have the news as soon as they could spare me..."

"Your face does not look good, zun," Fox said. "I gather you have unpleasant, but not wholly disastrous, news?"

"Yeah, pretty much," Yorker admitted. "We, uh, well,

Lord Entiyti's wing was getting pretty necrotic; it was badly infected, and we were worried about sepsis an' gangrene an' shit, so..." He shrugged. "We...had to amputate it. I'm sorry, but we all discussed it—Zarnix, and Zebra, and Dr. Eretigen, and Dr. Hissheth. They even asked Ooossi and me. But we just couldn't see how to save the wing; it was in too bad a shape. And if we'd left it, tried to save it somehow, it was only gonna kill him. When we'd finally gotten him stabilized!" The medtech met their combined gazes, his own earnest and concerned. "I'm...really, really sorry. We all are." He shook his head. "It must be so cool to be able to fly...and now he can't." Yorker hung his head.

"Zun, don't take the matter to heart," Fox said in a soft tone. "We were just discussing this very possibility. We all knew, from the time he was injured, that this was a likely outcome. From what I understood from Suud, here, even his bodyguards recognized that Pul would probably lose that wing, as the firefight was going on, aboard the transfer station."

"Indeed," Suud confirmed.

"We do what we can do," Raiit agreed. "We none of us are Creator. The only ones to blame are the wurg responsible for the attack."

"As one of my Agents might say, 'Lotsa that,'" Fox affirmed. "Go back to the rest of the medical staff and thank them for us, Yorker, for saving his life. And that includes you."

Yorker perked up a bit at that, and returned to the medical facility wing of the manor house.

* * *

"My friends, on that note, it is time for me to go," Raiit said with a sigh. "I hate like yngdru to leave, but if Pul is stable, then I need to at least go back to the university and get things into a little better order..."

"What do you mean, Lydhuu?" Suud wondered.

"What I mean is, I am going back only tentatively," Raiit explained. "I will help when and as I can; all you need do is call. I intend to set up the department and my classes with my colleagues, so that if need be, I can step away at a moment's notice. Should the Coalition begin to go to yngdru in a woven carrier, I will return to command the extra fleet, the one we formed for the Battle of the Great Hunter Nebula, to help PGLEIA forces maintain the peace. If...something should go wrong with, with Pulgey, CALL me. I will drop everything and be here as fast as I can." She waved her antennae in the Ergisol equivalent of a shrug. "He is a father figure to me, and the two of you are like older brothers, never you mind mentors. I know," she began, then broke off.

"Know what, Lydhuu?" Fox asked softly.

"Perhaps I am not supposed to know this, but...I have long suspicioned," the female Ergisol murmured, "that the three of you consider yourselves brothers of a kind...and there was the, the inheritance discussion..."

Suud and Fox exchanged glances. Then Suud nodded.

"It is somewhat more than that," the Reptoid admitted, "but yes. We do, and we are."

"So I was wondering...might I be a niece, of sorts? I think that is the correct term, is it not, Fox? I know I am a good bit younger than you three, and less experienced..."

Fox and Suud exchanged another look. Abruptly both males smiled.

"That is the correct term, meyn kind," Fox affirmed, then his throat tightened. "Ahem. But, uh, well, I mean, um..."

"Lydhuu, I think what Franz is trying to say is, you already are," Suud finished for him.

"That," Fox agreed. "And have been, for quite some years, now."

"Likely since before you were Pul's chief bodyguard," Suud added.

"Oh!" Raiit fairly chattered her mandibles in happiness. "Thank you, Uncles! Then let me gather my few things and be on my way. I will come back when I can, and sooner if needed."

"That's fine, Lydhuu," Fox said with a smile. "I'll call Zero and tell him to let your flitter through the force field when you call up."

"Thank you, Uncle Franz," Raiit said, and Fox recognized the Ergisol equivalent of a smile on the female's face.

"Meanwhile, Franz," Suud decided, "I suppose you and I should see about setting up a more regular guard shift around Pulgey, now that he is stable."

"Good plan, alter khaver," Fox agreed. "And maybe we need to see where Taas is in his investigation, so we can start playing detective to work out who did it and why. We can walk Lydhuu out while we're about it."

* * *

Omega went back to her quarters, ditched jacket, tie, and weapons holsters, then headed straight for the kitchen, where she threw together a quick two-egg omelet with some pre-sliced mushrooms and a bag of grated cheese—it was hot, tasty, reasonably healthy, caloric, and filling, and that was all that was important just then. She turned it out on a plate, set the hot pan aside to cool, then carried the plate to her dining table and ate alone.

Damn, I miss Ace, she thought, as she finished the omelet and carried her dishes into the kitchen to clean up behind herself. *Since we started dating, we've been spending even MORE time than usual together in our off hours, and it's awful lonesome, sitting around here by myself. Maybe he'll be home a little later, and we can watch a movie and smooch, or something. Or just talk for a while.*

She wandered into the bedroom and changed into black jeans and t-shirt, then went back into the den, flopped down in her recliner, and reached for the TV remote.

Omega channel surfed for a couple of hours, never really finding anything to catch her attention, and always aware of the cell phone sitting on the end table at her elbow—the cell phone which didn't ring—as well as the front door that never opened, and the empty back door, with a dark apartment beyond.

Bedtime came and went, and Echo had not arrived. Omega

129

doggedly continued watching the television, waiting for her companion, even as her eyelids grew heavy; it had been an extra-long day, what with the six-hours-early wakeup call.

This is getting ridiculous, she thought, checking her wrist chronometer against the wall clock. *Fox was never THIS busy, and I can't believe Echo can't expedite all the paperwork, especially with the Boys helping him. What's going on?* Then a poisonous thought struck. *Maybe he just doesn't WANT to be here.*

She shook her head. *No, no, no,* she told herself firmly. *That's the PTSD talking. Zz'r'p has told you as much, girl. So just stop it, right now.* She very deliberately fingered the engagement ring on her left hand, watching the faceted hyper-diamond sparkle in the light. *See? This right here. He LOVES you. So just stop that shit.*

Then where is he?

BUSY, dammit. Now shut up, you.

And surprisingly, the poisonous little voice...did.

Just then, the cell phone rang with Echo's identifying ringtone, and Omega snatched up the device, activating it and holding it to her ear in one motion.

"Hey, Ace!" she practically sang. "I was starting to wonder if the paperwork had reached singularity size, and you'd gotten sucked into a black hole."

There was a monumental snort on the other end of the line.

"Hey, baby; I knew you'd still be up," Echo answered. "Believe me, there've been moments today I've been wondering about a singularity, my own self. And just when I thought I was about to get done in time to at least kiss you good night, something else has gone down."

"What's happened now?" Omega wondered, worried.

"Two things, and I thought you'd want to know both," Echo explained, "especially because you might get hit up for a galactic media interview about it, though I'm trying to divert all that shit off on Sugar..."

"Uh-oh. Let's hear it."

"Well, first off, the news hit the media that Pulgey got caught in an assassination attempt," Echo elaborated. "Fox, Suud, and that Ergisol lady think it was a 'press release' of sorts—a tipoff—from whoever was behind the attempt. Anyhow, the initial reports had it that he and all his bodyguards—making it sound like there was at least a dozen, when I have the report from Division Five that there were only three—got wiped out, along with a significant number of bystanders. But the Division Five report shows only one bodyguard died, and—get this— there were NO bystanders, because the bystanders mostly got clear before the assassination attempt ever went down."

"Ooo," Omega murmured, thoughtful. "Somebody really didn't want witnesses, even more than they wanted to make a big spectacle."

"Exactly. But Fox and the others at Pulgey's home were all over it, with some help from the acting chairbeing, one Teela Krimnet—you haven't met her, but if I'm remembering right, she and Fox were an item, years ago, before he met Zebra—and they got out a press release in about twenty minutes that gave the truth of the situation, without giving away too much info to any bad guys that might be watching for intel."

"Oh. Well, that's good. Way to go, Fox, for being on the ball."

"When is he not, really?"

"True. Although he was close, last night. I've never seen him that rattled before."

"I have, once, I think," Echo's voice was thoughtful as he responded. "Back when he and I got drafted into the Agency. But it was a different kinda rattled."

"Oh, I get it. Yeah."

"Anyhow, you need to be aware that the appropriate response to a question from the media is, 'No comment,'" Echo gave instruction. "I got a message from Fox expressly about that, a bit ago. You and I are the most likely to be hit up in Division One, and since we're just filling holes while Fox helps out an old friend, we know nothing. I mean, we do, but not officially."

"Right. I gotcha," Omega averred. "So if a reporter tackles me, I wince...to show I'm worried about the situation, and therefore have a heart...then say, rather regretfully, 'No comment. Thank you, please excuse me, I have work to do, et cetera.'"

"Bingo," Echo's voice now held a grin. "I knew you'd be all over it like a duck on a June bug."

"Heh," Omega snickered. "I haven't heard that expression in entirely too long."

"Want me to use it more often?"

"Yeah!"

"Be careful what you ask, baby; I'll unleash all the Texan slang on ya!"

"I'll turn loose the 'Bama shit on you, then!"

They laughed together for several minutes. Finally Omega got control of her laughter long enough to ask, "Okay, so what's the other update?"

The laughter on the other end silenced almost instantly.

"Uh-oh," she said, growing worried again. "I dropped a lead brick in the conversation, huh?"

"A little bit," Echo admitted. "There's good news, and bad news."

"Let's hear it, then."

"Which one first?"

"I dunno. Just tell me."

"Well, they have the worst of the holes patched up, plenty of blood and saline replenishing his blood volume, and Pulgey is going to live."

"That's great!"

"Yeah, but the bad news is probably something you're going to relate to, baby, pretty closely—they had to amputate the damaged wing. Pretty much at the shoulder. Fox said there's nothing there but a stub, now, and that compression-bandaged, to minimize bleed-out."

"Aw shit," Omega breathed, a deep sympathetic pain shooting through her chest. In response, she grabbed her shirt front in her free hand as her face crumpled, but she fought off the tears that threatened. "Aw shit."

"Yeah."

They were silent for a long moment.

"You gonna be okay, baby?" Echo wondered, when the silence had grown awkward.

"Y-yeah," Omega murmured, choking back emotion. "I just...just feel for him."

"I knew you would. Ex-rocket jockey, skilled high-performance jet pilot, dogfighting spacecraft pilot—I think the things you love to do the most all involve flying of SOME sort. If there was ever an enhancement Slug mighta given you that you WANTED, it woulda been wings. And of course, he didn't. Damn him."

"Heh. Yup." The sound was dark, lacking any real humor. "You know me well, Ace."

"I try, anyhow." He paused. "Listen, those two tidbits of info were two of three reasons Fox contacted me. The third is that he left his personal tablet here in the office, and he needs it. So I'm gonna have it couriered to him A.S.A.P., and since it's a Director device, going from Acting Director to actual Director, I have to hand it off to the courier personally, AFTER packaging it up a certain particular way. I gotta find the special travel charger, too. I'm gonna do all that here in a few minutes, just as soon as I get off the phone with you. But it looks like being a couple more hours before the special courier arrives, so I'm stuck here."

"Well, DAMN!"

"Yeah, but in the meantime, Lima and Bravo are looking at getting us ahead of the game for tomorrow," Echo said. "Which might actually mean we can at least have a meal or two together, you and me."

"That's something, I guess." Omega chewed her lip in thought, opened her mouth to say something, but thought better of it and closed her mouth again.

"What, baby? What is it?"

"I didn't say anything."

"No, but I know you better than that—you started to. I heard you inhale. What's wrong?"

"Um, nothing, really. I mean, I know better, I just..."

"YES, I'd much rather be with you right now, than sitting here packing up Fox's damn tablet and waiting for the mailman. Preferably sitting on the couch with you, making out."

"Oh! Okay," Omega said, feeling comforted. "Well, I can have a kiss waiting for you when you do get home."

"No, honey. I appreciate the thought, but it could be HOURS. The courier is a special one and he has a route, and he won't be here for..." there was a pause, "three more hours, and that's if there aren't any delays. Go on to bed. It's way past our bedtime, and we were up damn early this morning as it was."

"But Ace! You gotta sleep sometime!"

"I know, and I will. I've found Fox's secret hidey-hole...or rather, Bravo showed it to me...and I'm gonna go in there and crash until the courier gets here; the Boys will come and wake me when the courier arrives, they said. It's kinda cool—it's really a saferoom, a tiny studio apartment that's an extension of the emergency warp tunnel system and connected to it, but he's got it outfitted with a cot, recliner, mini-fridge and hot pad for heating food, a cabinet stocked with said food, a wet bar, TV, all kindsa shit like that. That way he can grab a few minutes' down time without having to go all the way to his quarters and back."

"Oh, nice," Omega decided. "Now we know where he goes when he disappears and nobody saw him go out."

"Exactly. And the Boys have a couch in the corner of their office, and have been taking turns on it."

"So...I need to go on to bed now, and you'll be home when you get home."

"Pretty much. I'm really sorry, baby. This is not going at all the way I expected."

"Yeah, I know. I'm wondering if this is the reason why I got a bad feeling about it, last night," she pondered. "My day wasn't great, either."

"What happened?"

"Well, there was this new partnership in the department..."

* * *

"Aw shit," Echo grumbled, when Omega had finished telling him about her day. "Day two, round two."

"Yeah," Omega sighed. "Same shit, different day. But between us, me an' Romeo an' India think we got 'em set straight."

"Well, that's something, I guess. Look, head on to bed, baby. I'll find the charger, package up the tablet and catch some Z's myself, then come home after I hand this thing off to the courier."

"Okay. Good night, Ace."

"Good night, Meg. Love you."

"I love you, too. Ni-ni."

"Night."

And they ended the conversation. Omega grabbed the remote and turned off the TV, rose, stretched, and headed for the bedroom.

* * *

Omega had been asleep for some four hours when she felt a gentle embrace, and dragged herself from slumber. Her sleepy eyes cracked open to see the dimmer lamp on the nightstand had been switched onto the lowest setting, and a familiar and much beloved face hovered inches from hers—Echo sat on the bedside.

"There you are," he breathed, just as his lips came down on hers. "I thought I'd pop by for that kiss you promised. I missed you today, baby. But I'm finally home."

"Good. I missed you, too," she murmured, repaying his kiss...with interest.

Chapter 6

"Did you reach Echo?" Suud asked, coming into the office.

"Yes, I did," Fox said, satisfied. "He had already found it, and wondered that I didn't bring it with me. He's arranging to have it special-couriered to me, along with the travel charger—I told him where that should be—so I oughta have it in only a few hours."

"Oh, very good," Suud decided. "Your 'outboard brain,' as Pul likes to call them, will be most useful to us, I think."

"Yes, because with all the Director-level functions, I can set up the guard schedule around Pulgey, and have it automatically issue the schedules to the guards," Fox agreed. "But we can do it the old-fashioned way in the meantime. I don't think we need to wait any longer. We need to sit down and work out a formal guard schedule, rather than just having everyone standing guard, and sending a few off here and there to rest."

"Agreed," Suud declared. "That way lies failure, and the possible loss of our brother and the galactic leader. We can transfer it into your tablet later."

"Exactly." Fox pulled out the paper and pen that Suud had given him earlier. "So let's list everyone we have available for guard duty...yours, mine, and the Slliith City Office..."

The pair bent over the desk and commenced work.

* * *

"Oh, I think that will work very well, do you not think?" Suud said, roughly an hour later.

"I think it will indeed," Fox concluded, looking at what they had laid out. "Let's head for the guard barracks wing and start getting this under way. Then we can go see Taas and find out what he's discovered."

* * *

"Of course we would love your help, Fox, Lord Guurn,"

Director Siisshiiss declared, unequivocal, as the three stood in the sitting room outside Entiyti's office. "In fact, as soon as I was certain Lord Entiyti was stable and your concerns had been eased, I planned to approach you. But I did not wish to bother you when your minds were already filled with worry."

"Ah," Fox said, shooting a meaningful glance at Suud, and both males understood that the reason they had not been included in the investigation was thoughtful consideration for their anxiety, not a desire to exclude them, nor territoriality. "Well, while there is still some concern, it's our understanding that Pulgey—uh, rather, Lord Entiyti—is out of danger."

"From his injuries, at least, if not future attacks," Suud added, making a point, and the other two males nodded.

"Indeed," Siisshiiss agreed. "And now you both, as former chief bodyguards, especially given his current bodyguard is severely injured, desire to be involved. More so as Fox is a division director himself, and both of you are effectively admirals of Coalition fleets."

"When it is needful," Suud replied, modest.

"Well, I certainly have no objection to the additional assistance, let alone the political clout," Siisshiiss averred. "You both have a knowledge of Lord Entiyti's personal history that is apt to shed light on this situation, and frankly, I welcome the help."

"Then let us be seated and discuss the matter, and you can brief us on the latest information," Suud suggested.

"That is a pleasant way to do the thing," Siisshiiss agreed, and they chose seats in the corner of the room. "Now, let me think. I had intended to do this in a more organized fashion, most likely on the morrow once I had a chance to prepare, but even so, I should be able to make you aware of events fairly readily. So. We believe there were some eighteen or twenty assassins in the private-shuttle concourse of the transfer station. Nine bodies were recovered, all with weapons on their persons that were out and very recently active..."

"All one species?" Fox queried.

"No. There were six Ke!endarians, one Teludal, one Zargothian, and one being that we at first believed to be a Ke!endarian, but now suspect may have been a disguised Cortian."

"Shit," Fox cursed. "Any prisoners?"

"Five. Two Zargothians, a Teludal, a Reptoid, and a Ke!endarian. We have a top team of Deltiri interrogators on the way, but we have already extracted some information."

"Let us hear it," Suud said.

"It seems that many of the perpetrators 'had it in for' Lord Entiyti, as you might say, Fran-er, Fox," Siisshiiss said.

"You can call me either one, here, Taas," Fox noted. "I was known as Franz Levy to the galactic community for decades while I worked on Pul's security staff. Only on Earth is my code name important."

"Oh, good," Siisshiiss said, relieved. "I know you as Fox from the Division heads meetings, but many of Lord Entiyti's friends and associates know you as Lord Franz Levy. I did not wish to offend, but working with this group, it tended to get confusing."

"Not a problem. And when it's just us, I'm not going to stand on ceremony, either way. So they had it in for Pul, huh? Let me guess," Fox tried, reckoning off fingers. "The Zargothians were kin of the late Lady Zzs...Grrzzuus, I think we found out her clan name was. The Teludal was a littermate of 'Kenny' and 'Cartman,' aka Slettek and Relamu Frunflin, out for revenge for their siblings' deaths—one of which was a formal execution for egregious crimes committed. And the Ke!endarian was a member of the former H!nar kre Naese!en!Re cult."

"All correct," Siisshiiss responded, surprised. "How on Emdali did you know?"

"Because 'Kenny' was killed by my agents, and 'Cartman' captured by one of those same Agents with the aid of the civilian who then became his partner, who also assisted—with that partner—in uncovering the reality behind the Ke!endarian cult and taking out several assassins sent to Earth to kill the Ke!endarian Vice-President; the same two Agents were ultimately responsible for Lady Zzs' death when she was part of an assassination squad sent against the American President, earlier this year. The Cortians were shown to be the slaver pirate scum they are by those same two Agents, by the way—Alpha One, Agents Echo and Omega."

"Geessht," Siisshiiss cursed. "So we have a history of criminal activity among the associates, most notably attempted assassination, and a connection to Entiyti through the Division One Alpha Line's top Agents."

"Yes. And all of them would have reason to hate the Coalition leadership for, as they would view it, 'siding against them,' most notably Pulgey, I suppose. The Cortians are just out to destabilize the Galactic Coalition and take advantage of the fact; any vengeance they felt it wreaked would only be icing on the cake for them. The ones you found on the assassin team were probably crew from one of the handful of renegade ships that got away from us in the Battle of Orion. But I have no idea what part the Reptoids played in all this."

"Oh, that is easy enough to suuss out, at least for the one we captured, for he is a loudmouth and braggart," Siisshiiss noted with a shrug. "It was harder to get him to shut up than to find out what his motive was. In fact, he was the source of most of the information we have on the others, though it is only hearsay; once the Deltiri interrogators arrive, we can verify it. But he is just more of the same, saving he has not the assassination history, I suppose. The Reptoid, one Ulluuda Zziivux, is a career criminal, and resentful of the galactic government's 'interference' in Emdalian affairs—which, I might add, he views as the reason his 'profession' is illegal, never mind that theft, burglary, graft, fraud and the like were illegal for long millennia before Emdali entered the Coalition—but evidently he blames Entiyti, since he is far and away our world's most prominent galactic statesman."

"Well," Suud sighed, "I never claimed a normal distribution did not apply to the overall intelligence of the Reptoid population as much as any other."

"And if you comprise a high-end outlier, my friend, there must be someone to counterbalance you in the other tail of the distribution," Fox chuckled.

"Indeed," Siisshiiss laughed. "Not especially bright, that perp." Then he paused and rubbed a clawed hand over what passed for his chin. "None of them in this lot, actually," he admitted. "Which argues that these are simply the hired help..."

"And the real leaders of whatever faction is attempting to kill Pulgey are elsewhere," Fox finished for him. "Which fits with the release of the false information about the assassination attempt."

"Precisely," Siisshiiss agreed. "And while we have been looking for whoever put out the false report on that attempt, so far, we have no leads. The news reporters say it was an anonymous tip, and when they followed up on it, discovered the transfer station had indeed had an incident essentially matching the description provided by the tipster, and thus concluded it was true."

"Hm," Fox hummed, thoughtful.

"Perhaps you might want to call Echo again, Franz," Suud suggested.

"Because he had some involvement in pretty much all of it, and to a lesser extent, so did Omega?"

"Yes."

"That...is not a bad idea. I need to tell them to watch their backs. They could be secondary targets."

"And," Suud said, "I suppose it is not necessary to add... so could you."

Fox stared at him, stunned.

"Well, farkakte," he declared.

* * *

"Thanks for the heads-up, Boss, but that shouldn't be a problem," Echo told Fox a little later. Fox sat at Entiyti's desk once more, using the classified comm system to contact his deputy, and glad for the access. "Meg and I are staying damn busy, I'll admit, but it's all bureaucratic stuff—paperwork, departmental meetings, and the like. My schedule today, once I get there, just has—"

"Wait. Once you get there? Oh damnation," Fox said, suddenly realizing what time it was at Headquarters. "I'm sorry, zun. I didn't even think about the time, things have been so meshuginah here. I didn't wake you, did I?"

"No, I was already up," Echo said. "I'm dead on my feet, but I'm here."

"But...hold on. Dead on your feet? Why so tired?"

"Bravo and Lima got me an' Meg up six hours early yesterday so I could sit in on some unexpected negotiation with the Ganotian potentate, who was insisting that the Director be part of the negotiations...which meant me, since you weren't here. Then I spent ALL damn day in your office, trying to get through the paperwork, and had only just finished last night when you called, and then the courier was late, and..." Echo sighed. "Damn, Fox, I'm not sure I want this job after all. EVER. I dunno how YOU do it, but it barely gives me any time to sleep."

Fox sat in the desk chair for long moments, mentally cursing himself out, while Echo waited patiently on the other end of the communiqué. Finally the older man drew a deep breath.

"Forgive me, zun," he murmured. "You are obviously being very conscientious about each little bit of paperwork, when I had every intention of gradually introducing you to my shortcuts for determining what required careful scrutiny and what could be rubber-stamped...only I never had a chance to show you..."

"Oh," Echo said, voice very flat.

"All right, let me try to simplify it a bit," Fox offered. "Just from working with them, and getting Alpha Line applications from them, you should already have a good feel for which Offices, Stations, and other field centers have good, solid leadership, versus which ones need a bit of...help."

"Well, yeah..."

"Good. Then trust the reports and work coming out of the

ones with good leadership, and focus on the others. Put the other-planet reports somewhere in between—not because they have poor leadership; they don't. But they ARE entire planets, not merely field Offices. If you need to, get the Boys to screen the reports, especially from the other worlds in the Division, and flag anything that looks important. Don't do everything yourself; that's what Lima and Bravo are there for, and why there are TWO of them. The job will eat you alive if you let it. Don't let it. The operative word is 'delegate.' I know you do that with Alpha Line; you'll have to learn to do it with this, too. For instance, if there's a security question at one of the Offices, call the chief of Security at Headquarters—there's a reason each of you overall department heads are at HQ, and why I've been discussing with you about the possibility of basing small Alpha Line units at the other Offices, as the department grows, never mind starting to establish sub-departments on the other planets in the Division, using agents from those planets. Each one of the Headquarters leads are my overall leads, and I trust each of you to work through a problem and help out the other Offices. When a problem comes up, figure out which department it falls under, then contact that department lead and delegate the problem to him or her. If it seems to fall under more than one, determine which ones, then call them in and discuss it with them, and delegate to all appropriate, to work together on it. Trust me, the Office in question will be delighted you sent so much help their way, without having upper management—meaning you, or me—hovering over them."

There was silence on the transmission for several moments, and Fox could imagine Echo mulling over what he had just said.

"Yeah, okay, that makes sense," Echo agreed then. "All of it. I was so swamped yesterday by the sheer magnitude of shi- uh, stuff coming through, that I couldn't get my head above water to make sense out of it. I'll go into it with a battle plan today. Oh, and is there any sort of password that you use, to get all the...STUFF...to shunt to, say, your tablet, or your home laptop, or something? For the life of us, we could not figure out how to get that done yesterday, and Software said it was already handled, but wouldn't tell us HOW. Said it would violate Security, and then Security would be on their ass, and... Fox, I never made it down to the Alpha Line Room at all, all day yesterday, and Meg coulda used me for a couple things..."

"Oh, farkakte, that's a definite problem. Yes, there is a password, zun, and I'm about to send it to you in a ciphered blip," Fox said, engaging the high-level ciphering capability on Entiyti's virtual desktop, then typing in *Thi$jobi$apainintheA$$10Xover!* to the text messaging box and hitting <send>. "And I'm sure you'll agree with it in just a few moments."

They waited for some time, until Fox heard a *ding!* on Echo's phone.

"There it is," Echo noted unnecessarily. "Thank the good Lord. Hang on and lemme verify clear receipt."

Fox waited, lips twitching, while Echo pulled up the message and decrypted it, then read it. Abruptly the younger man burst into uncontrolled laughter, practically howling in mirth.

"Oh DAMN, Fox! Is it ever!" Echo exclaimed, still laughing, and Fox grinned widely. "Oh shit! That's PRICELESS! It's perfect! Oh! No, no, Meg, everything's all right, honey. No, I'm fine, it's, um, it's a howler of a joke, but it's kinda classified...yeah, it's Fox, but he just wanted to give us a heads-up about something—I'll tell ya in a minute—but he was giving me some advice on how to avoid staying in the office 48/7."

"Oh, good," Fox could just make out Omega's voice saying. "I'd kinda like to be able to work with my partner, AND see my fiancé once in a while, other than just over breakfast. Which is ready, by the way."

"Okay, just a sec."

"Mmm," Fox murmured. "Zun, don't react, but is she grumpy about it?"

"No, not particularly," Echo said. "Worried, I think, though. But Fox, I went for a solid thirty-three hours yesterday, and didn't even leave your desk for meals; Bravo fetched me food except for first lunch, and Meg brought me THAT. And I ate it all at your desk, while still working. And she couldn't even stay, because my work was classified."

"Damn, zun."

"Yeah. SHE may not be, but *I* sure as hell am. So I'm really glad to have these tips."

"Not a problem. I wish I'd had time to provide it before I left. I suppose, when I get back, we need to carve out some regular time to do that, in case I get called away on an emergency again. That way, you'll be better prepared, next time."

"Probably a good idea, yeah, and I'm game. Listen, Fox, I swear we'll keep an eye out, but I don't really think there's anything to worry about here, unless they infiltrate Headquarters to come and hunt us down...which, while not impossible, won't be easy...unless, I guess, they have a low-rez genetic duplicate of one of us, like Wright..."

"No, the last I knew, Security and Software were working together to gin up a combination audiovisual-slash-genetic identification system, and it was already being tested in Headquarters to their satisfaction. It was really just a matter of modularizing it, they said." Fox paused. "I think it was your partner's idea."

"Great! I'll notify Security and have 'em raise the threat level a notch, though."

"Good plan."

"Besides, like I said, I don't see Meg an' me being anywhere except dinking around HQ someplace...our quarters, or your office, or our office. I had thought about, if I could shake loose long enough, her an' me walking down to the deli for one of our lunches today, but if you don't think it's advisable, we won't even do that."

"Why don't you lay low for the time being, zun, both of you, and let us find out which way the wind is blowing?" Fox suggested. "I'd hate for something to happen, because we didn't realize it was bigger than we expected. Then, in a few days, if Taassass Siisshiiss—"

"Isn't that the Division Five director?"

"It is. If Taas and Suud and I feel like it's safe, in a few days, you two can start getting out and about again."

"Good point. Okay, we'll stay in-house for a while." Echo broke off to call, "Gimme 'bout another minute, baby."

"You need to go, before your breakfast gets cold," Fox noted. "Especially after the kind of day you had yesterday. Relax over a nice hot breakfast with your lady, at least. I'll keep you posted as best I can. And now that the critical point is past, and Pul looks like making it, if you need help, CALL."

"Okay, Fox. Thanks."

"No problem, zun. Fox out."

"Echo out."

* * *

"...And so Fox and Suud are apparently worried that whoever is behind the assassination attempt might try to target Alpha One as well," Echo told his partner over an excellent ham, mushroom, and Swiss omelet, shared at Omega's dining table.

"Because of the composition and background of the hit squad members?" Omega verified.

"Right," Echo said around a forkful of omelet. "You could argue that Pulgey was at the head of it because Coalition President an' the buck stops here, even though he wasn't the president for that whole time. But one way or another, even if you didn't know it at the time, you and I BOTH were involved in all of the rest of the mess, except for whatever's wrong with the Reptoid faction, I guess. And that might just be, like, a gang, or organized crime, or something, going after the home boy who made good."

"Well, I suppose they have a point," Omega considered, chewing a mouthful of egg and mushroom.

"Yeah. So we stay close to home, bump up Headquarters security, raise the threat status, and watch our backs," Echo decreed.

"Works for me. And you said he gave you some tips about

how to not get eaten by a paperwork monster?"

"Yup. I've already talked to Bravo and Lima, and they get what I'm asking, and said they do it not infrequently for Fox. But the schedule was all thrown off yesterday anyway, between me not being Fox, and the whole Ganotian negotiation taking way longer than scheduled. I tried to ease off the videoconference, but the potentate wasn't havin' it. In fact, I think she was happy it was me, because first contact an' all, so she glommed onto me." He shot Omega a wary glance. "In fact, well, they're humanoid and all, and she, uh..."

"What?"

"...I think she was trying to flirt with me."

"Aw, shit," Omega grumbled. "Just what I need—a planetary ruler tryin' to snag you."

"Come on, baby," Echo tried to soothe. "You know I'm not gonna go for it. It's YOU I'm crazy about."

"There have been such things as arranged marriages among state leaders before, hon."

"Yeah, but I'm not a state leader."

"Yet. But SHE is. What if she decides to make you a condition of the negotiations?"

"Simple. We say no."

Omega blinked, and stared at him, putting down her fork.

"Is it really as simple as that, Ace?"

"You'd be surprised, baby. And remember, I got that degree in diplomacy."

"Yeah, that's true," Omega sighed. "Okay, that makes me feel better. And so do the tips you said Fox gave you. Maybe we can actually have a meal together today. Other than breakfast, that is."

"Yeah, I hope so too, and I was gonna suggest we walk down to the deli for lunch and get some sunshine, but Fox thinks we should stay in-house an' not wander too much. We can always come back to our quarters and fix something, or send one of the Boys out for Chinese, or whatever."

"Ooo, Chinese sounds good..."

* * *

"Ah, there we are," Zz'r'p said, as Omega entered his office for her next counseling session, later that morning. "And how are you today, my friend?"

"I think...I think I'm okay," Omega noted, somewhat hesitant. "Yesterday sucked, but I'm hoping today will go better."

"Oh? Tell me what happened..."

* * *

"...And so when Echo was so late getting off work, your first thought was that he did not want to be with you, if I understand correctly?" Zz'r'p pursued the concern.

"Yeah, it was," Omega admitted. "It was the whole knee-jerk thing all over again. But, um, see, this time I recognized it for what it was, and I think...I think this time I kinda beat it down a little."

"How so?" the Deltiri wondered. "You are saying you bested the knee-jerk reaction and stopped it, remaining confident about your relationship with Echo?"

"Yeah," Omega said with a shy grin.

"How?"

"This," she murmured, and held out her left hand, displaying the shiny bauble on her finger. "My engagement ring. I made myself look at it, study it, think about what it represents. I played with it, you know, rolling it around my finger an' watching it sparkle. And really, really THOUGHT about what it meant for Echo to give it to me. About what it meant TO Echo, to give it to me."

"And you realized...?"

"That Echo's never done that for any other living being," Omega pointed out. "Until me. EXCEPT FOR me. He's offering to share his life with me in a way that he's never done for anyone else. From now on. And that...helped," she declared. "Then he called and talked to me, explained what was happening, and told me to look after myself and not stay up too long; said I needed to rest. And I knew he meant, '...after everything that's happened lately.' So he was looking after me, too, even if he couldn't be there with me."

"Excellent, my dear girl, excellent!" Zz'r'p exclaimed, pleased. "I could not be happier with this. Your inner recorded dialogue tripped and began to play, and you not only stopped it, you countered it. Did you feel better about yourself and the relationship afterward?"

"Yes, I did," Omega averred. "In fact, by the time Echo hung up, I had kinda...have you ever heard the expression, 'warm fuzzies'?"

"I have. And I know what it means. So that is how you felt afterward?"

"Yup," Omega said, offering him another grin. "Then I did what he said. I got ready and went to bed and got comfy and dropped right off to sleep. And when he DID get home, he came by and woke me enough to let me know he was home, and we kissed, and then he went off to crash, himself. And oh, Zz'r'p, he looked SO tired." She shook her head. "And I knew then, that he had worked hard, the whole time, and was glad to see me, glad to be with me, by that point."

"Oh, this is what I was hoping would happen, Omega, my dear," Zz'r'p said with a smile. "I must say, I did not expect to see it quite so soon."

"So I'm getting well fast?" Omega wondered, pleased. "That's great!"

"No, no; do not make the mistake of thinking we are almost done," he admonished. "Your anxieties are much deeper-seated than THAT. But you are at least starting to see what I have been telling you—that you are loved, and worthy of that love, and you are starting to regain some of your confidence. And that is a very good start."

He paused, telepathically reading her reaction—disappointment, consideration, puzzlement, and finally determination. "There we go. That is where I wanted you to end up with that thought. Now, let us discuss why you became afraid he was avoiding you in the first place..."

* * *

"Hi, baby," Echo said in a cheerful tone, entering the Alpha Line Room shortly before first lunch. "Man, is it good to see you."

Omega sat at her desk, reviewing reports on her computer. He moved to her side, and they both glanced out the door and adjacent observing window, ensuring no one outside was watching. Then he bent and gave her a gentle, brief kiss, which she returned with pleasure.

"Oh, is it that time already?" Omega wondered then, glancing at her wrist chronometer. "Wow. It's my turn to run late today, Ace. I haven't finished the departmental report collation yet."

"No sweat, baby. I'm a little early; that marathon paperwork session yesterday got us a little ahead of schedule today, for a wonder. Bravo volunteered to run out and get us Chinese takeout for lunch, when he fetched his and Lima's first lunch. He's gonna swing by here and leave it for us."

"That sounds good. What did you order?"

"Hot and sour soup, egg rolls, and pot stickers, for starters; chicken with black bean sauce—it won't be as good as yours, but it won't be half bad, either—and chicken curry, for entrees, with fried rice on the side," Echo said. "Green tea ice cream for dessert, assuming they pack it good, so it stays frozen. If not, green tea soup, I guess." They laughed.

"That sounds nummy, Ace," Omega declared. "You got any idea when he'll be back with it?"

"Oh, it'll be a while," Echo said. "I headed out only a couple minutes after he did."

"Then I might just be able to get this departmental report compiled from the individual Agents' reports, and have it ready for you later, when you go back to Fox's office," Omega decided.

"Nah, we got things worked, finally," Echo said, sitting down at his own desk and booting his laptop. "I'll be working all that mess from here, starting now, like we planned originally. Hey, didn't you say you wanted to have that new team,

Alpha Twenty-Four, come by to kinda socialize with us and get to know us?"

"Yeah?"

"Well, now I can be here and actually DO it," Echo said. "Those tips Fox gave me this morning are really panning out."

"They're helping?"

"Immensely." He waved a hand. "So don't worry about me. I'm here, and I'm gonna be here, probably the rest of the day. Finish your report and pop it off, and by that time, lunch should be here."

"That sounds good."

"How did your counseling session with Zz'r'p go this morning?"

"Pretty good, I think," a thoughtful Omega said, pausing her work. "Zz'r'p seemed to believe I was coming along. He did tell me I had a long way to go, longer than I'd hoped, which...makes sense, I guess. But he seemed exceptionally pleased with the progress I'd made overnight."

"Why's that?"

"Aw, you're gonna think I'm silly, 'cause it's stupid."

"It was you worrying about me not coming home last night, wasn't it?"

"Yeah."

"So tell me."

"Well, it's just that I'd already pretty much talked myself into ignoring that annoying little voice that tells me nobody could love a 'thing,'" Omega said, and Echo noted that she didn't add her usual, "like me."

"That sounds promising," Echo decided.

"Yeah, Zz'r'p thought so, too. And then you called, and basically confirmed what I'd talked myself into realizing, and..." She shrugged, then offered him a smile. "I behaved myself, went to bed, and slept like a baby until you arrived for your bedtime kiss."

"And after that?"

"I went back to sleep and slept like a baby some more, until the alarm clock went off this morning."

"That's great, sweetheart! Oh, and by the way, I, uh, I did something this morning, myself," Echo said, flushing a bit. "I thought maybe it might be good, since you pointed out some pertinent issues this morning over breakfast. And I figured if nothing else, it would make you feel better, more secure about things."

"What?"

* * *

"I had a long chat with Sugar about the Ganotian potentate's possible crush on me," Echo said, feeling his face heat. "I wanted to make sure that he was aware that that wasn't on the table for negotiation—that *I* wasn't on the table for negotiation. He seemed surprised, then got thoughtful, decided I might have a point, and said he'd take care of it."

"Good," Omega said. "And Echo?"

"Yeah, baby?"

"Thanks, hon. The fact that you took my silly little worries seriously, and acted on 'em, means worlds to me."

"Well, that's just it, Meg. The more I thought about it, the more I realized there might be something there to be concerned about—I've known that to happen in a couple of negotiations, not anything Earth did, but when Fox was head of Diplomacy and X-ray and I escorted him to some conferences and council meetings and the like...yeah. I've seen it happen. So it's not silly, at all." He shrugged. "Anyway, I'm not available, and Sugar is going to make sure the potentate knows it."

"Does Sugar know about us?"

"He does now. But he'll be discreet, and he's been a good friend ever since the whole Cortian shit went down. I didn't have any hesitation telling him, ya know?"

"Yeah."

"He said, uh," Echo broke off, feeling his face heat again. "He said to tell you that you managed to make a damn fine catch." He cleared his throat, self-conscious.

"Aw! I sure think I did," Omega agreed with a smile. "Did

he tell you anything about me? Like, 'boy, did you pick a nut-case,' or something?" she teased.

"Yeah, he did, but it wasn't quite that insulting," Echo shot back, letting the wording convey the quip. Omega gave him a raspberry, then they laughed. "Nah. What he really said was that I was a lucky man, and maybe one day he'd be half as fortunate."

"Aw!"

"He's right, ya know," Echo told her, earnest. "I AM a lucky man. A damn lucky man."

"Well, um," Omega began, face reddening. She tucked her head. "Wait until you know everything before you decide that, okay?"

"No need, baby. There is nothing you can say, no secret you can hide, that is so bad it will ever convince me otherwise."

"Just...wait," Omega reiterated, then made a show of focusing on her report. Echo watched her for a long moment, understanding that she was still struggling with whatever bothered her. Finally he sighed and resumed his own computer work.

Five minutes later, Omega hit a rapid sequence of keystrokes.

"THERE," she announced. "That damn departmental report is done. Should be in your inbox in a couple secs."

"There it is," Echo noted, pulling up the reporting module.

"And stop right there," Bravo ordered as he came through the door with two large take-out bags. "Lunch has arrived!" He deposited one of the bags on the credenza along the back wall between Echo's and Omega's desks, then turned to Echo with a smirk. "Permission to take first lunch, sir?"

"Permission granted," Echo chuckled. "If it tastes half as good as ours smells, you'll be in great shape. Get outta here, and you and Lima snarf down whatever y'all got."

"Getting out, sir!" Bravo laughed, all but skipping out the door.

"That dude has as many hollow legs as Romeo," Echo declared. "I swear, if we ever get the two of them together for a meal, we'll have an earthquake, 'cause the buffets of New York's boroughs will be shaking in fear."

"That sounds intriguing," Adam declared, coming in the door. "I didn't know chie-uh, Agent Romeo had that much of an appetite."

"Echo, this is Alpha Twenty-Four," Omega introduced the Agents, "Adam and Torino. Guys, this is the Alpha Line chief and currently Acting Director, Echo. I thought it might be nice if we had a casual little sit-down over first lunch and really got to know each other."

"That sounds good," Echo agreed, as he and Omega dug around and fished out the various dishes that comprised their meal. "I didn't know it was a first-lunch meeting though, or I'd have ordered more..."

"That's okay, sir, we brought plate lunches from the deli," Torino explained, waving a take-out bag.

"Great! Pull up some chairs and let's sit down and get to know each other," Echo said with a smile. "I gather y'all got brought in under kinda emergency circumstances while Meg and I were off on a recent extended mission..."

"Yes sir. Fox had a situation developing, and we had some pertinent experience, but it needed to be done under Alpha Line auspices. So Romeo and India tested us, and brought us in when we passed the testing," Adam elaborated, then shot a guilty glance at Omega. "Which is why we had a little bit of confusion yesterday about who ran the department..."

"No sweat," Echo reassured. "And since it's just us four, no need to call me 'sir,' either. If it was a staff meeting, sure, but this is just a group of colleagues getting to know each other."

"Bingo," Omega agreed. "I didn't call y'all here to dress you down or anything. I just figured, under the circumstances, it would help if we all actually got to know each other."

Torino and Adam exchanged surprised glances, then grinned.

* * *

"Fox," Zero called down from the *Genesis*, "they're here."

153

"Who's here, Zero?" Fox wondered absently into his cell phone, watching Zebra, Zarnix, and the others tend Entiyti.

"The interrogators. The Deltiri interrogators."

"You've confirmed identities?"

"Yes, sir. And I know a couple of 'em personally. My cousin dated a Deltiri for a while."

"Ah," Fox murmured, stifling amusement. "I'd bet that was an interesting experience."

"In aaaaall kinds of ways, sir," Zero noted, tone wry. "Shall I let 'em into the 'tabernacle,' sir?"

"Yes, Zero, please do. I'll notify Suud-er, Lord Guurn, and Director Siisshiiss, and we'll probably all three meet them in the front yard."

"Yes sir. I'll pass on that information."

"Thanks, Zero."

"No prob. Zero out."

"Fox out."

* * *

Three Deltiri in formal robes emerged from the station-to-ground shuttle, their blue fishlike faces inscrutable, as a human and two Reptoids came forward to meet them. Several Division Five agents stood near the door, prepared to assist should something go amiss, and to protect both their leaders and the arriving interrogators.

"Greetings, Lord Levy, Lord Suud, and Director Siisshiiss," the one in the lead remarked, bowing slightly "I am Tt'r'n ob Rr'ndir, of Deltir; these are my colleagues, Pp'k'r ag Or'nit and Qq'k'l ob Sii'stek. We were told to meet the three of you to be briefed. This involves the assassination attempt on Lord Entiyti?"

"It does," Siisshiiss averred. "We have managed to capture several of the would-be assassins, and require your assistance to extract pertinent information. Come with us and we will brief you more fully."

The six beings turned and filed into the main house, Siisshiiss in the lead; the agents scanned the area, then brought up the rear.

* * *

"...And so you have a conspiracy of some sort, because of the many different species involved," Pp'k'r ag Or'nit observed, as the six beings stood in Entiyti's office.

"Precisely so," Fox noted. "And since some of the assassins got away, and someone else notified the press that Lord Entiyti had been killed—even though he hadn't—someone is still out there, running the show. And whoever it is now knows that Pulgey survived the attempt."

"And may therefore try again," Tt'r'n ob Rr'ndir finished.

"That is our fear," Siisshiiss agreed. "Because of course to prevent chaos erupting in the Coalition, we had to counter with our own media release, thus revealing that their first attempt failed."

"Then we have our work cut out for us, as the humans say," Qq'k'l ob Sii'stek decided. "Gentlebeings, if you would have someone show us to our quarters, we will prepare ourselves to perform in-depth interrogations, according to the appropriate protocols."

Suud stepped to the door, opened it, and gestured. The house steward, an imposing and reserved Reptoid, came to the door.

"If you would follow me, sirs, lady," the Reptoid requested, "I will show you to your rooms."

"Once you've settled in, come back here," Siisshiiss said, "and I will personally take you to the holding facility. For obvious reasons, it is in a different structure."

The three Deltiri nodded, bowed slightly, and followed the steward out of the office.

Chapter 7

"...All I know, Meg, is that the order said to send you to the medlab," Echo told her as they sat in Fox's office, Echo behind the desk, Omega in front in a visitor's chair. "It didn't say why."

"Huh. I wonder what's up," Omega pondered. "Did you tell anybody I had a funny feeling about the next few days?"

"No, I haven't told anybody," Echo noted. "Speaking of which, have you managed to dredge up any particulars?"

"No, I haven't, even with Zz'r'p's help," Omega murmured, "but it keeps feeling an awful lot like the whole Cortian thing...but not. There isn't a first contact coming up, is there? Something like that to get bollixed?"

"Not that anybody's told me about," Echo said with a shrug. "And in the circumstances, as Acting Director, I think they'd HAVE to."

"Yeah. Okay. Maybe I'm all wet, and only nervous about running the department all my own self."

"Maybe. But I'm taking it seriously just the same, baby. Keep me posted if you pick up something definitive. Trust me, I'll listen and act on it. DAMN, I learned my lesson with the Cortians."

"Wilco, Ace. And...thanks." She rose. "I guess I'mma head on to the medlab, then."

"Okay. I'll come down in a bit and see what's going on with that. I just need to dig out of some paperwork here first."

"Roger that. See you soon."

* * *

"Okay, y'all, I'm here," Omega declared, entering the big outer room of the medlab. "WHY am I here?"

"It's because they need to do a little augmentation, Omega," Psi, the medic on duty and a new recruit, said as he met her in the outer office. Zz'r'p, the Arcturan ambassador and resident telepath, stood behind the medic; his usual blue skin tone seemed somewhat pale.

"Augmentation?" she asked, with carefully-hidden trepidation. "What kind of augmentation? And who is 'they'?"

A doleful Zz'r'p answered.

"Our team of physical psychologists has been extremely... intrigued...by you, Omega, ever since it was discovered that you had been—restructured—by Echo's old enemy. Especially after your defeat of Tt'l'k, one of our most gifted telepaths. Your on-again, off-again telepathic skills, so unique to humans, and so useful in the past, have been a challenge to them. One they believe they have overcome."

"In what way?" Omega asked, instinctively becoming guarded.

"They've developed an implant for you, Omega," Psi responded. "By implanting a special biotech chip in your brain, you can become a full, functional telepath."

"Hm. No offense, Zz'r'p, but...I don't want to be a full telepath." Omega was decided. Psi sighed.

"I was afraid you'd say that," the medic said. "All right, guys, come get her."

Orderlies poured into the room by the dozen, and Omega stood in shock as they surrounded her.

"What the hell?!" a startled Omega exclaimed.

"Orders, Omega," Psi responded.

"From Fox?!" Omega asked, shocked. "Echo??"

"No, higher—the Ennead," Psi answered, pulling a face. "Dammit, Omega, I'm sorry. Take her into surgery, guys." The orderlies reached for her.

"Zz'r'p??" Omega appealed. The tall blue alien bowed his head.

"I am truly sorry, Omega. I protested to the Council in the strongest possible terms—the chip is still in development—but was overruled. We intended it as..." suddenly the Arcturan's voice sounded in Omega's mind, *a wedding gift,* before he continued normally. "We never conceived of its being used like this. And, diplomatically-speaking, I...can do nothing."

"Well, I can!" Omega shouted angrily, and before anyone else could react, the room had become a battleground. Orderlies flew in all directions, slamming into the walls; some rose again, slow but active, and resumed their attempts to take down the female Agent, while others lay where they fell, unconscious.

Just then, Echo walked into the room.

"What the hell?!" he exclaimed.

* * *

Echo stopped dead at the sight of his partner and fiancée at the center of what appeared to be a small riot.

"STAND DOWN!" he shouted. "THAT'S AN ORDER FROM THE ACTING DIRECTOR! CEASE AND DESIST IMMEDIATELY!"

Omega stopped.

The orderlies didn't. They grabbed at Omega and tried to restrain her.

"I said STOP! Dammit, what part of ORDER do y'all not get?!" Echo cried. "You're all on report! Hang on, baby! I'm on my way!" He waded into the orderlies ranked between him and the woman he had chosen as his partner for life, blocking, judo-throwing, and generally plowing his way through bodies.

But, unwilling to risk seriously injuring their colleagues, even Alpha One found they could be overwhelmed by sheer force of numbers. Echo was driven back against the wall, while Omega's arms and legs were pinned to her sides.

* * *

"Echo! ECHOOOOOO!!" Omega screamed, as she felt herself lifted off the floor; all-too-vivid memories of her adolescent self, caught in a tractor beam by a psychopathic alien criminal and lifted off the ground, overlaid themselves on reality. "Oh, dear God—not again! NO! ECHO! *HELP ME!!!*"

At that desperate shriek, Echo fought like a wild animal, struggling to free himself and make his way to his partner, no longer caring if the orderlies were hurt. The angered orderlies fought back in kind, but slowly gave ground before the enraged Agent. Zz'r'p, pained, raised one hand.

STOP.

The incredibly powerful mental command froze everyone in their tracks, essentially paralyzing them, and all eyes turned to the telepathic ambassador.

"That is better." Zz'r'p turned to the orderlies. "Release them."

The orderlies didn't move.

"You're all on report," Echo snarled. "Every last damn one of you! You've disobeyed a direct order from the Acting Alpha Line Chief, an Ambassador, and the Acting Director. I'll send all of you to Confinement for this."

"No, Agent Echo, you will not," came a strange voice from an adjacent room. "Because you are no longer in charge here. I am."

A Zumbirian stepped through the doorway; his orange skin was flushed, his bright green eyes scowling. His bushy, greenish-tinted hair stood on end. Echo thought he resembled no one so much as the star of that alien-conspiracy show on the history network—no surprise, the star was Zumbirian—though this one looked rather haughtier...and at the moment, very angry.

But I'll see his anger and raise it, and then some, Echo thought in implacable fury. "Who the hell are you?" he demanded.

"I am Lord Ordik Adita, of Zumbir; you may know it as Beta Ophiuchi 7," he declaimed, arrogant. "As a duly-appointed member of the Ennead, I do hereby take charge of the Division One Agency."

"Oh, shit," Omega murmured.

"Lotsa that," an annoyed Echo replied in kind.

* * *

"...I don't give a damn if you're the acting Ennead chairbeing, which I happen to know you're NOT," an incensed Echo declared. "You canNOT just waltz in here and usurp the system of command that has been set up, and you cannot come in and order physical and medical modifications made to my agents without their consent!"

"Let's, um, all kinda settle down here," Psi suggested, seeming uncertain. "Orderlies are dismissed; if you need treatment, run over to the emergency room wing."

The orderlies filed out by ones and twos; a few threw dirty glances at Alpha One, and Omega in particular. Some had to help colleagues; two had to be carted out on antigrav stretchers.

* * *

"In here," Psi said then, leading the way into the nearby conference room, once the orderlies had all departed.

"After you, doctor," Adita remarked, aloof.

Once Psi, Zz'r'p, Adita, Omega, and Echo had entered the conference room and closed the door, they sat; Adita automatically assumed a position at the head of the table.

"Now, you were saying, Agent Echo?" Adita said, disdainful.

"DIRECTOR Echo."

"You were saying, Agent?"

"You cannot come in and usurp the duly-authorized hierarchy here, and you can't order my agents to be modified against their will," Echo reiterated.

"He's right, Lord Adita," Psi agreed. "I tried to tell you earlier."

"Ah, but I can," Adita said, calm. He produced a palm device and tapped several keys. "There. My orders are now on your cellular devices. I am here to take control and see that the two top partnerships in Division One are sent on a very special mission, with all the preparation required to ensure mission success. And if you will not do it, Doctor Psi, I have brought physicians who will, and highly trained guards who will restrain the patient."

"The hell you say!" Echo snarled.

* * *

"Why don't you try explaining, Adita?" Zz'r'p suggested, cool. "You will find, with humans, it goes much farther than issuing orders without explanation, and attempting to override personal autonomy. Which latter does not legally 'fly' on Earth, generally speaking, in any event." He neglected to note that some countries were more lenient; since the USA was not one of those, it was moot in this instance.

Adita glanced at Zz'r'p in some scorn. Zz'r'p remained calm and unruffled. Abruptly everyone in the room heard the Deltiri's irritated mental voice.

Adita, stand down from your high perch and listen to reason. You have just seen what only one of them can do. You had little chance to see what two of them can do, but believe me when I say that I have, and that the equation is not additive, nor even multiplicative, but exponential. Let me show you something.

* * *

Zz'r'p reached for the controls on the wall-mounted video monitor, intended for displaying data and such. He activated the screen, then searched for and brought up a particular training video that Alpha One remembered creating a couple of days before, queueing it to the last few moments, when Alpha One had taken out well more than one hundred 'zombie' Nazis and concentration camp inmates in a matter of moments. Then he initiated the video.

Omega studied the video; it was the first time she and Echo had seen it, and they had never seen themselves in full-out action before. She turned to Echo.

Whoa, she used one of their subtlest codes to signal him. *Did you have any idea we looked like THAT in a fight?*

Hell no, Echo replied in kind, eyes widening. *That, um, don't take this the wrong way, Meg, but that just impressed the hell outta ME. That looked...*

...Like a movie special effects fight, she finished for him.

Exactly. He shot her the faintest excuse for a grin, something Adita would be unlikely to see, or particularly notice if he did. *You and me are damn hot stuff, baby.*

I think I'm starting to see what Zz'r'p has been trying to tell me.

Which may be a secondary reason he just showed it to us the way he did, Echo pointed out.

Maybe so. But I hope Mr. UFO-nut over there sits up and pays attention.

Ain't that the truth.

* * *

Adita watched in what appeared to be dumbfounded amazement, until the scenario ended and the video cut to black. The Deltiri used the remote to switch off the screen. Then Zz'r'p turned back to the Zumbirian.

There. Perhaps that gives you a better feel for what they are capable of achieving in battle. The ONLY reason they were less than successful just now is because they were fighting their own colleagues and did not wish to cause them serious harm. Should you set your own personnel upon them, all such reservations will be cast aside. I put it to you that these two can likely subdue your entire entourage unaided, but four of them can certainly take down you and all your highly-trained attendant beings, and you would scarce know what happened. And rest assured, if they do not call for Alpha Two as backup, I shall, and as many MORE of Alpha Line as I deem necessary. Not for nothing is Alpha Line comprised of the top Agents in the Division, and Alpha One and -Two the top of THOSE. Would it not be better to give them the facts of the case, and try to get them to see your point of view? To work WITH you, instead of FOR you?

Adita seemed to consider this argument.

"Very well," he agreed at last. "You make an excellent point. I am still unconvinced that they could prevent my team from doing what is required." Adita hesitated, and they realized he was lying; he knew if it came to a fight, he was unlikely to win, but his pride refused to allow the admission. "However, it is undoubtedly better that they obey willingly, rather than be-

162

ing forced to do so, and risk injury."

"Finally," Omega grumbled.

* * *

"All right, Echo, Omega, let us try again. Here is the latest intelligence available to the Ennead—the Persis Federation has amassed a significant, heavily-armed force on the boundaries of the Galactic Coalition." Adita met their eyes; his own face was deadly serious. "The Persis Federation is a very old empire from what you humans call the Andromeda Galaxy. They lean toward militarism and expansionism. Rather than attack immediately, however, their Premier has made diplomatic overtures...though it is our understanding that this was not according to the advice of his counselors, who desire to invade. As their home galaxy is on this side of the Great Spiral, the decision was made to send the top agents in the entire sector to respond to that request. Those top agents are Alpha One and Alpha Two. It was well considered, Agent Echo, that you are experienced in first-contact missions, and have a degree in diplomacy yourself. Because it is the feeling in the Ennead that, if this diplomatic overture fails, there will be war."

"What?" Omega gasped. "War?!"

"War, Omega," Adita reiterated. "Of the intergalactic variety. I am old enough to have seen such things; you are not, nor have not. Believe me when I say it would be devastating, and entire systems might cease to exist. Whole planets could be sterilized of life. Intelligence information filtering back to the Council indicates that, if the Persis Federation does not find it advantageous to ally with the Coalition, they may very well try to take it over by force instead. And they are powerful enough to give us an extremely difficult time of it, if they do."

"Let me guess," Echo anticipated grimly. "They want to see the top agents from each Division, as they work their way into our galaxy?"

"Good guess, Echo," Zz'r'p replied.

"And they're demanding, unpredictable, and easily pissed off."

163

"Right again."

"Business as usual," Echo sighed then. "Damn. This ain't good."

"Exactly," Adita said. "We need inside information, and we need it swiftly. That is where you come into play, Omega."

"Using the chip, I walk into the middle of 'em, read their minds, and tell y'all what they're planning," Omega summarized succinctly.

"Yes."

"But they can scan me and find the alien DNA fragments. They'll know I'm potentially capable of doing something like that."

* * *

"The Ennead's specialists tweaked the implant," a subdued Zz'r'p explained. "It will...disguise your modifications. And those tweaks will render it largely undetectable to their scans; only a properly-encoded medical scanner will detect it, and Agent India's personal scanner will be modified in this fashion immediately upon implantation."

"Yeah, I've seen the schematics. All they'll be able to read is normal human," Psi added. Omega winced. Echo glared. Zz'r'p frowned. Psi shut up quickly.

Adita watched the unspoken interaction, and suddenly nodded.

"Ambassador Zz'r'p, this is the human agent who was modified by the psychopathic gastropoid, correct?" Adita confirmed.

"Yes, Lord Adita, she is. And it was not a particularly pleasant sequence of procedures, performed unanesthetized; nor was she given a choice. And she was a child. So while it was telepathically suppressed for most of her life, when the plot was uncovered and she was deprogrammed, that suppression was removed, and she now remembers all of it. It has caused... some psychological distress. And that...is very significant, in light of our current situation...and the approach to it which is being used."

"Yes, I see that now, and I begin to understand it...and her reactions and responses, as well as that of her partner, who, honorable being that he is, is trying hard to protect her, to at least give her...options. Yes, yes, I see. Omega, my apologies, but we...desperately...need your abilities, especially as they would be enhanced by this implant. If it proves...disturbing, you can have it removed after the mission," Adita said. "You have my word. Does that help?"

"A little, I guess," Omega decided, wry. "I'm still not keen on it."

"...I understand. Perhaps if Ambassador Zz'r'p explains more about it, it will alleviate your concern...?"

* * *

"...And the chip will enable you to turn your telepathy on and off, Omega," Zz'r'p said, attempting to soothe, as they discussed the situation and what few options were on the table. "It does not have to be continuous."

"What about, um, our sessions, Zz'r'p?" Omega wondered, tap-dancing around exactly what she meant.

"They will have to wait for your return, I suppose," the Deltiri responded with a sigh. "I would not have chosen this timing, but such things tend not to subject themselves to our preferred scheduling."

"And the Agency?" Echo pressed. "You're not sending Meg off on her own, that's for sure. But I'm Acting Director, diplomacy degree or no. I can't go."

"No," Adita observed. "Not now. That is the principal reason I am here. You WILL be attending your partner, and the Alpha Two team will also be in attendance. While you are gone, I will oversee the Division. You are the Alpha Line chief and senior Agent, as well as being officially relieved of the Acting Director responsibility," he held up a hand, as Echo started to protest, "effective immediately, per order of the Ennead, which has specific orders waiting for you, pertaining to this mission. Alpha One are the principal Agents involved; Alpha Two is there for backup as needed, physical and medical. I want Alpha

One and -Two to prepare for a two-week mission aboard the Persis Federation's imperial flagship, the...what was it called?" Adita paused to consult his notes. "Ah. The *Rtxrxs*. You will be meeting the Premier, Hsrs."

"And what exactly is the objective of our mission?" Echo pressed.

"To avoid war via any and all diplomatic means," Adita stated. "Barring that, to gather as much information as possible, to enable us to win—or at least, successfully defend the Coalition—should war become inevitable. In deference to your position, Director-level orders are waiting on your device."

"Does Fox know about this?"

"I was told he would be informed. I do not think you need concern yourself with that."

"Mm," Echo hummed, sitting back. He threw a glance at Zz'r'p, who returned it, and the two were silent for long moments; Omega realized Echo was consulting the Arcturan in a private mental conversation.

* * *

Zz'r'p, is this legitimate? the senior Agent thought at the Deltiri, who immediately glanced away from him to deflect suspicion.

I am not at Ennead level, Echo, Zz'r'p responded, *so I am not privy to all the matters under consideration here. But yes, it seems it is legitimate, I am afraid. He really is in the Ennead, and he really has been sent here to take over from you. And there IS an extragalactic threat, and it does originate from the Andromeda Galaxy; this Hsrs is the leader of the potential threat. Invasion appears imminent if they are not appeased in SOME fashion. More than that I do not know...because Adita does not know.*

Whoa. You've been trying to read him?

I have not been merely 'trying;' I HAVE been reading him. But he knows no more than he has told you, at least nothing that I can glean. Evidently this information is being heavily compartmentalized. I suppose it makes sense, in the circum-

stances.

So there's nothing I can do to hold off on this, or keep him from taking over, until Fox gets back?

Nothing, Echo. I am sorry. I am also worried about Omega; the implant was never intended to be presented to her like THIS, let alone forced upon her. And it is still only a prototype, and in our Deltiri technicians' minds, unfinished. Never mind the interruption in her counseling, just when we were beginning to gain some ground. Still, it should help her developing telepathic capabilities. Unfortunately, there is no time to prepare that capability.

Hellfire damnation, to all of it, Echo cursed. *There's just no good news here, is there?*

No, I am afraid not.

* * *

Finally the two seemed to come back to reality, and Echo sighed; Zz'r'p looked downcast. "Shit," Omega heard her partner mutter under his breath. Adita, who had been watching closely, frowned, confused.

Well, damn, she thought. *I guess that means not even Zz'r'p sees a way around those orders. Hellfire damnation, as Ace says.* Suddenly another thought cropped up in her mind.

"With all this going down, I suppose a little thing like an Agency charter amendment gets put on the back burner, huh?" Omega wondered.

"What charter amendment?" Adita queried.

"I guess that answers that question," Echo sighed. "Back to matters of Meg getting a say in things."

Omega shot a questioning look at Echo, who returned it impassively.

"Nope. Not this time. It's your decision, Meg," he said.

"What decision?" she replied, bitter. "The Ennead ordered me to be tinkered with, remember?"

"To hell with the Ennead," Echo said, scowling, and Adita frowned deeper. "It's YOUR CHOICE, Omega."

Omega's shoulders slumped.

"Some choice. Intergalactic war...or getting tinkered-with again," she muttered. She stood and walked to Psi. "Do it," she said in a low voice.

* * *

A loud bleat sounded from somewhere on Fox's person, and he pulled out his recently-delivered tablet from a warp pocket. A quick swipe across the screen woke it, and he studied the message that flashed up onscreen.

"They WHAT?!" he said, startled and displeased. "Alpha One is going WHERE? Oh no, no, no. That won't do. That won't do at ALL! Not my Acting Director and Acting Alpha Line Chief!"

Swiftly he spelled out a text message on the screen and sent it. Moments later the reply came back.

* * *

Echo, who gave you that order?
Where did it come from?

Ennead sent a dude named Lord Ordik Adita.
Orders came straight from the Ennead, near as I can tell.

Dont do anything yet.
Ill look into this.

Too late. Megs already been forced into accepting an implant.

She WHAT?

Yeah.
Deltiri developed a brain chip to boost her mental abilities.
Adita forced her to have it implanted.
Shes about to go into the O.R. right now.

Damnation.
Tell her stand by while I contact this Adita.
Do NOT let ANY procedure go forward until I say.

Wilco. Standing by.

* * *

A few quick inquiries brought up the contact information for Ordik Adita, and Fox sent a message.

Lord Adita, this is Director Fox, Division One.
I have it to understand that you have issued orders for
my four top Agents to attend an off-planet first-contact
mission.

That is correct, Director.

That is unacceptable, Lord Adita.
I am sure you are aware that Agent Echo is
Acting Director while I attend
Coalition President Entiyti,
and Agent Omega will be running
Alpha Line in the interim.
They are required at Headquarters
to perform these duties.
If you need a team to go off-planet,
check with Omega to determine if
she can spare Alpha Two.
Barring them, any Agents in Alpha Line
are more than capable of
handling a first contact.

I am afraid that is not true, Director.
We have a situation.
The first contact is to meet the Premier of the
Persan Federation from the Andromeda Galaxy.
We barely warded off an invasion force by same as is.

And there is concern in the Ennead
that the Persis Federation
may have masterminded the attack on Entiyti.
Please keep that in mind as you conduct
the investigation into the assassination.

That is still unacceptable.
It leaves no one in charge of Division One.

Not true. That is why I was sent, Director.
I will control the Division while you and they are
absent from it.

* * *

"Oh farkakte," Fox grumbled. "Maybe Teela can remedy this."
He began another message.

* * *

Teela, I was just informed that my Acting Director
and the Acting Chief of Alpha Line
have been co-opted and are
being sent off-Earth for some damn
first contact mission.
Thats a problem.

He waited several moments, then the reply came back.

I am aware of the mission, Franz, but I am sorry.
The matter is urgent, or it could wait until
the current crisis with Pulgey has been resolved.
You may not have been aware, but a
potential invasion force has been sitting
just off the Outer Arm for approximately
two Earth weeks. We must prevent their
attack at all costs.
If sending your agents as first-contact
emissaries is what it takes,

because of their reputation,
then that is what we must do.

> *Is it true they may have had something*
> *to do with the attack on Pul?*

If Ordik told you that, I cannot disaffirm it.

> *And you wont delay or modify*
> *the mission, either, will you?*

What would you have me do, Franz?

> *Either postpone it or send another*
> *team of Alpha Line Agents.*

I cannot.
The Premier specifically requested the top four agents.
That is Alpha One and -Two.
He is waiting now. He will not be denied.
I am sorry, Franz, but it is what it is.

* * *

"NO! Farkakte, verdammt, merde, glagaram, and argdun!" Fox cursed bitterly. "Why do I have a REALLY damn bad feeling about this?!"

"What is wrong, Franz?" Suud wondered, coming into the room in time to hear.

"Something's going down with a group from the Andromeda Galaxy, and while I'm gone, Alpha One has been co-opted to be the first contact team, along with Alpha Two...instead of running the Agency, like I'd planned," Fox grumbled. "Meanwhile, the powers that be have brought in a perfect stranger from the Ennead to run things, and from the sound of it, he has no clue how we operate."

"That...is not good," Suud decided. "What are you going to do?"

"I'm not sure yet," Fox said, rubbing his chin in thought. "I hate to leave you and Taas to run this investigation alone, never mind protect Pul. And Pul needs Zebra and Zarnix, so I'd be leaving my mate here, along with her boss, if I go back…"

"Mm," Suud considered. "I must admit, I was hoping to have you here. Director Siisshiiss is very good, but I have not so much detective skills as you and he. Pulgey was…less active, less prone to travel, when I was his chief bodyguard, and I had not so much wide-ranging experience, as a result."

"So you'd rather I didn't leave."

"I know Pulgey, and you know Pulgey, but Director Siisshiiss does not," Suud pointed out. "Oh, they have met numerous times, but they are not FRIENDS, they are not BROTHERS. He will not see the patterns you would, will not recognize possible past enemies."

"You would."

"True. But while you trained me well, I am not a…what was the word you used to use…I am not a sleuth. I am a good soldier, yes, a good commanding officer. But I do not have the mindset for this, Franz. You do."

"You want me to stay."

"Who is minding the store, as you used to say?"

"This Ennead councilor, Ordik Adita."

"Is he already making a sssshttt of things?"

"No, not that I can tell," Fox sighed, "although it rather sounds as if Omega got railroaded into some things…things that probably weren't good to railroad her into, at least given what she's already dealt with, of late. But no, I can't say that there's anything he's done wrong to this point."

"Did Omega agree to it?"

"In the end, yes, as I understand it. Though I expect she felt dreadfully coerced."

"Then what is the matter?"

"Hard to say. I just have a damn bad feeling about it, alter khaver."

"Mm. I remember when you had those. It behooved us to

pay attention. Well, we shall just have to stay in close touch with matters on Earth, and hope that this investigation resolves itself quickly."

"This investigation might tie in," Fox pointed out. "Evidently the Ennead is suspicious of the Persan Premier, and think he may be at least partly responsible for the assassination attempt, somehow."

"Huh," Suud said, looking blank; Fox adjudged it meant he had not considered the possibility until that moment. "Well, we do know there were others more intelligent behind the attempt, so it is possible, I suppose."

"Indeed. I guess there's no help for it," Fox sighed. "I'll stay here and help, and maybe the three of us can work out what happened faster, so I can get home and see that things are being properly managed." He turned back to the tablet and resumed texting.

"What are you doing?"

"Notifying Echo of my decision," Fox explained, sending the message.

* * *

Echo read the text message from Fox that had just popped up on his cell phone.

"Shit," he cursed with feeling.

"No options?" Omega wondered.

"Nope, doesn't look like it, baby," he sighed. "I guess we're boxed in on this one."

"Damn," she said, then sighed deeply and turned for the surgical area of the medlab.

* * *

Omega had just finished changing into the medical jumpsuit in the medical prep area when she felt the gentle, familiar touch.

"I am here, Omega," Dihl murmured in the Agent's ear, resting a light hand on her shoulder, before sanitizing her hands and donning gloves. "I will be the one prepping you for the procedure."

"Good," Omega sighed.

"Extraneous discussion will not be necessary, medtech," Psi said, crisp. Dihl silenced, and Omega raised an eyebrow. "It won't be as bad as you think, Omega," Psi continued, as a perturbed Dihl helped prep Omega for the procedure in the operating room. "It's fairly simple outpatient surgery; it won't take long."

"'Fairly simple'? It is her BRAIN," Dihl noted with some asperity.

"Medtech, if you can't obey orders and be quiet, get out," Psi barked.

"Cancel that! Dihl, stay put," Omega declared, incensed and scowling. "As the Alpha Line Assistant Chief, I'm overriding that order. Psi, let's get something straight, up front. Dihl is the medtech assigned to MY case, to MY body. THAT is why she is here. Of all the medtechs in this place, she knows me and my physiology best. She is here because I WANT her here, helping me, ensuring everything goes right. More, if memory serves, medtech she may be, but she has a medical doctorate in her own right." Dihl nodded confirmation, lips compressed. "She is therefore a specialist, NOT your personal servant. You WILL treat this woman with respect, or you will be placed on additional report. Do I make myself clear?"

"Huh? 'Additional report'? What the hell does that mean?"

"It means you overrode your Acting Director's orders BEFORE said Acting Director was officially replaced. Don't think Echo and I didn't notice that. Never mind overriding an Alpha Line Agent's orders—the acting chief, no less. And don't think a full debrief won't be performed to Fox, Zarnix, and Zebra upon their return. *I* will personally see to THAT. You're not waltzing out of here with no repercussions to your behavior. Do I need to explain THAT to you, as well?"

Taken aback, Psi could only shake his head.

"All right, then," Omega said, relaxing somewhat. "Remember that. ALL of that. Please continue."

"Um, o-okay." Psi was now badly shaken, and it showed.

"Uh, once the implant is positioned, it ah, it automatically links with your brain, by detecting the, uh, the 'telepathic nodes' was how the Deltiri guy termed it..."

"His name is Zz'r'p."

"Huh?"

"His name is Zz'r'p, and he is the Deltiri Ambassador from the Arcturus system," Omega said very clearly. "He should formally be addressed as, 'His Excellency.' Weren't you trained on how to address ambassadors when you were recruited to the Agency?"

"Oh, that. Unh, well, yeah..."

"Good. There's a reason for that protocol. Piss off the wrong ambassador, and Earth could be in the middle of a trade war...or worse, a REAL war."

"Oh..."

"So Zz'r'p said—"

"Waitaminit," an annoyed Psi interrupted. "You just get done lecturing me about His Excellency AMBASSADOR Zz'r'p, then YOU don't give him his title?"

"Zz'r'p and I are old friends; he gave me permission to drop titles and call him by his given name long ago."

"She is also on a first-name basis with Coalition President Pulgey Entiyti," Dihl observed offhandedly, by way of an additional dig. "They are good friends."

Psi paled.

"So Zz'r'p said it connected with the appropriate 'nodes' in my brain..." Omega continued.

"Oooo-kay. Um. So, uh, so...it, uh," Psi stammered, "i-it ties into the 'telepathic nodes,' detecting and tying into that frequency, or whatever frequency or frequencies your brain mostly uses; it isn't a physical connection. It's tucked into one of the sulci, the folds in the brain tissue—without damaging or removing tissue, let me add—but it isn't physically connected. Do you, um, get me?"

"Yeah, it's a Bluetooth for my brain," Omega said with a rueful chuckle.

"Exactly! And the insertion, well, all we really have to do is get it past the skull, and we got mad tools for that."

"Anesthetic?" Omega pressed.

"You want local, or general?" Psi asked. "We're outfitted to do either..."

Omega and Dihl exchanged glances.

"I really don't think I wanna be awake this time," Omega declared, cryptic.

* * *

When the outpatient surgery was complete, Echo went into the recovery room to see Omega, but she was already gone. So was Psi.

"How did it go, Dihl?" Echo asked his mother, careful to use her code name.

"It...went well, medically speaking, Echo," Dihl replied, subdued and obviously worried. "The procedure was delicate, and the first thing we had to do was calm Psi..."

"Why?"

"He was...rude...to me, and tried to control matters too much," Dihl explained. "It annoyed Omega, so she told him off rather thoroughly. It left him...rattled."

"Oh," Echo said, unsure whether to scowl or laugh. "One more black mark, I suppose."

"She said the same, yes. To Psi. I think that was what upset him."

"I guess I'll let her handle that one, then. So physically she's fine? The procedure went okay?"

"Yes. But I cannot say the same for her mental and emotional outlook. At least she was unconscious this time, and will not remember it."

Echo drew a deep breath.

"Well, I'm not surprised," he admitted then. "At any of that. Where is she?"

"She's gone. She went out the medics' entrance, Echo," the anesthesiologist told him. "Said she needed a few minutes alone. We threaded the thing up through one of the foramina, so we didn't have to cut bone or make a big incision. The chip was small, so it didn't take much." He held up index finger and thumb to indicate something perhaps a centimeter wide. "They hit all the little incisions with some regen fluid as they pulled out, so she's all healed up. She was alert and awake, handling everything fine, with good vitals, so I let her go. If I'd known you were waiting, I'd have kept her until you came in here." He glanced around, then added, "SOME of us still follow YOUR lead."

"All right, no big deal. I know where she'll be, then," Echo replied, nodding, and headed for the elevator.

* * *

Echo found her standing on the Headquarters roof near the little observatory dome, beneath a dark, starry sky, staring out over the city with a blank, thoughtful gaze. "Hi, Meg," he said softly as he moved to her side.

"Hi, Ace," she replied, subdued. *How does it feel to be engaged to marry an inhuman thing?*

"Meg," Echo said sternly, "you KNOW better than that. You're not inhuman, and you're certainly not a 'thing.'"

Omega shot him a sidelong glance.

"Guess I need to practice with this implant," she murmured. "You weren't supposed to hear that."

"You're still not certain of me, are you?" Echo said in sudden realization. "Not in here." He tapped her breastbone lightly. Omega turned away slightly.

"Echo...I love you, so much," she said softly. "By now, I reckon you know that. But no, I...I'm having a hard time believing this is real. It's like I'm dreaming this wonderful dream, and I keep waiting to wake up, for reality to catch up with me. Part of it's just...coming back from the depression. But...not all." She held up her left hand, tilting it and watching the starlight catch the hyperdiamond on her third finger. "I just can't imagine why you'd want me. You could do so much better."

"The hell I could." Echo wrapped his arms around Omega from behind and pulled her against his chest. She resisted at first, but eventually relaxed against him, leaning her head on his shoulder to look up into the heavens. "It's real, Meg. Trust me."

They were silent for long moments, looking up into the night sky.

"Do you wish you were holding Chase right now, instead of me?" she asked then, very softly.

"...Chase is dead, Meg."

"You didn't answer the question."

"Actually, I did," Echo replied. "Chase is gone, it's not an option, so I don't think about it. You're here."

"...Oh," Omega said uncertainly. The two Agents stood together, still staring into the heavens. There was another pause.

Echo, can you hear me?

"Hm? You say something?"

"Uh-huh. 'Listen,'" Omega said, reaching back and tapping his temple. "I need to practice."

"Oh. Okay, go ahead," Echo responded.

Can you hear me now? Omega asked.

Yeah, Meg. I'm with you. It's a little fuzzy, but I can hear you.

Can I ask you something? Something really personal?

Damn, Meg, you don't have to tiptoe around. Echo grinned. *You're gonna be my wife. I think that gives you the right to get personal with me.* A tender, intimate dream-image of the two of them curled up in bed together flashed between them. Omega blushed.

Well...give me the chance to get used to the idea, she said, and smiled. *Okay. I need to know if...are you...that is, do you have...*

Spit it out, Meg. It's hard enough for me to understand you right now without you stammering.

Doyouhaveanyartificialbodyparts?!

Huh? Do what? Slow down, honey. When I said spit it out, I didn't mean at machine-gun speed.

Do. You. Have. Any. Artificial. Body. Parts?

Oh. No. Echo turned her to face him. *Having the implant really bothers you, doesn't it? Apart from what it does to your telepathy.*

Yes. Omega visibly cringed. *Knowing there's...a thing in my head, that's not supposed to be there, that's not a part of me... after everything else that's been done to me...it's just squicky.* She turned and met his eyes. *I'm sorry. I know it's stupid.*

It's not stupid, Echo disagreed. *Different people have different hot buttons.* He pulled her against his shoulder. *This just happens to be one of yours.*

You don't have any hot buttons.

The hell you say! Sure, I have hot buttons.

Such as? Omega challenged, nestling her head under Echo's chin.

Anybody that messes with my partner, or tries to force her into something against her will, tends to get my attention, really damn fast, and not in the good way, Echo acknowledged, settling his chin comfortably on top of her head. *Among other things. I'm surprised you didn't figure that out in the medlab earlier. Hell, I was getting ready to take some folks out, if I had to. When I heard you scream, I...* He broke off and shook his head.

Yeah. I get that, Omega told him then. *Listen...thanks. I'm... glad it didn't come to that.*

Me too. But damn, do I intend to get some medical staff in trouble, once we get back.

Amen. Count me in.

They were silent for a while. Eventually Echo tilted his hand and glanced over her head at his wrist chronometer, then sighed, and Omega picked up on the unverbalized thought.

"We need to start getting ready to go, don't we?" she verified.

"Yes. The Persis Premier is expecting us at a certain time."

It was Omega's turn to sigh, as she reluctantly pulled away from Echo. "Okay. Let's go."

* * *

Omega was packing essentials in her bedroom when she heard a knock at the 'back door' between her quarters and Echo's, and heard his voice calling her name.

"In here, Ace," she replied, tucking the last items into the small duffel bag lying on the bed. It appeared to be a relatively normal overnight bag, but was in fact a highly-sophisticated piece of specialized luggage, containing multiple warp pockets; an agent could stuff in at least a week's worth of clothing, plus smaller items of equipment, with little effort.

"What's up?" Echo asked as she closed the duffel.

"Just finished packing, Echo," Omega answered, straightening up and turning around, to find Echo standing right behind her. "Oh!" she exclaimed, startled, jumping back into the side of the bed and losing her balance.

"Woops," Echo said, grabbing her before she fell. "Take it easy." He steadied Omega, holding her shoulders until she had recovered her balance, then slipped his arms around her waist. "You okay?"

"Yeah," Omega chuckled, easing her own arms around him. "You are the only being on this planet who can sneak up on me like that."

* * *

"This, or 'bout any other, probably. But only because you let your guard down around me," Echo responded with a grin. "Otherwise, you'd know every move I made, with those enhanced senses of yours." His dark eyes studied her thoughtfully. "You know, sometimes I wonder what your world is like, Meg."

"What do you mean?" Omega's face abruptly became carefully controlled. Echo shrugged.

"Nothing you need to worry about. I just wonder, with your senses, if you see the world—make that the universe—any differently than I do. Do you see more colors, more dimensions? Hear more frequencies? Does music sound different to you, food taste different? Do you see the same starry night sky that I do, when we stargaze together? Makes me curious sometimes."

Echo watched as Omega's head slowly drooped. "Meg..."

No answer.

"Meg, did I say it bothered me?"

"...No."

"Did I say I didn't like it?"

"No."

"What did I say?"

"...It makes you curious."

"And that means?" he pressed.

"I...don't know."

"It means my partner is really unique, and I love the fact, and one of these days, with her permission, I'm gonna ask one of the telepaths to help me see the world from her point of view—literally."

"Oh."

"So now look up here and give your favorite Agent a kiss."

"How do you know you're my favorite Agent?!" Omega protested, playfully dodging Echo's attempts to kiss her.

"Could have something to do with that ring on your finger," he deadpanned, firmly catching the back of Omega's head with one hand and clamping her tight against his chest with the other as he kissed her with his characteristic thoroughness. "Mm," he sighed then, and she echoed the soft sound.

* * *

"So...what did you want?" Omega asked—a bit breathlessly—a few moments later. She saw the gleam in Echo's eye, and rephrased before he could reply. "Why did you want me?"

The gleam grew more mischievous.

"Uh...what's u— no, better not go there, either..."

Echo stood grinning, waiting patiently, not helping Omega in the least, as she verbally dug herself in deeper and deeper.

"So, Echo...what's goin' on?!" she finally tried.

"Meg, why's your face so red?" Echo asked innocently, assuming a bland expression, then he ducked quickly to avoid the fist that came his way. When he saw the black-clad knee rising rapidly toward his bowed face, he instinctively stood,

181

right into Omega's headlock.

"Whoa!" Omega exclaimed, as Echo exerted some effort and deadlifted her clear of the floor. Overbalanced, they toppled over, bouncing onto the bed and laughing together. "Ace," Omega gasped through giggles, "have I told you lately that, under that tough shell, you're a lotta fun?"

* * *

"My partner tends to bring out that side of me," he deadpanned, sprawled atop her, grinning hugely.

"Is that good?" she quizzed.

"Do you like it?"

"Yeah!"

"Then it's okay." Echo gazed down for a moment into sparkling sky-blue eyes, and sobered as his own eyes dilated—the room grew brighter. He watched the mirth leave Omega's face then, to be replaced by a very different expression.

"Echo..." Omega whispered, sliding her arms around him and tugging gently, leaning up to kiss him. Abruptly, Echo made his decision—he pushed up and stood.

"C'mon, Meg," he said quietly, pulling her to her feet. "We've played around long enough for now. We've got work to do."

"But..." Omega gave him a slightly hurt glance.

"Meg." He kept his voice gentle but firm, still allowing a world of meaning in the tone. "I'm doin' my dead-level best to be the man you want me to be, baby. Help me out. Don't lay that in front of me." He drew a deep breath. "You have no idea how hard that was to walk away from."

"Oh. Yeah. You're right, as usual. Let's go."

"That's my gir—" Echo paused. "Huh. You really are."

They headed for the front door.

Chapter 8

"Well, the Deltiri pretty much confirmed everything our loudmouthed Reptoid conspirator told us," Director Siisshiiss informed Suud and Fox in Entiyti's office. "The Reptoid is indeed a career criminal and resentful of what he perceives as the galactic government's 'interference' in Emdalian affairs, and he blames Lord Entiyti. The two Zargothians are kin of Lady Zzs Grrzzuus, and they threw in with the assassins to get back at Alpha One, as it is becoming known that they and Lord Entiyti are close, and has been known for years that Fox and Lord Entiyti are old friends—a strike at Entiyti was therefore deemed a strike at Alpha One and their superior. The Teludal appears to be just a rogue, but the interrogators are delving deeper into his mind; he recognized and reacted strongly to the names Slettek and Relamu Frunflin. We do suspect he is likely kin, and therefore has similar motive to the Zargothians."

"It would make sense," Suud noted. "What about the Ke!endarian?"

"Yes," Fox said. "Is it Ke!endarian or Cortian?"

"The answer would seem to be 'neither,'" Siisshiiss said. "Unfortunately, we don't really know WHAT it is."

"What?" Suud said, confused.

"Huh?" Fox grunted in surprise. "I thought they were sending some of the same Deltiri that interrogated the Cortians. They should be able to recognize the same brain configuration."

"They are, and they can," Siisshiiss stated. "Whatever this creature is, it appears its mind is neither Ke!endarian nor Cortian. Nor is it apparently any other species known to the Coalition."

"Hm. That is interesting," Suud decided.

"Ain't it, though?" Fox agreed.

* * *

"But that isn't all," Siisshiiss told them, watching their reactions with interest, and realizing that they had not gotten the answer they had expected—especially Fox.

"What else is there?" Suud wondered.

"The Reptoid was hired by a small cabal of Reptoids AND Draconans," the Division Five Director continued. "And it seems that he is not the only one to be resentful of the galactic government's 'interference' in Emdalian affairs. I and my agents believe this cabal is likely an organized crime syndicate, and we have a good line on which of three known syndicates it is."

"Good," Suud grumbled.

"Yes," Fox agreed; the word was practically a growl. "I assume you'll be working with the local authorities to stamp out that little patch of plague?"

"Indeed," Siisshiiss averred. "They have been cooperating with us from the beginning of this entire giissht...mess, I believe you term it, Fox..."

"That's the word," Fox averred. "Along with a shtik drek, general pile of shit, Scheißestapel, tas de merde..."

"We have the idea," Siisshiiss said with a rueful chuckle. "I had heard your ability to curse was multilingual and creative, Fox, but really! I had no idea. You are positively masterful at it."

Siisshiiss and Suud watched with wide grins as Fox flushed in apparent embarrassment—a thing seldom seen in galactic circles, due to Fox's earned and well-deserved reputation as a smooth-tongued badass not to be trifled-with.

"Well, I've been around a bit, I suppose," he finally mumbled. "And seen plenty of the aforementioned drek to go around."

"Indeed, I expect you have, as long as you worked with Lord Entiyti," Siisshiiss agreed, sympathetic. "And forgive me for tweaking you, my friend and colleague; the investigation so far has been...unpleasant, and it was nice to be able to smile at something amusing for a change."

"Not a problem," Fox said, offering a wry grin himself. "I've had plenty of days like that, too, and I know what you mean. So I assume you'll be working closely with the local police to handle matters?"

"Yes, and with their intense gratitude and cooperation," Siisshiiss confirmed. "They have had trouble with the syndicates for some years and are ready to quash the illegalities once and for all. Unfortunately, given PGLEIA's jurisdiction is interstellar, and heretofore those syndicates have been strictly on-planet, we have been unable to assist. This incident changed that, however. Evidently the syndicate in question, one Ssllitthhssshhtt urr Hiiisss, believes if they can only force Emdali out of the Coalition, they would have free rein to operate. And they think this may best be done by assassinating the current President, who is from Emdali."

"Huh," Suud grunted. "They are truly 'Bastards of Hell,' as their name renders in that polyglot of Reptoid and Draconan."

"Appropriate," Fox noted. "Especially when you consider that your word for 'bastard' is literally translated in most Earth tongues as, 'shit-born.'"

"Most certainly," Siisshiiss agreed. "They are all that, and more. But this time I think they have rather egregiously overstepped, without realizing it. We will send them to Hiiisss if it becomes necessary. And without compunction."

"Sounds like a plan," Fox said. "Let me know if Suud or I can help, and if you would like the loan of some Division One personnel as backup, I'm sure I can oblige."

"That is much appreciated, Fox," Siisshiiss replied, grateful. "Certainly I expect the two of you can help; I will notify you as soon as certain matters come to a head, in fact. As for the offer of a loan of personnel, that is also appreciated. I do not think it will be needed, but given what is going on, I will not say nay, either." He shook his head.

"Not a problem. Just give me enough heads-up to get them here when required; that's all I ask. Anything else?" Fox wondered.

"Well, yes, and it may be one of the areas where the two of you can help," Siisshiiss added. "In fact, Lord Guurn, if you would be so kind as to come with me—you were part of the original rescue party, were you not?"

"I was," Suud affirmed.

"Good. Then perhaps neither of you would mind coming with me and looking at a map of the transfer station? I would like to ascertain a few things," Siisshiiss said, turning and motioning the others to follow. "I have the prisoners contained in the old gatehouse under separate force enclosures, as you already know, Fox, since the *Genesis* is providing the force fields. And my temporary base of operations is a room within the gatehouse; that is where we are heading. We have reason to believe the surviving assassins who are not already in custody are still on the station; my people confirm no unauthorized personnel have been able to leave, and a couple of beings matching Ke!endarian description have been seen very briefly, flitting in and out of the maintenance tunnels."

"Which means we need to reconstruct the fight, and locate where they entered the tunnels, so we can trace connections," Fox realized.

"And thereby determine where they may be hiding," Suud tag-teamed.

"You are both amazingly astute," Siisshiiss observed, pleased. "Yes, that is what we will attempt. Because we do NOT want them lurking among civilians, and there may be more information we can extract from them."

"I can certainly send some of my friends along, as well," Suud offered. "The ones that came with me for the initial sortie are ex-military and will be willing to help. They were giissht angry."

"I can imagine," Fox said. "I wasn't in any too good shape in that regard, either. And Taas, I'd recommend taking along one or more of the Deltiri. Keep 'em in the back, well-guarded, and let them pick up the thought patterns of your perps. I've done that before, and they make excellent trackers."

"Mm, that is a very good idea," Siisshiiss agreed. "I will discuss it with them, and see if any of them have had experience doing so, and would like to assist in such manner."

"Good job, then," Fox said. "Now let's go study the map and try to reconstruct their plans and escape routes."

* * *

In short order, the three beings had mapped key points on the transfer station, taking especial note of the locations where possible assassin sightings had been made.

"And the only real place to hide is in the maintenance tunnels," Siisshiiss pointed out.

"So we look for the nearest entry points to those maintenance tunnels," Fox added.

Moments later, they had the likely hatches identified.

"And look here," Suud said, tapping the map. "A tunnel junction with a storage room close by, in the same concourse."

"That is all inside the specialized blast- and fire-retarding section," Siisshiiss noticed.

"Bingo," Fox said with a smirk. "We got 'em."

* * *

"No, Fox," Siisshiiss ordered. "I am sorry, my friend, but you are a director in your own right, AND you are both admirals, and I will not risk you nor Guurn. I am not even going up to the station, but letting my field agents handle the matter, while I coordinate from planetside. My top agent in Division Five, Piradu Madru, is leading the team, and two of the three Deltiri are going with them. I will NOT send either of you, no matter how hard you protest. Especially with your mate here, tending Lord Entiyti. She would have my head, and rightfully so."

Fox huffed, but subsided.

* * *

Since the actual number of fugitives was unknown, Agent Madru took a contingent of fifty Division Five field agents up to the transfer station, while Siisshiiss called the station commander and coordinated matters. By the time the field agents arrived on the station, the commander had quietly cleared the maintenance tunnels of all legitimate workers, then sealed off the tunnels around the concourse in question, using the blast-and-fire suppression hatches.

"Excellent," Madru noted, studying the schematic on the control screen. "But internal sensors still show live bodies in the tunnels?"

"They do, sir," Station Commander Siinatuun Gaaligaat averred. "We estimate five, possibly six, persons—all inside the cordoned area."

"Very good. Now, is there a way we can introduce some gas grenades we brought with us?"

"Yes, there is," the big bronze-scaled Draconan said. "We have timed fire-suppression...I suppose you could call them grenades. They are intended to spread foam and decrease the oxygen in the volume in which they are released. So all of the suppression units aboard the station have small access chutes to allow complete distribution. But..." he paused, and his horns folded in concern. "Do you intend to suffocate them, then?"

"No, no," Madru said, offering a smile. "That would not be especially moral! Besides, there may be information we can obtain from them by capturing them. No, these are somniferous grenades, normally used in riot conditions. It will knock them out, and then we go in with oxygen masks, restrain them, and bring them out."

"And then we vent to space, and refill the air," Gaaligaat realized.

"Exactly," Madru said, as his smile morphed into a wolfish grin.

"Well then," Gaaligaat said, his own grin toothy, "let me show you how to access the chutes..."

* * *

Inside an hour, the trapped assassins were rendered unconscious, restrained, and carted out with hand-held antigrav devices. They were unceremoniously loaded onto a prisoner

188

transport, while Commander Gaaligaat saw to the venting of the soporific gas into the space around the transfer station, followed by the influx of fresh canned air, as he opened the maintenance tunnels once more.

Fifteen minutes after that, Division Five's top operative Agent Piradu Madru and his team were en route for the temporary Entiyti Estate Office on Emdali, complete with live cargo.

* * *

"Three more Ke!endarians, a Teludal, and a Reptoid," Siisshiiss reported to Fox and Suud. "And we know, because the Deltiri verified it, there are no more of the assassination squad aboard the transfer station."

"Make sure the Ke!endarians are really Ke!endarians," Fox pressed.

"We had already planned to do so," Siisshiiss averred. "As well as verifying your notion about the Teludal being a kinsman of your two Earth perps."

"And the Reptoid is probably part of the crime syndicate," Suud sighed. "There are times I am ashamed of my people."

"Don't be, alter khaver," Fox said, turning and laying a gentle hand on the other male's shoulder. "All species have people like these. Just as you pointed out that intelligence among a population has a normal distribution, so does the obeying of law, I think. Most of the population is fairly law-abiding, and just as there are those who are scrupulous about it in one tail of the distribution, so there are unscrupulous members in the other tail."

"He's right," Siisshiiss agreed. "Don't take it to heart, my brother Reptoid."

"I try," Suud sighed again.

"Well, let me get to it," Siisshiiss decided. "I shall notify you both as soon as I have anything to tell."

* * *

Echo and Omega, as already-certified spacecraft pilots, smoothly docked the Division One saucer *Helen of Troy* to the imperial flagship, while Romeo and India, in training, monitored systems.

"All right, Echo," Omega remarked, "instruments show docking port secure and latched."

"Copy that—secure and latched," Echo verified. "India, begin pressure equalization."

"Beginning pressure equalization," India replied. Moments later she announced, "Pressure equalization confirmed."

"*Rtxrxs* reports honor escort in place, Echo," Omega said.

"Cycle th' airlock, Echo?" Romeo asked. Echo glanced up from the pilot's console.

"Yeah, junior, go ahead," he answered. "Grab your gear, boys and girls, and let's go see the wizard."

* * *

Meg—how's it going? Echo thought at his partner as the mixed-species honor guard led the four Division One Agents through the alien vessel. Omega glanced surreptitiously at him.

What?

How's it going? Picking anything up? You're obviously still having trouble 'hearing' me...

Oh, okay, Ace, I gotcha now, Omega replied. *I'm reading our escort detail pretty well, all things considered. The one in front of us is the leader, and frankly bored stiff. The two on our right are curious as to exactly what sort of creatures we are, and a little put off by our appearance, and the one bringing up the rear is wondering what's for supper. So is Romeo, by the way. India's trying to mentally dissect the guards.*

Why am I not surprised Romeo's thinking about food? Echo grinned to himself. *So if you're doing so well, why are you still having trouble communicating with me? We've talked telepathically before—several times. In some cases, through some really extended conversations.*

Um. That's exactly why I'm having trouble with you, Echo, Omega answered. *I'm used to hearing you directly. It's like... having you in the room, versus talking to you on the phone. Sometimes the phone line just isn't clear.*

Oh. But you're sure you hear everyone else okay?

Yeah. It's a perception thing. Omega projected confidence.

Okay. Picking up any invasion plans yet?

No. But these guys are pretty much rank-and-file. It'll be interesting to see what I get from the Premier.

Yep. Speaking of which, that looks like the 'throne room' up ahead, Echo observed. *Put everybody on alert.*

Wilco, Ace, Omega replied. Seconds later, she 'spoke' to him again. *Romeo and India are on the ball, Echo. We're ready,* she told him.

Good. Are you okay with this?

Let's just say I'm handling it all right, hon', Omega said, with a subtle wince. *I'll be glad to get this over with and get the chip outta my head, though.*

Yeah.

You sound...disappointed, or something. Like...you don't want the mission to end? Echo, do you—I mean, are we—

Later, baby. Here we go. Concentrate.

The four Alpha Line Agents entered the main chamber with their escorts, and activity in the large, formal room ceased. They moved to stand before an imposing, gray, octopoid multi-limbed being 'seated'—at least that was Romeo's assessment, Omega realized, and she had to agree—on a raised dais.

"Ooolo saie aaoe, Uu Hsrs," Echo greeted the Premier.

"Gleetings, Agent Echo an' entoulage," the Premier replied through a mouth-slit in his upper body, waving two tentacles aloft as his skin changed color to a soft, warm peach tone. "Werecome aboald."

"Thank you, Premier," Echo replied. "I'm Agent Echo, and these are Omega, Romeo, and India." He pointed at each Agent in turn.

"Ah, velly good, Echo; you' gift is gleatry appleciated," the Premier beamed. "No otha pranet has been so genelous." He waved his tentacles again, changing to a deep red, and the escort detail surrounded Omega, Romeo, and India, herding them toward the Premier. A startled Echo grabbed for Omega, but succeeded only in catching her kit. "Omega, Womeo, an'

India wirr make hono'ed additions to my house. Take them to the halem loom," Hsrs commanded.

"What?!" India exclaimed, shocked.

"I think there's been a misunderstanding..." Omega murmured.

"Damn straight," Romeo agreed.

"The' is a plobrem?" the Premier queried.

"Got that right!" Romeo answered, before Echo could say anything. "I'm an Agent, not a present, an' AGENT India's my lady and my partner. We ain't goin' in nobody's 'harem.'"

"Ah, you ah correagues, an' you blought arong you' mate!" Hsrs nodded. "Folgive my assumption." He gestured, and the honor guard released Romeo and India, who quickly returned to Echo's side. "It is stirr an excerrent gift."

"Echo?" Omega inquired softly.

Echo met the blue gaze for a long moment, then he closed his eyes and turned to Hsrs.

"...I'm...pleased you like it, Mr. Premier."

"Echo?!" Omega's eyes widened in shock.

"Echo, whatchu doin', man?!" Romeo grabbed his shoulder and whispered urgently. Echo shook his hand off.

"We look forward to...dealing with you," Echo managed to choke out.

"Velly good, velly good," Hsrs said, waving the guards away with Omega.

"Echo? ECHO!" Omega called, as the guards, with some effort, pulled her resisting form out of the room. "What are you doing?! ECHO!!"

Echo thought hard at her. *Meg, just go.*

Echo? Echo, listen to me! Do you understand what he has planned? It's an orgy, Echo! and she showed him a scene of erotic alien debauchery, of such magnitude that it was doubtful the final condition of a human participant. *Echo, even if...if you don't really love me, don't let him do this to me! Please, Echo!*

Meg...

Echo, is this some sort of idea to get me close to him?

Please, don't! I can get all the information we need, just by our meeting with him! Do you understand, Ace? I'll be his property! Not even a wife! He can do with me as he pleases, any time he pleases! Even if you figure a way to get me out, there's no guarantee you'll...get me back in...my 'original condition,' Omega pleaded.

No more, Meg. Go. That's...an order. Echo met the sapphire eyes.

Echo watched as something in the blue eyes died, and the pale face hardened. She stopped resisting the guards then. But just as Omega disappeared through the arch, she made a throwing motion, and Echo saw something glittering fly through the air and hit the deck, to bounce to a stop at his feet with a soft pinging sound. He stared at it, then bent to pick it up.

It was the star-shaped hyperdiamond ring.

* * *

"Hell!" Romeo exclaimed vehemently, in the suite that had been assigned to the three remaining Agents. "Echo, what kinda damn fool thing're you doin'?! You gave away your lady, man!"

"He may have done more than that, Romeo," a furious India raged. "Meg mentally showed me what she was reading off IIsrs. She may not survive what Hsrs has in mind for her. His resemblance to an octopus is more than just looks."

"What?? Dayum! Echo!"

"Shut up," Echo threw over his shoulder as he stood, back to them, deep in thought.

"What?"

"Shut. Up."

"Damn, Echo, you're cold as ice," India said bitingly. "I actually thought you loved Meg."

"So did she," Romeo remarked cuttingly. "C'mon, India. Let's go to our room. I don' like th' company in here."

"I agree with you," India said.

Echo was left standing alone in the room.

* * *

Meg? Omega heard dimly as a frustrated attendant tried to teach her proper courtesan behavior. *Can you hear me, baby?*

I hear you, Echo, Omega replied coolly. *I'm afraid I really don't have time to talk right now. I'm being trained in proper behavior for the Premier's...bed, I guess you'd call it. I have to have certain 'skills' before I'm sent for. Nothing you'd be interested in.*

* * *

Echo, in the common area of the guest suite, winced in pain at the gibe. *Anything to report?*

Again, not that you'd be interested in.

When do you...see Hsrs?

He comes by to 'inspect' me tonight. I gather I have a couple days of preparation before the big night, Omega told him, sarcasm heavy and biting.

So you might pick up something tonight.

Maybe. I'll see what I can do, sir.

Meg— Echo began.

I'll let you know when I have anything to report, sir. Omega broke the link.

Two Alpha Line Agents, on opposite sides of the Persan imperial flagship *Rtxrxs*, sighed in pain.

* * *

Omega was stripped naked, her black Suit—and all the equipment it contained—taken away from her. In its place, she was given a thin, silk-like wrap that adequately covered her... barely. The mistress of the harem led her into the main harem room, and they wound around through several dozen lounging beings of different species, none of which was even remotely familiar to Omega, so she assumed they were all from the Andromeda Galaxy. All stared at Omega with various ocular organs. None appeared friendly, nor did Omega pick up any benevolent thoughts, except for the harem mistress, who had apparently taken a liking to the lovely agent.

What is SHE?

Another one. Damn her. But he's mine. I won't let her have him.

So that is the new addition. And she is not happy. I can work with that. Yes, this should work nicely.

How did that thing get in here?

What IS it?

What could Hsrs see in that creature? Never have I seen a more hideous being...

Omega chuckled humorlessly to herself. *Well, at least they recognize me for what I am,* she thought. *I guess Echo figured it out, too, in the end.* Tears came to her eyes then, and she bit her lip hard to maintain control. *Why couldn't he just tell me up front? Just...break up with me? Why do it like this? Oh. Maybe he wants a new partner, not just a new girlfriend. No, girl, settle down. I've got to hold on,* she thought, feeling desperate, *just a little longer. A couple of days. To the mating ceremony. By then, I oughta be able to get the info the Ennead wants. After that...well, if Echo doesn't want me, Hsrs isn't getting me.* Omega set her jaw grimly. Suddenly she thought of the image Echo had sent her only a couple of days earlier: The two of them curled up in bed together, murmuring and laughing softly, as bare skin was caressed. *Oh, Ace...* It was a mental sob.

The alarmed harem mistress spun to look at the despairing Agent, stubby antennae swiveling around in what somehow came across to Omega as a sympathetic motion, even as her lilac skin flushed a reddish-plum color. Swiftly she put a multi-tipped tentacle-arm about Omega's shoulders and led her back to the private quarters reserved for the Agent's preparation. There, the alien woman tenderly embraced Omega, then dimmed the lights and left her alone, to deal with her emotions in her own way.

Omega crawled onto the cushioned sleeping dais, buried her face in a pillow, and lay still.

* * *

Echo sat on his private sleeping platform in the quarters reserved for the three Alpha Line Agents, deep in thought. He had not even undressed, save to remove jacket, tie, and holsters...and those lay nearby. After a long time, he shook his head and sighed, then glanced around the room. Finally, he closed his eyes and reached out, the way his partner had taught him.

Meg? Meg, are you there? Meg...if you're listening, baby, answer me... and then, after a pause, an uncharacteristically pleading, *...please?*

There was no response but silence. Echo opened his eyes and glanced around the empty room again with another sigh. He loosened his tie, unbuttoned his shirt collar, and fished around inside his shirt for a moment, eventually retrieving a silver chain. Two pendants now dangled from it. One was a certain simple silver cross with filigree-like engraving, the same one that had been given to him by Omega the night they had become engaged, well after their 'family' had congratulated them and departed. He had worn it ever since, unbeknownst to her, carefully hidden beneath his shirt, not even removing it to shower. Beside the cross now hung the star-cut hyperdiamond ring. He stared at the two symbols of undying love, lying in the palm of his hand, then curled his fingers tight around them, making a silent request as he did so. Then he carefully replaced chain and pendants inside his shirt.

It was a funny thing, he mused to himself; even despite two previous partners, Echo had been essentially a loner for his entire adult life, at least until meeting Omega. But never had he felt so alone as he did now.

* * *

A distraught India and a disgusted Romeo paced around their sleeping room restlessly, late into their sleep period.

"I canNOT believe he did that," Romeo muttered. "Jus' givin' th' pretty lady away like that. Like she was...just a thing, an object. What th' hell was he thinkin'?!"

"I don't know, Romeo, but something has to be wrong," India worried. "Echo and Meg were so happy, just a few days ago! ECHO was happy! The psych profile they took during the Broadway-show mission proved it! That was no act, I'd stake my life on it. I've never seen him so relaxed, cheerful and out-going. It wasn't just Meg."

"I know whatcha mean, girl, an' I gotta agree," Romeo replied. "That's what makes it so surprisin'. You s'pose Echo's got sumthin up 'is sleeve?"

"Well, there's one way to find out," India said. "Let's go."

* * *

The harem mistress returned in plenty of time to prepare Omega for Hsrs's visit. Omega was bathed, massaged with perfumed oils, and dressed in another, more revealing, drape. Her platinum hair was released from its accustomed French braid to flow down her shoulders, her face cleansed and anointed with some special cream which left the skin velvety-soft.

I could enjoy the pampering, if not for what's coming, Omega thought ruefully, as the 'hands' of the harem mistress— four small tentacles branching from the end of four tentacular arms—gently massaged another lotion into Omega's flesh. *Talk about spa treatment. But I'd still rather it was Echo giving me the massage.*

A quick refresher on courtesan behavior, and the gentle harem woman was gone. *Hmm,* Omega mused. *Maybe I can play dumb blonde. Provincial hick. If I don't learn the right behavior, maybe... Well, why not? It's worth a shot. The worst that can happen is, I get killed. But I guess that's coming one way or another, anyway. Fast execution would be preferable to what I saw in Hsrs' mind.*

Moments later, Omega heard a chime at the extreme limits of her range of hearing, and Hsrs entered the room, moving along low to the floor on the lower of two ranks of suckered tentacles with an odd popping sound as the suckers adhered and released. Omega paled slightly at the strange sight, but stood her ground proudly, refusing to adopt the behavior the attendants had tried to teach her. This, however, seemed both to amuse and to please the Premier, who advanced slowly, one tentacle outstretched.

"Ah, Omega, do not be aflaid," Hsrs said gently. "I know

197

we ah velly diffelent beings. But I have seen much of the univelse, and I find you a velly beautifur femare."

So much for playing the country hick, Omega thought, hiding the disappointment. "Thank you," she replied hollowly. "You're...rather unique in that opinion, it would seem." She opened up and reached out mentally, activating the chip at maximum capacity. Suddenly her eyes went wide, and she swayed. *Ah! Too—too much! Overload...pull back, girl...* Recovering quickly, she said, "You...you have been many places, then?"

"Many." The premier perched himself on the edge of the sleep platform and gestured for her to join him, patting the cushioned surface with two of the upper row of tentacles, which apparently comprised arms, while the lower row were his legs.

Omega sat gingerly near him as she added, "I was once one of Earth's space explorers." She rested her chin on one hand and gazed at him, feigning interest as she endeavored to explore the alien mind. "Tell me about your travels, please. I'm curious..."

* * *

Romeo and India barged into Echo's bedroom without even bothering to knock.

"Echo, talk to us, man!" Romeo exclaimed, as the shirtsleeved older Agent sat up from his prone position on the cushioned dais. "What th' hell's goin' on?!"

Echo glanced around the room in what looked to the other Agents like a meaningful gaze, though neither could interpret it; then he looked calmly at Romeo, cocking his eyebrow.

"There's nothing to say, hot shot," he answered simply.

"Don't give us that, Echo!" India snapped. "You owe us an explanation."

Echo stood slowly, staring at his colleagues with an odd look on his face.

"I don't 'owe' you anything." Abruptly, he adopted a distant expression, as if his mind were suddenly miles away.

"Well, you owe Meg sumthin'," Romeo expostulated. "You owe her at least a rescue—"

"Be quiet."

"What?"

"Shut up a minute. I'm listening," Echo reiterated, and Alpha Two silenced, glancing at each other and then watching their leader.

* * *

Echo! Omigosh! ECHO!!

Meg? Meg, I'm right here. What's up? Are you okay? Have you got something?

Yeah, you might say that. A real bombshell. Where are Romeo and India? I want to make sure we all know this, just in case. Omega still sat in her boudoir, beside an increasingly friendly premier—who was now a deep shade of burgundy—trying to divide her attention between diplomatically fending off his advances and communicating with Echo.

Romeo and India are right here with me, Meg, Echo replied. Omega widened her mental 'view.'

Oh, okay, I 'see' 'em now. Hi, y'all.

We're here, Meg, India answered. *Are you all right?*

Hey, pretty lady, Romeo answered.

Yes, India, I'm okay for now—

Get with it, Meg, Echo grumbled impatiently, *if it's so damn important.*

All...all right, Echo. Omega tried to hide the hurt. *Try this out. Premier Hsrs is being fed his information surreptitiously by a member of the Ennead, the inner council of nine! There's a traitor on the Council. Is that good enough for you?*

* * *

What the hell?! Echo exclaimed, as India and Romeo offered similar mental opinions. *Who??*

The Celrian counselor, Omega answered. *Oh boy...* she thought, as the Premier's attentions grew more insistent.

N'Do? Echo pressed. *Ari N'Do?*

That's the one, Omega confirmed. *Blast it, get those suck-*

ers off me...

* * *

Meg? Are you in trouble? India asked, picking up on the aside remarks.

What kind of info is he passing, Meg? Echo followed up.

I'm...oh, no you don't...I'm working on it, Echo...I...no...stop... The tension in Omega's thoughts grew more and more pronounced. *Oh, dear God...not...not again...*

Meg? Echo got her attention. *Stay cool. Think. Look around you, and use your environment to plan strategy.*

Echo...I've got a problem here...Hsrs doesn't wanna wait... ohh, shit! and he's got more 'hands' than I do...NO!!

The link went silent suddenly, as three Alpha Line Agents sat tensely in Echo's bedroom, waiting. Abruptly, Omega was back—for a moment.

Ace...Echo, honey, please—

Silence. The telepathic contact was gone.

"Damn! The pretty lady's in trouble!" Romeo cried.

"C'mon, guys, let's go!" India jumped up from her seat on the dais. She and Romeo were halfway to the bedroom door when the harsh voice sounded.

"Stop. That's an order."

The two Agents froze in shock, then spun to face the voice's owner.

"Echo, you don't mean that," India pleaded. "She's still not over Wright's rape attempt..."

"I meant it," Echo said quietly, pale face set like stone.

"But, Echo—!" Romeo began.

"We don't even know where they're holding her," Echo pointed out. "If you go running out there right now, you risk blowing everything, including letting them know that Meg's telepathic...which could get her—and us—killed immediately, and plunge the whole damn galaxy into war. Now just calm down. Meg's good. Give her a minute."

India and Romeo sat back down, fuming.

* * *

"Hsrs," Omega told the amorous purple alien, "I-I'm not ready..."

"It is arr light," the premier smiled, the mouth-slit distorting with the expression. "You do not need to know thlone loom behavio'. You wirr not be in the thlone loom. I rike you rike dis." Clammy tentacles wrapped around her, finding bare skin and exploring it. Omega desperately suppressed a shudder.

"That...that wasn't what I meant," she tried to explain. "On Earth there is a custom—"

"Yes?" a blue-green Hsrs suddenly sat up, curious. "Ealth customs? Terr me. I have a, how you carr it, ah! A hobby. I correct customs flom the pranets I visit. To one with the tlaining, customs say much about the peopure who plactice them."

Thank you, God, Omega thought fervently. "Yes, it...this custom...it regards marriage—mating—ceremonies, and it comes from...from some religious beliefs..."

"You' lerigious beriefs?"

"Yes," Omega answered. "And I take those beliefs very seriously."

"Terr me."

"Well...I believe that...that a man and woman shouldn't... shouldn't..." Omega stammered, trying to express a very personal subject to a perfect stranger.

"Mate?" supplied Hsrs.

"Yes, until after the formal marriage ceremony, so that God will...will bless the union," she finished uncertainly. *That's stretching it,* she thought, *given that some Biblical marriages pretty much consisted of the guy declaring, 'This is my wife,' but the harder and faster I can make the rule, the better chance I have of holding him off.*

"This 'God'...He is the Deity?" Hsrs asked. "The Maker, some of your garactics carr it?"

"Yes."

"And It has tord you this?"

"Um, well, not me personally," Omega admitted, "but..." suddenly she thought rapidly, "if you'll let Agent Echo bring me my things, I can show you where the...the Deity...had it placed in holy writings."

"We wirr see," Hsrs said, and waved a dismissing tentacle. "And you feer velly stlongry about this?"

"Very," she declared, firm. *Given I was making Echo wait, I'm sure gonna make...hold on. I wonder if that was the problem with Echo. Maybe...he got tired of waiting...?*

Hsrs considered for long moments...as did Omega, though about different things.

"Velly werr. I wourd not wish the Deity to punish you fol disobedience. We wirr wait." He slid off the platform, then swiveled his face around to look at her. "I rook folwald to it."

"Thank you..." Omega whispered, as the Premier departed.

But she wasn't speaking to the Premier.

* * *

...Echo...? Omega's thought was weak, uncertain.

There you are. Right here, Meg, came the immediate answer. *Romeo and India are here, too.* Echo motioned at the two Agents sitting near him, and tapped his temple. Alpha Two relaxed slightly.

They're...there? With you?

Yep. Right here.

So you...couldn't figure out how to get to me, huh?

Dunno.

You...don't know? Didn't you try?

* * *

...No. A pause. *Are you...all right?*

Does it matter? Omega stifled a sigh of pained disappointment.

Yes, Meg. It matters.

Yeah, I guess it does. I have to stay intact long enough to get the invasion plans and pass 'em to you. After that, I'm that word you once told me never to use. Omega's thought was very quiet. She slumped on the corner of the sleeping dais, despondent.

What word's...that?

Expendable.'

And a heartbroken Omega broke the link.

* * *

Fox sat at Entiyti's desk, studying the reports from the Deltiri interrogators on the original prisoners, looking for something of significance that would point to the organizers of the attempt. When he got to the interrogation of the loudmouthed Reptoid, he sighed, rubbed his eyes, and laid it aside.

"No need for me to look at that," he murmured. "The idiot's life is an open book."

But when he reached for the next report, he paused, uncertain. Then he looked back and forth between the report he had just discarded, and the next on the stack.

"Mm," he considered. "My head says don't bother, but my gut says go over it with a fine-toothed comb. And as an old acquaintance once told me, 'Whenever an experienced investigator's gut is involved, it implies the mind, not the belly, has subconsciously deduced conclusions not immediately apparent.' So maybe I better."

He picked up the discarded report and began to read.

* * *

He had been at it for some little while and was starting to get bored, when a single statement caught Fox's eye. He stopped and reread it.

"Oh, farkakte," he whispered, staring at the page. "There it is. That's what we've been looking for, I'd lay everything I own on it!" He shoved back the chair, bellowing, "SUUD! Get in here!"

* * *

"...A Ke!endarian?" Suud noted, when Fox showed him what he had found. "But Franz, the Ke!endarians were part of the attempt. This is nothing new."

"No, alter khaver, you don't understand," Fox explained, patient. "It IS something new. If I'm reading this right, this is NOT one of the Ke!endarians who were part of the attempt. This is either the being behind it, or an emissary of that being.

The cabal on Emdali had no direction; they only knew they were dissatisfied, and felt that Pul's government and leadership was part of the problem—because they were looking for someone else to blame for the troubles they brought on themselves by their corrupt dealings. But they had no idea what to do about it, and none of them were audacious enough to consider offing the galactic president. If I've got this straight, they never even thought of it...until this Ke!endarian showed on the scene. It was HIS idea."

"Ohhhh," Suud groaned in understanding, as he began to grasp what Fox was trying to get across. "Then this being arrives and plants the idea in their heads..."

"Exactly," Fox said in satisfaction. "You see it now. And suddenly they're all hot to get Pulgey."

"What do we need to do, to confirm this?"

"For starters, go get Taas and the lead interrogator," Fox decided. "I want to see what else we can dig out of what we've already got."

* * *

"No, that is correct," Qq'k'l ob Sii'stek told them. "The Ke!endarian who approached the Emdalian group was not among those who actually carried out the attack. Or at least, he was not recognized, I suppose."

"Was one of the Ke!endarians who WAS there in charge?" Director Siisshiiss pressed.

"More or less, yes, I have gathered," Qq'k'l averred. "I am uncertain which one, however. I would need to go back and interrogate each of them again on this specific question. Which it sounds as if I should do."

"I think that's a good idea," Fox declared. "Taas, Suud, what do you say?"

"I think it is a good idea also," Suud agreed.

"Then let us do it at once," Siisshiiss decreed.

* * *

"That did not take so very long," Qq'k'l decided only a couple of hours later. "With the three of us on the matter, and only a few questions needful to answer, it was fairly simplistic."

"And so none of the participants recognized any of the Ke!endarians as this ringleader—or at least, instigator?" Fox pressed.

"No, though that does not mean that it was not," Qq'k'l pointed out. "The Ke!endarians have gotten rather good at disguise...at least the ones who were in the H!nar kre Naese!en!Re cult. Sometimes they cannot even recognize their own members...which is as those members wish it. But usually we can tell who those members are, thanks to their own thoughts giving away their guilt."

"Wait," Suud murmured. "Where are the most recent captives?"

"Oh, we did not include those as yet," Qq'k'l said. "We have yet to complete a full interrogation on them in any event. We will simply include this matter in the interrogation checklist and provide you a complete report when it is finished. If one of them is in fact this instigator in disguise, we should be able to tell."

"Excellent," Siisshiiss said. "I think we may have a lead at last."

* * *

"Fox, here is the second report from the Deltiri interrogators," Suud said several hours later, coming into Entiyti's office, where Fox used the desk computer to dig into the backgrounds of the known assassin conspirators. "This is...interesting."

"What is?" Fox asked, looking up and reaching for the printout Suud offered. "Can you give me a synopsis?"

"Yes. As you said, the Teludal is a relative of this 'Kenny and Cartman,' and the Reptoid is part of the crime syndicate. Apparently no Draconans were willing to obviously side against Pulgey, but there were several Reptoid volunteers." Suud sighed. "That is neither here nor there, I suppose. It is the three newly-captured Ke!endarians that are of interest—two are, as you suspected, part of the original H!nar kre Naese!en!Re cult, trying to generate a coup within the Coalition as 'payback,'" Suud noted. "The third...is not a true Ke!endarian. He is, instead, a disguised Cortian."

"All right," Fox noted, considering. "Not unexpected, either of those. What's so interesting?"

"The other Ke!endarian, the one captured earlier, claims to also be H!nar kre Naese!en!Re...but is not known to the newly-captured cultists at all."

"Huh," Fox said, thoughtful. "But that cult should be nothing but remnants now. I'd have thought whoever was left would be a small group..."

"This is precisely what is so odd," Suud pointed out. "They do not seem to practice any compartmentalization security, so it IS unlikely that they would not know each other. More, the first one claims to know THEM. All three of them."

"Even though one of 'em is a Cortian in disguise?" Fox said, raising a skeptical eyebrow.

"Just so," Suud averred. "I know that the lead interrogator said that they had gotten very good at disguising themselves, but this is more than that. There is a difference, Qq'k'l said, between not RECOGNIZING, and not KNOWING. 'Prisoner A,' let us call it, because I have not bothered to learn names, claims to know 'Prisoners B, C, and D.' Of course D does not know A, because D is the Cortian. Yet B and C not only do not recognize A, they have never heard of it. At least until they met on the way to the transfer station to initiate their operation."

"Oh, now that IS interesting," Fox decided. "And if memory serves, Prisoner A had a brain configuration that none of the interrogators recognized."

"Oh, that is right," Suud recalled. "I had forgotten that. But there is no physical evidence that it is Cortian or any other species than Ke!endarian; Qq'k'l seems to think this one might have a mental disease, and that is the reason for the difference."

"Which might also explain why it thinks it knows the others, when they don't know it," Fox mulled.

"Yes. But it is very...strange, nevertheless."

"It is, that," Fox agreed. "Well, just one more thing to factor into the entire case."

And he resumed his researches, as Suud headed out to see to Entiyti.

* * *

Echo had just gotten dressed after a restless, sleepless night when the door signal triggered. Through the bedroom door, he heard India's voice call, "I've got it." Moments later, "Echo?"

"Yes?" Echo opened the door, adjusting his tie.

Two guards stood there.

"Aaeai oool uu Hsrs a Omega iua," one pronounced.

Echo straightened up, hopeful, and he nodded. He ducked back into his room and emerged with Omega's duffel. He glanced at Alpha Two—who stood watching—with an elevated eyebrow, and raised the kit bag meaningfully; they all knew that Omega had recently taken to keeping some unusual and highly useful...'tools'...stashed in the warp pockets of that bag, in the aftermath of recent events...because she had told them, and instructed them how to handle her kit as a consequence.

"Back later," he said, and followed the guards out.

* * *

The guards led Echo through the huge ship, almost to the opposite side, changing decks in the process. An observant Echo took note of every detail of his surroundings, analyzing carefully as he went. He held his partner's kit tightly in one arm, carrying it close to his body like a football, feeling the flexible rectangle that was Omega's dead father's Bible as it rested comfortably against his side. Also in the bag were her blaster, brain bleacher, and Winchester & Tesla, as well as other personal items which might..."come in handy," as she was wont to put it; when those three items were found on her, the guards had carefully confiscated and brought them to Echo, and he had stowed them there.

Meg? Can you hear me?

Echo? Is that you?

Yeah, Meg. They're bringing me to you to give you your kit.

207

I think I'm close, Echo observed.

Good. That'll sure help. And I'll...be glad to see you, Ace... The thought was tentative, hesitant, seeming uncertain of its reception. *When you get here...are you going to get me out?*

No. Echo glanced at his escorts. *It might give you away, if I did. And that would be bad, all around. But with the stuff you've shown me in your kit,* I *probably don't need to.*

Oh. Good point.

The guards stopped at a door as the harem mistress barred their way, all four tentacle-legs splayed, all four arms out-spread, scowling face almost aubergine.

"Ee," she declared, brooking no resistance. That came across plain as day to Echo: no farther.

I'm here.

Okay. I'm waiting.

One soldier turned to Echo.

"Aaie oio uu a yoe eee yu."

Echo looked blank for a moment.

"Yoe eee yu?"

"Aa."

The black-Suited shoulders slumped slightly. Echo opened Omega's bag, dug around a moment, then pulled out the Bible, handing it to the guard. The guard took it, muttered, "Uuyu," and disappeared through the door with the harem woman. Echo and the other guard waited as they had been told.

Meg?

Yes?

It doesn't look like we'll be seeing each other today, after all. They stopped me at the door.

Oh. Well, once I get hold of the kit, maybe I can fix that.

Well, that won't be happening either, Echo explained. *They took your Bible and left me holding the bag—literally.*

Hm. That would explain why Hsrs just showed, Omega sighed.

Hsrs?? Echo replied, caught off-guard. *Why?*

Theology 101, Omega answered. *Comparative religion*

and marriage laws.

Oh.

Gotta go, Ace. I need my wits about me for this little conversation, and I can't afford to be distracted.

* * *

"Herro, Omega," Hsrs greeted the Agent softly. "I see you have you' hory litings."

"Yes, thank you—" Omega paused. "Uh. What...what shall I call you?"

"What wourd you rike to carr me?" Hsrs replied in a relaxed, almost casual fashion. "What wourd be applopliate on you' wolrd?"

"Well, I don't know," Omega admitted. "Are you considered royalty? Wait...you're a premier, so...yeah, royalty. Do you want me to address you formally?"

"No, no, I do not tink so," Hsrs mused. "Ret us keep it simpur. Carr me Hsrs."

"All right...Hsrs," Omega said, as the alien turned a soft red in pleasure. "Do you want me to show you the writings I told you about?"

"Yes, prease," the Premier said, 'seating' himself beside her on the dais.

"Okay, let me see..." Omega paused for a moment, thinking, then began thumbing through the old Bible.

"Whele did you get dis book?" Hsrs asked curiously, observing its worn condition. "It is velly old, is it not?"

"Yes. It was my father's," Omega answered. "When he... when he died, I kept it."

"You roved him."

"Very much."

"You' mothel?"

"She died, too."

"You ale arone?"

Omega looked away to hide her expression.

"Yes, I guess I am," she murmured softly. "I didn't think so, but..."

Hsrs stared at her for a long moment.

"Why did you not tink so?" he asked quietly. Omega blinked, and glanced at the Premier, suddenly on her guard.

"Well, I—I...I thought I had an...an adopted 'family,' but... but they decided to...to give me away..."

"Ah," Hsrs responded, "you miss dem. But it is arr light. You ale not arone now. I am hele, an' I wirr not ret you feer arone, pletty Omega." He smiled. "They gave you up fol a high hono'. I wirr make you one of my favolite mates." Hsrs gestured at the Bible. "Now show me the mating litings."

* * *

Echo waited for quite some time outside the door, the second guard sticking like glue. Finally, the first guard emerged, Bible in hand. He gave it back to Echo, then motioned, and they headed back the way they had come.

Meg? Echo reached out as he replaced the Bible in the duffel. *They didn't even let you keep your Bible?*

No. There was a pause. *Echo, are you gonna try to help me get outta here? I've scoped out the place, and there's flatly no resources in here that I can use to help myself. They make real sure of that in the harem. I expect I'm far from the first being to be put in here who didn't want to be in here.*

Echo closed his eyes momentarily as he walked between the two guards.

Don't ask, Meg. It's better if you don't know.

Echo thought he heard a sob before the connection broke.

* * *

After Hsrs left, the harem mistress entered the chamber and walked purposefully over to Omega. She pressed a betentacled 'hand' against Omega's breastbone, and carefully intoned, "O-may-gah..."

Omega smiled and nodded.

"O-me-ga," she reiterated, covering the woman's tentacle with her own hand. Then the Agent rested her other hand on the alien's chest area, and cocked her head.

"Yee-toy," the harem mistress promptly responded, enunciating carefully.

"Yee-toy?"

"Aa. Yeetoy."

"All right, your name is Yeetoy, and 'aa' must mean yes," Omega mused. "Damn, but I wish I'd had time to grab that Binary Language Translator. But I never expected to get separated from Echo..."

"Echoo?" Yeetoy's orange eyes widened, the odd, W-shaped pupils dilating, as the alien woman watched Omega. "O-may-gah y Echoo..."

"Uh-oh," Omega muttered, picking up a flurry of sudden understanding from the other female. "Why do I think I'm not the only one playing head games here?"

"Uu Hsrs?" Yeetoy asked, testing. Omega just sighed. Yeetoy nodded in understanding. "O-may-gah y Echoo. Echoo y O-may-gah?"

Omega mulled over the sentence inversion. Finally the meaning hit her.

"Oh! You're asking if Echo loves me! I love Echo; does Echo love me? Right?"

"Aa."

"I...don't know." Omega's shoulders drooped. "I don't guess so."

"Yee!" the harem mistress exclaimed suddenly. "Yeetoy yee Echoo!" And she disappeared through the door, a dumbfounded Omega staring after her.

* * *

Three dejected Division One Agents sat around the common area of their suite aboard the imperial flagship, struggling vainly to absorb the cultural information that the Premier had had delivered to them.

"Echo, can't we just try??" India finally burst out.

"No, India," Echo answered, stifling a sigh. "What good would it do, anyway? We're no closer now to knowing where she is than we were before."

"But—"

"Echo, man, they took you TO her," Romeo protested.

"No, junior, they didn't," Echo pointed out. "They took me to the main door of the harem, and no farther. I didn't even go INSIDE it. And according to what I've gathered from Meg's comments, the harem area is huge—she estimated something like fifty members, plus attendants, with associated living quarters and preparation areas and all that sorta shit. But I have no idea where SHE is in there. It's almost an entire DECK, and this is NOT a small vessel."

"We have to do SOMEthing," India began.

The door chime sounded. Echo put aside the document he held and stood to answer it. The harem mistress, obviously agitated and nervous, stood there, her normally-lavender skin nearing a bright amethyst in her anxiety; stubby, bulbous antennae on top of her head waved here and there, as if somehow watching for spies. She laid a tentacle-finger on Echo's tie.

"Echoo?"

"Aa," Echo replied, then stiffened as he recognized the woman. "Eiay a oiyu Omega ela?"

"Ee, ee, O-may-gah egge oiya ele," Yeetoy replied, and Echo relaxed slightly. Yeetoy smiled then. "Echoo y O-may-gah? O ee?"

A shocked Echo stiffened again, then turned away, as India and Romeo watched curiously. A gentle tentacle-hand wrapped over Echo's shoulder. He glanced back into the alien woman's deep orange eyes, and saw there a close spiritual kin of the caring blue eyes so familiar to him. He motioned the woman into the suite and closed the door behind her.

* * *

The alien woman promptly wrapped flexible, questing tentacle-arms around the Agent, turning him to face her and studying his dark eyes intently. Then Yeetoy smiled and caressed Echo's cheek with the tip of a 'finger.' Leaning forward, she murmured something to Echo, whose face lit warmly, and he responded in soft Persan.

After several more minutes of intense conversation with

Echo in her native tongue, Yeetoy departed hastily. Romeo and India stared at Echo.

"What th' hell was that all about?" Romeo asked.

"...Personal business, junior," was the only answer Echo gave, before resuming his study of the cultural documentation.

* * *

Late that night, Romeo and India were roused from sleep by the sound of the door chime. Romeo dragged himself off the sleep dais, threw on a dressing gown, and staggered groggily into the common area. India peeked around the bedroom door. Romeo stumbled to a stop.

Echo stood there, clad only in his trousers, with a scantily-dressed Yeetoy. He glanced up when he heard the other Agent.

"Go back to bed, junior," he told Romeo. "I've got it."

"Huh. Looks like it," Romeo muttered in disgust, glancing at India as Alpha Two turned and headed back into the bedroom.

* * *

The next morning, uncharacteristically, Alpha Two beat Echo up. They were dressed and eating the breakfast meal that servants had delivered, while Echo's door was still shut. They glanced at the closed door, then at each other, but said nothing. Suddenly the door opened.

A slightly weary Echo emerged, followed closely by Yeetoy. Both were dressed as they had been the night before; Echo had a satisfied smile on his face. When they saw India and Romeo, they both stopped dead. Echo shot a swift look at his wrist chronometer.

"Morning," Echo greeted Alpha Two, then turned to Yeetoy. "Aaeyei o-o lo, Yeetoy," he said, smiling warmly at the alien woman. Yeetoy wrapped a soft tentacle-hand around the angle of Echo's cheekbone.

"Aa," she replied, and quietly let herself out of the suite.

"Echo?!" India exclaimed in shock, as she and Romeo stared at the senior Agent in horror.

"So when's our next cultural exchange meeting scheduled?" Echo asked casually, ignoring the stares and grabbing a muffin-like item from the tray of food.

"Uhh...'bout three hours," Romeo replied, subdued.

"Good," Echo responded, taking a large bite out of the muffin-thing. "I'll be ready to go in three hours. Mm. This thing tastes pretty good. Probably better not to know what it is, though."

Echo disappeared into his bedroom and closed the door.

* * *

"Well, well, there he is! And how are you feeling today, Pul?" Fox wondered, entering Entiyti's hospital room.

"Not so bad, I suppose," Entiyti decided, morose. "Physically, at least. Tired. Discouraged, on several counts. But... alive."

"Tired, I can understand. What are the points of discouragement?" Fox asked, moving to sit beside the bed.

"About what you would expect, Franz," Entiyti sighed. "I lost my wing. I can no longer fly. The Coalition halls on Aleancë are so very cramped; I had hoped to spend some time at the glide park, as well as flying around the estate, while I was here. And now, I never shall again. And it is all my own damned fault!" he exclaimed in frustration and guilt. "Had I not been so blind, so stupid, so childish, as to run ahead of my guard contingent, there might have been opportunity to spot the trap, and none of this would have happened. Uussa would still be alive, she and Duuniiss would be marrying in a few months, Sigrund would not be maimed..." He let out a titanic sigh. "And it is ALL my fault."

"Hush that," Fox ordered mildly. "You had no reason to suspect."

"No, but I know better," Entiyti argued, all but slumped in on himself. "You and Suud both have been telling me for weeks—months!—that I needed a larger guard contingent, needed to be more careful. I simply did not want to believe it."

"Well, there is THAT, I'll admit," Fox agreed. "But you could have had twice, three times the number of guards with you, and it probably wouldn't have changed what went down... except maybe to increase the number of fatalities and casualties."

Entiyti tilted his head and gazed at Fox consideringly.

"Do you think so?" he asked finally.

"I'd lay a great deal of money on it," Fox averred.

"What would you have done differently?"

"Mm. Let me think." Fox pondered for a long moment, considering what he knew of the scenario. "If we had had any indication that there were groups gunning for you, we'd have made sure your arrival was unknown. Classified the flight information, entered the flight plan as a ciphered missive, maybe sent a decoy ahead, with guards to scout out the transfer station, see what was going on..."

"Keep going."

"Well, I guess my point would be, hindsight being 20/20, ASSUMING we had any advance warning of danger, I'd have found a way to spirit you in, maybe not even letting you set foot on the transfer station; just send a shuttle straight from the *Hsshthh* down to your estate." Fox shook his head. "But nobody knew anything was wrong, correct?"

"That's correct, insofar as I knew," Entiyti agreed. "And Sigrund would certainly have told me, and he is not derelict. Nor did anyone at Aleancë give me any sort of indication..."

"Then probably nothing I'd've done could have made a difference," Fox decided.

The two males were quiet for a time. Finally Entiyti broke the silence.

"Franz, how is Sigrund?"

"He's doing surprisingly well, I think," Fox said. "You'd have to ask Zebra or Zarnix, of course. But they kluged together a regen pod—like we used on Omega? You know what I mean..."

"Indeed. One of Doron's procedures."

"Right. And he's in there now. It took a bit longer than they thought, because there was more damage to his shoulder than they realized, else he might be out by now. I'm not sure; ask them. But he should be all right once they bring him out."

"So he will NOT be permanently maimed?"

"That's the plan, as I understand it."

"That is good," Entiyti concluded, relieved. "But that does not mean he will want to continue with me."

"I can't speak to that," Fox said. "But I would suggest that he has earned a nice vacation and time to recuperate. And there will be recuperation; he almost lost that entire arm."

Entiyti winced.

"Now, now, Pul," Fox soothed. "He did NOT lose the arm, and may not even lose much, if any, mobility. And there's plotting and planning going on in the background about your wing. We're going to do the best we can by you and your people."

"I know," Entiyti said with yet another sigh. "But Franz..."

"Yes, Pul?"

"I was wondering something...several things, actually..."

"What?"

"Who is on Earth, running the Agency, while you are here?"

"Echo, of course," Fox chuckled. He had discussed the matter with the physicians, and they had concluded not to worry Entiyti with matters of potential invasions, or Ennead interference in Division affairs—at least, not until he was much stronger. It hadn't occurred to them to wonder why Entiyti knew nothing of a possible invasion to begin with. "I think it was a pain in the tokhes, the first day or so, but he got the hang of it. And so Omega is running Alpha Line, and Whiskey is handling the medlab, him being third in command there."

"Very good, very good," Entiyti murmured, thoughtful. "This is more or less the group that you intended should supersede you, when you retired?"

"Pretty much," Fox agreed. "Zarnix would probably still be in Medical, but Zebra would come with me—she's already agreed—and Whiskey would move into the assistant chief of staff position."

"Hm," Entiyti hummed, eyes distant, considering.

"What are you up to, alter khaver?"

"Franz...come back to work for me."

"You know I'm planning to, Pul, just as soon as I retire."

"No, my friend. NOW. I mean now. Tender your resignation, or put in your retirement, and...just stay here. Oh, I suppose you and Zebra would need to go back and fetch your household goods, and we can find you a house, or build one here on the estate, for the two of you, and—"

"Whoa, Pulgey! Hold on a moment, here! I appreciate the offer, and it's very tempting. And I might. But there are a lot of things to be considered, first," Fox pointed out. "First of all, I need to find out if Zebra is willing to take that step yet, let alone ready. Second, I suspect we will need to allow Omega time to heal mentally and emotionally, after all the drek she's been through in recent weeks. And I think I'd really like to see the marriage amendment for the Agency charter go through, so we can get Omega and Echo married off...and hell, properly marry Zebra, under a canopy and whatnot, myself!" Fox offered his friend a grin. "So, while I might be willing, there are a few hoops to jump through first."

"Consider one of 'em jumped through, honey," came a voice from behind him.

Fox turned, to find Zebra standing in the door.

"I'm sorry, hon; I didn't mean to eavesdrop," she apologized, contrite. "I was coming by to see how Pulgey was doing, and overheard, the last bit anyway. And you know I have that wanderlust! I'd love to go exploring the galaxy with you, alongside your oldest friend."

"That is one hurdle down," Entiyti pointed out. "As for the marriage, if you move here, given you are already legally my brother, we can make you both legal residents of Emdali, and you can get married here, however you like. So there is a second hurdle down."

"But he's right about Omega," Zebra said. "She does need some time to get her head on straight, Pulgey. She's been through hell, and what none of us realized was that the whole thing that went down a year ago with Slug left her with a significant case of PTSD that she didn't let on she even had."

"What is PTSD?" Entiyti asked.

"Post-Traumatic Stress Disorder," Fox defined it for the Draconan. "It used to be called 'shell shock' on Earth, among war veterans. I think your people call it, 'hrrsst drrsst.'"

"Ah," Entiyti said, and bit his lip. "That. Yes, and I suppose the Cortian incident did not help that..."

"No, nor the crash landing on the protoplanet, nor a whole shitload of other crap," Zebra added. "It's amazing she's done as well as she has, for so long; I don't know of another agent that could have pulled it out like that, other than maybe Echo... and even that's iffy. And probably due to the tweaks, into the bargain. That poor girl has some shit to work out in her head. And that will take a while. And until it's worked out, she doesn't need the additional stress of being made the permanent chief of Alpha Line."

"And I still would like to get her and Echo married off, before we dump the leadership of the entire division on 'em," Fox averred. "Because, let's face it, she's going to be supporting him with everything she's got, in addition to running a department for him. But if we can push through the charter amendment, we might be able to accomplish the bulk of that in a couple of months, at most. Zebra? Does that seem reasonable?"

"I think so, honey," Zebra decided after a moment. "I did call Zz'r'p last night and ask him, as Omega's primary physician, how the sessions were going. There's only been a few, but he thinks she's doing well. He's giving her plenty of food for thought, real positive stuff, and she's taking it all in. She's even starting to put some of it to use, to counter the negative internal monologue."

"That's excellent!" Fox decreed in delight. "Our tekhter needed that!"

"He even thinks he found a way to explain to her that her conclusions regarding what Slug did to her were wrong, that he didn't succeed."

"Aha, even better." Fox turned to Entiyti. "In that case, Pul, if you can be patient a few weeks—"

"It's gonna take him that long to be ready to return to governmental duty anyway, assuming all goes well," Zebra pointed out.

"Oh," Entiyti murmured, face falling.

"Now, now, don't pout, meyn khaver," Fox said with a grin. "It sounds as if, by the time you're ready to need me, in my old position, I assume..."

"Just so."

"Then I can be here...along with a most excellent physician, willing to travel with us wherever you should choose to go!"

"What about Commander Dalgaard?" Zebra wondered.

"I think he has earned an extended leave of absence, in all honesty," Entiyti said, pulling a face...which was saying something, on a Draconan face. "Given my foolishness got him so badly injured, he may choose to find other, less dangerous, employment in any event."

"Well, now that you mention it, he was making noises about a vacation, just before we put him into the regen pod," Zebra recalled. "But I don't remember anything about a new job."

"Done, then," Entiyti decreed. "Tell him, when you take him out, that he has that vacation, as long as he wishes, and I will pay his expenses, for service rendered above and beyond, as the saying is. And then I shall make him chief of security for the estate, instead of having to travel everywhere with me. I know that was a hardship on him; he has a wife and young children who moved here when he came to work for me. And for just that reason, Suud cannot return to the position, at least full-time, either."

"I think Dalgaard'll be delighted," Zebra said, giving the Draconan a smile, as she began to check his condition.

* * *

When the Alpha Line Agents met with the Persan cultural ministers, they received several curious questions regarding Earth home and family life. The chief cultural attaché, a Ka'agand female with a barrel-shaped, bipedal body surmounted by a bulbous head on a thick neck, pointed at Alpha Two with an appendage.

"You mates, yes?" she asked. India and Romeo glanced at each other.

"Uhh...well, yeah, sorta," Romeo responded. The attaché turned to Echo.

"You?"

"...No," Echo replied briefly.

"No? No why?"

Echo remained silent.

"No why?" the minister pressed. "No why?"

Echo sighed but tossed off flippantly, "I don't seem to be able to hang onto 'em long enough to get through the wedding ceremony." He winced despite himself, but the reaction went unnoticed.

"'Wedding celemony'? What is 'wedding celemony'?" the woman inquired.

"A formal mating ceremony, either one of various religions, or civil," India interjected.

"Ah," the cultural minister said, comprehending. "You have wedding celemony?"

"Uh—no," India answered, glancing down and flushing. "Not yet."

"But you mates."

"Ummm..." India blushed deeper. Romeo looked blank, trying to formulate a response and coming up empty.

"The section of the Division One organization within the Sol system currently has no provision for a formal ceremony," Echo filled in smoothly, "and Romeo and India have done what they could to establish a mate relationship without it."

"We're tryin' t' get the Agency's charter changed to fix that," Romeo added.

"Why?" one of the adjunct ministers asked. "Mates mates."

"Huh?" Romeo muttered under his breath, confused.

"Mates are mates, junior," Echo murmured. "He's asking, 'why bother?'"

"Oh. Shit, that's easy," Romeo said. "'Cause I love 'er."

"Love now," the adjunct pointed out.

"Yeah, but it's a commitment thang," Romeo countered. "Th' big 'C' word. F'rever, an' all that." India smiled at her partner. "It shows God an' ev'rybody how much I love 'er."

The Persans mulled that for a while, conversing quietly among themselves, then turned back to Alpha Two.

"Hatchrings?" the attaché asked.

"No, not yet," India said with another smile, "but eventually, maybe."

"Mates, hatchrings—famiry," the minister declared. "Velly impo'tant to us. How wolk on you' pranet?"

India took a deep breath and prepared to plunge in, but before she could say anything, Echo answered.

"Maybe it would be easier if we talked to an expert in family and mating," he proposed. "Someone whose job is handling such affairs. We can compare concepts and traditions...directly."

"Hm. Idea good," the attaché agreed. "Who...?"

"Maybe...someone over the Premier's harem?" Echo suggested.

"Ah, yess, yess—Yeetoy good, yess," she answered. "Iss velly good. Yeetoy visit Diwision One Agents aftel she off duty. Yess?"

"That'll work," Echo agreed, ignoring the hard glances from his colleagues. "I—We'll be...waiting for her."

Chapter 9

"Herro, Omega," a dark-gray Hsrs greeted the Agent as he entered her suite. "I haf good news."

"Hello, Hsrs," Omega said quietly, watching the Premier advance across the floor of the room with that odd popping sound from his suckers.

"Ahh, I do rike dat," Hsrs sighed, coloring red.

"Like what?"

"Healing my own name," Hsrs told her. "I do not heal it often. Plemiel dis, Plemiel dat, You' Excerrency, how may we he'p mirord, arr dat. Honolifics. But nevel my own name. Being Plemiel iss velly ronery, sometimes."

"I get it. I never hear the name my parents gave me. Not anymore," Omega sympathized. "So I kind of understand."

"Why not?"

"The Division One Agency only uses codenames. The person I was before I joined the Agency...no longer exists."

"You ale an Agent?!"

"Yes."

"I thought you wele a gift flom the Agency."

"I'm...not quite sure how it came about, either," Omega admitted. There was a pause.

"Omega...what did you' palents carr you?" Hsrs asked softly, seeming sensitive to her mood; his skin deepened to that same charcoal gray shade again. Omega sighed.

"That person's gone, Hsrs." *Maybe she never really existed at all,* she thought.

"Prease...terr me." A gentle tentacle wrapped lightly over the top of her hand, the tip lightly, soothingly caressing her skin. Omega bowed her head, her voice a whisper.

"Megan...they named me Megan."

"What does it mean?"

"It means 'strong and capable,' according to some," she murmured. "Others say it means 'pearl,' which is a pretty gemstone produced by a shellfish in response to an...an irritation." *Which probably makes more sense than 'strong and capable,' in my case,* she decided.

"Megan," Hsrs echoed softly, lilting over the name. "Dat iss a velly pletty name. I rike it. You ale velly speciar, Megan. Do you know dis?"

"No, not really," Omega demurred.

"Yess, you ale. You do not know how speciar." Hsrs broke off suddenly, turning a deep shade of blue. "I bling news you wirr be preased to heal."

Omega studied him, picking up an unexpected sadness she was at a loss to interpret. *His thoughts are so alien,* she mused, struggling to read him. *Maybe I'm misunderstanding.* "What news?"

"Tomollow, at hou' fou' on my homewold..."

"Yes?"

"We wirr be mallied!"

"What?!" exclaimed a startled Omega. Hsrs smiled, still a soft shade of blue.

"I knew you would be sulplised," he said. "I put togethel a cclcmony based on you' hory litings. We wirr be plopelry mated. At the foulth houl as it is leckoned in de Pelsan capitor, you wirr become my wife."

* * *

"Yeetoy!" Omega called as soon as the Premier departed, "are you there? Yeetoy?"

"Aa," the harem mistress appeared in the door. "O-may-gah iio?"

"Um...lessee," Omega concentrated. "I oughta be able to pick up this. Iio...aha! Do I need anything!" Omega smiled. "Maybe this blasted chip is good for something, after all. So... the answer would be..." Omega accessed Yeetoy's mind again, "iia—yes, I need something."

"Aa! Aa!" Yeetoy smiled and wrapped tentacle-fingers together in delight. "Ho?"

Ho—what. What do I need? "Well...hm. How do I tell her?" Omega pondered. "If she isn't thinking of the word, I can't pick it up. I guess I'm back to sign language."

The pretty, exotic lavender alien with the sweet temperament watched Omega in patient bemusement, seeming to realize that the Agent didn't know how to express her need.

Omega made several unsuccessful attempts to get her concept across. Finally, she pantomimed drawing a sword. Yeetoy looked startled.

"Oooshu?!" she exclaimed, and Omega read, *Slasher?!*

"Aa!" Omega answered, holding her hands about eight inches apart, to signify a knife.

"A. Ushu," came the reply: *Oh. Knife.*

"Aa, ushu."

"Hu?" *(Why?)*

Omega mimicked plunging a knife into her body. The light-purple alien paled to almost white, horrified.

"Ee, ee, ee! Hu? Hu?" *(No, no, no! Why? Why?)*

Omega sighed and sat on the edge of the sleep dais, motioning the harem mistress to join her.

"I sure hope I say this right. Yeetoy, Hsrs y Omega. Omega y Echo. Echo ee y Omega. Omega ee y Hsrs."

"Ee, ee, ee! O-may-gah yoyo ba!" Yeetoy replied. *(No, no, no! Omega is...)* Omega couldn't grasp the last concept. Yeetoy continued. "Aia. Yeetoy uya O-may-gah." *(It's all right. Yeetoy will help Omega.)*

"Yeetoy uya Omega—ushu," Omega answered. Yeetoy stopped, studying Omega intensely, and suddenly Omega realized Yeetoy was an empath, as she telepathically sensed her own heartbreak, despair, and determination—but NOT her THOUGHTS—reflected at her.

"...Aa," Yeetoy finally said at last with a sigh. "Yeetoy uya O-may-gah. Yeetoy agaaga uumph, o nee." But before she could say more, before Omega could even attempt to telepathically translate, a low-pitched tone sounded and the harem mistress stood and hurried away.

* * *

Yeetoy returned to the entrance of the harem, where the cultural attaché awaited. They exchanged a few words in Persan, then Yeetoy nodded, and the attaché departed.

Yeetoy watched her go, then smiled to herself and ducked into her private room off the harem foyer. She emerged a few minutes later, carefully arranging her robes to disguise the slight bulge that now showed in her belly. Then she went out the harem door.

* * *

Echo waited impatiently in the common area, pacing, as Alpha Two watched, disturbed. The door chime sounded, and Echo moved swiftly to answer it.

"Ah, Yeetoy," he greeted the harem mistress with a smile. "Eeyea ooloui sou?"

"Aa," she smiled, pulling back the robes and patting the bulge in her belly. "Aa."

Romeo and India stared, horrified.

"Echo," Romeo exclaimed, "what th' hell you doin'?!"

"What do you think I'm doing?" Echo turned to look at them with an odd expression.

India and Romco could only watch as Echo and Yeetoy entered Echo's bedroom together and closed the door.

* * *

Once inside the bedroom, Echo turned to Yeetoy with another smile, and held out his hands. Yeetoy's eyes crinkled, and she parted her robes—

—To reveal a surreptitiously-obtained packet of information and schematics, strapped to her belly.

Echo spread the documents out over the sleep dais, and he and Yeetoy bent over them.

* * *

Human male and Persan female pored over the documentation late into the night, pointing silently and occasionally conversing guardedly in Persan. Yeetoy glanced about nervously once, and Echo nodded.

"Aa, iau o iiiyi." *(Yes, we're being observed.)*

"A ee!" *(Oh no!)*

"Ee, ee, yayaya ee oloiyo suu." *(No, no, right now they can't tell what we're doing.)*

"Hu?" *(Why?)*

Echo pulled a small gold rod from his pocket; it was a portable electronic scrambler, such as Omega had used when guarding the U.S. President in Dallas, back in the summer. "Ea." *(This.)* He waved it around the room, in imitation of the sweep he had performed before she arrived. "Oio eeilay su, o laaa ai, ii iau ou." *(It won't go far, or last long, but it'll do.)*

"A. Yeetoy e Echoo. Echoo ue." Yeetoy smiled. "O-may-gah oy yuoiea." *(Oh. Yeetoy likes Echo. Echo is smart. Omega has good taste.)*

Echo grinned. "Iou." *(Thanks.)*

Yeetoy sighed then, and rubbed a tentacle over her eyes. Echo glanced at her, considering.

"Yeetoy eia?" *(Yeetoy tired?)*

"Aa. Laaa oom." *(Yes. Long day.)*

Echo moved the diagrams from one side of the dais, plumped some pillows, then gestured.

"Ouy. Aeiae." *(Here. Sleep.)*

"Aa," Yeetoy sighed, accepting the invitation.

Echo bent back over the charts as the alien woman fell fast asleep.

* * *

Echo glanced at his wrist chronometer, then quickly gathered up all of the charts and documents, tucking them out of sight. Then he swiftly peeled off jacket, tie, shirt, shoes, and socks, tossing them aside. He stretched out on the sleep dais near Yeetoy and closed his eyes.

Just as a soft hum came from the surveillance equipment hidden in the room.

* * *

"...Today's the day of the ceremony," India observed anxiously as the three Alpha Line Agents assembled in the common area of their suite, later that day. Three invitations lay on the table platform. "Less than four hours."

"I know," Echo said quietly, turning away. Romeo and India glanced at each other.

"Damn, Echo, you gotta do somethin', man," Romeo told the senior Agent.

"You're right," Echo said, heading decisively for his sleep room. "Get your gear together. We're blowing this joint."

"Now that's what I'm talkin' 'bout!" Romeo grinned, as he and India ran for their weapons. "Let's go get th' pretty lady!"

"No," Echo said, sticking his head through the door. "Pack your things. We're leaving." Romeo and India stopped dead, staring at Echo in horror. "There isn't time to explain," Echo snapped. "Do it!"

India and Romeo turned back to their bedroom, and moments later, a sullen Alpha Two emerged, duffel bags on their shoulders. Echo came out of his room, a bag on each arm.

"Here," Echo tossed both kits at them. "Take this with you." Romeo snagged one, then frowned.

"What's this?" India asked, catching the other bag.

"Meg's gear."

"Damn, man," Romeo expostulated, "you not even leavin' Meg her stuff?!"

Echo ignored the question.

"Can the two of you prep the ship for departure by yourselves?"

"Yes, Echo, we're almost ready for our pilot certification test," India confirmed, puzzled, "but what about you?"

"You two head for the ship, but keep your heads down. Don't let anybody see you. Meg and I'll be there soon." Echo adjusted the settings on his blaster. Alpha Two glanced at each other as Echo looked up.

"Did you really think I'd let the Premier have her?" he asked them quietly. "Do I seem that heartless? Romeo, you, at least, should know better."

"But...but even Meg..." India began. An expression of pain flashed through Echo's eyes.

"I know," he answered. "But it won't matter for long anyway."

And he was gone.

* * *

Romeo and India followed Echo's example, slipping from the cabin on the Persan flagship and making their swift, silent way to their own ship's docking port.

Once at the docking port, India pulled her cell phone and keyed in a stealth code. Seconds later, their saucer had circumvented the *Rtxrxs* security, opening the airlock hatch and beginning stage one checkout without any flagship systems being alerted. India and Romeo slipped inside, closing—but not locking—the outer airlock hatch.

"Ready?" Romeo asked his partner.

"Let's do it," India answered. "The rest of the family's on the way."

* * *

Echo appeared suddenly in Omega's lonely chamber.

Her acutely sensitive hearing caught a slight sound; she turned, to find Echo rooted to the floor, staring at her with dilated, dark eyes.

* * *

Omega had already been prepared for the ceremony with Hsrs. Her skin was satin-smooth and pale, her body covered only with a filmy, translucent drape, expressly chosen for her by Yeetoy, the harem mistress, because it perfectly matched the blue of her eyes. Omega's platinum hair was long and loose, brushed until it resembled spun silver. Her feet were unshod. Echo could see that she wore no makeup, yet her features were as beautifully defined as if a master of that art had worked his magic. *Dear God, she is utterly beautiful,* he thought.

Slender hands toyed with the exotic, multi-tipped blade that the sorrowful, but understanding, Yeetoy had managed to smuggle to Omega. Echo felt himself pale slightly as he saw the weapon and realized its import.

"Echo?" Omega whispered, studying his face. Echo stepped forward, reaching out and running fingertips lightly along the velvet cheek.

"Damn, Meg," he breathed, "if we had more time, I'd..." He tore his gaze from her face and glanced around. "Where's your Suit?"

"I don't know. They took it away from me," Omega replied.

"Shit. All your gear, too. How well can you maneuver in that thing?" Echo asked, gesturing at the toga-like drape clothing her.

"You'd be surprised how well I can 'maneuver' in this thing," Omega replied drily, and Echo raised an eyebrow.

"Okay, then," he murmured, "come on. Romeo and India have the ship waiting."

"Echo!" Omega dropped the knife and flung her arms around him.

"No time now, Meg," Echo replied, disentangling them, "much as I'd like to. Hold that thought for later. Right now, I've gotta get you out of here before we're caught, baby. Come on." He led the way toward the air vent that had been his route into the harem prep room.

"Wait a minute," Omega said, putting out a hand and halting him. "Now that you're here to help me, it may be simpler than that. Let me check the other side of the hall door. It's the one the Premier uses for his visits, and doesn't go through the harem." After a few seconds of intense concentration, she said, "Okay, the guards just left in a hurry. We've got a minute or two before replacements show up."

"What did you do? You sent 'em away?"

"Yep. Simultaneous bellyaches—or what passes for one, in their species."

"So to speak," Echo grinned. "Meg, you're wicked."

"I have a lot of inspiration," Omega retorted with a weary smile, as Echo swiftly 'picked' the electronic lock and they slipped into the ornately decorated corridor. "Where to? I haven't a clue where I am..."

"Um, lemme think. This way."

The two Agents, working as a team, flitted from corridor to corridor like shadows, maintaining silence, communicating mostly via gestures and only occasionally by telepathy. Omega functioned as a sensor, detecting any *Rtxrxs* crew and helping Echo avoid them. Echo, in turn, navigated unerringly through the ship, thanks to memorizing the schematics Yeetoy had slipped him.

As they neared the docking ports, their surroundings became rougher, dirtier. Omega abruptly fell behind; Echo heard a soft grunt and a sudden telepathic cry of pain, and spun.

Omega leaned against a bulkhead, face crumpled in pain, biting her lip and holding one bare foot in her hands. Blood seeped between her fingers.

Oh shit! Meg?! Echo responded mentally, and quickly moved back to her side.

Blast, blast, blast! Omega grumbled. *Mmh, that hurts.*

What happened? Echo bent to examine the wound.

No shoes. Sharp metal edge. End of story. It's not TOO deep, but it's long.

Okay. I got this. Echo tore a strip from the bottom of Omega's drape, being as quiet as he could, then removed his tie, using the two to swiftly bind up the wounded foot. *There. India can look at it later; it looks nasty, with all the dirt an' grease around.* He turned his back to her and bent slightly. *Climb on.*

What? Omega looked puzzled.

You can't walk on that, Meg. Climb on my back. I'm gonna carry you.

'Piggy-back,' huh? Why not just pick me up? Omega scrambled onto Echo's back with his assistance, then clung to Echo's shoulders. Echo hooked his arms under her legs and resumed moving forward.

Wrap your legs around my waist.

Why?

Do it, and I'll show you.

Omega complied, and Echo promptly released her legs.

There, he told her. *Arms-free carrying. A Meg backpack. Reach inside my jacket, under my right shoulder. Your principal blaster's there; they returned your weapons to me, at least. I think they assumed you were my porter or something.*

Omega slipped her hand into his jacket and retrieved her weapon, setting it and holding it ready.

Do you have yours, too? she asked him as they progressed.

Yup. The principal one, at least. Ready to go. Like always. The other one's in my kit, to make room for yours in my spare holster. Let's go.

Echo, STOP!

Echo froze. *What?!*

Just around the corner, Omega explained. *A whole slew of crewmen. We almost walked right into them.*

Damn. Directly between us and our saucer. Shit, I didn't wanna have to do this. Well, let's do it the hard way, then. Echo reached inside his jacket for his blaster. *You cover our tails. I'll punch a hole through.*

Wait a minute, Ace. What if we steal a scene from the Shadow?

Huh? Oh, I get it. The bit about 'clouding men's minds?'

You got it, Ace.

Do you think you can, angel-baby? How many of 'em have we got?

Mmm... Omega counted minds. *Eight.*

Shit. That's an awful lot of minds, hon'.

Yeah. But if we start shootin' at this point, we'll alert the whole ship and never get away.

True. All right, give it a shot, Echo agreed.

Okay. But you'll have to move exactly where I tell you, how I tell you, when I tell you. Otherwise, it won't work.

Happy to. Echo glanced over his shoulder at her. *How?*

Omega pondered for a moment, then ordered, *Echo, close your eyes.* Echo obeyed. *Now put out your left hand and touch the bulkhead seam right here.* She pointed. Unerringly, Echo's left hand traced the seam.

What the hell?! I saw that! Echo exclaimed.

No, you didn't, Omega told him. *I did. Do you trust me to 'see' for you, to help you move?*

No hesitation, baby.

Then keep your eyes closed, and we'll do it just like this.

Okay. You know, a while back I said I was curious about how you saw your world. Now I know.

And?

I think...it's a LITTLE more...detailed, maybe? Sharper; clearer. But not that different. Let's go. Echo kept his eyes closed, prepared to move at Omega's signal.

Okay, just a minute... Omega began to concentrate hard. *Ungh...mmph...aaaAAGH! THERE! Now go!*

Meg?!

GO, Echo! Now! Head between the two on the left...

* * *

The silent, ninja-like pair walked right through the cluster of crewmembers unnoticed; Alpha One might as well have been invisible. Once out of their sight, however, Echo felt Omega sag against his back as he opened his eyes. She laid her head on his shoulder, and he felt her grip on his shoulders and waist weaken. The blaster in her hand drooped.

"Echo, a little help here, please, honey," she breathed in his ear, and he quickly hooked his elbows under her legs to support her.

"I've gotcha, Meg," he murmured. "Wrap your arms around my neck, and just hang on the best you can, baby. We're almost there."

"The coast is clear," she whispered. "I checked just before I threw in the towel."

"Good." They rounded another corner. "Here's the hatch. It's unlocked, so India and Romeo are waiting inside. Watch your head." Omega tucked her head into Echo's neck as he bent slightly and entered the airlock hatch.

232

Moments later, the hatch was sealed, and all four Division One Agents were strapped in. The small saucer detached itself from the Persan flagship, activated a sensor-scrambling field, and darted away undetected.

* * *

"All right, we're away," Echo decided when they had been under way for over an hour. "Time for some explaining. Quick."

His three companions glanced shamefacedly at each other as India finished treating Omega's foot.

"Echo, man," Romeo volunteered hesitantly, "we misjudged you. Bad. We're...sorry."

"Echo, I—" Omega began simultaneously. Echo waved a hand, and they all hushed.

"I meant it was time for me to explain," Echo elaborated. "I don't have long, so just listen." The others exchanged glances again, then gave Echo their undivided attention. "The orders I got from the Ennead were unequivocal, highly classified, and in two parts. One was direct from the Ennead to me as Acting Director. Send Meg to the medlab—"

"For the implant," Omega added, and Echo nodded.

"Right, except I didn't know that at the time; and the second part came through Lord Adita, after he'd taken over as Director: meet the Premier and give him whatever he wanted. I had no idea he would want Meg."

"Oh, wow, Echo," Romeo remarked, "no wonder you kept tellin' us t' shut up. You musta been rackin' your brains tryin' ta come up with a way out."

"I was." Echo nodded again.

"But why didn't you 'tell' me?!" Omega cried.

"I tried to sorta tiptoe around the classification," Echo explained, "but you couldn't understand me with the damn implant. And the situation played right into your insecurity, which Zz'r'p hasn't had a chance to finish helping you with, thanks to this Persan mess coming up when it did, and it just made it that much harder."

"Insecurity? What insecurity?" Romeo demanded.

"Meg thinks of herself as an unlovable, alien thing," Echo said succinctly. "Because of the DNA. Especially after the little episode with Wright."

Romeo and India stared at Omega in astonishment.

"Is that what you were dealing with, why you got so depressed, Meg? Back before your birthday?" India asked.

"Partly," Omega whispered, nodding.

"Aw, damn, pretty lady," Romeo pulled a face. "DNA ain't no thang. Not t' any real man."

Omega merely stared at the deck.

"Why didn't you tell us, Echo?" India asked.

"Well, aside from the classification levels being higher than anything all three of you have got? Because I knew we were being monitored, so I didn't want to be too obvious." Echo shrugged. "I used the bug sweeper, but the bug sweeper wouldn't really handle that amount of surveillance equipment too well, and neither of you picked up on my signals." He paused. "Same thing with Meg. I couldn't be sure we weren't being telepathically monitored—especially after I discovered they did have empaths—so I tried to be a little...indirect, and trusted to Meg to pick up the undercurrents, like she usually does. But..."

"I didn't," Omega finished for him, subdued. "Not this time."

Romeo studied his department chief skeptically.

"So what about the alien chick? The purple babe with tentacles?"

"Yeetoy?" Echo asked. "She was the harem mistress, and an empath. She knew how Meg and I felt about each other, without our having to say. She took a liking to Meg, felt sorry for her, and came to me to help me get Meg out. She fed me plans of the ship, showed me how to get into the harem undetected; she practically handed me the escape plan I used. At some considerable risk to her own skin, I might add. If they realize where I got my information, she may still catch hell."

"Oh," Romeo replied quietly.

"So how'd you get around the order, Echo?" India was puzzled.

"I...didn't."

Three heads shot up.

"But...but, Echo...a direct order," Omega stammered. Echo sighed.

"I know, Meg. That's why I said I had to explain quick. They'll be sending an escort to arrest me as soon as the Premier reports you're missing."

"What's th' penalty?" Romeo murmured, stunned.

"Brain bleaching and expulsion from the Agency. A dishonorable discharge, in effect," Echo responded quietly, watching Omega. Her breath caught, and her face paled as the ramifications hit her. "I know, angel. From the minute the Premier decided he wanted you, I knew I'd lost you. I just made up my mind HE wasn't gonna get you. I'm...sorry." Echo turned away.

"Oh, no..." Omega whispered, fighting back tears.

"Junior, would you and India mind keeping up with things?" Echo asked the agonized Agents. "I'd like to...spend some time with Meg—while I still can."

"Of course," India murmured.

"Sure, Echo," Romeo replied quietly.

* * *

Echo headed for his sleep station, and Omega limped along behind him on her wounded foot, the diaphanous drape billowing softly about her ankles. When he reached the door, Echo paused. Without turning or looking back at her, he spoke.

"Meg...this isn't how either of us wanted it...but we won't have another chance. Will you—?" He laid his hand meaningfully on the sleep station door. Omega understood the request without the need of telepathy. Her eyes filled with tears again.

"But, Echo...you won't remember it. Won't remember me..."

Echo turned and looked down at her, his normally-impassive mask gone, replaced by a gentle, tender expression that Omega knew came from the core of his being. Then he took her chin in his hand and tilted her face up to meet his eyes.

"No," he said softly, "I won't. But you will. I'll make sure of that." With his other hand, he brushed away the tears that spilled down her cheeks. "And since they can't brain-bleach you, they can't take the memory away from you. One of us, at least, will remember. That's...enough."

Omega's eyes glowed with a sudden light.

"You're right, Echo," she murmured, "it IS enough."

* * *

Some time later, as Echo and a Suited Omega re-entered the flight deck, India and Romeo looked up with dread in their faces.

"Echo," India said, "we were just hailed by a Coalition escort vessel."

"They're here," Romeo added quietly.

Echo nodded wordlessly, then turned to his partner, Alpha Line's assistant department chief.

"Per the Sydys Concordat, Paragraph four-two-seven, six-eight-three, I am surrendering myself to the ranking PGLEIA agent." He pulled blasters and brain bleacher from his jacket and handed them to his partner, then reached into the small of his back and extracted his Winchester & Tesla, placing it in her hands. Omega swallowed with some difficulty, then nodded, accepting the items.

"Per the Sydys Concordat, Paragraph four-two-seven, six-eight-four, you are hereby considered..." Omega paused, then forced out the words, "under arrest, pending a hearing."

"Meg!" India exclaimed.

"You not even gonna try to get away?!" Romeo blurted. "India an' I been workin' on—"

"Be quiet, Romeo," Omega barked, looking at Echo. "That's...that's an order." Echo saw sudden understanding in her eyes, as she remembered his commands on board the *Rtxrxs*.

236

"But—"

"Romeo, please," Omega said, turning to Alpha Two with agonized eyes. "Let it be. Don't make this any harder than it already is. Especially...for Echo."

"Coalition ship hailing," India reported, subdued.

"On audio," Omega ordered.

"This is Ennead *Bellatrix* calling Division One *Helen of Troy*. Do you copy?"

"*Bellatrix*, this is Agent Omega, in command aboard the *Helen of Troy*. What do you require?" Omega responded, voice flat, expressionless.

"Agent Omega, you have been reported, as a member of the Persan Royal House of Hsrs, missing, possibly kidnapped. Do you wish to return?"

"Negative. I am not a member of that House. I was about to be made a member against my will. I emphatically do not wish to return. Please convey my regrets to Premier Hsrs, and tell him...tell him I'm sorry, but I wasn't cut out to be one of the wives of a Premier."

"...Understood. Very well. We will...convey the message. Agent Omega, do you have Agent Echo aboard your vessel?"

"Affirmative. He has surrendered voluntarily and is in my custody, pending a hearing," Omega replied mechanically, eyes closed. The others watched silently as she rubbed her temple in pain. Echo unconsciously mimicked the gesture, running a hand through his hair.

"Excellent. You will accompany us to the Aleancë System. Your director will meet you there."

"Wilco. *Helen of Troy* out."

* * *

"WHAT?!" Fox exclaimed, as he stared at the small video screen in Pulgey Entiyti's office; he and Suud had essentially commandeered the office by this point, in order to ensure that the Coalition president's business affairs remained safe— given the initial 'press release' on the assassination attempt, it was probable that the assassination attempt was also a coup attempt, in which case galactic secrets might be at risk. The fact it also allowed them secure communications access to almost anywhere in the Coalition was a side benefit. Lady Teela Krimnet of Kor, Entiyti's second in the Ennead and current Acting Chairbeing, stared back at him out of the screen. "How in the NAME of HaShem did THIS happen?! Echo is under arrest for insubordination and disobeying a direct Ennead order? But there WERE no Ennead orders when I left Earth! Is this about that Adita drek?"

"Yes—well, the orders he delivered. It was a high-priority matter that came down after you left, Fox," Lady Teela noted, the green humanoid face sad and tired. "We got your emergency communiqué that you were en route to help Pul, so it went to Echo in your stead." She shook her head. "We need you on Aleancë as fast as you can get here. Unless...I mean...is Pul...?"

"Pul is better," Fox averred, "but Taas, Suud and I are a long way from figuring out what happened. And until we do, and we round up the people behind the attack, Pul isn't gonna be safe. And you may not be, either."

"I have doubled my personal guard, and increased security all around, my friend. Can Pul get along with Suud, for now? Especially with Director Siisshiiss working alongside? Surely you have a significant guard on him by this time."

"...We do, and maybe. Let me talk to Suud and Pul."

"Do that, my friend," the Acting Ennead Chairbeing said. "Agent Echo is being brought here in restraints even as we speak."

"Oh, abdab," Fox whispered.

* * *

"Oh no, no, no, that doesn't sound like Echo!" Zebra exclaimed in distress as she tended her patient, while that patient and his other bodyguard listened intently, in shocked surprise. "Not at all! Something's wrong there, Fox. He's been set up, or framed, or...or something."

"I am strongly inclined to agree with your mate, Franz," Entiyti averred, though his voice was still weak. "Something is

238

not right, here. That does not sound like the Echo I have known for so very long."

"I am in agreement," Suud said simply. "That young man has proven himself everything you thought he was upon our first meeting him, Franz. And more, beside. I cannot think this is all there is to the story."

"And to that end, I think you MUST go to Aleancë at once," Entiyti decided. "Suud and most of his friends and family are here, keeping guard. You brought a small contingent of guards, as well. I have your mate and her superior tending me, as well as several other physicians, including my family healer. There are trusted Division Five agents all about. And I have my own staff of bodyguards."

"Which is not nearly as big as Suud and I have been telling you it needed to be, ever since you went back into the Ennead," Fox scolded.

"I know, I know," Entiyti sighed in contrition, his flexible black horns wilting against the silver-white scales of his head. "I have already given Sigrund instructions to begin rectifying that, with Suud's help in verifying the recruits' bona fides, as you would say."

"Good," Fox grumbled, gruff. "About damn time. Where's Yorker?"

"Oh, we sent him off to bed," Zebra observed. "He's been sitting with Pulgey, here, even when he was supposed to be off-duty, just in case of something."

"Ah. Commendation time when we get home?" Fox wondered.

"I'd think, yeah," Zebra agreed.

"How is Sigrund doing?" Fox continued the questions.

"He's doing all right," Zebra noted. "Granted, we had to keep him in the regen pod for a couple extra days, but the damage to his shoulder is all healed. He's still got some physical therapy to go through before he's at a hundred percent, but he won't lose any mobility or strength."

"That is excellent news," Suud decided. "He has been frustrated, I think, with the current LACK of mobility."

"It's coming; he's gotta give it time," Zebra declared. "The only reason we haven't tried it on Pulgey yet is because...well, because the biochemistry for it is a lot different on a reptilian than on a mammalian, and not having had to use it on a reptilian yet, we're not sure. We're game to try it, and Pulgey's given his approval, we just want to make sure we have it right before we dunk him, as Whiskey likes to put it. So Zarnix and I have been trying to reach Doron for DAYS, for advice and recommendations, but he's not on Edeptis, he's off-planet handling some system-wide pandemic elsewhere in the Coalition, and not even his own people can reach him right now."

"Ah, that would be the Valestia system," Entiyti murmured, adjusting his legs. "I remember that report from before I left Aleancë; I was the one who suggested they contact Doron for help."

"Yes, I think that was the one," Zebra confirmed. "We've been trying to locate him THERE, but nobody seems to quite know..."

"Well, as you say, meyn teyere, give it time," Fox decided, then he met his spouse's eyes and dropped into the covert signaling he had once taught protégé Echo, using their subtlest private codes. *Bubeleh, if you wait too long, does that not cause problems in the regeneration?*

Yeah, it does, honey, Zebra responded in kind, checking Entiyti's vitals as she coded. *If we wait too long, and it starts to heal over on its own, we can lose the window for regeneration. So we're trying to keep the wound...raw...but that increases the discomfort...and at a certain point, it's gonna start forcing the issue anyway, just given the way Draconan tissues heal.*

So...he could end up permanently maimed?

Yes.

Damnation.

Exactly.

They were silent for several moments, as an uncomfortable Entiyti tried to shift position in bed. Suud and Zebra immediately began to assist him in repositioning himself.

"Ohhh, I think it's time for somebody's pain meds," Zebra decided, checking her wrist chronometer. "Yup, that's what I thought. Hang on a sec, Pulgey, and I'll take care of that."

"I am fine, my dear girl."

"I'll be the judge of that, Pulgey," Zebra said with a smirk, then addressed her spouse again. "Back to our original discussion. Fox, hon, you know I'll miss you, but I gotta think Pulgey's right. You need to go see about Echo. And Omega, too, probably; I'd be pulling my hair out, if I was her, right now."

"Oh, gronk," Fox groaned, smearing his hand down his face. "And her still trying to get used to the idea that they're in a relationship, and the Ennead about to jerk the rug out from under said relationship..."

"What?" Entiyti said, trying to sit upright; Zebra smacked his good shoulder, and he settled back down into the bed. "Are Omega and Echo...?"

"They're engaged to be married," Fox said with a grin. "You got the petition to change the Agency charter before this whole kappore went down, right?"

"Well, yes, but..." He shook his head. "I know you said you wanted to see them married off, but I did not realize they already...I thought you meant you were still playing matchmaker..."

"Didn't you look at the names on the petition?"

"Um," Entiyti hummed, dropping his eyes, as his horns crossed in embarrassment. "I saw you and Zebra on it at the top, and...well, I am afraid I did not look much farther, my old friend. I set it as the Ennead's top priority, effective immediately, barring no emergency proceedings."

"Aw," Zebra murmured, touched. Fox felt warmth spread through his being.

"What she said," he affirmed, voice even gruffer than before. "But yes, the other names on the petition were Romeo and India, the Alpha Two team...because they're the backup team to Alpha One, as well as India being the department medic, and Romeo being the number three in their command line... and Echo and Omega, the Alpha Line chief and assistant chief, never mind my second and his second. Quite a prestigious group of petitioners, if you ask me. But...it's been a rocky courtship with Alpha One, because of the whole mess that's been going down around them of late, plus..." Fox shrugged. "The entire business with what Slug did to Omega has created a bit of a psychic obstacle course from what I've gathered, talking to Echo."

"She's getting a little counseling, especially after that crazy Deltiri went after 'em and messed with her head, a couple weeks back," Zebra added. "You were still under a lot of fairly strong pain medication when we discussed that, so you might not remember it."

"Oh," Entiyti murmured. "Yes, that vaguely rings a bell. And I remember reading the report about the Deltiri...in a theatre, was it not?"

"Right. Never mind the whole 'forced mating' thing that Slug left behind for her. Thank HaShem that one failed," Fox added.

"Yeah—only by making her think Echo died, first," Zebra retorted. Entiyti winced.

"Oh, poor child. But it worked?" the Draconan asked.

"It did," Zebra explained. "Because Mark Wright—the guy Slug intended as Omega's mate, to rear a whole new generation of Echo-killers—see, his mental programming didn't have a back door we could use, like Meg's did. And it was predicated on Echo still being alive, to require this last-ditch plan. AND he was telepathically linked to Meg, and she couldn't block him completely. So once we figured out that whatever she knew, he knew, we convinced her that Echo was dead...and Wright's programming switched itself off."

"And we were waiting for that very thing," Fox tag-teamed. "We got him deprogrammed, threw him in a regen pod and reverted him to baseline human, then brain-bleached him and sent him home."

"End of story," Zebra said, "except for the mental and emotional stress that it caused to Meg. THAT was when the mentally-ill Deltiri caught her off guard and inserted ANOTHER telepathic program, which dogpiled the stress, and..." She sighed.

"It's been...difficult," Fox agreed. "But I really think our girl has come through the worst, and is out the other side, and improving."

"She sure made it hard on Echo, there, though," Zebra pointed out. "With him trying as hard as he knew how to convince her he loved her, and that damn programming telling her she was unlovable and worthless."

"Aw," Entiyti murmured. "Poor children."

"Yes, but Echo proposed a few days ago, and Omega accepted," Fox informed the injured Draconan. "They looked to be very happy...FINALLY. And now...this."

"Go, Franz," Entiyti added, voice soft. "They are your children; I see it in your eyes. And in this room you have your brothers in all but blood, and your own mate. That makes them our niece and nephew, and Zebra's..."

"Stepchildren, we decided, after Echo's mom went to work for us," Zebra interjected.

"Very good, then. And we are all three in agreement—this is what you need to do. If anyone can save them from this situation, it is you."

Fox drew a deep breath.

"Pul...you realize, don't you, that if I leave, and this doesn't go the way we hope it will, I won't be coming back? At least, not to work for you again? Maybe ever?" he pointed out.

"Wh-what?" the injured galactic leader stammered, taken off guard. "Why?"

"Because Echo is my chosen, duly approved and appointed successor," Fox reminded him. "If he is brain-bleached and ejected from the organization, I no longer have anyone ready to step into my shoes. And there is no one else who is even close to being able to do so. It will take years, possibly decades, to adequately train anyone else.”

“Aw, gronk,” Zebra grumbled under her breath. “Yeah.”

“Well, sssllltth ssshhiissh ttthhssiiss asssshh hiiisss geessht!” Entiyti cursed, dropping back into his native language. “That simply adds another layer of disappointment on top of everything.”

“I know,” Fox sighed. “Never mind the fact that it will lose me my oldest living human friend. I know. None of you are especially used to seeing me upset, because I learned very early in my life—in the concentration camp, as a boy—to hide most strong emotion; it caused fewer problems, that way, and drew less attention to me. Even Zebra does not see the true depth of my emotion; after so many years, it is...difficult...for me to completely drop the façade.” Abruptly Fox’s face contorted in implacable fury, and he flushed deeply as he gave full vent to his rage. “But DAMMIT if I am going to stand by and just WATCH while attempts are made to take two of my three oldest friends in the whole of the bloody damn UNIVERSE from me, in a matter of days!”

The other three fell silent in the face of Fox’s burning wrath. Finally his spouse ventured a comment.

“What are you gonna do, honey?” Zebra wondered, worried.

“I don’t know yet,” Fox admitted, having already regained control. “I don’t have nearly enough information. So the first thing I have to do is find out exactly what’s going on. THEN I can take action.”

“Then GO, Franz,” Entiyti said immediately. “Go, find out what is happening, and save Echo, even as you and yours are helping to save me.”

“But I do not think he should go alone,” Suud spoke up just then.

“What? Why not?” Fox wondered. “I’ll travel faster that way...”

“Because you bring up an excellent consideration, brother Franz. YOU are the proper Division One Director,” Suud pointed out. "We do not yet know WHY Pulgey was attacked. And now Echo, the Acting Director for Division One in YOUR stead, YOUR deputy and successor, has become embroiled in an accusation that does not sound right, that does not match his personal history, does not match HIM as we know him, and which effectively removes him from leading the division in your stead. As you say, two of your oldest friends...but also connected, by power, position, and status. As well connected by a significant number of the assassins on the transfer station. If someone is after the Coalition leadership—or even just a portion thereof," the Reptoid indicated the beings in the room, "you may well be on their list, as well. Remember, interrogation of several of the captured assassins revealed they had a vendetta against you and Alpha Line, Alpha One specifically."

Zebra stifled a gasp and paled.

"Okay, now I gotta agree with Suud," she murmured. "Maybe you DON'T need to go."

"No, no, sister Zebra," Suud soothed. "He does need to go, just not alone. And I think I may have a solution which will... what was that old expression of yours, Franz? Ah. 'Kill two fowl with one stone.'"

"And that would be?" Entiyti wondered.

"My eldest son Duuniiss hankers for something useful to do, to help us in this situation," Suud reminded them. "And he is mourning Uussa; he spends far too much time 'moping,' as Zebra put it the other day. Never mind his military training and experience. This will give him something useful to do, which will get his mind off his loss—at least to a point, I suppose—while also providing Franz with a very loyal, skilled bodyguard of his own."

Zebra, Fox, and Entiyti exchanged surprised glances.

"I think it'll work," Fox decided.

* * *

In the wake of Fox's departure, Entiyti grew thoughtful.

"What's up, Pulgey?" Zebra wondered. "That face of yours has an intriguing expression on it."

245

"Oh, it is nothing much," Entiyti replied with a shrug. "I was just pitying whoever is responsible for Echo's predicament."

"Huh? Don't you mean you feel sorry for Echo and Meg?" Zebra wondered, puzzled, even as Suud nodded his understanding.

"No, dear girl," Entiyti said, offering her a rueful grin. "How many times have you ever seen Franz lose his temper?"

"Oh, I've seen him plenty mad before."

"No, no. Not merely angry. How many times have you ever seen him LOSE his temper? Lose it sufficient to shout, as he just did? To flush and turn red in the face?"

"Um, well, just the once, I guess," Zebra decided, thinking back. "Just now. Fox doesn't LOSE his temper."

"Yes, he does," Suud averred, "but it takes something very, VERY serious to cause it. That was only the third, maybe fourth, time I have ever seen it, in all the octads I have known him."

"And woe betide to whoever caused it to happen, in our experience," Entiyti added, gesturing to Suud and himself. "They usually did not survive the incident."

"Oh," Zebra said in a small voice, suddenly grasping where they were going.

"Now you are catching on, my dear Zoë," Entiyti said with a wolfish grin. "These fools have angered, truly angered, our desert fox—for they threaten the one thing that means more to him than any other in this life, the one thing that has been taken from him once before: his family. And mark me well—there WILL be retribution."

Chapter 10

The pair of sentients, one human, one Reptoid, boarded the interstellar shuttle *Exodus* together, small kits tucked under their arms.

"Captain Prrt, do you have a course for Aleancë laid in?" Fox asked; in truth, the *Exodus* had two 'captains,' really pilots, since the *Exodus* was attached to the *Genesis*, and therefore had no true captain—Fox was the commanding officer over all. That said, the pilot functioned as the captain when the *Exodus* was free-flying, so Fox tended to offer the courtesy.

"I do, Admiral Director, sir," the Bastian female noted, having relieved Du'ven'de from the previous shift, some hours prior. "If you and your bodyguard would take seats and strap in, we can be off in a matter of moments."

* * *

Emdali and Aleancë were relatively close systems, galactically-speaking, and it required only a couple of hours to traverse the distance at emergency speeds. Soon Duuniiss was escorting the Director, his adoptive uncle, to the secure facility where Echo was being held.

"I'm sorry, sir," the guard, an exceptionally large Ergisol whose name tag read, 'Darg,' said to Fox. "You have clearance, Lord Levy; your bodyguard does not. You should be safe inside, however. This is the maximum-security facility." The Ergisol, an eight-foot-tall beetle-like creature, clacked his mandibles in dismay. "I have known Echo too many years to think he'll attack YOU. Or anybody but a perp. I cannot believe you are here for the reason you are. I really..." The guard broke off, straightening his stance...and his determination, Fox adjudged. "Your bodyguard can wait with me, sir."

Fox and Duuniiss exchanged a glance; Duuniiss nodded, and Fox continued on.

* * *

"Dammit, Echo, what the hell were you thinking?!" Fox rebuked the imprisoned head of the Alpha Line department and his intended successor, as he finally entered the small cell at the end of a very long, very empty corridor.

Echo sat on one end of a small cot, slumped in what looked to Fox like an uncharacteristic despair, elbows on knees, face in his hands. Omega knelt beside him, one arm around his shoulders, face pressed close to his, murmuring in his ear, apparently attempting to encourage him. India and Romeo sat in visitors' chairs nearby, watching the tableau. All four Agents jumped, startled, as Fox barged through the door without preamble.

"Fox! What are you doing here?" Echo wondered, obviously startled, as Omega pulled away, straightening her Suit jacket. They all rose to attention, but Fox waved them back to their seats; Omega chose to sit beside her partner on the bedside, rather than kneel beside him or take a chair.

"Pulgey sent me to see what the hell is going on," Fox declared. "I got the meshuginah notice that you four were being sent off by the Ennead on a classified mission a few days ago, then that you'd been arrested, mere hours ago."

"Is he better? Pulgey?"

"A little bit better, yes. Still not well—not at all. And he may not ever be...as good as he was, before. But he and I both felt he was far enough out of the woods that your situation took priority. Besides, Suud is still there, guarding him and trying to work out who attacked him. As well as what you'd term a shit-ton of other trustworthy guards." Fox gazed at his designated successor. "Now you lot tell me what's happened, and why you're being charged with the maximum levels of insubordination."

Echo sighed, as Omega and the others gathered in a tight knot around the beleaguered Agent.

"Sit down, Boss," he told the Director of Division One, pointing at the remaining visitor's chair. "This one looks like taking a while."

* * *

"So what in the Name were you thinking, zun, to disobey a direct order like that? Several, by the sound of it, and given the orders I left myself," Fox demanded, putting his fists on his hips. He never had taken the chair Echo offered, preferring to pace, to vent some of the anger he was still trying hard to control.

"That I wasn't going to let Meg be treated like an object, to be used—maybe killed —for one night of pleasure for the Premier," Echo replied curtly, his face darkening as he flushed in anger of his own.

"What?!" Fox actually took a step backward, in shock. His hands came off his waist, floating upward, almost into a defensive posture, as the full measure of what his deputy had said hit home.

"Fox, didn't they tell you what this was all about?" Omega asked the Director as she scooted closer to Echo on the cell cot.

"They told me Echo disobeyed a direct order to humor the Premier, and risked war in so doing. They had to do a diplomatic tap-dance to avert hostilities. And what you've just told me didn't contradict any of that."

"He disobeyed orders in an effort to keep the Premier from making me part of his harem!" Omega declared.

Fox stared at Omega, then—finally—calmly sat down in the chair across from Echo in the cell.

"Oy vey. Clearly there's far more here than I've been told," he understated. "All right. Go on, Omega. Your life was in jeopardy, as well, I gather, based on Echo's earlier remark?"

"Fox," India interrupted, "first off, the Premier looks a lot like a giant octopus. Anatomy appropriate to the form, except even more arms. And let's just say his sexual preferences aren't...human norms. Not anywhere close. I've seen some anime stuff that was...disturbing, but...damn." She paused, shaking her head. "Both ROMEO AND I would have been in the same boat, except Romeo wasn't bound by any orders,

249

and protested. When the Premier found that both of us were Agents, and Romeo and I were already...spoken for, mated to each other, he wasn't interested."

"Never mind all that now," Echo said impatiently. "Fox, what's important is that Meg found out that one of the Council members has been collaborating with the Persans, feeding Hsrs information."

Fox sat up straighter.

"Who?"

Ari N'Do, of Celro, Omega confirmed silently, raising a hard mental block around the five Division One Agents as she informed them telepathically, thereby guarding against being overheard in any fashion. *He's secretly given the Premier inside information and fed him special instructions. Exactly what, I don't know. Hsrs's thought processes are...kind of different from what I'm used to, and it was sort of difficult to figure them out. Okay, it was a LOT difficult. But I'm sure of it. He shouldn't even be AWARE of N'Do, let alone have the familiarity I picked up on.*

"Well, well," Fox murmured aloud. "Interesting. Let me see what I can make of that. Meanwhile, Omega, would you mind taking Alpha Two and allowing me some time to talk to your partner, here? We need to try to develop some legal strategy."

"Sure, Fox," Omega said, very subdued, as she led India and Romeo out of the small force cell. Fox reached out and laid a hand lightly on her shoulder as she passed.

"Omega, we're going to do everything we can to get him out of this."

"I know," she murmured, still subdued. "Thanks, Fox."

* * *

Once the force door closed behind them, Fox turned back to Echo.

"I gather the orders were classified?"

"At the highest levels, Boss. But you're at that level. I was, ONLY by dint of being Acting Director." He shook his head.

250

"If you had still been there, I wouldn't have known as much as I did. Even as your second, I wouldn't have been included in the classification. It was that damn tight."

"All right, zun, give me the order's details," he demanded.

* * *

While Fox was getting the full details, guards came and led Echo to an interrogation room, where he was left with Fox and a Deltiri interrogator.

"Director Fox, sir," the Deltiri said, "if you would not mind, we have our protocols..."

"And I'm not supposed to be here during the interrogation," Fox noted.

"Precisely, sir. I will notify you so you may come back once we are finished, certainly."

"In that case, I think I'll go check on my other Agents," Fox said. "Hang in there, Echo, zun. We'll get this worked out."

"If you say so, Fox," Echo sighed, as the older human left the interrogation room.

* * *

"Oh, that's good information to have, then," Omega decided, when Fox found her and told her about the interrogation, mere moments later. "Hang on a second, Fox, while I do something..."

"Hanging on, tekhter," Fox agreed, trusting his Agent fully, while Omega concentrated, her eyes closed, for several minutes. When she opened her eyes and focused on him again, he asked, "What was that all about, if I may?"

"Aw, I put up a little bit of a disguised telepathic block around some of Echo's psyche," Omega admitted, frowning. "I didn't want the interrogator stumbling across Echo's memories an' stuff of how we're hoping to circumvent this mess."

"Ah. And that is handled?"

"Yeah, it is now."

"Good. Then may I ask YOU a few questions?"

"Sure, Fox, I guess so. I'll do my best to answer what I know, anyway."

"Excellent..."

* * *

"Shit, merde, gl'ag'a'dr'b, abdab, and gronk! I can't believe...what the hell was the Ennead thinking?! It's meshuginah!" Fox ranted, when Echo had finished being interrogated and the Director could return to finish their aborted discussion. "And why did you even go along with it, zun?"

"I DIDN'T go along with the whole implant thing, Fox," Echo said, impassive. "The medic on duty that day was a new recruit; Whiskey was off-duty, I gathered getting some errands done, and was out of pocket. And what with Zarnix AND Zebra gone, evidently the new guy got some sort of direct orders from the Ennead. And the Ennead representative had him bring in a shit-ton of orderlies! THEN he ordered 'em to take Meg down and hold her while the medic performed the operation! I ordered 'em to stop, but this Lord Adita dude overruled me. And even if the medlab personnel had refused to perform the ordered procedure, Adita brought along physicians and guards of his own, and they weren't taking no for an answer, even from ME."

"Even despite the fact that you were nominally in charge of the whole Division, as my deputy?"

"Even despite that," Echo averred. "Because Adita was usurping the whole ball of wax, overriding everybody. Had you been there, he'd have overridden you, too—he told me so, at one point. If Zz'r'p hadn't already been present—because of the implant being Deltiri make—and pitched what Madrid woulda called 'a right royal fit,' to include one of his telepathic biosystems lock-ups, I'm not sure what would have happened, but Meg and I were getting ready to go full-blown, all-out Alpha Line on their asses."

"Oy vey," Fox whispered, shocked at the revelation, and its ramifications. "Somebody would have died."

"Probably," Echo admitted. "A few of the orderlies got hurt, as it was. And given that Adita's guards had weapons—and they weren't stun guns—it mighta been us. But they weren't leaving us any choice, Fox! Damn, you should have heard Meg scream. She had a flashback, I'd lay money on it. Lots of money. Like, everything I've got." He broke off, shaking his head, patently deeply upset. "They were getting ready to forcibly modify Meg, whether she wanted it or not! That's no better than what Slug did to her!"

"No, it's not, and I fully intend to have some serious and very heated words with any and all appropriate members of the Medical Department when I return, never mind the Ennead," a grim Fox agreed. "I expect some medical staff are going to end up in Confinement, if not brain-bleached and ejected from the Agency. But you shouldn't have been able to go on the mission anyway. You were the acting Director."

"Not once Adita showed on the scene," Echo pointed out. "Like I said, he pretty much usurped my authority from the get-go. He showed up with Ennead orders and assumed control of everything. He basically took over running the entire Division. Once I could get to your office after the whole debacle in the medlab, I DID call the Ennead point of contact, and verify Adita's authority, but they told me the orders he had were legitimate, and I was required to follow them to the letter."

"Shit, merde, abdab and gronk!" Fox cursed again, using the shorter variant of his favorite multi-lingual invective. "Is he still there? In charge, I mean?"

* * *

"I have no idea," Echo admitted. "If he's not, then there's nobody guarding the hen house. I've had my hands full." He waved his hands about the cell, invoking the entire scenario. "And I haven't been back anywhere near Earth since we left on the first contact mission."

Fox muttered something under his breath; Echo thought it sounded vicious, and he sincerely hoped his old friend wasn't mad at him. Given the situation, and the way it had been handled, there had been little else Echo could have done, at least that he could see. Just then, Fox looked up and caught his expression; the Director shook his head.

253

"No, zun, I'm not angry at you. The situation? Oh HELL yes. You? No."

"Good. I kinda wasn't left with much choice. They boxed me in, and any attempt to do anything different from what I did woulda just landed me here even quicker."

"I see that. But why did you go along with the meeting with the Persis Federation, to begin with? Especially the orders to...well, I guess it really wasn't that different from most first contact orders, was it?" Fox admitted, considering the matter more deeply.

"No, not really," Echo confirmed. "I mean, you figure a system leader would ask for trade relations, or technology exchange, or something like that—NOT a sentient being, let alone my partner, for a damn sex slave! Even the Cortians weren't stupid enough to be OPEN about it, and they were sla- vers! So I only realized what the ramifications were gonna be when the Premier decided to claim Meg, Romeo, and India for his harem."

"Romeo and India too?!"

"Yeah, but that all went down differently for them. See, Romeo didn't get those orders."

"Ah, wait, wait—I do remember India saying something about that, now you mention it. All right; I think I get it now, zun. And since Romeo didn't have the same orders you did, he was able to declare himself and claim India as his mate, which took them both out of the 'available' category..."

* * *

"Right. But I couldn't say anything, or I'd have been in direct violation of orders from the get-go." Echo sighed. "It scared Meg pretty bad, and seriously upset her. She thought... she thought I was dumping her, that I was gonna just...let him rape her and kill her." He raked a hand up his face and into his hair, perturbed.

"Why in the name of Heaven would she think such a thing?"

"Because she has this notion that nobody can love her like that!" Echo exclaimed.

"Haven't you told her that YOU love her like that?"

"YES!"

"But she doesn't believe you?" Fox was astounded.

* * *

"Evidently not! I mean, sometimes she does, but...if anything happens, well, like this, then she...she kinda reverts, and..." Echo sighed. "Dammit, Fox, I just wish she would let me in," he complained. "If she would, she'd KNOW I'm crazy about her. But she's so convinced what Slug did to her left her unlovable, she won't give me a chance! I think it's kind of a knee-jerk thing, but I can't seem to figure out how to bypass it. And it's been especially bad, after...well, after Wright, and then Tt'l'k, and all that shit that just happened. I keep thinkin' we got it licked, her and me. But it seems like every time I turn around, she's viewing my reactions through her own filters, and assuming I don't care, as a result." He shook his head, hurt. "I've probably just thrown away my career, and for that matter, the way of life I know and love, because I love her MORE— too much to leave her to die at the Premier's tentacles!"

"Calm down, zun, I know. Do you know what you're going to do to get out of this mess?"

"Maybe. If it works. Meg and I cooked up a plan, but..." He shrugged. "There's no way to test it until it actually goes down."

"All right. So you know she's here, you know she's all right, and you're still talking to each other?"

"Yeah. I think...I think it's okay again. At least until next time." Echo sighed again. "I only wish I knew what to do to stop there BEING a next time. Of course," he noted, more dejected than Fox had ever seen him, even after the boy Echo had been co-opted into the Agency, "it may all be moot now..."

* * *

"Echo," Fox began, hesitant and not entirely sure he truly wanted to discuss the matter, but feeling obligated for the couple he had come to think of as his own children, "has Omega told you WHY she feels unlovable?"

"Not...really."

"Then do you want me to tell you what I suspect to be the problem? You may not like it."

"I'll take whatever info I can get to help me work things out with her. Assuming we have a future to work out, given I'm in jail and may get brain-bleached back into diapers. And your suspicions are better than some peoples' supposed facts."

"All right, then. Let me see. Where to start? Ah. You'll be aware that she's had genetic recombination from multiple other sentient being 'donors,'" Fox quirked his fingers around the word, "because you two discovered that last Halloween..."

"Right. And I know it bugs her, but..."

"Hush, son, and let me finish—because that's not the part that bothers her."

"It's not?" Echo stared at Fox in surprised bewilderment.

"No. Well, it does, but it's not the worst part. The part that really bothers her, ESPECIALLY after the, uh, the 'forced breeding' attempt we had to deal with a few weeks ago, is the fact that I'm well better than 99% certain Slug ALSO spliced in genetics from NON-sentients...which is probably one way he got the whole 'forced breeding' thing to work, to begin with."

* * *

"Okay, I mean...wait," Echo broke off, as understanding slammed into his brain. "You're saying...Slug spliced..."

"Animal genes into her; yes, Echo, that's precisely what I'm saying. Not from Earth, granted, but animals all the same. And then forced their expression."

"Well, but that's not really...I mean, even standard Earth medicine uses things like pig hearts for transplants, and animal organs to fill in until a human one becomes available, an' shit."

"If that were all, then you'd be right," Fox agreed. "But that wasn't what Slug did, wasn't what he was trying to do."

"What, then?"

"This is going to be hard to hear, zun, so steel yourself."

"I already did, when you first started talking, Fox. TELL me."

"Good; be patient, I'm getting there. Now, I've discussed my suspicions with a couple of others, subject-matter experts, let us say, and they believe I'm likely right. So. As best I can figure, on a very fundamental level, what Slug was attempting was to create a 'customized,' controllable ANIMAL...with Omega's intellect. Not a human, not a sentient being. An animal. He started with a human, and...tried to degrade that human into a...beast. A killing machine. Something lower than even a feral human. Something that LOOKED human, that he could control and manipulate. Think, uh...oh. You like reading Tolkien, right?"

"Yeah," Echo averred, not sure where that remark was going, but sure he wasn't going to like it.

"Do you remember how Tolkien said orcs were made, in Middle Earth? Like that." Fox broke off momentarily as Echo stared at him in horror. "And she knows this now. She KNOWS, zun. Since...since at least last Halloween, I think. Mind, I have NOT seen her medical records on this matter, so I'm not speaking to this situation with anything like that level of authority; those records are private, and not even I have a need to know on THAT, unless something comes up pertaining directly to it. And even then, Omega would have to approve it through Zebra or Zarnix."

"How did you figure it out, then?" Echo wanted to know. "And how long have you suspected it?"

"Since...last Halloween, more or less. Though I admit, the full ramifications didn't really hit me until the whole farshtinkener balegan with Wright went down. See, I had to have enough of the genetics reports on what the medlab found, that I could re-open all those cold cases and solve them, Echo," Fox explained. "And I've been around the galaxy a few times, so I sort of read between the lines of what Zebra wasn't telling me, and of the data I wasn't provided, and after a while for it to percolate in my brain, I extrapolated the rest. I didn't mean to; it rather hit me all at once. See, there were something like a dozen or better different individual species identified, but only about half, maybe two-thirds, of those could be linked to cold cases. That left around a third to half of the species that had nothing to do with cold cases..."

"And therefore were not sentients," Echo said, understanding. "I get it now. Aw, poor Meg; I totally get how that woulda made her feel, 'cause I'd probably have reacted the same way. And that musta been what upset her so badly that night once we got home from that damn world-wide treasure hunt of a mission, after she got back from the medlab. I remember she only ate around half of what I expected her to eat, after winding up so strenuous and long a mission. And we'd planned a private chat, 'cause she'd asked for one, but then suddenly she didn't feel like talking..."

* * *

"That makes sense," Fox agreed. "I'm betting...see, that was around the time I began to realize there might be more than a standard partnership to your relationship, just from watching the two of you interact. And I suspected she'd picked up on that already...but you hadn't."

"Oh." Echo flushed. "I guess I can be kinda thick about stuff like that, after all."

"Hush, zun. Don't put yourself down like that. You had other things on your mind, and you were still recovering from a failed relationship of your own."

"Well, yeah, but...never mind. Keep going."

Fox shook his head and sighed.

"All right. Zun, I'd be willing to lay money that she asked for that chat because she wanted to discuss the possibility of a future with you, to get your take on it, your reaction to the idea...until she saw the genetic studies and realized the ramifications. ALL the ramifications. And she broke off having that conversation, because her innate sense of fairness meant she'd have to tell you 'what you were getting into,' as she would put it...but she couldn't bring herself to. She would have felt... horrified, utterly humiliated, ashamed..." He paused, and Echo gaped at him in shock.

258

"Aw, damn," the younger man finally murmured, wincing in sympathetic pain. "That...makes a helluva lotta sense, Fox."

"I thought so," Fox agreed. "So...how DO you feel about all that, zun?"

"How...am I supposed to feel about it?" a thoughtful Echo wondered. "I guess I see where Meg's comin' from, now. And I hurt for her, because like I said, it'd make me react pretty much the same way, I expect. But I don't see what it's got to do with the way I feel."

"It doesn't change your perception of her as a person? Doesn't make you view her as...LESS of a person? Because Slug intended her for an animal? Intended her for a twisted, degraded, depraved excuse for a human? A ravening, soulless beast, willing to kill even the person she was closest to?"

"Hell, no," Echo expostulated, angry at the very idea. "She isn't ANY of those things! What she IS, is intelligent, beautiful, quick-witted, strong, fun to be around an' with a wicked sense of humor, tough when she needs to be, tender when she wants to be—! Besides, I love Meg because of WHO she is, not what she may—or may not—be! I swear to you, Fox, on everything I hold dear, it doesn't change my opinion of my baby at all. She could, I dunno, start growing a tail on her ass tomorrow or something, and I wouldn't care! If she didn't want it, I'd help her find a way to have it medically removed. If it turned out she liked it, we'd make it work. If it turned out to be prehensile or something, I'd be brainstorming ways to use it in the field, and tryin' to help her learn to shoot a blaster with it!" Echo grinned, but Fox could see the sincerity in the younger man's eyes, as well as the love and esteem he held for his partner. "She could morph into a Grendel right this instant, and I'd still love her. As long as it didn't affect anything, uh, in the bedroom, you know, it wouldn't stop me at all. Hell, if it DID affect things in the bedroom, if it turned out we weren't compatible that way at all, I'd still find a way to ensure she enjoyed our intimate time."

"I didn't think you two had started..." Fox began, and Echo flushed.

"Well, I know you said you were gonna update the partnership, but I figured you probably never had the chance, once Pulgey got attacked. One of the first things I did the next morning after you left was to check the Alpha One status, and I confirmed you hadn't had time. So I planned on filing the life partnership paperwork myself when we got back from this first contact thing," Echo admitted, "then maybe running down to the chapel and having Father Papa do a little private religious ceremony for us. Not that it'd be official or anything, but I think it would make Meg feel better. Both of us, if I'm honest. I wanted to do it right, with her...and FOR her." His shoulders slumped. "I guess we'll have to wait and see what happens. But yeah, Meg was a little shy on that sort of thing."

Fox noted the use of past tense, and given the intimations Echo had given him earlier, during the explanation of recent events, he suspected he knew what the pair had planned to try to save Echo. He also knew that, given what he knew of the technique, certain things were apt to occur. But he decided to say nothing; the situation was delicate enough without adding embarrassment—and in Omega's case, possibly some moral and religious guilt, given her upbringing and beliefs—into the equation, if he were correct in his suspicions.

Which I may NOT be, this time, he realized. *As strong as those two are mentally, and as short a time as they had to accomplish what needed doing? I might be all wet about this one. I'll probably never know. And that's as it should be. Now for... the other thing. Oy.*

"All right, zun," he said. "Then I suppose it's time for me to confess something."

* * *

Echo's eyebrows shot up at that statement. Unwanted suspicion shot through him. *Damn, but I hope he's not trying to pump me for information to use against me at my own trial,* he thought.

"No, no, never that," Fox said, apparently having read Echo's expression sufficient to interpret it. "No. I'm on your side, zun. But I AM acting for someone else."

"Who?" Echo said, the unpleasant suspicion still lurking in his mind.

"Your partner," Fox said, voice soft. "Everything I told you just now was true, except for one thing: About ten minutes before I came back in here to finish talking to you, she confirmed it all. She's tried to tell you several times, but couldn't bring herself to do it. So she asked me to do it. She wanted..." Fox drew a deep breath, then sighed. "Like I indicated earlier, she figured she owed it to you 'to know what you were getting,' as she phrased it, before it got as far as a permanent, officially-designated relationship. She just couldn't choke it out to you herself."

"Wait," Echo said, pain shooting through him again. "She could tell you, but...she couldn't tell me?"

"I didn't say she told me, alter khaver," Fox pointed out. "I said she CONFIRMED it."

"Oh. So you told her your suspicions," Echo surmised, "and she...probably just nodded."

"That's exactly what happened. And...forgive me, but... she's been listening in, and talking in my ear, in case she needed to provide additional input, while I explained it to you. Which she did, a couple of times." Fox put two fingers to his right ear, pausing for a moment, and Echo realized he was listening to a covert-ops earpiece in that ear. "And if I had to guess right now, based on the silence and the occasional sniffing, I think she's probably crying."

"Crying?! Why?"

"Relief, zun. Sheer, unutterable relief. Remember, after the 'shit-ton' of junk recent events have dumped on her, her emotions are VERY close to the surface right now. She loves you, more than either of us could ever guess, I expect, but she was terrified to tell you, for fear of seeing the same horror and disgust in your eyes that she sees in her own, every time she looks in a mirror and thinks about what was done to her."

"Then tell her to get her cute little ass in here, so she can see for herself that it isn't there."

Fox paused for a moment, listening again, then said, "She's coming. Give her a minute; she was in another room."

"Okay."

* * *

Moments later, the door of the interrogation room opened. Omega stood in it. Her nose was pink, and her eyes looked like she had been crying, but her cheeks had been freshly scrubbed to remove the tearstains. Echo simply stood and held out his arms, and she ran into them.

Before he could even respond, however, she had stretched up as far as she could, standing on tiptoes, and suddenly he was being kissed as if his very life depended on Omega transferring as much of her life force into his mouth as possible. Automatically, his arms went around her, and he returned her kiss with equal intensity.

"I think I'll be leaving now," he dimly heard Fox murmur, followed by the sound of the door closing.

Yeah, the Boss knows good timing when he sees it, Echo thought absently, as he heard the door close. *Not to mention when his agents need a little privacy.*

* * *

No sooner had Fox left Alpha One in the interrogation room than he called Suud Guurn's son.

"Duuniiss," he murmured into his special cell phone, "are you still waiting with the chief of security? No? Oh, that's excellent. Where have you got us set up to stay, and is it close...?" He listened for a moment, then nodded. "I know it; wait right there. I'll be there in five."

He deactivated the cell phone and headed from the confinement facility at speed, all senses on alert.

* * *

It took a while before Omega was willing to come up for air. But when she finally did, she refused to let Echo go, preferring instead to cling to him and bury her face in his chest.

"You are so awesome," she murmured in a wobbly voice

after a few minutes.

"Shh, baby, hush. It's okay. It works both ways, ya know."

"If you say so."

"I DO say so." Echo tucked his curled fingers under her chin and nudged her head up to look at him. "So. I know, now. All of it. A hundred an' ten percent. Listen to me carefully, Omega, baby: I. Don't. Care. Whatever you've got in your genetics now, it doesn't matter a damn to me. You're not a 'thing,' not a beast, and you never will be. It's a who, not a what, that I fell in love with."

Omega offered him a tremulous, but very happy, smile.

* * *

Once Fox entered the hotel suite Duuniiss had reserved for him—noting as he did that the suite had an extra, smaller bedroom, into which Duuniiss had already moved, as Fox's bodyguard—he turned to the younger biped.

"Have you swept it?"

"Of course," Duuniiss replied, confident. "Pater gave me the latest devices for such things before we left Emdali, and I can promise you, the suite is secure in every possible way. You are safe, and you can make as many, and as varied, secure calls as you wish." He showed Fox a special device. "This ensures that nothing said in this room can be detected outside this room, by any other than the party to whom the communiqué is routed."

"Terrific! Zun, when all this farshtinkener mess is over, I plan to recommend to your Uncle Pulgey that he bring you on as his new assistant security chief. You'll make an excellent chief bodyguard some day, at this rate."

"Thank you, Uncle," Duuniiss murmured, as his scales flushed a darker shade of green. "That...means a lot. And I think I would like that...and...and so would Uussa."

"Good. Consider it done, then. Now, let me see." Fox pulled his cell phone and placed a very special call, routing it through various highly-classified and largely-unknown PGLEIA channels. "Lima? This is Fox. Yes, Lord Entiyti is as well as can be expected. No, he's got a long way to go, to be well. Is Bravo there? Good. Listen closely, both of you; we have a very large balegan landing on us, and I'm going to need all the help I can get. Yes, it's about Echo. Yes, I'm going to tell you all about it...but not quite yet. I need for you to get hold of Sugar and Whiskey, and get them and yourselves on the horn, WITHOUT this Adita kaker knowing it. Do you think you can do that in the next ten minutes? Good. Call me back when you've done so. Fox out."

Fox deactivated the phone, sat down at the desk, laid the phone nearby, and stared at Duuniiss, who stared back.

* * *

Ten minutes later, the cell phone rang with the 'interstellar incoming' tone. Fox answered it.

"Fox here. All four of you? Excellent. And this Adita doesn't know? Good. Now, just listen, kinder; I have a lot to tell you, and not much time to do it in..."

* * *

"...And you can confirm that, Whiskey? Oh, he WAS, was he? At gunpoint? Well, that explains a lot. No, no, if he was coerced into doing it, that's not his fault. No, I'm sure he would have. The orderlies? You already have it sorted, but Adita isn't letting you act? All right, I'll see about that when we're done here. Sugar, what do you know about this Adita? Oh, DO tell. Mm. That bodes ill, then. No, no; all I have as yet are suspicions, and I may be wrong."

Fox listened for several moments, while Duuniiss watched.

"No, that makes a certain sense," Fox agreed then. "Yes, I think so. All right, gentlemen, here's what I need you to do. I want the four of you to work together—Lima, Bravo, you co-ordinate this—I want the four of you to contact every facility head and department chief we have, and TELL THEM EX-ACTLY WHAT I'VE TOLD YOU. But you need to do it such that Adita has no idea. Yes, Sugar, that includes all the other worlds in the Division. Earth is the Division Headquarters, Alpha Line doesn't just handle Earth-based situations, and Echo is the Alpha Line chief, Assistant Director, and Director Successor. They ALL need to know. Oh, and Sugar? I want you to make sure Alpha Line knows what's going down. Every. Last. Bit. Yes, every single Agent in the department. They deserve to know what's happening to their chief. This is a railroading job or I'll eat my...well, we ditched wearing hats decades ago, so...my tie, I guess. No, I can't promise this won't end up with Echo gone, and Omega in charge. But I want as much leverage as I can manage."

Fox listened for a while longer.

"Yes, I do, and thank you for the concern. No, that'll be fine. I also want you to ensure the various leads tell the agents under 'em. Yes, that's right. I want EVERY DAMN AGENT in the whole bloody Division to know about this. And I also have a couple of questions I want each agent, regardless of location, to answer. Echo has a serious reputation in our Division, and within PGLEIA, he's fairly well-known. I want to see how many of our people will support him, and what I have in mind to do. Right. No, I'll pop those to you in a separate, ciphered blip. Bravo, Lima? I want you two to receive the responses, collate them, and send them to me in another ciphered blip, as soon as you can. Yes, this is VERY time-critical. Yes, I expect them to convene the Ennead hearing on Echo's charges later today, most likely. Exactly, zun, that's what I need. You have a good head on your shoulders. All right, then. When I get off here, I'll compose the specific questions and pop them to you. Then I'll wait to hear back." Fox glanced at Duuniiss and nodded. "Very good, kinder. Fox out."

Fox deactivated the phone, then pulled his tablet out of a warp pocket and began typing into it, using the touch-sensitive screen. He was a swift, accurate typist, so he was done in less than a minute; he ciphered the file, ultra-compressed it, and sent it to his assistants on Earth through the same channels he'd just used for the voice comm. Then he drew a deep breath, smearing a hand over his face.

"You are playing a dangerous game, Uncle," Duuniiss decided.

"Damn straight," Fox declared, face growing hard. "And if anyone knows how, it's me! Echo did nothing wrong; the wrongness lies in the orders, the way they were worded, and the lack of leeway for my people to respond according to ethical considerations. And that tells me this is a political matter. Arguably, it's an attempted coup."

"...I think I can see it, but please explain."

"Consider this, Duuniiss," Fox said, ticking off fingers. "We have a nearly-successful assassination attempt on the Coalition President. We have the usurpation of the rightful chain of command in an entire Division, along with an attempt to eliminate the second in command of that Division. All that's left would be a direct attempt on my life." Fox paused, as Duuniiss seemed to swell with determination. "I fully expect my next step to be stonewalled, and I expect I know how. But I have to try anyway."

"So what ARE you going to do now, Uncle?"

"Gird up my loins and contact this bastard, Adita, and tell him to get the hell out of my office, that's what," Fox affirmed.

* * *

But that proved even more difficult than Fox expected. Had Fox actually been present, it might have been doable, especially given the presence of a cadre of loyal agents; but with Fox on Aleancë, Adita insisted he be allowed to 'help control the Agency' by remaining in control of the Agency. Fox quickly understood Echo's predicament, for he came perilously close to insubordination himself, falling just shy of telling the Zumbirian where to get off.

"Which I can't do quite yet," the Director noted to his adoptive nephew, "because until I get done with things, he's still a member of the Ennead, so he outranks me, after a fashion."

"And the galactic head of the PGLEIA is also a member of the Ennead, right?" Duuniiss queried.

"An adjunct at most, but yes," Fox affirmed. "He isn't a representative member, but he does get a vote." He sighed. "And

I saw him in the corridor earlier; he was fairly glaring holes through me. He is NOT happy about this situation. Nor am I, but I think he may not know the background I now know."

"So this Adita is still running things on Earth?"

"After a fashion, yes," Fox confirmed. "And says he will continue to do so until I arrive home. At which time, I fully expect him to refuse to relinquish control...or try to do away with me, or both. But if I get the kind of response from my Agency that I expect and hope, I think he may be surprised, himself."

"He doesn't know how to run such an organization," Duuniiss surmised.

"It doesn't sound like it, no," Fox agreed. "Not from what my people were just telling me. He is autocratic, high-handed, and very militaristic in...wait a minute..."

"What?"

Rather than answering, Fox pulled out his tablet again and went to work on it, pulling up several files of information. He studied the files for long moments, then rubbed his chin.

"Well, that's interesting," he decided, but refused to say more.

* * *

In the Director's Assistants office—underneath the Director's office where Adita currently sat—Lima, Bravo, Whiskey, and Sugar stared at each other in dumbfounded amazement.

"This ain't good," Whiskey murmured. "I think I'm glad Dihl changed her plans and headed back to the Ranch after working with Omega; she doesn't need to see this shit go down. Man, I thought the whole thing with Medical and Alpha One was bad. But..."

"Indeed. It has just escalated at least an order of magnitude, perhaps more," Sugar agreed, and the others nodded. "Gentlemen, it is my considered, experienced opinion that we are in the midst of an attempted coup."

"How do you figure?" Lima asked.

"A nearly-successful assassination attempt on the Coalition President—never mind the initial report, from mysterious sources, that it DID succeed; the usurping of the rightful chain of command in an entire Division; an attempt to negate the second in command of that Division? All that would be left would be an attempt on Fox himself," Sugar pointed out.

"Oh shit," Bravo breathed. "That's why you asked about him having a personal guard."

"And why I was most pleased when he said yes," Sugar confirmed.

"We gotta get to work," Whiskey decided, "and work fast. This has to be stopped, as fast as possible. We can't let this guy get entrenched, or it might end up successful anyway."

"Then let's get you two out of here and back where you need to be, so we can," Lima averred, hitting a secret button.

A hidden hatch in the floor under Lima's desk opened; stairs led down into the yawning hole...which was part of the emergency escape warp tunnels that ran throughout Headquarters.

"Catch you later," Whiskey said, as he and Sugar disappeared into the escape tunnel.

* * *

Half an hour later, a text message from Lima arrived on Fox's phone.

Cannot provide data in timeframe requested.
Too much information back & forth.
Will collect, collate, & send ASAP
Sorry.

"Dammit," Fox grumbled. "Then we may not have it in time for Echo's trial."

"That is...not good," Duuniiss observed.

"Not at all," Fox sighed. "Well, let's get back over to the holding area. I want to provide as much support to him and Omega as I can, while I can."

They rose and headed for the door.

"I will stay in the security chief's office this time," Duuniiss informed Fox, "and I will be nearby during the hearing. You will sit in the gallery?"

"Yes."

"Then you will see me, but do not acknowledge me. I will provide a certain amount of...undercover...security. You will have your other Agents with you, yes?"

"Yes, so they can be the overt security. That'll work."

The door of the suite closed and locked behind them, and the two males headed out at speed.

* * *

A little while later, Alpha One, Alpha Two, and Director Fox had all 'reconvened' in Echo's tiny force cell.

"It just ain't right, man," Romeo grumbled. "Echo done the RIGHT thing, an' he's gonna get PUNISHED for it."

"I'm with my partner on that one," India agreed. "Fox, isn't there anything you can do?"

"If we can get past the initial, perfunctory investigation and hearing, maybe," Fox averred. "I've already got something in action, but it doesn't look like being ready in time for the initial hearing. As, I gather, does Alpha One, and it apparently IS ready. I only hope it works. All of it."

"Me, too," Omega murmured. "'Cause it's probably gonna take all of it to get Echo cleared."

"Damn," Fox grumbled then, as the guards approached.

"It's time," Echo said quietly, standing. "Meg?"

"Right here, Echo," Omega said firmly, moving to his side. "I'm not budging. Don't even try to convince me otherwise." She reached out and took one of Echo's hands, which hung limply by his side, lacing her fingers with his and holding tight. "Let's go."

* * *

The council chamber was an equilateral triangle; the nine members of the Ennead—the core of the Galactic Council—arrayed themselves along two sides with the chairbeing at the apex, and a moderately-sized, multi-tiered observers' gallery was situated on the third. The guards led Echo, in force cuffs,

269

into the center of the room, facing the Ennead. Omega stayed right beside him. Fox, Romeo, and India seated themselves in the gallery. Duuniiss Guurn sat nearby, keeping a close watch on Fox without appearing to do so, or even seeming to be part of his group.

"Agent Echo," demanded one of the councilbeings, "who is the entity with you?"

"This is Agent Omega, my partner and," Echo added, "my fiancée."

"Fiancée?" another councilor reiterated, puzzled by the unfamiliar term.

"...Intended mate," Echo elaborated.

"Ah, so this is the being for which you requested an amendment of the Division One Agency charter," one observed. "Alongside Alpha Two, Director Fox, and the assistant chief of staff of your Medical department."

"Yes, ma'am, she is."

"Enough inconsequential chatter," another councilperson interrupted impatiently; the watching Agents recognized him as Ari N'Do, the likely traitor on the Ennead. "We are wasting time."

* * *

"I'll just bet you think so, y' ol' bastard," an angry Romeo muttered in the gallery.

"Hush, Romeo," Fox reprimanded under his breath.

"Shut up, Romeo. Be quiet, Romeo. Hush, Romeo. Someday, I'm gonna get to say my piece," Romeo grumbled.

"Romeo, cram a sock in it." India elbowed her partner, who finally silenced.

* * *

"I demand the Interim Head of the Ennead put the questions," N'Do pressed.

"Very well, Councilor," Lady Teela Krimnet, a female Korian, replied with a sigh. Korian women reminded Echo of nothing so much as the alien slave women of a certain classic 1960's science fiction television series, only with a lot more gravitas; Lady Teela, in particular, bore herself like the galactic leader she was—she was the Acting Ennead Chairbeing during Pulgey Entiyti's recovery. "Agent Echo, did you receive the Ennead's orders regarding the Premier of the Persis Federation?"

"Yes, Ma'am, I did."

"Did you understand those orders?"

"Yes, Ma'am."

"Did you follow those orders?"

"To a point."

"Objection!" N'Do cried.

"Answer yes or no, Agent," Lady Teela instructed.

"To a point," Echo insisted. "The orders were not—"

"Answer yes or no," Lady Teela repeated, growing hard, as she signaled the guards. The big Grendel and its partner Tethanoid stepped forward, hefting their weapons.

"...No," Echo replied. Beside him, Omega stifled a sigh.

"No further questions are necessary, Head," N'Do crowed. "He has admitted his guilt."

"True," she admitted reluctantly, her lovely green face sad. "Agent Echo, you know the penalty?"

"Yes," Echo answered quietly.

"You may have a few minutes to say goodbye to your partner while your Director prepares for the holographic mnemonic re-encoding."

* * *

"Fox?!" Romeo exclaimed as the Director stood. "YOU gotta do this??"

"Yes. Meshuginah, isn't it?" Fox replied, pulling brain bleacher and goggle glasses as he moved toward the prisoner.

* * *

Echo turned to his partner. "Meg? Go, baby. Go now. I don't want you to see this."

"No. I'm not leaving, Echo," Omega replied, sliding her hands up his chest to his shoulders. "You might as well quit trying to convince me otherwise."

"Are you okay?"

"No."

"Well—are you ready?" he asked then.

"How the hell am I supposed to get ready for something like this?!" Omega responded, incensed at the situation, and not bothering to keep her voice low. "No, I'm not ready! Not one bit of this is fair, or right! But...I'll deal with it...somehow. And I swear—I'll clear your name and get your memories back, if it's the last thing I do in this life."

A gentle hand fell on each Agent's shoulder, and they glanced up.

"Kiss her, Echo—one last time," Fox ordered softly. It was an order that Echo obeyed without question, complaint or delay. The council chamber hushed respectfully as the two Agents made a tender, wordless parting.

When the goodbye embrace ended, Fox added, "Omega—take his goggle glasses."

"Fox—" Omega choked. Then she nodded wordlessly, slipping her hand into Echo's jacket and retrieving his goggle glasses. Echo never moved, simply watched her with warm dark eyes, a hint of yearning in his gaze. Omega, Fox, Romeo, and India, as well as all the susceptible councilors, guards, and eyewitnesses—which was, by design of the device, pretty much all of them—donned their own eye gear. Echo stood passively as Fox raised the pre-set brain bleacher and triggered it.

Immediately Omega ripped off her goggle glasses and flung them away, clutching her partner's shoulders and staring into his face.

"Echo?!"

The tall, dark-complexioned man blinked dazed brown eyes for several long seconds, staring blankly into space, unseeing.

"Echo? Say something, honey...please...?" Omega pleaded despairingly, face contorted in pain.

"...Damn, Meg, now I understand why you always gripe about seeing spots with this thing," Echo finally replied.

The room erupted.

* * *

"I demand to know what has happened!" Ari N'Do exclaimed, standing and pounding on his console with a balled appendage. "This is an outrage!" Omega and Echo glanced at each other, then nodded slightly.

"The entire Ennead agrees with your curiosity, Councilor N'Do, if not your sentiments," the Ennead head replied, cool. "Agent Echo, could you please explain why the brain bleacher suddenly fails to affect you? It has done so in the past, has it not? For...more disturbing events, whose memory is best forgotten, and the like?"

"Yes, it has. But maybe my partner can answer that question a little better than I could," Echo offered quietly, and the chairwoman nodded permission. "Meg?"

"As you know," Omega addressed the Ennead in a formal tone that Echo often thought of as her 'professor' voice, "I am what Echo likes to refer to as an 'enhanced human.' One of Echo's old enemies...modified me...when I was young, intending to use me as a tool in his plot against Echo."

The Council group nodded.

"One of those enhancements was low-level telepathy," Lady Teela added. "That is why you were a logical choice for the Persis assignment."

"True," Omega replied. "And with the implant provided by Ambassador Zz'r'p and his people for the mission, I am now a FULLY-FUNCTIONAL telepath." Members of the Ennead shifted uncomfortably; Omega raised a knowing eyebrow and stared each one down, which caused them to squirm worse. "I was, therefore, able to perform a technique on Echo that I recently learned from Ambassador Zz'r'p."

"And that was?" N'Do demanded, scornful.

"Nd't'lq transfer," Omega answered. "The process of transferring a 'psychic clone' of one being into another being. With my help and guidance, Echo gave me his nd't'lq."

"I...do not understand," Lady Teela murmured.

"One of the deliberate effects of Meg's 'enhancements' is that she can't be brain-bleached," Echo explained. "Therefore, by placing a...'backup' of my mind in Meg's mind—"

"In the form of an nd't'lq, which stays in constant contact with the original mind," Omega interjected.

"—I can 'reload' my own memories as soon as you 'delete' them," Echo finished.

"A 'hot reboot,'" Omega declared.

"Brilliant," Fox muttered behind them, just loud enough for only Alpha One to hear.

"Omega, why did you do this?" Lady Teela queried, shocked. "It was not without some risk to yourself, surely."

"Yeah," Echo agreed. "We weren't sure if it would make Meg susceptible to the brain bleacher, or make me immune."

"Why, then?" Lady Teela repeated.

"To save—or at least be with—the man I love," Omega declared unhesitatingly, as Echo's eyes flashed warmly. "To goad the Ennead into a demand for an explanation, so that the full details of the incident could come out—including the collaboration of a member of this Council with Premier Hsrs."

The Ennead erupted in a babel of voices.

"Order! Order!" Lady Teela called, and the room eventually quieted. "The Ennead shall recess for eleven standard time units, and then resume." Councilors began filing out of the room as the guards approached Echo and Omega. Suddenly Echo noticed the councilbeing at the head of the exit line.

Meg! Look! Quick! What's N'Do thinking??

He's planning to skip out during the recess! Omega read the alien. *He's trying to get away from me, so I can't read him!*

Stop him, Meg! Level an accusation! They'll have to hold him!

And Omega was in motion, running across the room, springboarding off a low table, and leaping to the top of the high console. "STOP, Ari N'Do!" she shouted, pointing a condemning finger down at the being. "I accuse you of collaborating with a potential invasion force!"

The room stopped dead.

Chapter 11

Fox, escorted by Alpha Two, with Duuniiss Guurn subtly flanking, had barely made it out the gallery door when a *ding!* sounded from one of the Director's warp pockets. Smoothly he turned to Romeo.

"Zun, find me a private room where I can give a quick look at my tablet without anyone being the wiser," he murmured. "And there is a young Reptoid following in our wake who is part of my entourage, but not openly; make sure he comes along."

"All over it, boss-man," Romeo breathed back. "C'mon, India babe, lessee what we kin find."

"If you can locate Lady Teela, the interim chair, she can help us," Fox added. "She and I...knew each other pretty well, a long time ago."

"Ooo," Romeo said with a mischievous grin. "Old girlfriend?"

"Actually...yes."

"Does Zebra know?"

"She does now," Fox said with a shrug. "When we decided to apply for life partnership, I gave her a full accounting of my personal past. Which, given how old I am, took a while, but we thought knowing things like that about each other was the honest thing to do. She's had a few significant others, and so have I. None of 'em are a factor in our relationship at this point."

"That's good, Fox," India murmured, as Romeo went off in search of Lady Teela. "Maybe I should be saying, 'Dad,' but you know what I mean. I'm happy for the two of you, and so is Romeo. We think...don't take this the wrong way, I'm just not coming up with a better word...we think you two are a cute couple."

Fox flushed, ever so slightly.

* * *

Within moments, Romeo was back with Lady Teela; Duuniiss hovered nearby.

"This way, all of you," Teela murmured, leading the way down an adjacent corridor, then turning right, into a small side hallway. "There is a private, secure room here, for when an Ennead member needs to take a personal call."

She unlocked the door and let them in. Fox turned and waved to Duuniiss to catch up, and the young Reptoid glanced around, then scampered inside. Teela raised a green eyebrow.

"Is that..." she began.

"Suud's son," Fox confirmed. "Clandestine security for me. Suud insisted, and for that matter, so did Pulgey." He shrugged one shoulder. "And Zebra appreciated it."

"I can imagine," Teela agreed. "She is good for you, Fox."

"I'm glad you think so, Teela. I agree."

"Is this about Pul...?"

"I don't think so, but I don't know for sure," Fox admitted. "I got an alert that a classified message had arrived on my tablet, and needed to get someplace out of observation to have a look. It's probably work stuff from home, but..."

"Ah. All right. And you still don't know who did it...?"

"Not yet, no. I swear I will keep you posted on that, Teela, as best I can, given circumstances."

"Thank you, old friend. Let me leave you in peace now, so you can do your job."

* * *

Lady Teela left, and Fox extracted the tablet, awaking it and opening the messaging utility. Then he located the new message, opened it, and studied it carefully.

"Hm. That's interesting," he decided.

"Is that the data you were expecting?" Duuniiss wondered.

"Yes, zun, it is. Oh, let me introduce you; Duuniiss, this is Agent Romeo and his life partner, Agent India; together, they comprise Alpha Two, the backup and support team for Alpha One. Romeo helps run Alpha Line when Alpha One is away from Headquarters, and India is the department medic. India,

Romeo, this is Duuniiss Guurn, eldest offspring of Suud Guurn, the Reptoid who became Lord Entiyti's chief bodyguard when I...left...to help found the Agency."

"Hey there," India murmured with a smile, shaking the young male's hand.

"Pleased t' meetcha," Romeo averred, doing likewise.

"I am very happy to meet the two of you," Duuniiss replied with a wide smile. "I have heard much about you from Pater, Uncle Franz here, and Uncle Pul."

"'Uncle' Franz?" India murmured. "I knew your given name, Fox, because Meg insisted we all read the unabridged history in our departmental handbooks. But how did you get to be a Reptoid's uncle?"

"Adoptive uncle," Fox explained, still studying the information on the tablet, "same as you're my adoptive daughter. And Romeo, and Echo, and Omega..."

"Oh, right," India said, nodding.

"Pater told me there was a special ceremony, Uncle," Duuniiss protested mildly.

"There was," Fox confirmed. "Years ago though it's been. Given that Pul, Suud and I were, at that time, all single, with no offspring, and the three of us the best of friends, we wanted to ensure that..." Fox broke off and looked up from his tablet, staring into space for a moment. "Well, if something happened to one or two of us, whoever was left could...kind of, see to things," he continued, "if you know what I mean. Legal things, like living wills, or actual wills, or just giving the medics permission to do certain procedures, or whatever. Only it turned out that, to make it all legal, we had to have a legal kinship status. So Pul put us all three through a Draconan 'blood brother' ceremony. That made it a legal kinship on Emdali, and so that, in turn, made it legal...pretty much anywhere in the galaxy."

"Thus the Lords Franz Levy and Pulgey Entiyti are my uncles," Duuniiss said with pride.

"So I guess that makes us cousins, kinda," India decided. "We have an interesting clan, here."

"Fox, you got the craziest damn family," Romeo said with a lopsided grin.

"Don't I know it," Fox shot back with an affectionate smirk. "Jews and Gentiles, black, white, Oriental, Native American, Draconans and Reptoids and Ergisols—Lydhuu Raiit is now a semi-official niece—and HaShem knows who all else, before He brings me to His tabernacle to stay." The Division One Director chuckled. "But for me and mine, it works. And...well...I don't use this word very often, and I suppose never before to you three, but..." Fox bit his lip, then murmured in a husky tone, "I love every damn one of you."

"And we love you, too, Fox," India said, slipping an arm around him to offer a hug.

"Group hug," Romeo said softly, and he and Duuniiss joined in.

"If you so much as breathe of this moment to another living soul, I will kill you all," Fox declared.

They all laughed.

* * *

Five minutes later, Fox had finished perusing the data, and nodded, satisfied.

"Was it what you hoped, Uncle?" Duuniiss wondered.

"It was, indeed," Fox averred, "and more than I had hoped. Now, let's go find Alpha One and see what we can do to bolster them a bit. Duuniiss, now that Teela knows who you are, you can probably come with us, if you like."

"Probably," Duuniiss agreed, "but that does not mean that I should, necessarily. I think I may still be of more use to you outside, watching, without telegraphing the fact that there is a relationship between us."

"And that makes good sense, and I have no qualms with it," Fox decided. "Let's go."

* * *

"Excellently played, you two!" Fox said with a smile, as the Earth Agents all talked in Echo's cell, not five minutes later. "Great idea, using Omega's abilities like that—"

There was a soft thud in the corner of the cell. They all spun, and suddenly Echo found himself kneeling on the floor beside his partner, gathering up her unconscious form.

"Damn!" Echo exclaimed, alarmed. "India, get over here! Look at her nose!"

* * *

India scrambled over, whipping out a medscanner as she observed the trickles of blood in Omega's nostrils. After a few minutes of examination, she looked up at Echo with worried eyes.

"It's the implant chip. Her body's rejecting it."

"Whazzat mean?" Romeo asked.

"It means her immune system considers it an invader and is trying to destroy it," India elaborated.

"But it's in her BRAIN," Fox protested.

"Exactly," India replied grimly, adjusting settings on her medscanner and passing it over Omega's limp body repeatedly, gathering as much data as she could.

"Is this a leftover reaction from Slug's drek?" Fox wondered. "Maybe trying to prevent us from changing something, or tagging her, or the like?"

"It's possible, I suppose, but I don't really think so, not in this instance," India answered, studying the readouts on her scanner. "No, I think this is just normal immune-system response. I'd expect a Slug-tinkered reaction to have happened pretty much immediately after the implant and be way more... acute. Not that this is...well."

"India? Be straight with me. How serious?" Echo asked, face slightly paler than normal.

"Very serious," India answered quietly. "This has probably been developing since shortly after the implant was emplaced. Meg's probably covered up the symptoms because of needing to use the damn thing, one way and another, but it's gotten too bad to hide, now."

"Can you remove the implant?" Echo asked. "Will that help?"

"Yes, it'll help," India confirmed. "If I remove—"

"No," came a weak voice from Echo's shoulder. Omega opened her eyes, which were somewhat dilated and mildly unequal.

"Meg, it could kill you," India explained gently. "It will almost certainly cause brain damage if we don't do something, and soon."

"India, I am not letting Echo go," a determined Omega answered, trying to sit up. Echo propped her against his shoulder, and she continued. "I know now, he was fighting the whole time to get me back, and I'm damned if I won't hang on just as hard! But since we did the nd't'lq transfer with the chip in place, I can't be sure I can maintain the transfer if you remove the chip. And I have to maintain it until I'm sure Echo's out of danger."

"Meg—" Echo began, staring into Omega's eyes.

"Ace," Omega replied, meeting his gaze firmly, then they both fell silent and the others realized that an unseen debate was occurring. Finally, Omega held up a hand and said, "No, Echo. I hear you. But my mind's made up, Ace. End of discussion."

A frustrated expression flashed across Echo's face.

"Meg, you are damned stubborn, baby."

* * *

"I had a good teacher," she grinned. "Not that I wasn't, to begin with. But I'm not foolhardy, hon. I've got an idea." She turned to India. "Have you got any immunosuppressants in your medikit?"

"You know, come to think of it, I've got some imprazine." India brightened up. "It's used for severe allergic reactions, so I think of it as an antihistamine, but it works because it has a powerful immunosuppressant effect."

"Shoot me full, then," Omega said, resting her throbbing head on Echo's shoulder. "Gimme the biggest damn dose you can, and let's just hope I don't run into anybody who's sick. Oh, and a nice, strong analgesic would be awfully appreciated, too." Omega rubbed her temple.

"Your wish is my command, honey," India said with a grin, setting to work.

"As I was saying, it was a brilliant solution, Omega," Fox commended. "It really solved the problem of Echo's brain bleaching."

"It helped another problem, too, didn't it, Meg?" Echo said softly. "A personal one."

"More or less." Omega nodded, blushing slightly. "I'm... still trying to process it, around everything else going on. So it's...um. Still a problem, but getting there, I guess you could say."

"Which is better than not," Echo noted.

"Yeah, I guess," Omega agreed.

"What problem?" Fox asked curiously, as India finished treating Omega.

"Meg's insecurity," Echo answered succinctly.

"Aha," Fox responded knowingly. India smiled.

"I don' get it," Romeo muttered.

* * *

"Meg thought she was unlovable, Romeo, remember?" India reminded him. "Now, she and Echo are in each other's heads—"

"About as far in each other's heads as it's possible to get," Echo amended. "Or, well, I'm in HER head, I guess..."

"And I know exactly how Echo feels about me," Omega finished softly. She glanced up at him, to find Echo watching her with warm, dark eyes. "It's how I knew, when, um, when Fox and Echo talked, that..."

"I get it," Echo murmured.

"So do I," Fox added.

Romeo and India watched the brief exchange, then nodded, and Omega knew they weren't going to press to know what the discussion was about.

As it turned out, that didn't mean that Romeo wasn't curious about other matters, however.

* * *

"So...izzat what you two were doin' alone together on the saucer?" Romeo asked. "Playin' head games?"

"...Among other things," Echo affirmed, stone-faced, and Romeo grinned.

"Uh-huh," he said knowingly. "Meg?"

"Romeo, you know a lady never kisses and tells," Omega teased. Romeo noticed, however, that she didn't blush as she spoke, which made him wonder exactly what she wasn't telling, and what 'other things' actually were.

'Cause they's both old-fashioned, he considered. *Echo done made that REAL plain. So I wouldn't think it'd be THAT. Leastways, not th' obvious 'that.' 'Cause Meg'd turn a hundred an' twenty-eight shades o' red right now, if it was. So what th' hell WAS it?*

"But—" he began.

"Junior, I think Meg told you recently to let us handle our own relationship, didn't she?" Echo prodded.

"Yeah."

"Then what we do—or don't do—is our business, right?"

"...Yeah." Romeo sighed. *So much f'r ever findin' out, I guess,* he thought. *Then again, I guess that's the way it should be. I just wish I could ever get m' damn curiosity satisfied 'bout shit. I always get told t' shut up b'fore I ever get any answers. Eh, f'rget it, Romeo. None o' my business nohow. Not this time.*

"Good. Now let's plan strategy. Hm. They're probably monitoring," Echo mused. Then he glanced down at the woman leaning against him. "Meg? I hate like hell to ask you this, baby, especially since I know what the implant rejection is doin' to you, but...are you up to providing a private conference for us?"

"I think so, Echo. I'll try, anyway. Try to keep it brief, okay? Here goes, everybody..."

* * *

...Sound good to you, Fox? India asked, and they all sensed the Director's nod.

I haven't been too pleased about the high-handed way the Ennead has handled this anyway, Fox answered. *Something isn't right, here. I had a long-distance meeting not long after I arrived on Aleancë, to explain what I knew of the situation, to Whiskey, Sugar, Bravo, and Lima. They weren't too pleased, either. It didn't take 'em all that long to pass the word around to the department chiefs, who passed it to their people, and get ALL their responses back to me—without, let me add, Adita knowing word one about it— and yes, Romeo, that was what the classified communiqué a bit ago was about.*

Score! I done got one'a my questions answered! the younger Agent exclaimed, and the others snorted. *Finally!*

One and all, the other agents felt like there had to be more to the situation than they had been told...at least, by Adita, Fox continued. *So I notified them, through Bravo, Lima, Whiskey, and Sugar, of why you're on trial, Echo. Your fellow chiefs were outraged. And they thought Alpha Line would riot. I think the Agency will go along.* Fox's irony was heavy. *Oh, and by the by, I ALSO informed one Lord Ordik Adita that his services were no longer required, and that the Division One Agency Director, namely me, was back in charge. I relieved that bastard from duty...or so I thought and hoped. According to Limu, he refuses to leave until I actually arrive on-planet to hand over... surprise, surprise. AND...he is enforcing their compliance with his personal guard. At least insofar as he knows of any non-compliance; they're having to be cautious in their communications.*

Shit. That's not good, Omega decided.

Nope, Echo agreed. *Hellfire an' damnation. Not one bit of it.*

Indeed. I suspected the two of you would think so, Fox observed. *I have my suspicions, but there are a few things I am investigating...*

So...I gather everyone knows now about Meg and me? Echo asked, curious.

Yes, Echo, Fox replied. *They're delighted. Everyone says it's a perfect match.*

Oh, Echo said, stifling a sigh.

* * *

Echo? You sound...displeased, Omega observed with some trepidation. *You didn't want anyone to know about us?*

Not...particularly, Meg, Echo responded with a shrug. *Not yet, anyway.*

Oh...

Everyone felt the strong mental block go up swiftly around Omega, but not fast enough to stop a surge of humiliation and pain from getting through.

Meg?! What's wrong, baby?

Noth...nothing, Echo.

* * *

It was Romeo who figured it out.

Th'pretty lady thinks you're ashamed of 'er, Echo. Thatchu don' want anybody knowin' you love an... 'inhuman thing.'

What? Meg, is that true? Is that what you think?

Well...isn't it? Omega replied quietly.

'Isn't it' what?

True.

* * *

You're getting tired, aren't you, angel? Echo asked gently then. *Holding together this telepathic conversation, especially with the chip causing so many problems, and the immune system rejection and shit. You're reading 'static' again.*

You didn't answer me, Ace.

Actually, I did. What with the nd't'lq thing going, I'd have thought you'd know better at this point, but you're so tired and stressed, you're not reading things straight. No, Meg. I'm not ashamed of you. I'll never be ashamed of you, honey. You've never given me any sort of reason to BE ashamed of you, EVER. Given the fact that I trained you, I'd say it's the exact opposite. I'm so proud of my protégé and partner, I could bust. Come on, Meg, you know me. I just wanted to keep it private, is all. Now, when we get back, everybody's gonna want to know all about it, throw damned parties, make us the center of attention, and all that shit. Hell.

* * *

Echo, India interjected with a smile, *most brides like having 'all that shit' made over 'em. It's their one big chance to be special.*

Bride? Echo sounded bemused. *Huh. Yeah. I guess so.* Suddenly they all shared a brief mental image of Omega in a white confection of satin and lace, a filmy veil over her face, and they realized it was the picture conjured in Echo's mind by the thought of Omega as his bride. *Meg? You really want all that fuss made over us?*

...It doesn't matter, Echo. It's not important.

That wasn't what I asked, honey. Guys? Echo addressed the other three Division One Agents. *Would you excuse us a minute? Meg and I need to chat. And I think we've finished planning strategy anyway.*

All right, the others agreed. *But Echo,* India added, *Meg really is awfully tired. Keep it short.*

Wilco.

* * *

The three colleagues exited the mental link, and stood watching as Alpha One silently talked, Echo sitting beside Omega where she lay on the cot, gazing into each other's eyes.

After several minutes, brown eyes and blue resumed an alert gaze as they exited the telepathic conversation.

Omega's face was drawn and tired, but the sapphire eyes shone. Echo's face wore its characteristic neutral expression, but the dark eyes held a smoky smile.

"Well, I think we got that worked out," he said.

* * *

Fox emerged from the high-security confinement area, signaled Duuniiss to follow him, and they stepped into a privacy alcove.

"Yes, Uncl-uh, milord Levy?" Suud's eldest offspring queried.

"Duuniiss, do you have your comm unit on you?" Fox wondered.

"The 'cell phone,' I think you call it, Uncle?"

"No, the emergency family thing. The quantum comm device."

"Ah. The Emdalian family signaler? Of course," Duuniiss noted, getting out the device and checking it. "Why? I have heard nothing from Pater, so he and Lord Entiyti are all right..."

"No, I had an idea, and there's less chance that your unit is being monitored than any of my comm," Fox explained. "Or, for that matter, that it CAN be monitored. It's a little tighter tech, and longer distance, than our phones. I could just go back to the special Ennead conference room, but I'd rather not be seen using it again, especially so soon, and I don't have time to run back to the hotel..."

"Oh," Duuniiss said, understanding. He pressed a couple of buttons, then offered the communications device. "Here."

Fox held the device to his ear, and almost immediately heard his old friend's voice. "Duuniiss? Is everything all right? Is Franz well?"

"I'm fine, alter khaver," Fox said with a slight smile. "Everything is...all right, if anything can be said to be all right when my adoptive brother has so nearly skirted death and is likely permanently maimed in any event, and my adoptive son is teetering on the brink of being exiled from me. I borrowed your son's emergency communicator to contact you directly; forgive me if I frightened you. I have a task for you, which may shed a little light on this verdammt conspiracy."

"Name it, my friend."

"The Ke!endarian-that-nobody-knows...you still hold it? Nothing has happened to it?"

"We do, and it has not."

"Good. Go over everything it has, and tell me what you find."

"We have already done so. We have found nothing unusual."

"Hm. Well, if you have to, shackle it, strip it naked, and do a body cavity search."

"...All right. THAT will not be pleasant...for anyone. Why? What am I looking for?"

"Anything unusual. Anything not Ke!endarian. Anything that might tell us who or what it is, and where it's from."

"You have a...what is it you used to call it, Franz...? Ah—a hunch."

"Well, I do, Suud."

"What do you expect us to find?"

Fox drew a deep breath, considering.

"No," he finally decided. "I don't think I'm ready to go that far, yet. I may be wrong, and I don't want to risk biasing your search. Just look for anything you wouldn't expect to find, and let me know what."

"Very well, Franz. I will get right on it."

"Do you need Duuniiss to come back to help?"

"Will you want to see whatever we may come up with?"

"Most definitely."

"Then yes, send him back; he will serve as the courier. You have bodyguards there, yes?"

"I have half of Alpha One—sort of, and all of Alpha Two."

"That will work, then," Suud said, with the hint of a grim chuckle. "Stay close to them; we do not want you falling to the enemy, too. Have Duuniiss fetch his kit, and..."

"I'll make arrangements for his transport back there, Suud, no worries," Fox offered.

"Very good, then. I will expect to see him soon. And Franz?"

"Yes?"

"Take great care, my friend. This appears to be a couple of very convoluted piles of sssshttt we have fallen into."

"Is it? I wonder," Fox murmured. "But not to worry, Suud. You know I'm always on guard, and I have three excellent Agents...well, make that two and a half, at the moment...to assist me in that. You be careful as well. Sedate the unknown being, if you have to; I'd rather that than one of you get hurt when it gets pissed."

"Affirmative. I was already considering that option."

"Excellent. Fox out."

"Guurn out."

* * *

"Well, we wound up back here, anyway," Fox said in the hotel room, after Duuniiss had hurriedly packed his duffle, with the human's help. Within moments, the room's door latched behind them, and they were headed across the lobby and out of the hotel. "Let's get you back aboard my shuttle as fast as possible, and we'll send you to your father. I have the feeling he's going to find something quite unusual that will blow the case wide open."

"I hope so," Duuniiss grumbled, as they strode swiftly toward the ultra-secure hangars reserved for the Ennead and affiliates. "I have already submitted a request to be present for the execution of the bombers. Given my father's status, and the fact that my beloved was killed, the Emdali High Council is considering allowing me to assist in the executions."

"Are you sure that is wise, meyn kind?" Fox asked in a soft voice. "Do you want to continue the entire mess?"

"What do you mean?" Duuniiss demanded. "Surely you are not arguing that we do not punish them!"

"No." Fox sighed. "There is murder, and there is war, and then there is rabid-dog slaughter. In my humble opinion, this went far beyond the first, and since there is no war—at least, nothing official—the second does not apply...though I am beginning to wonder if that was not the intent. No, this was a serious attempt at rabid-dog slaughter, and rabid dogs cannot be saved. The fact that only one of the intended targets has died so far—your beloved—is rather beside the point, as we are only fortunate that no innocent civilians were caught in the blast and subsequent firefight. No; by the time a sentient reaches the point of willingness to cause such atrocities, there is something very, very wrong with it...something that is unlikely ever to allow it to revert to a more peaceful means of..." he paused, then his face twisted in something akin to distaste as he finished, "communication."

"Then what the ssshhrr do you mean, Uncle Franz?"

"I mean, zun," Fox murmured, meeting the younger male's gaze, "that it is one thing to be the official, governmental executioner in such a matter, and quite another to usurp that role for the sake of personal revenge. And isn't that what you would be doing, if you are the one to...'throw the switch,' let us call it?"

"But it is legal on Emdali," Duuniiss pointed out.

"It is. But that does not argue that it is wise. I have seen the vengeance wars among families, among clans, that it can tend to perpetrate. First-hand. As has your father. As has your Uncle Pul." Fox met the young Reptoid's gaze once more. "Are you sure you want to do that? More, do you think UUSSA would want you to do that?"

"Oh..." Duuniiss blinked wide, dilated eyes at the addendum.

"All I am asking is that you think on that, my young friend, my...adoptive nephew," Fox told him, all while thinking, *Romeo is right. My family is so meshuginah. But family they are, and family they shall remain, until my dying day...and beyond, if I have anything to say. If HaShem continues as merciful to me as He has been to this point.*

"Um, all right," Duuniiss agreed, thoughtful. "I will give it...a great deal of consideration, Uncle. Not least because you, of all people, advise it."

"Good. Get on, now," Fox said, nudging him toward the shuttle's hatchway. "I've instructed the captain of the *Exodus* to travel at emergency cruising speeds, and maintain maximum security for the duration of the flight and any subsequent flights she may need to make with you, or any of our people involved. You'll be on Emdali in about two hours, and since this is a small planet-to-space craft, it will put you down directly on Pul's estate. And given it's usually a drop-ship from the *Gen-*

esis, they can probably open the usual force-field gate to allow it entrance."

"Good, sir," Duuniiss averred.

"Off with you, then."

"Yes, sir!"

* * *

When the Council session resumed, Echo had a companion—other than Omega—with him in the dock: Ari N'Do. The councilor glared at the Alpha One team.

If looks could kill... Omega observed telepathically.

Yep, Echo agreed in kind. *Fox would be looking for a coffin for us.*

Don't you mean 'coffins,' plural?

Nope.

Huh?

Just the one.

Oh. Omega thought for a moment. *Okay. But...why?*

From now on, we go together, you and me. Everywhere. In life, and in death.

Omega closed her eyes, lips curving up gently as she grasped his meaning; Echo glanced around the room.

Heads up. Teela's about to resume the session. Are you ready?

You know it, Ace, Omega replied confidently. But Echo could sense the mental and physical strain through their link, and he worried for her. *Stop that,* she told him then.

Uh. Sorry. But I can't help it, baby.

I know. And I appreciate it. But we got this.

"The Ennead will now begin a new session," the chairwoman made the traditional announcement. "We shall now hear testimony from Earth Division One Agents Echo and Omega as to the details behind Agent Echo's apparent disobedience and Agent Omega's accusation of Councilor N'Do. Agent Echo, please begin. Agent Omega, as his partner and betrothed, feel free to interject as you deem appropriate."

"Thank you, Ma'am," Echo said, and Omega nodded an

290

acknowledgement. "As you know, my orders were in two parts: Send Omega to the medlab—there was no mention of the reason—which I did. Meg wasn't too happy about that when she got there and found out why. The medic's interpretation of the Ennead-issued orders was that he should insert the implant whether Meg was willing or not. And your Ennead representative, Lord Ordik Adita, came with a medical team and his personal staff of guards, all prepared to do so if our medlab staff proved unwilling."

"Given Agent Omega's history, that was...unfortunate," Lady Teela observed, raising a decidedly disapproving eyebrow.

"Rather," Omega remarked coolly.

"It is also not how those orders were intended to be executed," Teela added.

"Oh, now THAT'S interesting," Echo murmured.

"Adita then proceeded to usurp Echo's authority as Acting Director of the Agency, overruling him and attempting to force the issue," Omega tag-teamed. "Deltiri Ambassador Zz'r'p had to all but browbeat him into even telling us what the problem was, and why the implant chip was important to the mission that we didn't even know we had, at that point."

"Hm. So the mission started...inauspiciously," Lady Teela remarked. "With a great deal of...obfuscation."

"Damn straight," Echo agreed. "Still, Meg and I, as well as Romeo and India, the Alpha Two team, went along, once we understood the nature of the mission. A lot was at stake, and we put aside our personal feelings and responses—"

"The way we always do," Omega added as Echo nodded agreement.

"—To get the job done," Echo finished. "So part two of my orders was to provide Premier Hsrs with anything he wanted or expected. I was NOT prepared, either mentally, emotionally, or morally, for that to include my colleagues."

"Colleagues—plural?" a councilor verified.

"Yes," Omega confirmed. "Myself, Agent Romeo, and

Agent India."

"For what reason?" the chairwoman asked.

"He considered us gifts, and intended to make us his... consorts," Omega explained. "Which, aside from questions of personal autonomy, might well have been fatal to us—Persan physiology and human physiology aren't exactly very compatible. And that's completely aside from issues relating to sentients becoming property, AND sexual mores."

"Agent Romeo, who received no such orders, spoke up then," Echo continued, "and indicated that he and India were already 'spoken for,' as Romeo put it, given their mating and life partner status. Apparently not willing to 'share,' as it were, the Premier therefore released them both."

"But Echo was stuck, trapped by his orders; consequently, so was I," Omega added. "We weren't officially life partners yet, since Director Fox had to leave to attend Lord Entiyti before the paperwork could go through, so I had no protest I could make...and Echo couldn't say anything, because it would violate his orders, which were classified at a level so high that, had he not been the Acting Director, he wouldn't have even been allowed to SEE them. He certainly wasn't allowed to tell any of the rest of us about them. So we were trapped between orders and duty on one side, and emotional, moral, and religious convictions, on the other."

"I presume the latter won out," Lady Teela remarked drily. Echo shrugged.

"Omega's here, isn't she?" he observed. "Chairwoman, are you familiar with Earth history?"

"Somewhat," she acknowledged. "A basic knowledge of the history of all Concordat-signatory planets is a prerequisite for Ennead membership."

"Does the word 'Nazi' mean anything to you?"

"It does," Lady Teela admitted, aloof and reserved. "What, exactly, are you intimating, Agent?"

Omega stared for a moment at Echo, seeing the golden spark of anger in his cocoa eyes; she raised an eyebrow.

Shades of that last training-room session, huh? she asked, and he turned to look into her eyes, deliberately telegraphing to the room that they were conversing mentally. What both Agents found interesting was that, while recognition of that fact was obvious and immediate, no one ventured a protest.

Hell yeah, he said then.

Do you want me to handle this explanation?

Probably better if you do, baby, Echo replied. *As mad as I am right now, I'm apt to say too much, which won't do my case any good. I'm likely to start making blunt comparisons they won't care for. Diplomacy be damned.*

Are you sure?

After a moment, he nodded. *Do it.*

"What Echo is trying to say, Madame Chairwoman," Omega said softly, "is that the Nazi soldiers obeyed orders and carried out their duty. They followed the letter of their law down to the last detail. But they were morally WRONG. If the Nazi soldiers—from the officers all the way down to the rank and file—had exercised proper moral judgement on what they were being commanded to do, Earth's Second World War likely would have followed a very different course of events...IF it had happened at all. And the German armies would have been a lot less...cohesive."

"I...see," Lady Teela remarked thoughtfully, and the other members of the Council nodded in consideration. "You are saying that the orders, at least as they wound up being executed, violated Agent Echo's moral code, and he chose to be true to his morals, regardless of cost."

"Damn straight," Echo replied, steely-eyed. *Declaration of Independence, baby,* he prodded.

Ooo, of course, Omega responded, then addressed the Ennead again.

"Echo and I both come from a nation on Earth where a declaration was made at its founding that spoke of certain 'unalienable rights,'" Omega noted. "Rights that come from the Creator, as we feel, and that cannot, and should not, be abrogated. And 'among these are life, liberty, and the pursuit of happiness,'" she quoted. "The sanctioning of presenting us as slave gifts to the Premier, whether as Agents or autonomous sentients, is in violation of ALL those rights."

"Hell yeah," Echo averred with force. "I got no desire to work for a government that has no consideration for a person's rights."

"And that goes for the entire Division One Agency," an authoritative voice said behind them, booming the words across the Council chamber. All attention focused on the voice's owner; Fox stood in the gallery, closing his cell phone even as he moved forward. "The orders issued to both Agent Echo and physician Psi were so broad and inflexible that they left no room whatsoever for individual objection on any grounds; had Ambassador Zz'r'p not intervened to allow Omega a modicum of personal autonomy in the implant decision, Doctor Psi—who was coerced with a brandished weapon—was prepared to disobey orders also."

"Ooo," Omega murmured. "There's interesting news. Good for him."

"I've been in communication with Agency Headquarters on Earth—NOT through Lord Ordik Adita, let me add; nor is he even aware of it—and the agents around the planet and across the division have now been fully informed of events," Fox continued. "Let me add, they were completely in the dark that ANYTHING was transpiring until I instituted a means of communication that circumvented Adita. And since being informed, they've been submitting their responses to this situation in the form of a vote, at my request, and those responses have been tallied by my assistants, again without Adita's awareness. In point of fact, this was necessary because Adita has been interfering with the proper running of Division One—issuing improper orders, violating regulations, refusing to relinquish control to myself or any of several of my duly deputized subordinates, all while claiming Ennead authority; this has made no one in our organization happy, and that includes the other worlds in Division One."

"Oh dear," Teela murmured, frowning. "That is not right. He does not have that authority, nor was it even considered..."

"I suspected as much. In addition," Fox continued, "the leaders of several governing bodies on Earth have been contacted, from the current U.S. President to the UN Secretary-General, and a number of others beside. The collective decision of our agents and the planetary leaders is unanimous—Echo did the right thing, and we want no part of the Sydys Concordat or the Galactic Coalition if this council decides otherwise. If you condemn Echo, Earth secedes and becomes a neutral planet. All non-Terrans will be expelled, contact severed, our out-system security maximized. AND...we take our information on N'Do and the Persis Federation with us." He paused. "Other worlds in Division One must make their own decisions...but I have it to understand that none of them are at all happy with the Ennead just now. And you have Adita to thank for that."

A buzz filled the room, as startled Ennead members mulled this unanticipated sequence of events. After a brief discussion ensued, the chairwoman addressed the room.

"The Ennead will adjourn for deliberation until further notice. Director Fox, you are courteously requested to join this discussion, though it is at your discretion. Guards, you will take Agent Echo to a minimum-security cell, where his companions may join him if they wish, and place Councilor N'Do in Echo's former cell."

The guards saluted, and once again the room emptied.

* * *

In the Division Five 'Entiyti Estate Office,' a temporary office and detention facility set in the old gatehouse of Entiyti's property just outside the main force field dome provided by the *Genesis*, Suud Guurn—galactic admiral; former chief bodyguard of Galactic Coalition President Pulgey Entiyti; former protégé of Lord Franz Levy, now Division One Director Fox; and brother-in-all-but-blood by ancient Emdalian ritual to both males—oversaw the body search of the assassin of mysterious antecedents. Next to him stood Taassass Siisshiiss, Division Five PGLEIA chief from the Slliith City Office, though Division Five Headquarters was elsewhere.

They stood inside an observation room with one-way windows overlooking the interrogation room, and adjacent to it. Inside the interrogation room were five Division Five agents of various genders; since the unknown being also had an unknown-to-the-Coalition gender, and given there was an outside possibility it was not even the species it appeared to be, the chief had decided to have multiple genders available in case it complained, as well as to provide witnesses that nothing untoward was attempted against the alien being...body cavity searches notwithstanding; there were certain procedures for those, and the attempted assassination of a galactic leader invoked specific protocols. A small video camera in the corner near the ceiling also recorded the events, to similar purpose.

The agents assigned to the body-cavity search were clad crown to foot in waterproof, disposable clean suits with full-head enclosures, to protect them from any inadvertently—or deliberately—released bodily emissions. One agent was medtech-trained and stood near the door with something in hand. The others went straight for the prisoner.

When Beletana Ve!eresh, no longer unquestionably presumed to be from Ke!enda!ar, was finally restrained by no less than four agents—which took some time, as it put up a lengthy fight—the fifth agent stepped forward...

...And in one smooth motion, produced the object in its hand: a micropore osmosive hypodermic, and injected its contents—a powerful galactic sedative—into the prisoner's neck. Within moments Beletana slumped, unconscious, remaining upright only by the agents holding its arms and legs.

"On the table," the lead agent—Piradu Madru of Tath—noted, gesturing at a portion of wall. The agent who had wielded the syringe moved to the wall and brought down a panel, hinged to the wall on one side, forming a sturdy table about the right size for standard medical procedures on most bipedal sentients—it had been installed by the agents earlier. The four 'restraint agents' carted the limp, feather-covered body to this platform, and eased it atop the table.

"All right," Madru declared. "This will be a bit different than most such body-cavity searches, since this being may NOT be the species it appears to be. I'll take the head; I want each of you to take a quadrant—one arm or leg, and associated attachments—and use your sensory appendages to search it closely for anything out of the ordinary. This includes something inside a body cavity, an unexpected subcutaneous bulge, ANYTHING like that."

A chorus of "Yes, sir," was his answer.

"All right, let's get started," Madru ordered.

The detailed body search of the mysterious, unidentified assassin began.

* * *

Guurn and Siisshiiss watched as the search went on for nearly half an hour with no significant results. All at once, one of the Yelfflan agents called, "Sir, I've got something!"

"Show me." Madru moved to the left leg where the Yelfflan worked. The Yelfflan held the assassin's ankle firmly in her left hand, and carefully pushed aside feathers on the outside of the thigh with the other.

"There, sir," she said, indicating an oddly-square lump under the skin.

"Mmm," Madru hummed. "Let's see here..."

He pressed the lump gingerly with the flat of his hand, palpating carefully—

—And abruptly the being morphed into something they had never seen before.

* * *

Beletana Ve!eresh, formerly brightly-feathered and plumed, now had slick, moist, almost slimy skin. It had two 'legs' which an inhabitant of Earth would have said most closely resembled those of an octopus or squid, complete with suckers in areas that might be expected to contact a surface.

The body was barrel-shaped, surmounted with a bulbous head on a thick neck, more a tapered extension of the torso than was typical of necks upon bipedal species in the Coalition. Unlike the legs, which were highly flexible, muscular, and apparently boneless, the torso appeared to be reinforced with something more rigid than cartilage, but not as hard or inflexible as bone. The outline of this reinforcing structure was just visible under the skin and musculature of the body, and appeared as a network of ribs and vertical struts, rather like multiple spines; the whole formed a cage-like structure. This cage flexed lightly as the being breathed. There were no obvious genitalia, though there were several sphincter-type openings to be found between the legs.

Its arms were similar to its legs, save that each one ended in a kind of hand comprised of what seemed miniature tentacles, six on each hand, equally spaced and clustered in a circle around the end of the arm, capable of splaying a full three hundred and sixty degrees, and all essentially opposable. Each 'finger' ended in a single sucker-like appendage like those on the 'feet.'

The facial features on that bulbous head consisted of a soft, V-shaped mouth; large black eyes possessed of a thin, pale-pink, nictitating membrane instead of lids, currently partly closed; and what might have been ear holes arranged in an arc around the back of the head, from side to side; there was no nose. No internal bracing could be seen within the head, though it was possible it was buried so deeply that there were no surface indications; the medical scan—admittedly, made well BEFORE the embedded device triggered the alien's reversion to what the agents assumed to be its true form—had shown the brain to be inside the head, with a skull-like structure protecting it, though this structure bore little resemblance to a Ke!endarian's. That said, the medic's scan had not, Suud thought as he watched, indicated any lack of bone structure in arms or legs. *At least,* he thought, *not that I noticed. Then again, I am no physician.*

The being had a dull liver color overall, and gill slits on its neck; these flopped gently as it breathed.

"What in the bottomless pit is THAT thing?!" Chief Siis-shiiss exclaimed, shocked. "And how the inferno do we re-strain it?'

"That is an assassin unknown to the Coalition as a whole," Suud noted, "though perhaps not so much to certain beings within it; and I would recommend a fetter around the waist—it appears to have what Director Fox would likely call 'cuttle-bone' in the torso, to provide stability and likely protect inter-nal organs—and that fetter, chained to the wall."

"Condemnation, I wish we had proper force field cells close enough to work with!"

"I know, but we have no facility near enough, with high enough security, for one Coalition Presidential assassin, let alone more than two hands full," Suud pointed out for the thou-sandth time. "I cannot count the number of times I, as Pulgey's chief bodyguard, recommended an upgrade to the nearest facil-ity to this estate, but no one listens. It is a shocking oversight, so close to the Coalition President's ancestral home, but, as Franz says, 'That's bureaucracy for you.' This incident may see it done in future. At least here, the *Genesis* has the main house enclosed in a hard, triple-field dome, with this facility in a secondary, projected dome, of nearly equal strength. If noth-ing else, it is certain that the assassins are neither going any-where, nor are they able to reach Lord Entiyti."

"True," Siisshiiss sighed. "Forgive me, Lord Guurn; I am merely frustrated and perturbed by this entire..."

"Mess," Suud finished for him.

"...I have never heard that term before this incident, at least used in that fashion," Siisshiiss said, the corner of his mouth betraying a hint of amusement, "but it seems apropos enough."

"It is an Earth expression I learned from my old friend Franz," Suud said, letting his own lips quirk slightly. "'A shtik drek' is another of his expressions that...fits."

"And it means?"

"'Pile of sssshttt,' in essence."

"Ah. As you say, it fits."

"It does."

Abruptly both males' attention was drawn by Agent Madru, who let out an elated exclamation. Madru reached into one of the larger gill slits on the unconscious being's thick neck and produced a small pad, roughly the size of a Cerebellar Holographic Mnemonic Re-Encoding Induction unit. Madru held it up to the one-way window, a questioning expression on his face.

Chief Siisshiiss hit a button on the wall beside the window, which immediately converted to two-way. He and Suud both nodded; Suud offered Madru a thumbs-up, as well.

* * *

"What did you call it? 'A shtik drek?'" Siisshiiss noted, as he and Suud studied the sophisticated electronic device in the room that passed for the Chief's office.

"Yes, and yes," Suud decided. "Hmm. It LOOKS like a Zumbirian memory pad...an 'outboard brain,' as Lord Entiyti likes to call those sorts of devices. I wonder where it got one."

"But I've never seen a keypad entry system that looks like this, on ANY device," Siisshiiss observed.

"No. But look at the being's 'hands,'" Suud pointed out. "The tentacle-things at the ends of its arms."

"Oh," Siisshiiss said, face going blank for a moment. "I see. The keypads are shaped to fit the suction-cup things on the tips of its...fingers."

"Or whatever they call them," Suud agreed. "Would that Lord Entiyti were conscious at the moment. He could tell us."

"Is he all right?"

"Yes, but in some pain. Zebra and the others felt he would do well to sleep, so they gave him a rather powerful medication. But he would know what it is."

"Are you saying YOU recognize this creature?"

"Vaguely," Suud sidestepped the question. "I think Pulgey's flagship encountered a few of these beings when I was very young, and still peeling gissht in the ship's mess."

"Would any of the ship's crew still recognize them?"

"Possibly, but that was many octads ago. All of them will have gone on to other places in their lives by now...if they are still alive. I have no idea where to begin looking..." Suud paused, as an eureka moment hit, "except for one. And I will lay odds HE will recognize the species of this being."

"Who?"

"Lord Levy. Director Fox."

"Who runs Division One, and has been a part of this investigation from the beginning," Siisshiiss realized. "Excellent." He hit the intercom. "Agent Madru?"

"Yes sir?" came the almost immediate response.

"Please obtain a full visual scan of our very mysterious prisoner in his CURRENT form, and send it to Lord Guurn and me as soon as it is completed."

"Yes sir. You think you have it identified?"

"No, but we may have a line on someone who can. And he's part of our system. Is the prisoner conscious yet?"

"No, sir. It's still unconscious."

"Even better. Get that visual record as soon as you can, then. Best if the thing is unconscious while you're imaging it. And then get it restrained like Lord Guurn recommended, again preferably before it wakes up."

"Understood, sir. I should have the visual scan on your tablets in five minutes, no more than ten at the outside, and the being restrained two minutes later."

"Good."

"Huh. He reminds me of Agent Echo," Suud murmured, unaware the intercom was still active.

"THANK you, sir!" Madru exclaimed, a broad smile on his face.

Chief Siisshiiss merely snorted with a frown.

* * *

"Lord Guurn, I am not comfortable with sending it away," Siisshiiss protested, as the Reptoid studied the imagery now residing on his personal tablet, showing it to Duuniiss, who had just arrived. "It is, after all, an important piece of evidence."

"And this is exactly why Lord Levy needs to see it," Suud argued. "He is the one who recommended we search for just such an item, and he knows more about Lord Entiyti and his history than you and I together—he lived a large chunk of it alongside him, and is closer to him than any other living soul; I was the solitary witness for their secret blood-brother ceremony, as it is still performed by the old families—and it may mean something to Fox." He neglected to mention that he had participated in that same ceremony himself. "Besides, my son was Emdalian Military Intelligence when he served; he couriered classified information over half the galaxy! I have little doubt he can take it to Fra— Lord Levy, Director Fox, for his study and general perusal, and still bring it back to us safely for our use in trying the bastard."

"Basss—?" Siisshiiss tried.

"Earth term," Suud sighed, raking a hand across his face in a gesture that human friends would have said looked very like Fox. "Like ssllitthhssshhtt in our tongue. It means an illegitimate offspring and is generally NOT considered a...compliment. Nor did I intend it to be so. Evidently more of my vocabulary was influenced by Lord Levy than I had realized."

"Which is not a bad thing, Pater," Duuniiss pointed out. "He is a good, honorable being."

"No, son, it is not, and yes, he is. I suppose I simply had not realized how much influence he has had upon me, until working closely with him to keep Pulgey alive these recent days."

"Ah." Siisshiiss turned to Suud's son. "And you were EMI?"

"Yes sir."

"Grade?"

"Giirrsht, first rank," Duuniiss replied, "with an Ultra clearance level."

Siisshiiss' eyes widened in surprise.

"Impressive," he decided. "I should have thought you

much younger than that rank and level implied."

"He is," Suud said, trying to keep his chest from puffing out with pride. "He was exceptionally good. And quite skilled."

"My pater was a good teacher, and he learned from two good teachers. I can take care of myself, and any items I courier, quite well, Chief," Duuniiss declared, confident.

"Very well, then," Siisshiiss concluded. "We will send the memory pad to Director Fox via retired Giirrsht Duuniiss Guurn, for him to study alongside the imagery of our strange prisoner. Hopefully he can determine what we are working with, around dealing with his most recalcitrant Agent."

Suud and Duuniiss both hid scowls at the disparaging reference to Echo.

* * *

In short order, Duuniiss Guurn was back on the *Exodus*, Fox's personal long-distance shuttle, headed for Aleancë again, a very special couriered package in hand.

Also on the *Exodus* was a diminutive little being known as a Sluuite. It looked like nothing so much as a little purplish-red salamander, but unlike Earth salamanders, it was intelligent. Nargiss Nesh hailed from Sluu in the Kepler-969 system, and she was aboard in a desperate effort to earn sufficient funds to adequately feed her brood of children, after her mate was killed in an accident aboard the starship where he had performed sanitation work, the year before. After all, she considered, it was not as if Sluuites were particularly large compared to the average sentient, and most galactic species could readily step on them if they were not careful. Not that she held resentment toward the crewmember who had tripped and fallen on her husband. She missed him, but had rarely seen him in any event, because of his job. And the last time he had been home for shore leave, he had left her gestating a new brood.

Now that brood had hatched, and she needed to provide for them. And there was little on Sluu any more to provide; as fast as the Sluuites bred, by the time their culture developed significant technology, the small planet's resources had been maxxed out, and it was often necessary to find work elsewhere. So she had left the tads with her own parents, and set out to find work, sending funds home as she could...which wasn't nearly as often as she would have liked.

Consequently, when the odd stranger with far too many wriggling fingers had approached her on the transfer station where she had paused her interstellar perambulations, she had tried not to think too much about why he might want her to do something for him. Instead she remembered the brood at home, more than thirty little mouths to feed, and accepted the job. It had taken a bit of doing to maneuver herself into position, and she had hopped through more star systems than she cared to think about, but she was where she needed to be now.

If she failed, she knew, it behooved her to vanish, and quickly. And since she had never seen any creature like it before, she doubted she would have trouble disappearing; he obviously was not from the Great Spiral—perhaps one of the satellite galaxies. Fortunately she had had sense enough not to give the strange being her real name.

* * *

"Hello there, young Guurn," the *Exodus'* pilot/captain greeted Duuniiss as he came aboard. Behind him, a small purplish-red streak shot around the airlock hatch door and disappeared in the shadows of the aft flight deck.

"Hello, Captain Du'ven'de," Duuniiss replied. "It seems I am back again. You and Captain Prrt may be seeing a lot of me for a few days, at this rate."

"Not a problem, youngling," Du'ven'de decided. "Do you want me to stow that package for you?"

"No, I need to hold onto it. But thank you."

"All right, then. I have instructions to get you to Aleancë at maximum emergency speed. That means we will be there in only a couple of hours. So sit down, don the harness, and we shall depart Emdali."

"Consider it done."

Duuniiss was the only passenger—that anyone knew

about—so he tucked the couriered package into his jacket, sat in the co-pilot's seat, and commenced fastening the five-point harness. Given his specialties when he had served in the Emdalian military, both Du'ven'de and Prrt had given him permission to sit in the co-pilot's seat, knowing if anything untoward came to pass—such as an attack directed at Fox—the young Reptoid would be more than adequate at the weapons controls. Which, they had told him, would be very useful while they ducked and dodged.

While he strapped into his seat, Du'ven'de strapped into her own with practiced speed and finished checkout, closing the airlock hatch remotely. She made a quick call up to the *Genesis* for departure approval, and moments later, Du'ven'de smiled.

"Hang on, youngling," she said. "Here we go!"

The *Exodus* lifted off the ground and eased forward, through the narrow opening in the bright-yellow triple-layer force field, then aimed heavenward and accelerated.

* * *

That is not good, Nesh decided, watching as Duuniiss tucked the package safely inside his jacket. *I cannot possibly reach it if he keeps it there. I am small and light compared to him, but not so much that he will not notice.*

She found a safe place to handle the acceleration of the small, swift interstellar shuttle, and waited as the craft shot spaceward.

I shall just have to keep watch, she decided. *Surely he must go to the hygiene facility and relieve himself or something. And then I will have my chance.*

* * *

Shortly after the *Exodus* activated its Alcubierre drive, Duuniiss did indeed unstrap and rise, aiming for the head; given Reptoid physiology, the g-forces of ground launch tended to force the fluids through his kidney-equivalents and into his bladder. He headed aft, down the passageway to the head, entering and securing the door behind himself.

305

Not before a tiny purplish-red sentient slipped through.

* * *

This is far more about Reptoid anatomy than I wished to know, Nesh thought in something between embarrassment and distaste, watching as the young male relieved himself at the urinal. *But there is his jacket, hanging to one side. Perhaps I can scurry up the wall.*

She turned and, using her highly-adapted hands and feet, scuttled the two feet up the bulkhead to the draped cloth. In seconds she had darted inside and begun systematically searching the pockets.

But to Nesh's dismay, there was no sign of the couriered package in the Reptoid's jacket pockets.

Just then, she felt the entire jacket picked up as the Reptoid finished his business and began to don the item of clothing. A frantic Nesh scurried out the rear of the collar and onto the upper back just as the Reptoid settled the jacket in place on his body. A desperate leap took her from the Reptoid's shoulders onto the vanity by the sink, thence to the deck...

...Barely in time to dart out the door behind him.

* * *

Duuniiss, more comfortable for the break, settled back in the co-pilot's seat, not bothering to strap in this time.

"Better?" Du'ven'de wondered.

"Much," Duuniiss averred. "Planetary launch does that to me almost every time. I've learned to deal with it for a while, if it is not convenient to go, but..."

"When you are just waiting to get there, might as well, eh?" the captain remarked with a chuckle.

"Exactly," Duuniiss said, shooting her a grin. "What is our ETA?"

"Oh, given how Prrt and Fox and I have hot-rodded this little girl, around two Earth hours, give or take," Du'ven'de decided, after checking her instrumentation. "Not long."

Behind them, in a tiny nook underneath a passenger seat, a small creature drooped in disappointment.

* * *

Du'ven'de was as good as her word, and Duuniiss did not move from his seat, nor reveal the hiding place of the couriered package, for the rest of the brief trip. Less than two hours later, the *Exodus* arrived at the special dignitaries area of the Aleancë spaceport, and Duuniiss thanked Du'ven'de, then debarked.

In his wake, a tiny sentient slipped through the *Exodus'* hatch, and watched in dismay as the incredibly tall—to her—Reptoid strode away, up the gate bridge, at a pace the little Sluuite could not hope to match.

Nargiss Nesh sighed.

"I guess I will have to feed the babies some other way," she murmured to herself. "Time to disappear."

She scurried to the nearest bulkhead, found an air vent, and slipped inside.

* * *

"...And so the interrogation is now complete," Qq'k'l reported to Director Siisshiiss.

"To judge by your face, it was...unusual," Siisshiiss noted.

"Insofar as interrogating a heretofore unknown species is unusual, yes," Qq'k'l agreed. "It is a male, and his name is Beletan Veersh—minus the Ke!endarian beak clacks. He is a Persan something or other—I fear his name for his species does not translate well for us; like so many, it simply means 'the people,' so I cannot give you that—but he is part of a larger coup and invasion attempt from a faction of the Persan Federation. He was part of the assassin team to see that it went as planned. Which of course, it did not. And he is frightened of what his superior will do to him, but we could not obtain a name for that superior. I am uncertain if that is because he does not know it, or because there is a more sophisticated mental technology at work. His mind appeared...mm, compartmentalized. I am certain the information is there, but we are still ascertaining 'how far is too far'—we do not wish to destroy his mind while obtaining the information, but we do not yet know how far we can press this new-to-us species."

"Sssllluutth ssshhiissh ttthhiissiiss oosssshh hiiisssht ssshhrr," Siisshiiss cursed with feeling.

"I did not know hell had sixteen levels," Qq'k'l replied calmly.

"It does in Emdalian lore," Siisshiiss retorted, a bit sheepish. "Forgive my language. That is simply not at all good news. Especially given the matter Director Fox has gone to deal with, I suspect."

"You sent some evidence to him via classified courier to identify, did you not?" Qq'k'l pressed. "To include hopefully identifying the creature?"

"I did," Siisshiiss confirmed. "Now we must wait."

"Yes, now we wait," Qq'k'l agreed.

Chapter 12

Left to themselves in what was essentially a force-field-encased studio apartment—rather larger and more comfortable than the cell in which Echo had originally been housed—three Alpha Line Agents attempted to convince their exhausted companion to have the chip removed.

"No," Omega responded, determined. "Not yet."

"Then at least rest," India coaxed, "while I pump you full of imprazine again."

"Fair enough," Omega agreed. She removed her jacket and rolled up one shirtsleeve before slumping down in a corner of the small sofa. "There we go. Okay, India, go for it." She leaned back and closed her eyes.

* * *

Romeo, Echo, and India exchanged glances. Echo jerked his head over his shoulder at the bed; Romeo and India nodded. Echo moved to the end of the couch and swiftly bent down, scooping up Omega before she could react.

"Echo?! What are you doing?" Omega exclaimed as Echo carried her across the room.

"Putting you to bed," he said firmly, laying her on the bed and proceeding to remove her shoes, tie, and empty shoulder and waistband holsters over her protests. "Now lie down and rest."

"But Echo—"

"Sweetheart," Echo murmured very softly, sitting on the edge of the bed as Romeo and India backed away to give the couple some privacy, "whether you realize it or not, you're damn sick. Remember, I can feel the strain on you through the mind link, no matter how good a face you try to put on for us. You're pale, your head's splitting, you're feverish, and you feel like shit. Am I right?"

Omega sighed, then nodded.

"Yeah," she admitted. "Yeah, hon, you nailed it. Across the board."

"So lie back and stay here, let India treat you, and rest while you've got the chance, baby. I'm not a doctor, but I'd bet the less you move around, and the more you just shut down and try to relax and rest, the better off you'll be. Right, India?"

"Right, Echo," India affirmed, moving to the other side of the bed and beginning to check Omega. After several minutes of scanning, India glanced across the bed at Echo, then prepared an osmosive syringe. Omega caught the look.

"What is it?"

"Meg, you can't let this go on much longer," India answered. "Your immune system is trying to form an abscess around the chip."

"Damn," Echo whispered, looking away to hide his concern.

"Just a little longer, India," Omega pleaded. "Keep it going just a little while more. Please. Fox is in there with the Council. He's a diplomat; he founded the Diplomacy department! He'll convince 'em Echo was right, if they don't think so already."

"Okay, Meg, but it's against my better judgement," India sighed, administering the hypodermic, then refilling it. "I only hope we don't regret it later. There. That should stave off the rejection a little longer, and ease your pain. But this one will make you sleep for a bit."

"Good," Echo said, watching India administer the sedative.

Within seconds, Omega grew drowsy, and India and Echo stood to join Romeo on the couch. Echo felt a gentle, sleepy mental touch.

Echo...don'go...

What? Echo turned to look at his partner, and India paused. *Don'go. Sit here with me. Please.*

Echo glanced meaningfully at Alpha Two, who nodded in understanding, then he sat back down on the bedside, as India joined Romeo on the sofa. Slim fingers sought out his hand, tucking themselves within it. He glanced down at the small hand in his, as he wrapped his own fingers around hers.

Meg? Are you all right, sweetheart?

Umm...would you be dis'pointed in me 'f I said I was...was scared?

No.

Okay. I'm scared.

Of what the implant will do?

Yeah, that. But mos'ly...what if Fox can't convince 'em? What if we secede? What if the Persans invade? Worl' War Two'll be like a snitz nex' to that.

Wha-huh? What the hell is a 'snitz'?

Uh, you ever feel like you gotta sneeze, only it never quite makes it out? So you kinda stand there going, 'AH-huh, AH-huh,' an' tryin' to get your breath? That's a snitz.

Oh. Echo chuckled. *Those things; I didn't know they had a name. Annoying as hell, but nothing much, really.*

Exactly. An' all on 'counta me, sorta.

Ssh, Meg. It's not your fault, and it's not my fault. Somebody did a damn bad job of planning and issuing orders. And maybe somebody else is trying to grab more control than he's supposed to have.

Adita?

Yeah. Don't worry about it right now. Just relax and go to sleep.

You gon' go? Omega yawned prodigiously, putting the back of her other hand to her mouth as she stretched slightly. Echo grinned gently, affectionately, at his partner's childlike state.

No. I'll stay here, if you want me to. It's not like I can go too far, anyway.

Tha's true. Omega giggled sleepily. *Talk 'bout a captive audience.*

Echo groaned, then snickered despite himself.

So you want me to stay?

'Es, please.

All right. Quit fightin' the meds and go to sleep, Meg. I'm right here.

Okeydoke...

And she was out.

* * *

Echo sighed and glanced over at Alpha Two. "Finally."

"She asleep?" Romeo asked.

"Yeah. She fought it, though, really hard. She's worried about the whole situation," Echo confided. "She knows she has to play this just right, and I don't think she's very comfortable about it."

"I don't blame her one bit," India commented. "Intergalactic war is a little beyond me, too."

"I think it's a little beyond all o' us," Romeo agreed.

* * *

"Tsu aldi rukhes," Fox said blankly, looking at the video imagery on the tablet screen Duuniiss presented, as they met once more in the private Ennead room. "You're kidding. This is what the mystery assassin really looks like?"

"Apparently, Uncle Franz," Duuniiss averred. "Pater was there for the...reveal, I suppose we may call it. Do you know what it is?"

"Well, it's been years," Fox admitted. "But it sure looks like a paramilitary band we encountered about a year after I'd signed on with Pulgey. Damn, that was a long time ago! Rumor had it, they weren't from ANYWHERE around here, as in nowhere in the Milky Way." He paused and frowned, thinking hard, trying to pull the species name to the front of his mind. "Kugel...no. Kanda...Kag...Ka-ahgh! I give u— Oh!" he exclaimed. "That was it! Ka'agand! It's a Ka'agand!"

"Where are these...Ka'agand...from, Uncle?"

"That, I couldn't tell you for sure," Fox confessed. "Like I said, rumor had it they were from outside the Milky Way, but that's as much as I know. Somewhere in the Local Group for sure, because anywhere past that is rather too far to travel for most races' lifetimes, at least with our current level of tech. But they could be from the Sagittarius Dwarf like the Cortians, or one of the Magellanic Clouds, or the Carina Dwarf, or even the Triangulum or the Andro—" Fox broke off abruptly.

"Uncle Franz?" Duuniiss said, laying a hand on the human's shoulder. "Is everything all right?"

"I don't know, zun," Fox murmured. "I don't know. Either...well. I've got another hunch, and either we're about to solve this whole thing, or we're about to fall into one farshtinkener meshuginah shtik drek. Maybe both. In which case, di zakhn zenen gegangen tsu gehenem in a khandbask."

"I didn't understand a word you said, Uncle Franz," Duuniiss complained.

"That's all right, zun; you will, soon enough, I'm afraid," Fox sighed.

* * *

"...And Adita really went missing for over two weeks?" Fox wondered, as he discussed some private concerns with old flame Teela Krimnet over drinks in her private office.

"He did, yes, about an Earth year ago, but it turned out, it was only an extended holiday," Lady Teela averred. "He had had a very busy time of it with the influx of system applications to the Coalition, and him the principal focus for the evaluations. It seems his personal assistant lost the travel information, then panicked when Ordik could not be reached..."

"But why?" Fox pressed. "Why would the assistant panic over something he, she, or it knew was going to happen?"

"The assistant tried to cover its tracks, according to what I understood," Lady Teela elaborated. "Ordik was QUITE unhappy when he got back from his holiday to discover the uproar."

"Mm," was all Fox said. "Do you know what happened to the assistant?"

"Well, of course its position was terminated," Teela noted. "Ordik said he could not tolerate such incompetence, and frankly, I did not blame him."

"Where is the former assistant now?"

"I have no idea, Franz," Teela said with a shrug. "Honestly,

I am uncertain what this has to do with anything."

"It may, or it may not, Teela," Fox said, deliberately vague. "Let's just say I'm...sleuthing...and leave it at that. If I find out anything of import, I'll notify you as soon as feasible."

"Very well," Teela agreed, good-natured. "Would you care for another drink, my old friend?"

"Thank you, Teela, but no. I have more sleuthing to do, and I need my wits about me to do it."

* * *

Fox, the faithful Duuniiss in tow, headed back to the hotel, deep in thought. There, Duuniiss arranged for a light meal to be sent to the room through secure, trusted means to ensure his adoptive uncle's safety, while Fox proceeded to dig deep into the Aleancë records databases, searching for tidbits of information. When Duuniiss brought him a sandwich suited to human consumption, he ate it one-handed, never looking up from his search; Omega was not the only Division One agent who knew how to do research.

Nearly four hours later, he found the telltale tidbit he was looking for, and sat back in mingled satisfaction and concern.

"Well, well, well," he murmured. "That IS disturbing."

"What is, Uncle Franz?" Duuniiss wondered.

"I've just finished digging back through news reports and PGLEIA records," Fox explained. "Did you know Ordik Adita went missing for more than two weeks, almost an Earth year ago?"

"No, I did not."

"He did. Then showed up abruptly at the end of a fortnight, explaining he'd decided to take an extended vacation, after a period of intense work for the Ennead...which work he had indeed done. There were no less than eight systems that had petitioned for either Coalition entry, or increased trade rights, during the previous quarter. And him in charge of the work preparing those systems for increased participation."

"All right..."

"So...he disappears, then comes back...and not even his assistant knew where he was, because according to Adita, the assistant was incompetent and lost the travel itinerary...then tried to claim Adita never told him he was traveling."

"That seems an odd excuse to use," Duuniiss said, thoughtful. "It would be easily dispelled by the employer."

"Or the investigators, because the assistant, a Valestian named Pwizeen Ashurgrubon with a heretofore impeccable record, was the one who reported Adita missing, when he didn't show up at his office as Ashurgrubon expected, for two consecutive days after disappearing."

"Oh my," Duuniiss said, slit pupils dilating in surprise. "That IS interesting. And very odd."

"Ain't it?" Fox said, quizzical. "It gets MORE interesting."

"I am all hearing membranes."

"When Adita suddenly showed back up after his extended absence, he and Ashurgrubon had a bit of a row of sorts," Fox went on. "It seems that Ashurgrubon felt something was wrong with Adita, 'not right,' he put it per reports, and—contrary to previous commendations of Ashurgrubon—Adita now claimed that Ashurgrubon was, and always had been, a complete incompetent. But just when the PGLEIA-assigned investigators were ready to telepathically interrogate Ashurgrubon, Adita fired him and sent him away."

"Meaning this Ashurgrubon knew something Adita did not wish known," Duuniiss decided.

"More than likely, yes," Fox said, "though it could have been as simple as an affaire de coeur that he wanted secret, because of political exigencies or the like. Still and all, this Ashurgrubon all but dropped off the face of the galaxy for the next three or four months...when his body was found, washed up on the shore at one of Valestia's sleazier oceanic shipping centers."

"Let me guess," Duuniiss said, quirking his mouth. "Cause of death unknown, but the body had many contusions."

"Said as if you had been reading the news report, zun," Fox said, wry.

* * *

"They're here, Fox," Bravo murmured into the comm line a little while later, and Fox nodded to himself.

"Good work, kinder," he said, keeping his voice low for the sake of his personnel on Earth. "Golf, Easy?"

"Right here, Fox," Golf replied.

"Good. Given that Echo is still in custody pending a verdict, and Omega is...not well...and Alpha Two is with them, providing support on several levels to include medical, I'm afraid I'm going to have to give an order to Alpha Line directly. That assumes you all still recognize me as the Division One Director..."

"Like hell we're gonna recognize GreenHair CarrotFace as director," Easy grumbled. "Of course we do, Fox. Every last damn one of us. And believe me, Golf and I polled everybody in the department."

"We had a meeting in the warp tunnels, which tunnels Adita evidently doesn't know about," Golf averred. "It was kinda cramped, but we managed."

"Excellent. Then here is what I need you four to do, as best you can, because it will require a bit of strategy."

"You may fire when ready, sir. We are ready to copy and execute."

"Lima, Bravo, I need you to contact the Deltiri embassy on the sly and have Ambassador Zz'r'p and his top interrogators standing by. Alpha Four, I want you to round up all of Alpha Line that you can get hold of, because the first thing you need to do is start taking Adita's 'entourage' into custody. I want all of his props taken out from under him, and then I want HIM taken into custody. DO NOT underestimate ANY of them, kinder. In my considered opinion, and based on evidence already discovered in the assassination attempt investigation, any one or all of them may not be as they appear. They all look to be Zumbirian, correct?"

"Yes, Fox," Lima confirmed. "There's a shit-ton of 'em, too, as Echo would say."

"How many?"

"Fox," Golf said, "Alpha Line has already been investigating that situation. By our estimate, he has about fifty 'security guards' here at Headquarters, helping him maintain control, and probably ten each at..." Fox heard several beeps, as Golf apparently checked his 'outboard brain' for the information, "Atlanta, Chicago, Los Angeles, London, Geneva, Moscow, Tokyo, Hong Kong, Rio, Sydney, and Gaborone. So figure a total of a hundred and sixty, or thereabouts."

"A brokh," Fox kvetched. "And—what?—around fifty Alpha Line Agents?"

"Yeah, less Alpha One and Two," Easy agreed. "But we're no slouches, Fox; trust us on that. Echo and Omega trained us well, and we were all good field agents to begin with. Now, if you won't consider me a braggart, our department is a small army unto itself, *I* think. And we also have the 'regular' field agents firmly behind us; Adita's been interfering in the patrols, and the result has been...some problems."

"Farkakte, verdammt, merde, rab'dr'ib, glagaram, gloob a flop, and argdun!" Fox cursed with feeling. "This is going to be a giissht mess to clean up after, isn't it?"

"Afraid so, Boss," Lima sighed. "So we better get to mopping as soon as we can, before they have time to get too entrenched and it gets worse."

"Lima, let me ask you and Bravo something really quick..."

"Go, Boss," Bravo said.

"How deep has Adita been able to get into the system?"

"Not very," Bravo averred. "He doesn't have any of your passwords, we haven't given him any—we said that you and Echo had your own, and kept them to yourselves, so we were clueless—and he ticked off Security and Software pretty much right off the bat, by trying to run roughshod over 'em, especially when everybody started realizing he'd ousted Echo as Acting Director. So they've been dragging their feet about getting him access to Director functionality on the servers an' shit."

"And yes, we made sure to fill them in on what you already

told us, like, A.S.A.P.," Lima added. "So he ain't EVER gettin' access. Now, whatcha need us to do next?"

"Right. Well, then, I'm going to have to leave a certain amount of this to your discretion, gentlemen," Fox decided, "but use what resources you have, the four of you work together, and start at the most distant Offices, taking Adita's stormtroopers into custody and immediately interrogating them, preferably with Deltiri. You'll have to move fast, and get them into custody before Adita finds out..."

"I think we're already on that, Fox, because Sugar decided we had some sort of coup under way, and he told us as much when he notified Alpha Line of the situation with Echo. We have a number of different plans already laid out for clearing this buncha trash," Easy noted. "And Sugar and some of his people have been working surreptitiously with us, too. What we figure we need to do is cut the supports out from under Adita, then take him in hand. Right?"

"Exactly, zun."

"We can run with it," Golf declared. "And we'll squeeze as much information out of 'em as our Deltiri colleagues can wring. All we were waiting for was word, and if that didn't come soon, we were gonna take it in hand our own selves, if we got brain-bleached for it."

"Good man!" Fox exclaimed, pleased. "All of you, the whole damn department, good men and women. And that goes for Field, Diplomacy, Security, and Software, too. Use all of 'em as you require, gentlemen. Call in offworld allies if you think you'll need 'em, though you might have to come up with an excuse as to why they're suddenly showing up."

"We're all over it, Fox, I swear," Easy affirmed. "Say the word, and Operation: Kickass is under way."

"The word is said," Fox declared.

"Then let's roll, boys," Golf said. "O. K. Command out."

"Fox out."

* * *

"That was good news, and bad news," Duuniiss observed,

as Fox sat silently, pondering the situation.

"It was," Fox agreed.

"You have very good people," Duuniiss decided. "Led by very good people, assuming that Echo is released. Well, even if he is not, though I do not wish to think about that possibility."

"Indeed I do, and I don't want to consider that, either, zun. I hope my people are up to it, though," Fox worried. "If what is going on is what I am suspecting more strongly with every hour that passes, we may already be in the midst of a cold war verging on becoming hot."

* * *

A gentle hand lightly shook a sleeping shoulder, and a deep, familiar, and much-loved voice called softly. "Meg... Meg, wake up, baby. The guards are back. It's time."

"Mmmfh," Omega grunted as she roused groggily from a deep, drug-induced sleep and sat up. "Oooh. Smaller dose next time, India."

"Sorry, honey," India replied, tying the laces of the shoes she'd just slipped on Omega's feet. "They came for us sooner than I expected."

"There better not be a next time, one way or th' other," Romeo observed, stern but sympathetic, standing at the foot of the bed, holding Omega's discarded outer clothing and holsters. Item by item, he passed them to Echo, who put them on his woozy partner.

"Good point, junior," Echo remarked. "You with it now, Meg?"

"More or less, Ace," Omega replied, swinging her feet off the bed and standing with her partner's aid. She wobbled badly, and an alarmed Echo grabbed her, steadying her and ensuring she stayed upright. "Urgh. Y'all might have to keep me vertical for a few minutes, but I'll pull out of it 'ventually, here. I really wish I had a cuppa coffee, though."

"I'm sorry, Meg," India noted. "That's one thing I don't have in my medikit. Though a couple caffeine pills in there might be a good addition, now you mention it. I'll see what I can do about that once we get home."

"Maybe we kin get th' pretty lady some coffee from th' guard station," Romeo suggested. "I noticed earlier that they had a coffeepot. An' Earth trades in th' stuff, so it oughta be th' real deal."

"That might be a plan," India agreed. "We'll stop by on our way to the hearing chambers and see."

"Here, baby, lemme get this," Echo said, wrapping his arms around Omega from behind to quickly knot his partner's tie, then handing her the empty waistband holster, which she tucked into the small of her back. "The guards will give you your guns in a minute." He smoothed her platinum braid somewhat possessively as India brushed down Omega's Suit jacket, then handed it to her.

"Okay, let's go," Omega said quietly after shrugging into the jacket, and they followed the guards out.

* * *

Breaking up into specialized teams and spreading through the Offices, the Division One agents took surprisingly little time to round up the distributed teams of Adita's enforcers. In a few cases it was as simple as creating a distraction sufficient to draw the entire group of enforcers together to investigate, then tossing a somniferous grenade into their midst.

"Evidently Adita does not select them for their intelligence," Sugar observed.

"Doesn't look like it," Golf agreed.

* * *

"Normally, I would only call forward the accused," Chairbeing Teela began, as the Ennead reconvened. "However, since another sentient's future is so intimately bound with the accused's: Team Alpha One of the Division One Agency of planet Earth, Sol system, step forward so that judgement may be rendered."

Echo and Omega moved to the apex of the triangular room, facing Lady Teela. From their vantage point in the gallery behind Alpha One, Romeo and India could see two hands, one

320

large, one small, making light, surreptitious contact as Echo and Omega stood silently, close together, awaiting the verdict. Romeo felt a hand laid gently on his forearm, and without even looking, covered his life partner's hand with his own.

"Agent Echo."

"Yes, Ma'am."

"The Ennead, as well as the full governing galactic council—who were convened for the express purpose—has considered your case carefully and at length. We have also, at a suggestion from your Director," the alien woman gestured at Fox, now seated beside her, "carried out some investigations of our own. We have found that Ari N'Do was given at least partial responsibility for the wording of the orders sent to you. Interesting, in light of the suspicion now cast upon him. We also found that Ordik Adita has grossly exceeded his boundaries in the way in which he executed the orders...and is not responding to our communiqués to recall him. More, there is emerging evidence of manipulation, both subtle and gross, in his positioning to be the entity levying those orders. We also found, after reviewing those orders—specifically the wording as they were, in fact, issued to you, which was not how they came from us—that you responded properly in violating them. It was certainly never intended by this Council to permit what amounts to enslavement of its law enforcement agents. We have no desire to be...'Nazis.' About which group, I might add, Director Fox most kindly gave us considerable additional enlightenment, based on his...extensive...personal experience." Lady Teela paused. "This Council therefore finds your actions justified. Guards, release Agent Echo, and return his weapons."

Echo showed no reaction, except, perhaps, a satisfied gleam in his eyes, but Omega staggered in titanic relief. Echo steadied her, then accepted his proto-cyclotron blasters from the guards, placing them in his empty shoulder holsters, before tucking his Winchester & Tesla in the small of his back.

"Agent Omega? Are you well?" Lady Teela queried considerately, on observing the female Agent's unsteadiness.

"I will be now, Madam Chairwoman," Omega responded with a tired, grateful smile.

"Good. Then you can telepathically link the Ennead and show us exactly what evidence you obtained against Ari N'Do. The matter is an urgent one, as I am sure you will agree."

Omega glanced up at Echo, and both were aware of thinking the same thought: *Uh-oh...*

"I'll try, Ma'am," Omega responded, hesitant. "But that's a lot of minds. And I'm not real experienced at this telepathic business yet."

"We understand," Lady Teela replied. "Do your best. That is all we ask."

"And all Meg ever gives," Echo remarked, looking his partner in the eyes in encouragement. "And her best can be truly amazing." Then he added silently, *You can do it, angel baby—just relax.*

"Okay—here goes..." Omega said, closing her eyes and trying to focus.

* * *

Omega struggled, but somehow managed to link all the minds, both human and alien. Echo began to grow concerned as the link progressed, however; he could sense through the nd't'lq the tremendous strain she was under, and tried to lend her some of his strength through their private link, with only moderate success. Nevertheless, Omega stepped the Ennead through her meeting with the Premier in her private suite, and what she discovered in his mind.

As the tale wound toward Hsrs' sexual move on Omega, Echo felt the stress in his partner build swiftly, and he realized in consternation that she was essentially reliving the events to relate them to the Ennead. He also became very aware that she was associating it with the far-too-recent sexual assault by a brainwashed Mark Wright. More, as Echo watched the memory alongside the others, he realized that same association had made Hsrs' behavior seem far worse to her than it actually was.

He was flirting with her, certainly, the Agent decided, keeping his thoughts behind the rudimentary block Omega had taught him. *And caressing her, which in the wispy dress-thing they put her in, was inappropriate, at least by our lights. But she wasn't in danger of actual sexual violation, that I can see. He's actually avoiding touching her breasts, or her crotch... like he already knew the human anatomy, and what was off-limits. There's more going on here than meets the eye. And I'm starting to suspect what.*

But Omega's tension was building rapidly, so he decided to interject a cautionary remark.

Meg, take it easy, honey, Echo warned through their private link. *Back off some. Get some emotional distance.*

Echo, I...Echo... Abruptly, Omega spoke to the entire assembly. *Everyone, I think I've...I can't...Echo, help...get India...I...Echo? Are you still there? Echo...please...Echo...?*

And suddenly Echo found himself sitting on the floor of the Council chamber, with an armful of his limp soon-to-be life partner in his lap, as India bent over them.

* * *

"How are we gonna do this?" Golf wondered, as the combined Alpha Line and 'regular' field agents, along with quite a few combat-trained Diplomacy agents—some two hundred, in all—met in Sub-Basement Three, out of sight and surveillance...at least, that Adita knew how to access. The field Offices were clear of Adita's henchmen, but now they needed to clear Headquarters before word could get back to Adita. "We gotta get 'em away from the Core, and keep Adita in the dark until it's too late and we got 'em all..."

"I suggest a diversion," Sugar noted. "Perhaps in Grand Central Station. It could look like a scuffle broke out when a perp was taken into custody..."

"And then another team cuts in, maybe objecting to the way the first team handled it," Monkey brainstormed.

"Like, one of 'em is Fox-and-Alpha-One-schooled," Nuts suggested, "an' the other one is suckin' up to this Adita guy."

"And they get in a fight," Easy added. "Which ought to

bring in the 'enforcers' pretty quick."

"That should work," Sugar decided. "What do the rest of you think?"

"Quick show of hands," Golf declared. "In favor?"

Most of the hands went up.

"Opposed?"

No hands went up.

"Those who didn't vote...you don't have any ideas?" Golf pressed. There was silence for a moment, then the abstaining agents, none of whom were Alpha Line, shrugged and shook their heads; some scuffed feet in embarrassment. "But you're okay with us running with this?"

"Yeah, man, sure."

"Go for it," another said.

"We'll back ya, but you're Alpha Line," a third replied. "Just tell us what to do on this one."

Golf and Easy glanced at each other, then nodded together.

"All right, we're gonna run with it," Golf declared. "Now, we need some volunteers."

"With that plan, you prob'ly want one Alpha Line team and one standard field team, right?" Kappa wondered.

"That seems logical," Sugar offered, for the benefit of Alpha Four.

"Me 'n Nun can be the standard team," Kappa said, a bit hesitant. "I mean, we're not gonna be a team no more, 'cordin' to Fox, but we can do this. Right, Nun?"

"Sure, Kappa," Nun said quietly. "We can roll together on one last mission."

"Okay," Golf said, keeping his voice even; most of the agents there knew how serious it was to break up a partnership, and while they had not particularly liked Kappa's behavior, they still hurt for the pair. "In that case, I guess we need an Alpha Line team. I'd suggest me an' Easy, but we're kinda left at the top of the department hierarchy, so..."

"So you need to stay in the back," Torino averred. "Adam, are you game?"

"I think we could do that, Torino," Adam said with a wicked grin.

"All right," Golf said. "We have our initial teams, and we'll need an alien who's in on this, to serve as the 'perp.' Anybody got ideas for who?"

"I volunteer," a voice came from the back, and the group parted to allow a short, muscular being with richly-colored dark mahogany skin to move forward. She was less than half the height of most humans, with pincer-like hands and elephantine feet; as was normal for her species, which dwelled on a super-Earth with three times the gravity, her breasts barely pushed out the front of the black jumpsuit uniform she wore. Her head was a squat cylinder barely bigger than her neck, with ear holes, nose holes, and a mouth slit; her eyes were slightly larger than human-sized, but the color was indeterminate—they were shielded by a thin nictitating membrane that protected them against daylight, making them appear glazed.

"And you are?" Golf asked.

"I am Slekuwiss Jostek," she said, "an exchange agent from Exinul—what you would know as Luyten b. I think I look different enough from you humans to make a good offworld perp, do you not think?" The mouth slit curled in a grin. "And I know your regulations, for they are mine as well. I can dress in other clothing," she tugged the collar of the black coverall, "and use my native tongue at first, and no one will know I am not a tourist."

"This works!" Easy declared. "We have our diversion team."

* * *

"I know it'd prob'ly be the field team that'd be followin' Adita, the bastard," Kappa noted, as he and Nun met with Jostek, Alpha Twenty-Four, and Alpha Four to work out details. The rest of the teams would remain in the near vicinity except for a few teams selected to wander the Core, to keep Adita believing all was normal. "But I just dunno if I could do that an' keep a straight face, fellas."

"Me neither," Nun admitted.

"I mean, if you guys think it's essential, we'll give it a shot," Kappa offered.

"No, that's cool," Torino decided. "I get that. Adam, you think if we play the collaborators, you can act the part?"

"I can try, I guess," Adam agreed, somewhat reluctant, but understanding the need. "After all, by now everybody probably knows about our misunderstanding regarding who led the department; we can play off that, I suppose. So...what? You two take her into custody in the standard fashion, then we come along and tell you to let her go, because Lord Adita is offering amnesty for all perpetrators in the division..."

"You're kidding. You made that up," Nun declared, shocked.

"Don't we wish," Torino grumbled, as Adam shook his head.

"Sonuvabitch," Nun expostulated.

"That," Kappa agreed.

"Okay, we'll play it that way," Golf declared. "Let's go get set. It goes down in fifteen."

* * *

An Exinulic in civilian clothing, a small overnight bag over one shoulder, meandered down the concourse toward Grand Central Station, having appeared innocuously from one of the restrooms near the maglev gates as a train disgorged passengers from the Penn Station spaceport. She stretched, looked for the 'Baggage Claim' sign, then ambled that direction.

Just then, two agents slid smoothly into line with her from behind, one on each side.

"Come with us, ma'am," the taller of the two said. "We've been waiting for you."

"What?!" the Exinulic declared. "I don't know what you're talking about!"

"Oh, I think you do," the other agent said, easing a hand under her arm. "We've seen the warrant issued for your arrest. Kappa, grab her!"

"I got 'er, Nun!" Kappa caught the woman under the other arm, and they began hustling her out of the main traffic flow; as short as she was, they would have tried to lift her, but Exinul had gravity three times that of Earth, and any sentient being that could function there without servo-suits was too heavy for humans to lift unaided. Upon realizing what was happening, the new visitors hurried away, clearing the concourse as fast as they could.

"No! STOP! I've done nothing wrong!" Jostek cried. "Someone help me! Please—HELP!"

Just then, two more Suited Agents ran up.

"What's going on here?" the woman demanded. "What do you two think you're doing to this poor woman?"

"Ma'am," Kappa explained, "there's a warrant out for this woman's arrest. She just arrived as a fugitive from Division Four. We're taking her into custody."

"The hell you say," the female Agent's partner declared, even as a cluster of five Zumbirian enforcers wandered up the concourse, drawn to the shouting, and watched, curious. "You KNOW Lord Adita has issued amnesty orders for our less-fortunate brothers and sisters."

"I don't care if he's issued candy f'r everybody," Kappa averred, insolent. "Division Four has a warrant out f'r her arrest, and Nun an' I aim to see it gets done!"

"Not any more," the male Agent insisted. "We're Alpha Twenty-Four, so we're in charge here, and we're overriding you as of right now!" He turned to Jostek. "No worries, ma'am, you run along now. We'll set these jerks straight."

Jostek scampered away as fast as her short, stocky build would allow, and Nun and Kappa did a not-so-slow burn.

"What the HELL do you think you're doing?!" Kappa demanded, getting up in Adam's face. Adam put both hands on his chest and forced him back.

"Yeah! She's a damn KILLER!" Nun added. "We can't let her run around loose! How many did the warrant say she'd murdered, Kappa?"

"Six, maybe eight," Kappa disclosed. "Two of 'em kids!"

"Are you two going to settle down and go about your business or not?" Torino asked.

"That's what we were DOIN', ya bimbo, when you two interrupted!" Kappa shot back.

And then he swung.

The roundhouse apparently connected Adam's jaw with a resounding thud, and the Alpha Line Agent spun, nearly falling. Torino tackled Kappa, jumping onto his back, clawing and hitting; Nun grabbed her and dragged her off his partner, just as Adam leaped at Kappa.

At that, four of the enforcers immediately dived into the fight, pulling Kappa and Nun off Alpha Twenty-Four; the fifth pulled a communications device and called for backup.

All four agents turned on the enforcers, however, and the fifth threw in his weight to no avail. Within moments all five were gagged and restrained via force cuffs on wrists and ankles, before being dragged out of sight by a contingent of other agents who briefly emerged from hiding places around the concourse. The four agents who had been in the altercation panted briefly, looking around.

"Oh good, they got the civvies clear," Nun observed, as Jostek returned to reset the scenario for the backup enforcers.

"Yes," Sugar said. "Golf contacted Security and asked Uncle to hold back visitors from this concourse, so once our cover passengers were clear, no one else would enter. Uncle, in turn, contacted Flight Control, who happily rerouted further incoming craft to avoid the gates on our concourse. Provided we can keep this little operation confined to this area, we should be good."

"What about Adita?" Golf asked.

"His Excellency Ambassador Zz'r'p said to leave that to the Deltiri Embassy," Sugar added.

They all grinned.

* * *

Fifteen minutes later, another batch of enforcers had been

taken into custody. This time there were eleven.

"Sixteen down," Easy noted.

"'Bout thirty-something to go," Golf added. "Maybe this'll be smoother than we thought."

The agents quickly reset again.

But when the new batch of reinforcements showed, all hell broke loose.

* * *

"Take them all out!" the lead enforcer snarled to his contingent of more than thirty Zumbirians, upon encountering the fighting agents; hidden eyes watching the scene determined this group comprised the rest of the enforcers, who apparently really were not chosen for their intelligence. "I care not who they are! Calling for reinforcements twice in a matter of moments speaks of resistance!"

Abruptly they all produced an offworld version of a black-jack—a small depletalloy weight in a sophisticated, flexible-polymer mini-club—and waded into the four mock-fighting agents.

But the instant one of them swung his weapon at Kappa, the agent went into berserker mode, lashing out with both fists and both feet. Several enforcers went flying across the concourse, slamming hard into walls and not getting up. Nun, Torino, and Adam followed suit, though with slightly less ferocity. Unfortunately, that only angered the Zumbirians, to a being...who, interestingly enough, were not normally known for fierce anger, as a species. Their response was ferocious.

Within moments, and before any of the hidden agents could react, Kappa went down, with at least half a dozen enforcers dogpiling him alone, all beating him with their blackjacks; Alpha Twenty-Four also disappeared under a dozen or more enraged Zumbirians.

A horde of black Suits suddenly appeared around the concourse and ran for the beleaguered agents; within moments, Alpha Twenty-Four, who had gone back-to-back before being overborne, came out of the mêlée.

But Kappa suddenly let out a scream, and one of the enforcers yelled in triumph as his blackjack splattered blood.

Nun let out a howl of raw fury, snapped the neck of the enforcer fighting him, drew his blaster, and began firing at the pile of enforcers on top of his partner. In moments, all six enforcers lay dead, scattered around a badly-wounded and unconscious Kappa, his head swollen and misshapen, as blood trickled from nose, mouth, and ears.

"STAND DOWN!" Golf shouted. "Zumbirian forces, stand down at once! Surrender now or face the consequences!"

But he was ignored. In response to Nun's use of deadly force, the other Zumbirians pulled their own weapons and began firing into the mass of Division One agents.

* * *

Alpha Eight, who had made a beeline for the downed Kappa, intending to get him to safety, proved the first victims of the newly-escalated battle, as Kako staggered back with a gasp, his hands going to his belly.

"Kako, what's wrong?" Monkey said, already kneeling beside Kappa. "Get over here and help me, buddy. He's in a bad way."

"I...cannot, moy drug," he said, and Monkey spun on his knees. Kako stood there, his hands holding tight to his abdomen; blood seeped between his fingers. "I...I am...shot..." He crumpled to the floor beside Kappa.

"*NO!* MEDIC!" a horrified Monkey bellowed. "MEDIC! I got TWO MEN DOWN!"

"WE HAVE NONE!" Sugar called back, targeting several Zumbirians' legs and literally taking them down. "They're being watched too closely! We must clear diese verdammten Schlägertypen before we can take them to the medlab!"

"Then it's time to clear the damn goons!" Monkey declared. He flung himself to the ground and pulled out both blasters.

* * *

"Golf!" Sugar said to the Agent currently directing Alpha Line. "The agents are trying to spread them out, to get them away from our casualties! This is spilling back toward Grand Central main concourse! We cannot let them get—"

"Already handled," Golf noted, calm, taking out a Zumbirian that was trying to flank him with a snap kick to the face. The alien being flew backward, unconscious before it hit the floor. "Uncle said he would set up a perimeter. Nobody in, nobody out."

"Ausgezeichnet!"

Just then, Torino screamed in pain and went down, as one of the Zumbirians jumped on her back, landing with both feet and forcing her to the floor, then stomping. Adam shouted in outrage and swung at the enforcer; the goon grabbed his forearm, yanking hard, even as he swung his blackjack at Adam's shin. Two loud crunching sounds marked the failure of Adam's shoulder and tibia, and Adam fell beside his badly-injured partner, whose legs were not moving. The vicious Zumbirian raised his blackjack to deliver a killing blow to Adam's head.

"Oh, no you don't," Golf growled, targeting the Zumbirian responsible, not bothering to wound. The Zumbirian's body fell, its newly-detached arm beside it...but its head was gone.

Enraged, another Zumbirian whipped out a firearm and took aim at Golf. Before Golf could react, two things happened.

The Zumbirian enforcer fired...

...And Agent Uniform leaped in front of Golf.

* * *

A furious Monkey was firing with both blasters, having gotten Alpha One to teach him some gun-fu techniques several months earlier, and he had practiced diligently in the training facilities in the interim.

Consequently, numerous Zumbirians' legs were disappearing, which made it damned difficult for them to reach their intended targets. Nun saw what he was doing and joined him, shouting, "HEY GUYS! TAKE OUT THE LEGS!"

The Division One agents threw themselves to the floor behind various objects for cover, and began doing just that.

* * *

Golf promptly dispatched his would-be murderer, then knelt beside Uniform, who had dropped at his feet. Blood poured from the hole in his shirt front.

"Aw, man," Golf whispered, trying to stanch the blood, but knowing it was unlikely to happen, given the location of the wound. "What'd you go and do that for, Uniform?"

"Y-you're runnin' this...shindig," Uniform panted. "Do-doin' a...a damn fine...job. You an'...an' Sugar, an' Uncle... you're gonna do it, man. Gonna cl-clear these...these guys out. Gotta...gotta keep you...goin'..."

"Hush," Golf soothed. "I get it. Save your energy, pal."

He felt a light hand on his shoulder, and knew Easy was there; his partner's voice was murmuring into electronics, judging by a certain quality to the sound, and Golf realized he was notifying the medlab, hoping to get instructions for how to save their dying comrades...how to save Uniform.

Easy knelt beside Golf, who glanced at him, and saw the grim expression and tight lips. *No saving him, then,* Golf thought. *Damn, damn, damn. And he's dying to save me.*

"Dude," Uniform blurted then, as Easy rose, drew his blasters, and defended the pair. "Golf? Are you there?"

"Right here, pal."

"Tell...tell Kilo...I'm sorry. Tell him...I'll wait for him... on...on the other...side."

"Hush that," Golf said, signaling Kilo, who saw who Golf held, and came running. "You can tell him yourself."

"Y-you...you know that...I won't. Won't make it..."

"Yeah, you will. 'Cause he's right here."

Kilo crouched beside the two, then groaned.

"Aw, Uni," he whispered, "what did you do, buddy?"

"Saved my life," Golf murmured, "for which I'm no end grateful."

" 'S...'s okay, Kilo. 'S okay, Golf," Uniform said, voice growing weaker as his face paled. "It's okay, pal. I don't...don't regret i—"

And he was gone.

* * *

By the time three Alpha Line Agents—Monkey, Golf, and Easy—and two standard field agents—Nun and Kilo—had added the full measure of their cold fury into the fight, those few enforcers who were not lying on the floor with missing limbs fled down the concourse toward Grand Central Station. Golf whipped out his cell phone and hit a speed dial.

"Uncle, get ready—you got about eight or ten headed your way at a dead run. Yeah, no quarter asked or given. We got enough prisoners here to get info out of 'em. If they give you a hard time...take 'em out." This last was delivered in a growl. Easy laid a light hand on his shoulder; he turned to his partner, who wore a concerned, querying expression, and nodded. Then he hit another speed-dial.

"Whiskey, this is Golf. Get your people down here A.S.A.P. We got wounded on both sides, and one of ours has already passed over. I don't want more joining him if we can help it."

* * *

Within moments, medics and medtechs were pouring from the emergency warp tunnels, and Security agents were moving among the wounded Zumbirians, restraining them where necessary, even as Deltiri interrogators went to work. The majority of the Zumbirian wounds were cauterized by the blaster beams even as they were made, so while the aliens were in pain, few of the survivors were in danger of expiration, and it was nothing that could not be repaired in a regeneration pod if necessary.

"Though I'm all for letting 'em deal," Easy snarled. "They cared little enough for our people."

"No shit," Golf agreed. "But that's not for us to decide. The medics will take care of this. Let's round up the unwounded agents and see about taking down the head of the monster."

* * *

Lima and Bravo met the battle-hardened agents as they filtered from the warp tunnels into the Alpha Line Room off the Core.

"He's still in Fox's office," Bravo murmured to Alpha Four, "and doesn't seem to know anything's wrong, so the Deltiri must be doin' it right."

"Did you get the upper floors of the Core cleared?" Sugar asked.

"We sure did," Lima averred, eyeing the blood on so many white shirts, "ten minutes ago, no questions asked. How'd it go downstairs?"

"One agent dead, at least ten injured, four severely," Easy noted, seeing Golf was in no mental state to answer, at least not tactfully. "And the severely injured...might not make it. But a lot of the Zumbirians are dead or injured. They just wouldn't stop."

"It's like they were soldiers with orders, or something," Nun decided. "No stopping, no giving in, they'd die rather than surrender. And take as many of us with 'em as they could, in the process."

"All of which needs to get reported to Fox," Bravo decided. "Because that'd sure fit in with the whole coup scenario. Have the Deltiri started interrogations?"

"Right alongside the medics," Easy noted. He glanced at his grim, silent partner, whose shirt front was nearly red with Uniform's blood. "Let's go get Adita and get it over with. I'm tired of this shit."

"Ain't we all?" Bravo noted.

* * *

Within moments, the entire Core was filled with black Suits. A grim Golf stepped forward, triggered an app on his cell phone, and raised it to his lips.

"ORDIK ADITA!" his voice suddenly boomed through the large volume as if projected from a megaphone, hard and unyielding as adamant. "YOU ARE UNDER ARREST. COME OUT AND BE TAKEN INTO CUSTODY IMMEDIATELY."

Visible through the bay window, a figure at the desk rose and looked out. Abruptly the lights in the office went out, though movement could just be seen via reflected light; evi-

334

dently Adita didn't know the windows could be opaqued...or didn't know how.

"ATTEMPTS TO CALL FOR YOUR HENCHMEN ARE USELESS," Golf added, scowling. "THEY HAVE ALREADY BEEN TAKEN INTO CUSTODY...THOSE WHO SUR-VIVED."

The Director's office remained quiet for several more moments. Golf decided he had had enough. More than enough.

"ADITA, YOU HAVE THIRTY SECONDS, OR WE *WILL* COME IN AND GET YOU," he ordered, raising his arm to glance at his wrist chronometer. "ALIVE OR DEAD IS YOUR CALL. AND...MARK. TWENTY-NINE...TWENTY-EIGHT...TWENTY-SEVEN..."

Abruptly the office door burst open, and Adita emerged, personal weapons in hand...

...To stare into nearly two hundred blasters, all targeting him. He stumbled to a stop.

"I am from the Ennead!" he blustered. "You are rebelling against the Galactic Council!"

"We. Don't. CARE," Golf declared.

Chapter 13

"No, no, the procedure went well. It was a simple matter to remove the implant and stop the immune response," Lady Teela's personal physician told the Division One Agents gathered in the small medical conference room off the Ennead offices. "Agent Omega will be awake and mobile shortly."

"Did she suffer any brain damage?" India asked, glancing at a rigid, anxious Echo.

"No, she did not, thanks to the imprazine. My compliments upon your excellent medical care, and my thanks for your assistance in locating the implant with your scanner."

"It's my job, sir," India said with a slight smile, as Echo relaxed ever so slightly.

"Echo, can you still feel the mental link?" Fox asked quietly.

"I'm not sure, Fox," Echo responded after a few seconds' concentration. "She's probably still under the anesthetic, and I can't tell if the link's gone, or just...dormant."

An attendant came to the door of the room. "Agent Omega is awake, and asking for her partner," she said. Fox glanced at Echo.

"I guess that answers that question, old friend."

"I guess so," Echo replied; then, under his breath, added, "damn."

* * *

Echo slipped into the room to find a pale Omega apparently asleep in bed. *Meg?* he thought hard. *Meg, can you hear me?* Omega lay quiet in the bed, unresponsive. Echo sighed.

At the slight sound, Omega opened her eyes. Echo immediately moved to the bedside and sat down carefully, to prevent jarring her.

"Hi," he said softly, smiling at her. "How are you doing?"

"Okay," she murmured, her voice very low. "Got kind of a nasty headache." She paused for a moment. "Where are you?"

Echo sat up straight, startled, and shock and dread slammed through his being like the proverbial runaway train. He waved his hand in the air over her face as he said, "Meg? Can't you see me? They said there wasn't any brain damage—"

Omega reached up and unerringly caught Echo's wrist.

"No, no," she said, and his tension eased as his gut unknotted. "I meant, 'where are you?'" she continued, tapping her temple. "I...can't find you. It feels like you should be there, but..."

"I dunno, Meg," Echo answered, puzzled himself. "I know what you mean. It's...mmm...like a carrier wave, but no signal."

* * *

"Yeah; good analogy. Maybe the link's still there, but I'm... not strong enough to access it right now, or can't access it without the chip, or...or something."

"Maybe," Echo replied. "But I'm betting it's me that can't access it. It's not like your nd't'lq is in me this time, see; it's the other way 'round, and I'm not a telepath. Which means, I guess, that it was good you were stubborn and waited until all chances of me getting brain-bleached were past. At least it doesn't feel like a big raw hole this time."

"True. You sound disappointed, though," Omega observed. "Just like you did on the Persan ship, now that I think about it. Why?"

Echo shrugged, then glanced away. Omega studied the averted face.

"Echo?"

"What?"

"You like being able to talk to me telepathically, don't you?"

"Well, it's a good way to have a really private conversation, I'll admit," he hedged. "It flat blows surveillance technology out of the water."

"Uh-huh," Omega responded skeptically, smiling at her suddenly-uncomfortable companion. "So is it only with me, or does Mr. Privacy like telepathy in general now?"

Echo met her eyes then, and Omega could have sworn she 'heard' Echo say, *What do you think?*

* * *

"So when are they letting you out of here?" Echo changed the subject before Omega could analyze it; the truth was, he liked the intimacy of a telepathic connection with the woman he loved. But Omega was right; he WAS a very private man, so admitting as much was difficult for him.

"Pretty much any time, I think," Omega thought out loud, sitting up and holding the sheet around her nude form. "I need to get dressed..."

"Need help?" Echo grinned.

"Ah-ha-ha," Omega grinned back. "You wish." She started to wave her left hand in front of his face in a teasing fashion, then stopped. "Oh..." Her head bowed, ashamed. "Oh." Omega closed her eyes, and Echo watched as a tear squeezed out between the silver-white lashes.

* * *

"Is this what you're missing?" Omega heard Echo say softly as she felt something hard slipped onto her finger. She opened her eyes to see the star-shaped hyperdiamond solitaire back on the ring finger of her left hand. It was very warm, as if he had been carrying it close to his body.

"You...you kept it?"

"Of course. I've had it hanging on the chain with the cross you gave me, ever since. Right here." He patted his chest, over his heart. "I never planned to abandon you, baby. I just didn't know how to FIND you, in that damn big ship. And I needed a plan, some sort of strategy; I kept hoping I could figure out a loophole, see..."

"Why didn't you TELL me about the orders?!"

"And get YOU in trouble over violating those damn orders, too? No way in hell, sweetheart. I knew it would get ME brain-bleached. But you can't BE brain-bleached. It would have gotten you imprisoned, maybe for life."

"Aw! Oh geez. Echo...I-I'm so sorry...I did it all wrong..."

"Hush that, baby," Echo shushed her, then pulled her head against his shoulder. "It's all right. Only trust me next time, okay?"

"I do! I...I just...there was so much input...I was SO confused, and horrified, and...and when you didn't..." She hid her face in his shoulder. "But I didn't know about the orders! So I thought...And I already—"

"Wait, what? Confused?" Echo interrupted.

"Yeah," Omega admitted. "I didn't tell anybody, but I flat didn't know how to handle the full telepathy. I could turn it on and off, yeah, but when it was on, it was wide open. I could 'hear' everybody in the area. All at once. No filters. No volume control. No gain adjustment."

"And no wonder you had trouble understanding me," Echo realized. "Damn! That must've been bedlam, sweetheart."

"Yeah. Apparently nobody remembered I wasn't born a telepath, and didn't know how to do all that. And there wasn't time to ask anyone to teach me." Omega sighed.

"You were winging it the whole way, sorting out thoughts and figuring it out as you went. In the middle of the roar from hundreds of minds thinking at once."

"Uh-huh."

"Could you even concentrate?"

"Not...very well. I had to work hard at it, focus with, like, laser intensity, just to make out what one person was thinking. Even you." She slumped. "Then I'd have a headache after, usually. Especially after reading the Persans."

"Shit. I wish you'd told me," Echo murmured quietly. "I would've tried to be a little clearer in my explanations. I had no idea it was that hard for you."

"I didn't really think that...I mean, there wasn't...it all happened so fast," she sighed. "When I was at Headquarters, I thought, MAYBE I can handle this. But when we got on the Persan flagship and I got fairly bombarded by all these thoughts from brains that don't operate like ours...I knew I was in trouble."

"Aw shit. And by that time, it was too late, and Hsrs claimed you, and everything went to hell in a handbasket," Echo realized. "I still wish you'd told me."

* * *

"I know. And I should have. But I was so confused and upset! It was...it was like...jackhammers comin' at me from every direction! I couldn't even hear MYSELF think, for everybody ELSE thinkin'!"

"Damn."

"Yeah. Look, um. Can we...maybe...chalk it up as our first real miscommunication as, as almost-sorta-kinda mates, and let it go, hon?" Omega suggested hesitantly, slipping her arms around Echo with affection. "I'm really, really sorry—I can't even begin to say how much—but I had all I could do just to keep functioning..." She sighed again, and rested her head on his chest, slumping against him, deeply tired.

"Okay, on one condition," Echo replied, easing his arms around her in turn, letting his fingers caress the bare skin of her back.

"What's that?"

"Look up here at me, and I'll show you."

Omega looked up into dark eyes and caught her breath, then smiled happily as Echo bent his head over hers.

* * *

Echo joined India and Romeo in the gallery of the Ennead room a little while later; Duuniiss Guurn sat nearby.

"Hey, Echo, where's th' pretty lady?" Romeo asked. "I thought it was s'posed t' be just outpatient surgery, once they got th' immune response under control. She's okay, right?"

"Yep. Meg's fine, or she will be, soon. But she's got a damn nasty residual headache, pal," Echo explained. "Nothing serious, but she took some pain pills the doctor gave her, and decided—finally—to give it a rest. She'll be along when her head feels better."

"'Not t'night, honey, I've got a headache,' huh?" Romeo teased, and India ribbed him hard with her elbow. Echo merely ignored him and seated himself as the Ennead resumed its session. By invitation, Fox was with them again, and sat down next to Lady Teela.

* * *

"Ari N'Do, step forward," Lady Teela commanded. "To the charges of collaboration and treason, do you have a response?"

"I admit collaboration, but I emphatically deny committing treason," N'Do replied vehemently.

"How can that be so?!" one of the other councilors exclaimed. "Collaborating with a potential invasion force, passing government secrets—"

"I passed no state secrets," N'Do replied calmly. "Agent Omega never determined the specific information which was passed."

"Agent Echo?" Lady Teela scanned the gallery. "Ah, there you are—where is your intended?"

"Still recovering, Ma'am," Echo answered, standing. "Do you want me to get her?"

"Is it advisable to let her rest?"

"She's got a helluva headache," Echo admitted, "and she's kinda tired, but I think it'd be all right by now. We might have to accommodate her being somewhat below her normal physical and mental condition, and I'm glad our department medic is right here, but it should be safe."

"Very well, then. Please ask her to attend, if you would. We will take all due care of her possible, and be as understanding as in us lies, given the surgical procedure she has just undergone. We will pause the proceedings until she has had an opportunity to join us."

* * *

"I don't know," Omega said blankly, blinking at the Ennead members from the floor. "I'm sure the information was there. But there was...so MUCH information..." Omega's voice tapered away. After a moment, she sighed wearily, rubbed her aching head, and glanced around, searching the room.

"Whatcha need, Meg?" Echo asked softly, just behind her on her right, ready to support her if she needed it.

"Well, a chair would be awful nice. I kinda feel like over-cooked asparagus right now..."

Lady Teela gestured, and an assistant quickly brought a human-proportioned seat to the center of the room. A weary Omega eased into it and leaned forward, folding her hands and tucking them between her knees, before closing her eyes and bowing her head. Her forehead creased. Echo knelt beside her.

* * *

"Meg? What's wrong? You look like you're hurting."

"That's 'cause I am. See, I remember it all, Echo. I'm just trying to sort through it, to see if I can pull out the right one of the Premier's thoughts. It'd be awfully good if my head would stop poundin' so I can concentrate, though. Whenever I try to concentrate too hard, it feels like it's gonna explode or some-thing."

Echo frowned, glancing up at India in concern. India pursed her lips, considered briefly, then shook her head in the negative, mouthing, 'She needs to stop that,' while making a cutting-off gesture across her throat with one hand. Echo turned his eyes to Fox, a plea for assistance—of some sort—in his gaze.

* * *

Fox looked satisfied as he leaned toward Lady Teela and murmured something. Lady Teela nodded. Fox rose and walked to the chamber door, opening it and gesturing to some-one outside.

"Omega," he said, turning, "I thought you might need some help, so I asked an old friend of yours to stop by. Actually, I sent a special shuttle to fetch him, as fast as he could get here. He was...a bit busy, but he dropped everything, handing the work off to the other members of the embassy, to come to the side of his favorite pupil."

"Welcome, Ambassador Zz'r'p of Deltir, in the Arcturus

system," Lady Teela intoned formally as the tall blue alien entered the room, attired in formal robes.

"Zz'r'p! Am I ever glad to see you! Bless you, Fox!" Omega exclaimed with a glad smile. Zz'r'p's eyes tilted in pleased amusement as he offered the Agent the Deltiri equivalent of an answering smile; he immediately moved to the female Agent and crouched beside her. Echo stood to give Zz'r'p room, but didn't move away. Instead of resuming his seat with the Ennead, Fox stood nearby as well, ready to help if needed.

* * *

"All is well now, Omega," Zz'r'p soothed, rubbing gentle fingers across her puckered brow. "Just relax, my dear. I can also ease the telepathic part of the headache, though the surgery aftermath will remain until it heals properly. Good, good. There we go. That is much better."

"Oh, wow. Yeah, it is," Omega murmured, as she felt the pain subside. She slumped in relief, and rubbed one temple with her fingers. Zz'r'p took that as a cue and replicated the motion, as Omega felt his gentle telepathic probing soothe the nerves of her face and scalp, easing the tenseness in the muscles there.

"Good," he told her, as the Ennead looked on. "Very, very good. You are an excellent pupil, Omega; you 'catch on' to what I need you to do very swiftly. No, no, child, do not denigrate yourself so—no, do not try to deny it, either, for I see it in your mind. Hush that. Relax and show me the memory. I will undertake to sort it out and show it to the Ennead for you."

Omega relaxed as commanded, closing her eyes. A second later, her body shuddered slightly as the Arcturan entered her mind. Seconds after that, the chamber's occupants were looking around at each other, puzzled.

* * *

"N'Do's telling the truth," Omega said, bemused. "He really didn't pass state secrets."

"No, just private ones," Echo observed, eyes narrowed. "VERY private ones."

"But why'd he tell Hsrs t' put you, me, an' India in his harem?" Romeo wondered from the gallery.

"Especially after making sure Hsrs already knew Alpha One and Alpha Two were engaged to be married," India added in distaste. Echo gazed consideringly at Lady Teela, eyes still narrowed.

"That's exactly why," he said cryptically. "Right, Lady Teela?"

"You are perceptive and intelligent, Agent Echo," Lady Teela replied, and smiled. The other Division One members, including Fox, stared, perplexed, as the Ennead members all began smiling, leaning back in their seats. "Resume your position, Ari, if you please. Thank you. It was well done." The accused councilor took his place at the Ennead console.

"I...don't understand," Omega said.

"It was a test, Meg," Echo explained. "The whole damn mission was a test. Was there ever really any danger of invasion?"

"At the very first contact with the Persans, yes," Lady Teela acknowledged. "Most definitely. But by the time you four met with them, no; Pulgey went to some effort to ensure the matter went peaceably. In fact, by the time the Ennead approached him with our little test, Premier Hsrs was rather amused by the scenario. That is why he agreed to help us."

"Amused?!" an indignant Omega expostulated. "Romeo, India and I could've been killed! Echo was almost brainbleached! For what?!"

"Calm yourself, Agent," Lady Teela said, holding up both hands and keeping her voice placating. "I understand your reaction, but I assure you we would not have allowed anyone to be hurt. Nor would Hsrs. He is a brilliant actor, and was very careful not to overstep his boundaries any farther than the role required. We saw, however, that—given recent events in Alpha One's history, of which Fox made us aware only hours ago—it still proved far more disturbing to you than we ever intended, and for that we deeply apologize; we were unaware of some of those events, until he told us."

"Oh," Omega murmured, gaze faltering. "I...never mind. You're right, now that I think about it, I guess. When I actually told him flatly to stop...he did."

"Precisely. Hsrs became quite fond of you, by the way; I think he would like for you to visit and perform a cultural exchange of a more traditional kind of first contact, if you might be willing...later, when you are more recovered from...recent events. Perhaps along with your partner and mate, by that point. And speaking of your partner, had Echo been successfully brain-bleached, we would have immediately downloaded his memories back into his mind, as has been done for other agents in different circumstances. Your solution to the matter was creative and...rather startling, I admit, and I think the rest of the Ennead agrees! As to our reason: It was background research for your request."

"Say what?" Romeo interjected. "You mean the charter amendment?"

"Precisely," N'Do replied, his attitude much softer; even his voice was gentler, lacking the stridency of earlier remarks. "We desired to see the level of commitment and fidelity you had for each other. The situation was deliberately set up to force you into violating your orders, if you had significant feeling for one another at all. Ordinarily, we would never send agents off on first-contact missions with such inflexible orders as those, impending war or no."

"And?" Fox demanded. "What were your conclusions?"

"The events were intriguing to watch," one of the other councilors volunteered. "Particularly the reaction to Agent Echo by his colleagues. We expected more...understanding."

"Especially by his betrothed," N'Do added.

Romeo and India, in the gallery, hung their heads. Omega, already in physical pain and near exhaustion in the aftermath of the stress and the powerful immune response, could take no more. She put her head in her hands, hiding her face. Echo saw her shoulders shake once, and a trickle of liquid escaped between her fingers, tracking slowly down the back of her hand. A worried Zz'r'p looked up at him and shook his head slightly. Echo turned to the Ennead, expression determined.

"I object to the implied blame," he said, quietly but firmly. "They had no knowledge of my orders, I was unable to tell them due to the security level of said orders, AND I knew we were under continual surveillance. The anti-surveillance equipment provided for this mission was entirely inadequate to the task of overcoming the large amount of surveillance equipment being used—which I am sure was exactly how you intended it. Consequently, I had no way to tell them the reason for my actions. Appearances were entirely against me."

"That is true for Romeo and India, but not for Omega," Lady Teela pointed out.

"No," Echo disagreed. "She and I have already discussed that problem. Since Meg wasn't trained as a full telepath, and wasn't born that way, she was so swamped by foreign thoughts and sensations, it's a miracle she was even able to function. A lesser-willed being would likely have become catatonic from the sheer onslaught of information and general sensory overload. And the implant actually interfered with communication between the two of us."

"Hmm..." Zz'r'p murmured, as the Ennead members glanced at each other.

"But I still should've known better, Echo," a miserable voice came from the chair beside him.

"Goes f'r us, too," a subdued Romeo agreed. India nodded.

"So it means we need to work on our communication a little more, for situations like that." Echo shrugged. "We've never worked through a scenario like what we had on this mission, so we'll add some, and use 'em to figure out strategies and means of communication. That's what all the department training is for, really." He knelt and poked Omega's arm teasingly. "I'm kinda looking forward to it," he murmured just loud enough for her sensitive ears to hear. Lady Teela smiled.

"They ring true every time," she observed to the Ennead.

"No matter how many obstacles we place between them, they come back together." She turned to the Agents. "The implant's interference was deliberate, Alpha One; we introduced it in the modification to hide Omega's recombinant DNA. Forgive us for 'breaking' it, Ambassador Zz'r'p; our technicians can show you what was done, and I feel sure that the implant, as originally designed, will work much better than what we used! We are impressed with Agent Omega's determination, however, as well as her ability to sort through such confusing and overwhelming input to go on with the mission. The fact that Omega overcame the equally-deliberate omission of training to successfully complete the mission, is an outstanding testament to her intellect and determination, traits demonstrated by all four Agents in their resourcefulness. Frankly, we had not considered Omega might pick up Ari's subterfuge in Hsrs' thoughts! My congratulations, Lord Levy, on four very fine Agents. And my apologies for keeping you in the dark, my old friend. I can only say it was necessary. But let me also add that, although unexpected, your Agency's overall response is indicative of a high level of teamwork, trust, and the highest moral standards. It is good to know that there is an organization in our Coalition willing to hold accountable even the Ennead to moral responsibility."

"And Lord Entiyti's near-assassination?" Fox demanded, outraged. "Was that necessary, too? For I can tell you of a certainty, that he knows nothing of this..." he waved an angry hand, "little 'test.' I've already communicated with him, and with Suud Guurn, on the matter."

"Oh," Lady Teela said, voice growing quiet. "No, Franz, we are all as upset as you at the attack. Pulgey is well-liked by the Ennead, and none of us would wish him harm, certainly not to get him out of the way for something like this—or any other reason."

"No," N'Do agreed, perturbed. "In fact, this little fact-finding mission was concocted largely AFTER he was injured; prior to that, he was our source of information, since you and he go so far back, Lord Levy." N'Do sighed. "He has such a wealth of knowledge of humans, partly from your long friendship, as well as that with Agent Echo, and he was able to start explaining what needed inclusion in this amendment to your charter..."

"And then he was injured, and no one was certain what would come of matters," Lady Teela noted. "We were worried—personally, and professionally—that he might not survive, certainly, but from a practical standpoint, such things are always prepared-for, at this level of government." She sighed. "It seems hard-hearted to me, and in some respects, I suppose it is. But it is also necessary, nevertheless."

"But you were pressing for the amendment, and without Entiyti, we needed to find another information source," N'Do explained.

"And THAT...is a LIE," Fox declared. "One of your own is, in fact, a sleeper agent infiltrated into the Ennead in order to invade this galaxy and overthrow it."

The room erupted in chaos.

* * *

"Explain yourself, Lord Levy," a suddenly-imperious Lady Teela all but snapped.

"I should be happy to, Lady Krimnet," a scowling Fox responded in kind, not a whit less authoritative and commanding. "After effectively evicting my duly chosen and trained successor, Echo, here, and sending him and his partner on a mission that he KNEW would end up like this," he waved a hand around to evoke the hearing so recently concluded, "because he maneuvered to make it so, Ordik Adita proceeded to take over Division One Headquarters with a shipload of trained shock troops. At least fifty of these troops were stationed around Headquarters, charged with ensuring that the agents there obeyed Adita...and no one else. He then sent additional troops to the most prominent field Offices around the planet, to extend his sphere of influence. Having thereby taken over the Agency, he proceeded to extend his reach to the other planets in Division One. Subsequent orders appear to have been calculated to upset the structure and balance of power, by among other things, refusing to allow the field agents to properly police Earth, or any of the other planets in the division, and giving known criminals free reign."

A disturbed murmuring filled the chamber, from gallery and Ennead alike.

"What proof have you of this charge, Lord Levy?" Lady Teela pressed, less certain than she had been moments before.

"A great deal," Fox declared. "Including copies of those various orders, surreptitiously passed to me by certain agents who objected to the way he was running the Agency, indeed the Division. Never mind the fact that, when I contacted him to stand down as interim Director, as I was now capable of focusing on the operations of the Division, he refused."

"Surely he could be expected to wait for your arrival—"

"As well as the fact that we have now tied him into the assassination attempt on Coalition President, Lord Pulgey Entiyti of Emdali," Fox averred.

The entire room abruptly fell silent. The tension was palpable.

⁎ ⁎ ⁎

"Ambassador Zz'r'p, if you please?" Fox said, and stepped back as the Deltiri rose to his feet and addressed the Ennead.

"As Fox is the rightful and duly-appointed Director of Division One, whose presence on-planet has never been required for his orders to be obeyed," Zz'r'p reported, "it was not hard to line up the various field agent units, under the overarching command of Alpha Line, to take Adita's troops into custody. And yes, they were indeed shock troops and enforcers—I myself witnessed a field agent severely beaten at Headquarters a few days ago for failing to follow Adita's orders, but instead following the standard Agency protocols established years ago for field operations. And the very public beating was issued on Adita's command, as he stood and watched."

* * *

A gasp went up. Fox scowled. Echo balled his fists. Even Omega, in her obviously weakened condition, leaped to her feet.

"Who was it?" she demanded.

"I was gonna ask the same thing," Echo averred.

"So was I," Fox agreed.

"It was Agent Orange," Zz'r'p said, and the inadvertent reference to military terminology caused Romeo, in the gallery, to desperately stifle a snort of laughter, given the name and mode of address; a scowling India gave him a sharp elbow in the ribs, and he sobered. "He is still in the medlab, being treated, and may need a regeneration procedure to fully recover, acting chief medic Whiskey said."

"Please continue," Lady Teela said, very quiet.

"Because of this sort of thing, the matter had to be handled carefully and surreptitiously," Zz'r'p explained. "No one wanted more agents needlessly injured. So Alpha Line, under the command of Alpha Four—given that Alpha One and -Two were here, and Alpha Three is the very excellent Enigma code-breaking team but not so much intended as a field team—rounded up the rank-and-file field agents and started at the outlier Offices. They made more than adequate use of their intimate knowledge of the various facilities, and coordinated operations among multiple teams. Each team consisted of two Alpha Line partnerships leading anywhere from twenty to fifty standard field agents, and there were five teams. Each was assigned an Office, where they were tasked with taking all the enforcers at once at a handful of facilities—there were only some ten or twelve enforcers at any given field Office, since they generally are not nearly so large as Headquarters—before moving on to the next facilities on their schedule."

"Waitaminit," Echo interrupted. "Just how many shock troops did Adita HAVE?"

"Precisely one hundred seventy-eight, total, by our final count," Zz'r'p answered. "Though the arrival of the majority was clandestine and did not take place until after Alpha One's departure from Earth. Prior to embarking on their Director-Fox-approved mission to rid the Agency of these shock troops, Alpha Four prearranged with my embassy, and we ensured that each squad of agents had at least one skilled Deltiri interrogator with them. The rest of Alpha Line remained at Headquarters, keeping a watchful eye upon Adita and his minions, and ensuring things remained quiet and looked normal. In a matter of hours, over a hundred and twenty of Adita's troops across eleven Offices were in custody and interrogated. Then the agents turned their full attention to Headquarters, which was...more difficult." Zz'r'p paused. "There were a good fifty-some enforcers billeted there, and several agents were hurt, including a recent Alpha Line applicant, Kappa, who was badly wounded when a group of enforcers jumped him at once. His most recent partner, Nun, dispatched the half-dozen enforcers responsible, having to resort to lethal force to do so. Kappa may have brain damage, for they beat him about the head and shoulders rather viciously; the medlab was considering whether a regeneration procedure would rectify it. Also, several agents have been injured; around a dozen in all, I believe. This included several Alpha Line agents, notably Kako of Alpha Eight, and Torino and Adam, the Alpha Twenty-Four team, who were all severely wounded. According to Dr. Whiskey, Kako took a projectile to the gut; Adam had a broken leg and dislocated shoulder, and Torino suffered spinal damage. Worse...Agent Uniform, one of the 'rank-and-file' field agents...was killed outright. He died honorably, saving the life of Alpha Line Agent Golf, who oversaw the operation."

"Shit," Echo grumbled. "Damn, damn, damn."

"Dammit t' HELL an' back!" Romeo vented loudly from the gallery, but no one complained this time, not even India.

"Echo, do you need Romeo and me to go back?" India wondered. "I can at least help see to our injured." She shook her head. "With Zarnix and Zebra out of pocket, the medlab is probably short-staffed..."

"I've already checked on that, India," Fox noted, before

Echo could respond. "Given most of the violence occurred at Headquarters, Whiskey was able to call in assistance from the Atlanta and Chicago Offices, and had the wisdom to do so in advance. He specifically said to tell you they're good." He turned to Echo. "Still, the Alpha Line chief can send you back if he so wishes."

Echo considered for a moment, studying Omega, Fox, and India. Omega abruptly shook her head, apparently having picked up on Echo's train of thought in some fashion.

"Nuh-uh. I'm okay, Ace," she told him. "If you think they need to head back, send 'em."

"That's not your call, baby," he told her, then turned. "India? What's your prognosis on Omega?"

"Meg, honey, come here a sec." India stood and eased over to the railing at the front of the gallery, extracting her med-scanner. Omega moved to stand in front of the medic, who promptly scanned her from head to toe, intently studying the readout. Then India looked up at Echo.

"She's still recovering, and she needs to take it easy and rest as much as she can, to allow everything to heal properly," India diagnosed. "But she's doing well, and that hyped metabolism of hers is clearing things up right along. Do NOT let her overdo, under any circumstances. Feed her good," she admonished, by way of closure.

"Then yes, I want you two on a ship to Headquarters as soon as possible," Echo ordered.

"But you might want to wait until the entire report is finished, Echo, so they know what they're getting into," Fox suggested.

"Good point," Echo agreed. "So don't leave until this whole ball o' shit is finished."

Alpha Two nodded, and Echo turned to Fox and Lady Teela.

"Please forgive the interruption, sir, ma'am," he said, sketching a slight bow. "Alpha Line is fairly tight-knit, and we do our damnedest to take care of our own, AND our other colleagues, regardless of department."

* * *

"And that is admirable," Lady Teela declared, "and after what has already transpired, I would expect no less of you and your people, Agent Echo. Lord Levy, Ambassador Zz'r'p, would you please continue?"

"You're the one who brought the report, Zz'r'p," Fox noted, deferring to the Deltiri.

"Yes, well," Zz'r'p said. "The good thing about it was that essentially all of Headquarters was in on it EXCEPT for Adita and his personnel, and even despite the violence, it was all accomplished very swiftly, away from the Core, and without civilian casualties, or any of the enforcers managing to issue a warning to their leader."

"So Adita did not know what was happening," N'Do realized.

"Precisely," Zz'r'p averred. "And my embassy assisted in 'keeping him in the dark,' as the humans like to say; it is very difficult, but we have our little tricks for...I believe Agent Omega calls it, 'clouding men's minds.'" He offered her a slight smile. "Though it tends to leave us all rather...debilitated, for a time. So it is not without cost, and we had to be very careful that those who were keeping Adita...distracted...were not among those who would be needed for interrogations. So when the rest of Alpha Line gathered and went for Adita—with the Core filled with field agents to back them up, let me add—while Adita blustered and threatened, and did indeed attempt to call for backup, by that time there was no backup to be had. He put up a brief fight at one point after being taken into custody, but he was not in the kind of physical conditioning he seemed to think he was—at least, not with respect to Alpha Line Agents."

"So Ordik and his...henchmen...are in custody," remarked Mrrp Prrow, the Bastian representative on the Ennead.

"They are," Zz'r'p agreed, "but he is not Ordik Adita. Neither is he a Zumbirian, nor from Beta Ophiuchi 7. Or anywhere close, for that matter."

353

"I knew it," Fox grumbled. "He's Uzshei, isn't he?"

"Yes," Zz'r'p confirmed, as every member of the Ennead looked blank. "He and all his entourage were either Uzshei or Ka'agand. Using the same type of disguise the Division Five investigators found among Lord Entiyti's assassins, according to the reports I had from colleagues involved in that investigation. But the false Adita was evidently the leader. His real name is Humn Aggum. As it turns out, even though I 'read' him initially upon arrival and at Echo's request, it took more than a cursory telepathic scan to ascertain he was not Zumbirian, let alone that he was lying. He had what fiction writers sometimes call a 'neural trap'—his brain itself had been compartmentalized and the information that he was a sleeper agent carefully hidden. Extracting the information from him was dangerous and exacting."

"Ooo," Omega murmured. "Interesting. And damn sneaky."

"Yes," Zz'r'p agreed. "I do not yet know if neural traps are innate to the Uzshei or not, though I suspect not, based on the shock troops taken into custody...all one hundred seventy-eight of which proved to be Uzshei, Ka'agand, or a hybrid of the two, as well."

"Please excuse my interruption, Ambassador, but...what in the name of the Abyss is an Uzshei?" Lady Teela wanted to know. "Surely not the mythological race of multi-limbed beings! And Ka'agand? What are they?"

"They're two of the more common races from the Andromeda Galaxy, Teela," Fox explained. "And believe me, they aren't mythological! Most of the species there are very different from anything we know in our galaxy, or even in the satellite galaxies. Many have strong resemblances to various mollusks found on Earth, notably gastropods—squid, cuttlefish, octopus, and such."

"And you know this, how?" Ari N'Do wondered.

"Because back when I worked with Pulgey-er, Lord Entiyti," Fox said, "somewhere around, oh, forty Earth years ago, we encountered a scouting party from the Andromeda, and the small craft was fairly swarming with them both. The closest any of the peoples of our own galaxy would be to them might be the Lambda Andromedans—that's what we humans call them, in reference to our constellation designation of their system's star; you'd know them as...mm, ah, Alaygoons. It's only coincidence that the Andromeda Galaxy happens to lie in that same constellation, as viewed from Earth."

"Ah," N'Do commented. "I was about to ask."

"Although, now that I think about it, maybe not so much coincidence. As it happened," Fox continued, "the communications officer aboard Pul's flagship was Lambda Androme-uh, Alaygoon, and we discussed it with her a bit. See, there seems to be a slight etymological relationship between the Alaygoon and Uzshei languages, and Beebop thought that, based on the legends and myth of her people, they might once have been a colony founded by an explorational team from the Andromeda Galaxy. Except it's been so long since that colony would have been founded that they began to evolve differently, adapting to their different environment, and now they're not the same. But the various colonizing parties from that ancient time may be the origins of the galactic myths-that-aren't."

"Why was the scouting party even here? Why did not the Premier approach us back then?" N'Do asked again.

"For one, they were here as the prelude to an attempted invasion," Fox said, grim, "and fought harder than a pack of angry Cortians when we ran across 'em. They didn't want any witnesses left of their incursions...which sounds vaguely familiar, with respect to what went on during the assassination attempt at Emdali. Two, the round trip from where we found them to the Andromeda Galaxy is not short. And three, they neither gave nor asked for quarter...so we gave them none, either." Fox raised an eyebrow. "None of them survived to go home. Had they tried diplomacy, Pul and I were willing to meet them halfway. They didn't."

"Neither did the shock troops at Headquarters," Zz'r'p added. "Agent Nun—who has a military background—noted they acted like seasoned soldiers, rather than simple henchmen."

"I'm not surprised," Fox averred.

Everyone else in the chamber sat in stunned silence.

"So...they already planned to attack us?" Prrow asked.

"They did at that time," Fox said with a shrug. "Or at least, that group did. I can't speak to the Premier's actual motives."

"I can," Omega spoke up. "Now that Zz'r'p helped me sort it all out, I can tell you several things. One, Hsrs wasn't Premier forty years ago; he's too young—he's a little older than Echo, generally, and his particular species should have a lifespan comparable to a human, if I'm understanding certain stuff correctly. Yes, I think he'd have been alive then, but just a small child—his FATHER would have been the Premier. Now, his father might have authorized it; I dunno. But given Hsrs' memories of his father, I'm inclined to doubt it. Two, Hsrs didn't want to invade to begin with; it was some of his advisors who were pushing for that. He was actually pretty relieved to establish peaceful diplomatic relations; he's generally an easygoing guy. Not a playboy by any means, though—he's got strategic smarts. If he WANTED to fight us, he could, and give us a time of it; he just doesn't want to. And three, he doesn't seem to know anything about any of this."

"I would not expect him to," Zz'r'p agreed. "Nor do I believe the current Premier's father would have known of that incursion, Fox—I agree with Omega on that. Because when I personally interrogated this Aggum, I found that setting up shop within the Great Spiral was only the first phase of his plan. He fully intended to take over Division One using whatever means necessary, ensure Lord Entiyti died, instigate unrest in the Coalition at large—taking out as many Ennead members as he could along the way, to ensure a large leadership void—then step into the power vacuum himself. Once that was accomplished, he has henchmen aboard the Premier's flagship who would then assassinate Hsrs Syrsh and declare Aggum the rightful ruler. A double coup."

"With him at the top of no less than two major galactic empires," Lady Teela almost snarled. "He would rule virtually the entire Local Group."

"He would," Fox agreed. "Which is why I sent a classified, priority message to Premier Hsrs as soon as I was notified a bit ago, warning him of the attempt. His response indicated trusted personnel were sweeping his ship for the traitors. He, in turn, asked for an update on Alpha One and -Two—which I will personally remedy shortly. Then he requested and obtained instructions for returning Omega's Suit and gear, and sent a message for Echo."

* * *

"Oh?" Echo said, turning to Fox.

"Yes. It seems the assistance you had in rescuing Omega was somewhat planned," Fox said with a wry grin. "Even as you were instructed to do what the Premier asked, the harem mistress was told to do whatever the lot of you needed to help you resolve the situation. You, Echo, she was able to help readily, though she was concerned that perhaps her orders did not extend to what she actually did. I have been assured, however, that she is not being considered a traitor in helping you, given those pre-existing orders." Fox cast a glance at Omega. "She was not entirely comfortable with what a certain other Agent asked for, but in the circumstances, it was understandable, and she tried hard to ensure matters timed out to...negate the need."

Omega nodded, shooting a self-conscious glance at Echo, who nodded back, tight-lipped.

"I understand," was all he said.

* * *

Abruptly, a recollection hit, and an alarmed Omega leaped back to her feet.

"Oh shit OH SHIT *OH SHIT!*" she exclaimed, horrified. "They're in the harem!"

"What?" Fox, Echo, and Zz'r'p exclaimed at once. "Baby, what's wrong?" Echo added.

"I get it now, guys! There was this concubine in the harem—every time I encountered it, its thoughts were cold, calculating, and treacherous. It did NOT like me, and I sensed, without getting any direct thoughts, that it planned to get me in trouble somehow. And it liked Hsrs even less, and that's how it was going to try to get me in trouble! The assassin is embedded in the harem!"

Fox and Teela exchanged concerned glances. Then she directed several hand gestures at one of her personal guards, who nodded and left the council chamber.

"We will get that information to Hsrs right away," Teela declared.

* * *

"So what will happen to Adita-uh, Aggum?" a relieved Omega wondered, getting the discussion back on track.

"As far as the Coalition is concerned, he and his co-conspirators will be brought to Aleancë and tried as accused war criminals," Lady Teela decreed. "Then he will be handed over to the Persis Federation to be tried, and assuming we obtain convictions all around, we would then negotiate with the Persis Federation regarding whose punishments are enacted first."

"But if they are convicted—" Fox added.

"Which is probable, given what information my colleagues and I obtained from them," Zz'r'p interjected.

"...Don't expect them to live very long lives, Omega, tekhter," Fox finished. "And Teela? I would swiftly start an investigation here, into the bargain, to ensure there are no more of Aggum's embedded agents. Especially if he intended to take out multiple members of the Ennead. He was here almost a year, and had plenty of time to set up matters."

"Point," Lady Teela agreed. "And we also need to find out whatever became of poor Ordik."

"I do have a few feelers out on that, as well," Fox noted. "Duuniiss?"

"Yes sir?" the young Reptoid stood in the gallery. "You wish me to report?"

"If you would, zun. Members of the Ennead, this is retired

358

Giirrsht, first rank Duuniiss Guurn, eldest son of Admiral Suud Guurn. Duuniiss has been acting as my personal bodyguard and assistant investigator, as it were, while I have been on Aleancë. Please give him your undivided attention."

"Very well, Lord Levy, sir," Duuniiss said. "Esteemed members of the Ennead—upon instruction from Lord Levy, earlier today I contacted some of my...friends...from the military, who are now in various positions in the PGLEIA. Having once been a military intelligence courier, I had...contacts...appropriate to this sort of investigation, and I made use of them for Lord Levy. I passed on to them the information that Unc-uh, Lord Levy had already found, namely that the real Adita had disappeared last year, that not even his personal assistant knew what had happened or where he went, and that when Adita, as presumed, returned, he terminated the assistant's employment, and within months the assistant was found dead on another world under unusual circumstances."

"Cause of death, multiple blunt force traumas," Fox added. "Of a kind consistent with a severe beating with clubs."

"Which sounds very much like what the shock troops used in Headquarters," Zz'r'p observed.

"Oh, dear Creator," Lady Teela murmured, shocked. "I did not know the youngling had been killed."

"I then told my friends that we—Lord Levy and I—had reason to believe the Adita who returned was not the Adita who left, and the matter needed to be handled delicately and urgently, as it might pertain somewhat to the Presidential assassination attempt," Duuniiss continued.

"And?"

"They understood, and undertook to reopen the investigation in a quiet fashion," Duuniiss said. "I have it to understand it was difficult, especially after all this time, but they were able to trace Lord Adita's whereabouts after his presumed disappearance. They subsequently ascertained that he seemed to have truly vanished in the Myarana system. It is a sparsely-populated system, and at that point, they feared they had lost the trail. But they persevered, and eventually found a body on Ahaw, the moon of planet Myara of that system."

"The forensic report? Were they able to identify it?" Fox pressed.

"They did, milord," Duuniiss averred. "I received notification not an hour ago. It was Lord Adita. The REAL Lord Adita."

"Farkakte, geessht, grubdrfrutz, gloob a flop, and abdab," Lady Teela cursed bitterly, revealing a talent for cursing which rivaled Fox...and likely had been learned at his hand, given the Yiddish. "He was a good friend, once upon a time, though we had not been close in some few years."

No one else said anything.

* * *

"I believe I am going to call for a hiatus," Lady Teela finally said, shoulders slumped. "There is much that needs to be done to ensure no one else joins poor Ordik, and it needs to be done as quickly as possible."

"Excellent decision, Teela," Fox murmured. "Would you like for me to fill in Premier Hsrs on matters, or do you wish to do that?"

"Perhaps it would be best if we did it together," she considered. "He has interacted with me, but the warning came from you."

"That's an idea," Fox decided. "You can formally introduce me that way."

"Very good," Teela agreed. "This session is now adjourned. We will resume in four standard time units."

* * *

"Now, be aware, Fox," Teela told her companion in the private consulting room off the Ennead chambers, while she routed the communication to the Persan flagship. "Hsrs sounds a bit...well. He sounds rather like one of those stereotype Asians from the Earth comedy show we watched that time. But it is because his particular species is, or was, amphibious; I haven't been able to ascertain if it's current or past tense yet. At any rate, imagine what his speech would sound like underwater, and it will make sense. And help YOU make sense of what he is saying," she added. "It sort of...bubbles."

"Ah, I get it," Fox said with a nod. "You want to make sure I don't laugh, or react oddly."

"Exactly!" she said with a chuckle. "I still remember that devilish sense of humor of yours! I know you are a consummate diplomat, my dear old Franz, but I thought it would be better if it did not catch you off guard. And I can definitely see where a mating between his species and yours would be...difficult. In looks, at least, he reminds me of your Agent Burbulon Vex."

"Ah. And now a great many things Omega and Echo told me make sense," Fox said, eyebrows shooting up. "Klack has a devilish sense of humor as well; does this Hsrs, also?"

"In his way," Teela considered, "I suppose he does. But it is more...subtle...than Klack's. More like yours, actually, when you are in one of those big diplomatic affairs that has gotten too boring for words."

"Ah yes," Fox said, smirking. "You never have let me forget that one banquet."

"I never shall, so why should you?" Teela shot back. "Honestly, Franz, you and your practical jokes. PEANUT BUTTER. To a DRACONAN." She shook her head. "I watched that tongue and jaw of his work and work, and he turned greener and greener, the longer it went. And that, through his scales! I truly did not think he would make it past the hors d'oeuvres course."

"Oh, that. That was nothing, really; his dentist took care of matters inside fifteen minutes, once he finally got sick enough of it to see the being. You totally missed the really big one, Teela."

"And what was THAT, pray tell?"

"Brussels sprouts. Right before he had to climb into a spacesuit for a diplomatic meeting with the Oord."

"Oh. Dear. Creator," Teela said blankly. "I remember the

dreadful time I had of it after you fed some of that to ME, and I don't even have a Draconan digestive tract. How did he not suffocate in his own fumes...?"

"I have no idea. I'm just glad I wasn't in the suit-up room when he came back," Fox noted, smirk growing wider. "I did hear from the techs that the air inside the visor had a distinctly greenish tinge. And so did Pul's face, for that matter. Considering he has those silver-white scales, that must have been quite a feat. And the techs weren't any happier with me than Pul was, because THEY had to deal with it when they opened the suit. I have no idea how they cleaned inside it."

"They had to CLEAN it?!" Teela gaped. "You mean he...I mean, did...?"

"From what I was told, yes. Accidents do happen, I suppose. I know he had a rather griping bellyache for several days thereafter, so I felt rather badly about it, and didn't try it again. But the communiqué is finally connecting, so I'll hush."

They paused for several moments while Teela desperately tried to regain her decorum, waiting and watching the vid screen flicker.

* * *

"Hello, Hsrs," Lady Teela said when the image of the Persan ruler finally came up on the vid screen, having managed a relative calm by that time. "You've already communicated with him, but I have someone I want to introduce to you. This is Division One Director Fox, sometimes known to the galactic community as Lord Franz Levy, the overseer of Agents Echo, Omega, Romeo, and India. He is a good friend, and a good friend as well to Coalition President Entiyti."

"Herro, Teera. Ah, yes, yes, we have tarked, Fox and I," Hsrs said, bobbing up and down in the Persan approximation of a nod, as his skin turned a warm mustard-yellow in greeting. "I am velly preased to meet you, Dilector Fox. And thank you fo' dat wa'ning earier; my tlusted bodygua'ds found mo' dan ten of Genelar Aggum's so'diers on my ship, PRUS the concubine in da halem. Dey a' in what I think you wourd carr

362

the blig."

"General?!" Lady Teela exclaimed. "This Aggum who infiltrated our inner council is a Persan military general?"

"Yes, I am aflaid so," Hsrs sighed. "One of the mole ladical of my adviso's, dat one. I had thought he was on a mission to settur some unlest on one of our flontier pranets at home; he has been gone a rong time. And hele I find he has infirtlated you' councir! Kirred one of you' councirors! He put Omega and Echo at lisk! DERIBERATERY! I am most unhappy with him."

"But you yourself are safe?" Lady Teela verified.

"Oh yes, quite safe," Hsrs affirmed. "My chief bodyguald is confident we have arr of the conspilato's. And he has tlipled the guald on me, just to be sule. I am fine."

"Excellent," Fox declared. "I'm glad to know you found them before they could get to you."

"Yes, it is good," Hsrs agreed. "I thank you, velly much. And how is my pletty human fliend Omega, who saved my rife by discoveling de assassin in de halem? And her beroved Echo? Ale dey werr? And the a'ready-mates, India and Lomeo?"

"They're fine, Hsrs," Fox said with a smile. "All of my...'children'...are doing well, or getting there."

"Chirdlen? You sired them?"

"No, no, not literally," Fox said, smile widening. "But I am considerably older than I look, older than a human can normally be and still be as active as I am, thanks to galactic medicine and caring friends. And I've been around some of my agents since they were younglings. And...we grow attached. So..." He shrugged.

"Ah, I undelstand," Hsrs said, nodding. "It is how it is, sometimes, fo' those of us who goveln. Those we ale in chalge of, we come to cale fo'. As you say, we glow attached."

"Indeed. And so they're my children in a sense. And Omega, she has no other family..."

"Yes, she tord me dis. She said the othels and you wele her famiry."

"We are," Fox said with a nod. "Or at least, we try to be. Sometimes we fail each other despite our best efforts, but we try hard."

"As is tlue of arr who rive, yes," Hsrs agreed. "We arr make mistakes, but we rove dem and we tly to do light by dem."

"Yes, we do," Teela said softly, smiling. "Fox, you wanted to tell him about Omega and Echo, I think? At his earlier request?"

"Yes-yes, prease," Hsrs averred. "I undelstand that this rittur pran set up Echo to get into tlouble, but thele was nevel a..." He broke off. "Teera, it was supposed to be tempolaly, yes?"

"Yes, Hsrs, and we played it all the way through," Lady Teela averred. "Echo figured it all out when Omega revealed she discovered one of our people had communicated with you. And then this whole conspiracy and attempted coup came to light, and they and their colleagues, including Fox, here, have proven the saving of us all."

"Oh, dey ale smalt," Hsrs said, flushing a deep rose in pleasure. "I knew Omega was velly interrigent, and that meant Echo rikery was, too, though I had rittur oppoltunity to tark to him. Velly, velly good." Then he sighed, turning an ashy shade with distinct blue undertones. "Prease excuse. I am a rittur envious, I feal. They ale werr-matched, yet fole arr my halem, I have not found my tlue mate. And Omega was appearling to me mentarry. I know she finds me flightening as a potentiar mate, and I do not know that it wourd wolk, even if she wele flee to mally; we ale too diffelent, in too many ways. I would not wish to hult he', and I think I might, wele we to try to mate. And she roves Echo in any event, and he is an honolaburr being; dey berong togethel. And if Yeetoy terrs me collectry, he roves her much, as werr. It wele better not said befo' him, I think, but Yeetoy said he was armost beside himserf, to flee her flom de halem. But Omega was fliendry to me, and she undelstood much. She has a good healt, as does Echo, I think. I would velly much rike to be theil fliend, aftel arr dis."

"I think they would like that, also," Fox said. "In fact,

Omega defended you when one of the Council suggested you might have known about the coup attempt, and I know Echo was worried about the possibility he got Yeetoy into trouble. He holds no ill will toward you and your people, nor does Omega. We have sorted out the mess that happened on our end, and it turns out it was your general who caused all the complications, with his attempt at a double coup. It seems he seized on this attempt by the Ennead to glean information from us while providing a first contact experience for you, and it is a mercy we did not wind up in an altercation of some sort."

"When none of that was ever intended," Lady Teela added. "It was all in how Aggum set it up to play out."

"Yeessss," a grim Hsrs drew out the word, even as his skin grew dark gray and his forehead creased in what looked like a scowl. "I am VELLY dispreased with him. I do not know how it is in you' coarition, but we wirr have a plopel and fail tlial, and if he is convicted of tleason—which seems rikery, based on what Fox sent—as the readel of ou' peopur, I dictate the punishment. And I plomise you, it wirr not be preasant fo' him."

"We too will have a trial," Lady Teela agreed. "It will likely be presided over by a judge or arbiter and a council of beings, who will not only determine guilt or innocence, but will set the punishment. But in our case, he and his allies will be tried as war criminals, since they attempted an invasion and overthrow of the rightful government."

"For which the penalty is death," Fox added. "In general, even the high civilizations in our Coalition have found that rabid creatures must be put down; there is little that can heal or rehabilitate them."

"Yes, that has been ou' expelience as werr," Hsrs agreed. "It is sometimes sad, and arways a waste, but it is what it is. But once dis unpreasantness is behind us, Fox, I shourd rike to tark to you and Arpha One about a curtulal exchange."

"That's fine, Premier—" Fox began.

"Carr me Hsrs, prease," the Persan leader offered. "Rady

Teera does, and Omega does. You shourd, as werr. As shourd Echo. And I do not hea' it enough."

"Thank you, Hsrs; I'm honored," Fox murmured. "I will pass that invitation along to Echo, as well. And we will definitely begin discussing a cultural exchange, perhaps even a diplomatic visit to Earth. But that all might have to wait a little while; Omega is healing from several things, some of which happened not long before your arrival."

"Oh!" Hsrs said, dismayed. "She is irr? Is thele anything my physicians can do to herp?"

"Thank you, but no, our people are on it," Fox said, holding up a hand and trying to soothe. "Part of it is psychological; an old enemy of theirs keeps coming back to haunt them, and put her in a bad way, especially mentally, about a month ago."

"Is she getting counsering?"

"She is," Fox averred. "But it had to be put on hiatus in order to meet with you."

"Aw."

"And the biochip I told you about," Lady Teela added, "appears to have caused a rather severe and unexpected immune system reaction. The chip had to be removed only hours ago, before it caused permanent brain damage."

"Oh NO! Is Omega arr light?"

"A bit headachy yet," Fox observed, "but otherwise healing well, yes. She'll need rest after this, and good, nourishing food, but she really is quite amazing, and I'm sure she will be fine. Echo is taking good care of her, with help from India and Romeo."

"Ah, he' famiry," Hsrs said, turning a soft pink as his lips curved in the Persan equivalent of a smile. "Dat is velly good."

"Yes, it is."

"Werr den, we wirr just have to be patient and wait," Hsrs declared. "I rike her and I wourd rike fo' her to be hearfy, not sick. So whire I wait, thele is much in dis garaxy of you's fo' us to exprore, and with the Councir's pelmission, I wourd rike to do so. And when I letu'n to my own garaxy, pelhaps some of you may come to visit, as werr?"

"I think that would all be very nice," Lady Teela agreed. "I will certainly put it before the Ennead, but I cannot imagine they would take issue with the idea, especially now that the traitor's little conspiracy has been broken."

"Yes, and that is not arr dat wirr be bloken by the time I am thlough," Hsrs grumbled, in his displeasure turning a mottled shade that Fox privately likened to a charcoal briquette...which was already ignited. "I expect we wirr have to take tulns with punishment."

"Probably," Fox noted. "And if capital punishment winds up being the sentence, we'll...flip a coin, or something."

"That wirr wolk," Hsrs agreed with a chuckle.

"Very good, then," Lady Teela said. "In that case, unless either of you have something to add, gentlebeings, we have a few more urgent matters to take care of here..."

"Velly good," Hsrs said. "No, Teera, I am satisfied. I berieve our garactic peopurs wirr be excerrent fliends, when arr is settured."

"I think so, too, Hsrs," Teela said with a smile.

"Likewise," Fox averred. "You'll hear from me about that visit from Alpha One soon, Hsrs."

"Wondelfur!" Hsrs exclaimed. "Hsrs out."

"Ennead chair and adjunct out," Teela said. The viewscreen went dark.

Fox and Teela turned to look at each other.

"Let's go see about infiltrators," they said simultaneously.

* * *

"Don't sweat it, Fox, Lady Teela," Echo said when the pair returned from contacting Premier Hsrs; Duuniiss Guurn stood nearby, having stayed with Lady Teela's own bodyguards while she and Fox were conversing with Hsrs. "We've got this under control. Councilor N'Do contacted their Security people, as well as Chief Gwag Wuxullian..."

"Galactic head of the PGLEIA, eh?" Fox pondered. "That ought to do it."

"It should," Lady Teela agreed.

"He didn't want to listen to Echo, though," Omega murmured, perturbed. "I dunno if he hadn't heard about the not-guilty verdict yet, or what."

"Or what, baby," Echo sighed. "I'm not sure he thought the Ennead's rationale was good enough to excuse my behavior—never mind the morality of the thing. Fox, I'm afraid my Agent Badass reputation is in the toilet and flushing down the sewer fast. Unfortunately, it may be taking Meg's with it."

"Uh-oh," Fox said, frowning. "What happened?"

"Aw, it wasn't any big deal," Echo said with another sigh.

"Was, too," Omega disputed.

"I gotta agree with th' pretty lady," Romeo averred. "Dude didn't EVEN give 'im no respect."

"And I have to agree with Romeo and Meg," India agreed. "Chief Wuxullian would barely give Echo the time of day, and when Meg tried to explain, he snorted and turned away in disgust. Lord N'Do and Ambassador Zz'r'p had to stop him and MAKE him listen."

"No, no, no," a distressed Teela said, putting her hand to her forehead. "This will not do. It was never our intent to destroy the reputation of possibly the most respected Agent in the entire galaxy...AND his partner, who has heretofore been deemed a most worthy ally and associate."

"Well, no offense, Teela, but setting up the man to risk being charged with insubordination wasn't going to do his reputation any favors," Fox pointed out.

"But it was never supposed to reach that point!" Teela exclaimed. "It only went that way because of Adita's— uh, General Aggum's interference!"

"Whoa, th' dude's a general?" Romeo picked up.

"Apparently," Fox confirmed. "He was supposed to have been quelling unrest in a backwater of the Andromeda Galaxy, when in fact he was here, fomenting unrest in ours."

"Well, however it wound up where it is, my reputation appears to be shot," Echo pointed out. "Fox, if you'd like, I can tender my resignation as Alpha Line's chief, and...I guess, as your successor, into the bargain. I don't think it's gonna be good to have someone who isn't trusted by YOUR colleagues running the department, let alone filling in for you when you're out of pocket."

"Aw, Ace," Omega murmured, deeply distressed. "Please don't do that."

"You'll do fine, baby," Echo told her. "I can, I dunno, take a back seat someplace. Maybe be your unofficial advisor or something. We'll talk about it."

"I don't WANT to talk about it!" Omega fretted. "You're a damn good Agent, honey! You're terrific at running the department, and once you got your sea legs, you had things humming at Headquarters, almost as well as Fox could, I think. At least until that damned Adita, or whoever the hell he was, stuck his nose in! Fox, don't let him resign!"

"I'm not resigning from the AGENCY, sweetheart," Echo protested. "Just from the management roles."

"No, you're not," Fox declared. "I'm going to see what we can do about that whole reputation bit."

"And I will help," Teela averred, then dropped her gaze in something like shame. "To be honest, this was my idea, anyway. I...should have just contacted Fox, I suppose. But I did not want to cause problems with Zebra, if she was the jealous type..."

"She's not particularly, but the thought is appreciated, my friend. Well, first things first," Fox said. "Let's get the more time-critical matters dealt with, so we aren't all gunned down before we can act, then we can worry about exonerating Echo. What became of the search for potential additional conspirators?"

"By th' time us four," Romeo indicated Alpha One and Two, "an' Zz'r'p an' Councilor N'Do got done talkin' to th' head o' Security an' Chief Wuxullian, I think we got th' message across. Those two headed out, talkin' ninety ta nothin', coordinatin' a search an' investigation, draggin' poor Zz'r'p along with 'em an' pumpin' him f'r info th' whole way."

"In the first five minutes, they flushed out a probable conspirator, with Zz'r'p's help," India added. "The threat risk for the entire Houses of Council facility has been raised two levels, every councilor now has two bodyguards escorting 'em everywhere, and Lady Teela has had half a dozen personal guards shadowing her ever since you two came back from your conference with Premier Hsrs."

"And you've had Suud's son, plus a couple more that Wuxullian added," Echo told Fox.

"Indeed," Duuniiss murmured from behind. "They were kind enough to introduce themselves. But they are functioning as shadows."

"Which I don't mind, though I'm still pretty damn good in a scrap myself," Fox agreed. "Still, it enables me to concentrate on other things, which is good right now. And now I'm satisfied about THAT matter, let's turn to more personal ones. Teela, we can't let Alpha One's reputation go to hell like this. They're GOOD, and they EARNED that reputation legitimately, both of them."

"I know, Fox," Teela agreed, concerned. "I'm thinking that, perhaps while Security and PGLEIA are routing the last of the coup, you and I should go off and compile a media release about Echo's situation. Maybe with Ari N'Do's assistance; he really is very good with wording such things. That's why we chose him to muddle the original orders...never realizing the fake Adita was going to make them far worse than Ari ever did, or would."

"And that needs to go into our release," Fox realized. "That sounds like a good plan, Teela. Duuniiss, have you heard anything from your father?"

"Yes sir," the young Reptoid said, his scaly face somehow conveying intense unhappiness. "Specifically, he said Zebra wanted you to know that, well..."

"What, zun?" Fox wondered, as the others frowned. "This doesn't sound good."

"It is not," Duuniiss said, shoulders slumping. "Zebra said it took too long to find Doron—which they have yet to do, by the way. Uncle Pu-er, I mean Lord Entiyti's wing stub has already started to heal over, despite their best efforts. It is too late to use the regeneration procedure on him."

"He lost a wing?!" Lady Teela gasped.

"Yes, and it sounds like it will be permanent," Fox said, pained. "They were trying to keep the wound viable for the regeneration procedure Doron taught us, but given that Draconan and Reptoid biochemistry and physiologies are very different from human, Zebra and Zarnix were uncertain how to set it up. They were trying to reach Doron, who has worked on Pul, but..."

"But Dr. Doron was off-planet," Duuniiss continued, "handling a pandemic in the Valestia system..."

"Which, if memory serves, Pulgey recommended him for, just before leaving on his holiday. And so they were not able to reach him before the wound became unviable for the procedure," Teela realized.

"Exactly, meyn khaverte," Fox said with a deep sigh. "My poor, poor friend Pul. I know how much he loved those moments in the air—more so as his life grew too busy to do it much."

"Indeed," Teela said, near tears. "I know, as well."

The small group was silent for long moments, saddened by the news.

Abruptly, Omega's legs buckled under her, and she sat down hard on the floor.

"MEG?!" Echo exclaimed, wheeling and crouching beside his partner and intended mate. "What's wrong, baby? Are you okay?"

India was already kneeling on Omega's other side, her medscanner out, as the others swiftly clustered around, adopting protective postures, even as several guards moved forward to form a perimeter around the group.

"I'm...I'm okay, Ace," Omega said, rubbing the back of

one hand across her eyes. "I'm just...remember how I said I felt like overcooked asparagus? Back when I entered the Council circle?"

"Yeah?"

"Well, that asparagus is fallin' apart in the boiling water now," she decided.

"And that's a good way of putting it," India confirmed, looking up from her medscanner readouts. "We should have sent her back to bed after she was done testifying for the Ennead. She went and overdid it after the surgery, as a result."

"Uh-oh," Echo said, worried. "So we need to get her back to the room and lying down?"

"That would be my strong recommendation," India declared. "I was just about to ask if you were ready for me to head for Earth and see about helping Whiskey, but maybe I need to stay here instead."

"I'll be okay," Omega averred. "I promise I'll be good. I'll go back and rest some. I dunno if I'll lie down, or just sit in the room and make like...I dunno, creamed corn or something."

No one said anything, but everyone stared at her, puzzled and concerned at the apparent non sequitur.

"Aw c'mon, y'all," Omega complained. "Do I gotta explain it? Corn. Vegetable. Vegetate. I'll go back to the room and vegetate, already."

Echo, Fox, and Romeo all snorted loudly; Teela snickered, India rolled her eyes, and Duuniiss let out a hissing laugh.

"I'd still rather you laid down and tried to nap, Meg," India said then. "I can give you something to help you sleep, and stay with you while—"

"No, no," Omega protested. "The department needs you at Headquarters. We got teammates HURT."

"YOU are hurt, baby," Echo pointed out. "Tell you what. India, you get in touch with Whiskey and find out how bad the need really is there; I could see him giving Fox the high sign because of everything that's been going on here, while being hip-deep in aggilators, himself."

"Aggilators?" Romeo repeated.

"He picked that one up from me," Omega volunteered, still sitting quietly while India continued scanning for as much data as she could get. "Swap out the G and the L in 'alligator,' and you get 'aggilator.'"

"Oh," Romeo said, somewhat blank, even as Teela abruptly nodded, as if suddenly comprehending the pun.

"I'll take care of calling Whiskey, Echo," India offered. "If you're right and he's putting on a good face, he's more apt to give me the straight poop than the man who was Acting Director until Adita's Coup. Let's you and me and Romeo get Meg back to her recovery room, and maybe Lady Teela and Fox can work up some sort of media report that'll help exonerate you."

"They need guards, too," Fox suddenly realized. "Alpha One and Two, I mean. As things stand, three of the four are still in the line of succession for the department and the Division."

"We have matters in hand, sir," one of the guards said. "Ambassador Zz'r'p was very explicit that you all needed guarding. We recognize that, as PGLEIA agents, you are all quite capable, yourselves. But you have also been very busy and distracted with everything going on. So we have been providing unobtrusive, clandestine watch."

"Which is probably good, given I'm gonna carry Meg," Echo acknowledged, scooping up his partner and performing a reverse squat to stand up.

"Ace," Omega protested. "I can walk!"

"With the way your legs buckled a second ago? Your foot only just healed up from that nasty slice it took on the Premier's flagship, honey."

"Ooo, that's right," India remembered. "And the first thing I had to do was clean it out so it wouldn't get infected! Meg's healing functions have been operating on overtime for a while, now. We need to get some proper food in her, too; she hasn't eaten since...?" The physician shot a querying glance at the other female Agent.

"Uh," Omega grunted, coming up blank. "Um...maybe

back on Hsrs's ship? And not much, then."

"And that, several days ago, tekhter," Fox chided. "And the stress on you has been high. That won't do. No wonder your knees buckled."

"Her blood sugar level's probably in the third sub-basement," Echo decided.

"I'll see she has a proper meal sent to her recovery room," Teela offered. "For that matter, I'll have a communal meal sent over, because I'd bargain that none of you have eaten as you should. That goes for you, too, Franz; I've known you too long to think otherwise."

Five black-Suited Agents looked anywhere but at Lady Teela. She turned to Suud Guurn's son.

"What about you, young Guurn?"

"I...have managed," Duuniiss averred.

"Not as well as he ought, because he's been keeping up with me," Fox pointed out. "Never mind zipping back and forth between here and Emdali. So he needs to eat, too."

"All right, Fox; you, young Guurn, and I will join your Agents for as long as it takes to eat," Teela determined, pulling out an electronic tablet and typing out a message, "and then you and I...with Guurn and our other guards...will go see about a media release for Echo's reputation." She tapped out a specific sequence. "There. By the time we can get to Omega's recovery room and get her settled, my personal assistants will arrive with a meal for seven, suited to five humans, a Reptoid, and a Korian."

"This will work," Fox decided.

Chapter 14

"Sir? Sir," a tiny voice piped from somewhere near Zz'r'p's feet, as he scanned the area for signs of a Ka'agand or Uzshei mind.

"Mm?" the Deltiri said somewhat absently, then, recognizing the danger, quickly performed a telepathic scan of the area for threats, picking up nothing of concern.

"Down here," the voice piped again, and he felt a tug on the hem of his robes. He looked down.

A little Sluuite stood there, a reddish-purple female, looking up at him and tugging on his robes.

"Well, hello there, little one," he said. "May I help you?"

"I think I can help you," she said. "Could we talk?"

* * *

Soon Zz'r'p had the whole story, and he took Nargiss Nesh in hand—literally—to meet Administrator Wuxullian.

"And he won't be mad at me?" Nesh asked with a quavering voice, as she rode Zz'r'p's shoulder while he strode down the corridor. "I only wanted to feed my babies..."

"I understand, and I think he will, too," Zz'r'p soothed. "In fact, you might be eligible for a reward, for recognizing this being as wanted by the PGLEIA, and reporting it."

"Oh, that would be nice," Nesh said, wistful. "What would be even better would be a safe job, where I could raise my babies in peace. Scavenging all the time...it's SO hard. I'm always hungry, because if I get paid well, most of it has to go home..."

"That might be doable," Zz'r'p agreed, pulling a small snack bar he had secreted in one of his robe's capacious pockets and offering it to the tiny being, who devoured it swiftly. "I will suggest the matter to the Administrator. In fact, I will strongly recommend it. If you could work for him in some capacity and move your family here, would that be good?"

"That would be wonderful!" a delighted Nesh exclaimed.

* * *

"Oh! Franz, come with me," Teela said, as they all headed for Omega's recovery room. "I just thought of something—we need Ari involved with this, but more importantly, we need to line up the appropriate clearance information for that media release, which will take time, so we ought to do that now. Young Guurn, if you would attend, I would be glad of the additional protection around Lord Levy."

"But what about getting Fox and Mr. Guurn fed?" India wondered.

"This will only take a few moments," Lady Teela vouched. "But Fox and I both need to do it. We will be there by the time the food has arrived, or very shortly thereafter."

"She's right," Fox agreed. "There are protocols we have to set up. It won't take long, kinder."

"I am here, and so are the other guards," Duuniiss averred, "just not as visible."

"Not that your guard duty has been especially obvious," Lady Teela pointed out.

"Very true. Let's go, then," Fox said.

* * *

"No, Whiskey said they really were doing all right," India explained, once the three Agents managed to get Omega tucked into bed over her protests. "He did ping Zarnix about something a few days back—I think it was details for getting Orange into a regen bath—but he's got Rglfrz and Psi, and they'd already called in half a dozen guys from the Chicago and Atlanta Offices, like Fox said. So settle down, Meg. I'm not needed back at Headquarters. As a matter of fact, as acting chief of staff, Whiskey ordered me to stay here with you, given everything that's happened. He was kinda worried when I explained you were weak, and your legs gave way."

"But I'm fine," Omega protested. "I swear I am."

"Then explain why your ass hit the floor in the Ennead

chamber," Echo demanded.

"I'm just tired."

"Then you're not fine."

"Yes, I am! India needs to see to people in more serious shape than me!"

"Meg, your head isn't completely healed yet," India pointed out. "The abscess that was forming is still clearing itself. We're really lucky, all things considered, that you haven't stroked out or something bad like that. And despite the prognosis I gave during the Ennead session, you're probably not completely out of danger of that yet; I just didn't wanna scare you. That's why I really want you to rest, and why I'm not comfortable going off and leaving you. To be honest, I thought that's what was happening when your legs buckled."

Echo paled, and Romeo grabbed a chair and shoved it behind him.

"Here, you," he ordered. "Sit."

To everyone's surprise, Echo sat without protest.

"Ace?" Omega said softly, eyes wide. "Are YOU okay, hon?"

Echo said nothing for a long moment; he simply sat and stared at his partner, his expression blank. Finally he roused himself.

"All right. I'm still Alpha Line chief, at least for the time being," he said, "so here's the way things are gonna be until such time as Fox may relieve me of duty. And yes, these are orders, so treat 'em as such. India, you and Romeo are staying here, and you're gonna look after Meg and make sure nothing happens, like that stroke shit you were just talking about. Omega, you're going to stay in that bed and rest until India says it's safe to get out of it."

"What about food?" Omega asked, dismayed. "The food is supposed to get here soon. And once y'all brought it up, I realized I'm HUNGRY."

"I can help you eat," Echo offered. "But I want you in that bed, resting, while you eat. And afterward, India, I want her asleep. No waiting to drop off on her own. Give her something so she sleeps. Not as deep as you had her when I was still in confinement; just a little something to get her to nod off, but she needs it, and I want her to have it."

"All right," India agreed, as Omega huffed. "We can manage that."

A knock came at the door, and Romeo went to check who was there.

"Oh, good timing," he declared. "Th' food's here already." He opened the door.

"What about Fox and Lady Teela?" Omega wondered.

"Right behind the food, tekhter," Fox said, following the servant with the tray, Lady Teela and Duuniiss accompanying. "Verifying the servants are legit. Let's eat."

* * *

Several hours later, everyone was well fed, Omega was sleeping comfortably, and a media release had been composed and sent out, explaining matters and clearing Echo...and by association, Omega. After a quick conclave, Fox and Teela also decided to send the same release to every Office in every Division of the Pan-Galactic Law Enforcement and Immigration Administration, thereby hoping to make the rest of that organization aware of the way Alpha One had been manipulated by gaming the system.

"And I've already gotten some positive feedback from it," Fox noted when once he had rejoined his Agents.

He, Echo, and Alpha Two sat in a corner of the private recovery room—which was a cross between a hospital room and a tiny studio apartment, the latter apparently provided for family of the patient—and chatted in soft tones while a worn-out Omega slept peacefully in the bed nearby, aided by a mild soporific India had given her.

"In fact, the first was Taas, my friend and fellow director who runs Division Five," Fox continued. "He was a bit...disrespectful...toward Alpha One after things went down, according to what Suud said. But he called me at once and apologized, then told me he was forwarding the release to his entire Division. His top agent was especially glad to hear it, I gathered."

"Well, that's something, I guess," Echo decided, still a bit morose.

"Give it time, zun," Fox soothed. "Most of 'em will come around. And those that don't were probably jealous to begin with, and looking for an excuse to bad-mouth you. And that won't change, regardless of what happens."

"Yeah, but how long's it gonna take?" Romeo wondered.

"And what are Meg and I gonna have to put up with in the meantime?" Echo added.

"That, I can't say," Fox admitted. "But I do plan on getting the matter on the agenda for the next Division Directors meeting, so I can make sure they ALL KNOW that I still trust and rely on you and your discretion and integrity. That should help, too."

Just then, a light knock came on the door.

"Come in," Fox called softly.

Duuniiss cracked the door and peeped inside. "Uncle Franz, the Ennead is reconvening. They wanted you all to know, in case you wanted to attend."

"Let me get Meg," Echo noted, rising and heading for the bed. "I'll never hear the end of it if she's not there."

"I'll go get 'er some coffee from th' guard station," Romeo offered.

"And I'll fetch an antigrav wheelchair," India said.

* * *

"So...the whole thing was to find out—what? If we were worth allowing to marry?" a weary Omega asked bitterly from her antigrav chair, when the little matter of what was coming to be called 'Adita's Coup' had been handled and the Ennead reconvened.

"No, Omega," Lady Teela said gently. "You are each beings of great worth, regardless of recent events and what you believe, child. Given your personal history as discreetly explained by Fox, the brief public interaction between yourself

379

and Ambassador Zz'r'p told us much of your mindset, without his having to actually SAY anything, at least to us. You are a... unique...individual, yes; that may cause you disquiet, but so is your partner unique; so are each of your friends. And you are, indeed, worthy of love and happiness, child. I have lived many hundreds of your years, and have much experience, so please listen to what I say, and consider it."

"Then what th' hell was it all about?" Romeo asked, puzzled.

"It was to understand the relationships," Lady Teela explained with a sigh. "Please forgive us. We are not familiar with mating customs on your planet; we have never had to be. We needed to understand what you are requesting, and how this differs from working partnerships, cross-gender or not—of which you are already excellent examples."

"Why didn't you just ask?" Echo wondered.

"We did, and your diplomatic lead—who is, by protocol, designated as the recipient of such inquiries—attempted to explain, but," Lady Teela sighed again, "it seems Sugar is, as he put it, 'married to his job,' and was...not much help, I am afraid."

"And the very notion of 'married to the job' was confusing to us at first," N'Do added. "We wondered if THAT factored into what you were asking, at least for a time."

"Oh," Omega murmured, comprehending. "Yeah, Sugar is a nice guy, but he IS kind of a workaholic."

"True," Echo agreed. "Not that we aren't; we just have a different situation than what he's got. The Diplomacy department doesn't use a partner system. They tend not to get as close to people...and for good reason, I guess. You start to wonder, when you're all negotiators, who's giving you the straight shit, and who only wants something."

"Yes, you do," Fox averred. "Which is one reason why I accepted the Directorship, instead of remaining as head of Diplomacy."

"Yeah, man," Romeo concurred. "Alla that."

"I believe we can grasp that," Teela decided, thoughtful.

"Indeed," N'Do agreed.

"Do you understand now?" Fox asked. "Our request, I mean."

"In part," N'Do replied. "Agent Omega's explanation to the Premier was most useful, particularly with its religious overtones—and he was careful to pass it to us, in detail and entirety, via all of that 'surveillance equipment' Agent Echo mentioned earlier. And we do know there are other beliefs on Earth to consider, in addition to those she explained to Hsrs, as well as those with NO beliefs. We think we now understand sufficiently to at least begin drafting a proposed amendment. But there will be questions, even so."

"We'll do our best to answer them, sir," Echo replied, glancing at Omega, who nodded agreement. "How about it, guys?" He turned to Alpha Two. "Y'all think, between the lot of us, we can help 'em set up a proper marriage amendment, with enough flexibility for everybody?"

"Absolutely," India agreed. "I don't think it'll be that hard."

"You know it, m' man!" Romeo responded enthusiastically. "An' what India said, too."

"Add Zebra and myself into that tag team," Fox noted. "Anything to help speed matters along."

"Very well," Lady Teela said, pleased. "Ari, you will draft the amendment, placing it at the top of your priority list. And you will make it a little more....'user-friendly' than the last such document that came from your pen." Teela fairly smirked, and everyone smiled. "Human Agents, expect to hear from him as he requires your assistance. And, Alpha One and Two, when you send out your wedding invitations, do not forget the Ennead or the Premier of the Persis Federation. This Ennead session is—at long last—dismissed."

And as the councilors filed out, two black-Suited couples sighed and slipped arms about each other in relief and expectation.

"Let's go home, guys, and see about helping to mop up,"

Echo declared.

* * *

In the end, it was another day or so before they left for Earth, to allow Omega to rest and recover. But in short order and with the combined forces of Council Security and PGLEIA, Aleancë was cleared of conspirators, much to the relief of the Ennead. Zz'r'p contacted the Deltiri delegation to the Council and got them heavily involved in the sweep, which helped the PGLEIA agents considerably; once they knew what to look for, the Deltiri readily identified the unique configuration of Uzshei and Ka'agand brains.

"...And it seems they were preparing to set another bomb, in the Ennead chamber this time, to wipe out the entire Ennead, not just Lady Teela," Administrator Wuxullian informed Fox and the rest of his party, as they walked together toward the special spaceport used by the Ennead and their guests, to return home. "Fortunately, they had not done so yet—I don't think they anticipated matters with Echo happening so soon, or taking so long—and not only were the Deltiri able to identify the bomb-maker in their group immediately, they pulled out the location of his equipment. That little concern has been neutralized."

"Excellent," Fox determined. "Sir, if you would be so kind as to keep me informed on the entire matter as you progress, I would appreciate it."

"I can see why," Wuxullian admitted, nodding in a friendly fashion at Echo. "I'll send Ambassador Zz'r'p on a priority transport right behind you, but we had a long conversation, which I'd like to continue, before he goes. Aside from the fact that I now have a most excellent little office assistant courtesy of that Deltiri, I understand some other things MUCH better now." He held out a hand to Echo. "My apologies, Agent Echo, for misunderstanding your circumstances earlier. Truthfully, I have long admired you, and came to admire your partner as well, and was bitterly disappointed in the reports I had most recently heard. I have the full story now, and you both hold my respect...and continued admiration. You did well, both of you. I'll do my part to help you recover your reputation, as Teela informed me."

"Thank you, sir," Echo said, shaking his hand; Omega shook it in turn. "That means a lot."

"It sure does," Omega agreed.

"You have confinement cells prepared for General Aggum and his forces?" Fox asked. "The last I heard, a prisoner transport caravan had already left Sol system, en route to Aleancë for war crimes trials."

"Yes, and when I leave you, I'll be heading for the maximum-security confinement facility on Armik."

"That's Aleancë's moon, right?" Omega verified.

"Yeah, Meg," Echo confirmed. "A lot like Earth's Moon. No atmosphere, hellish in the sun, hell frozen over in the shade, not someplace you can survive without a shit-ton of resources."

"Which is why it makes an exceptional maximum-security prison," Fox added. "There's a plan on the table to do something similar on the lunar farside, but we have to coordinate it with the drydocks at the L2 point, so we don't put 'em at risk. We've been talking polar farside for the prison, because that minimizes potential—if extremely unlikely—contact with the drydocks."

"Ooo," Omega murmured, thinking. Fox and Wuxullian chuckled at her expression.

"Get on with you, now," Wuxullian said, nodding at the nearby gate. "Go home. I expect there is a good bit to clean up there, too, even if the riff-raff have been collected and thrown out."

"Yes, and I dread it," Fox sighed.

"You have excellent help, here," Wuxullian pointed out, waving at the Agents, "and you need only call me if you need more, or more specialized, help. I have people I use for similar...if SMALLER...situations on other worlds; I would be happy to send them your way."

"I may take you up on that," Fox averred, and they chuckled.

Then the humans boarded the starship as Wuxullian waved farewell.

* * *

By the time Fox, Alpha One, and Alpha Two arrived home at Headquarters, Entiyti was sufficiently out of danger that Dr. Eretigen and Dr. Hissheth declared they could handle matters. And between them, Suud and Dalgaard had managed to get Entiyti's security staffing up to proper standards.

So Captain Prrt ferried Zarnix, Zebra, and Yorker, as well as the Earth security contingent, up to the *Genesis* on the *Exodus* shuttle, and the big dreadnought returned to Sol system, Dog in the pilot's seat and Zero in command. Fox met Zebra in Grand Central Station, and with a sigh, they embraced.

Yorker and Zarnix stood nearby, gazing elsewhere, allowing the couple a moment of privacy for their reunion. Then everyone was all business once more.

* * *

It took a bit of doing—and the better part of a Division week—to straighten out everything the fake Adita had deliberately bollixed, and Fox was infuriated by what the being had done to his office, but 'the Boys' pitched in, along with Echo, and soon matters were more organized.

"And less bloody damn militaristic," Fox grumbled, "my office, at least. We finally got all the weird-shit 'trophies' out and gone. The weapons as well as the heads." He shook his head. "The farkakte giissht Persan animal skins—at least, I HOPE they're animals—he has plastered everywhere will take a little longer."

"Well, that's something. And most of our injured agents will be out of the medlab soon," Zebra told them all, over the remains of a delicious familial dinner in the quarters she shared with Fox. The group everyone thought of as 'Omega's family' now sat and chatted over after-dinner drinks at the big dinner table which Fox had acquired specifically for such intimate but larger gatherings—Fox, Zebra, Echo, Omega, Dihl, Romeo, and India. "Though we still have some serious work to do on Kappa and Torino. I only hope we can return 'em to normal eventually." She sighed, and the others sobered.

"How bad?" Echo wondered, and Zebra pursed her lips.

"Torino still has some spinal injury in the lower thoracic region—say T10 through T12. There's no way she can walk until we can get that repaired. Zar and I are looking at the most efficient way to formulate a regen bath for her, and we FINALLY reached Doron! So he's consulting with us on all this mess. Kappa...well, he's conscious and alert, and he understands what's happened, but..." She sighed again and shook her head. "He's got definite impairment of higher-level cognitive function. General loss of coordination to limbs, moderate to severe aphasia, things like that. Think...think severe stroke patient, and you'd be close."

"Damn," Romeo murmured.

"That," Echo agreed. "A lotta that. I mean, I know he gave me an' Meg a hard time, but in a bass-ackwards way, he meant well. He wanted to make sure Alpha Line lived up to its reputation, when you get down to it."

"He just wasn't very respectful about how he went about it," Omega noted. "But I wouldn't have wished THIS on him for anything. 'Cause I've been there, and almost went there again, this go. Only I was fortunate, and everything worked out."

"Thank the good Lord," Echo muttered.

"Amein. For whatever it's worth," Fox noted, "I've decided to postpone separating Kappa and Nun until we have a better idea of Kappa's prognosis. There's more than enough uncertainty about Kappa's future as it is. I thought it might be good if he had Nun as an anchor in his recovery."

"And I think that was an excellent decision, honey," Zebra averred. "Because you never know; if we can get him properly patched up, this might be the wake-up call he needed. Or the injury might...affect his personality, and make him less full of himself, by the time we get him out the other side. There's hundreds of ways it could go."

"I know," Fox said. "Consider it...a wait and see, I suppose."

"Makes sense to me," India decided. "I agree, though, it's a good plan, Fox."

"Yes," Dihl affirmed. "It is always good to have a friendly, supportive face nearby, when one is fighting a serious medical condition." She shot a glance at Omega, and smiled.

"Very much so," Zebra agreed. "But I have to say, Dihl, I thought the medlab did great under Whiskey. You were here for at least part of it, and then came back from the Ranch to help with the mop-up, from what I heard; what did you think?"

"He did excellently well," Dihl affirmed, nodding agreement. "Psi and some of the orderlies are...perhaps not as good, I think. But that is not for me to say."

"It sure is for you to say," Zebra declared. "I had it to understand from Meg that Psi was NOT respectful to you."

"Psi wasn't respectful to much of anybody, except the fake Adita," Omega pointed out ."I guess he's a good enough physician, because I coulda had a bunch of problems just from the insertion of the implant, even had a stroke, they told me... afterward."

"AFTER?!" Zebra exclaimed. "They didn't tell you the serious possible repercussions up front?"

"Nope. I've been thinking about all that, but...I dunno. I mean, I get that Adita threatened him to make him cooperate, but still. I'm not sure if it's just that he doesn't yet understand our system, or if he doesn't take it that seriously, or maybe he's a bad judge of character...or if there's something more broken going on in there."

"There has already been a meeting between myself, Zarnix, Zebra, and Whiskey about the matter," Fox noted. "We are discussing how to handle matters."

"And we're not sure if Psi is going to stay with us or get retired, not yet," Zebra said. "I'm not gonna say any more about it right now, though, because personnel files an' shit."

"Right," Echo agreed.

"Damn straight," Romeo sighed.

"I never had any real interactions with him," India said, "so I'm afraid I have no input, guys."

"As for the orderlies," Echo almost snarled, "I want every damn one of 'em that continued tryin' to take Meg down after I ordered 'em to stop, thrown in Confinement."

"Way ahead of you, zun," Fox said, scowling. "In fact, Whiskey got together in private with Alpha Four before they cleared Headquarters, as it turns out, and had the orderlies who followed 'Adita'" he quirked his fingers in air-quotes, "locked up as a precautionary measure. They didn't want to risk 'em pitching in with the coup."

"I'm wondering, though, how many there were that just didn't understand the situation," Omega pondered.

"We discussed that, too," Fox said. "Don't worry, tekhter. We won't be hasty in our decisions. We'll get everything sorted in the wash. And yes, Echo," he added, "there will be repercussions. And considerable remedial training for those who, as Omega says, didn't understand."

"Good," Echo grumbled.

* * *

Just then, Zebra's cell phone let out a really loud, annoying bleat. Everyone at the table jumped.

"What the hell?!" Echo exclaimed.

"Oh, that's my reminder," Zebra declared.

"Of what, bubeleh?" Fox asked.

"Come on in here, everybody," Zebra said, standing up and heading for the den. "No, no, Meg, India, leave the dishes for the moment. You can help me get 'em later. Right now somebody's waiting for us."

Zebra got everyone settled around the wide-screen television-slash-vidcomm unit that Fox had acquired right after Omega's birthday party, having been impressed with Romeo's setup. Then she picked up a special remote and hit a button, timed off thirty seconds, and hit another.

387

The screen lit, to display a master bedroom on a planet far from Earth. A white-scaled Draconan sat up in the bed, propped on pillows; in a chair beside the bed sat a certain Reptoid. In a corner sat a deactivated medical hoverchair. A certain younger Reptoid stood guard near the door, already clad in the deep-burgundy livery of the Guard of House Entiyti, a uniform Fox knew well.

"Oh my," Dihl whispered, shocked, and silenced.

"Pul! Suud!" Fox exclaimed, and the others murmured in delight. "And young Duuniiss standing guard!"

"Hello, Franz," Suud said with a broad grin, as Duuniiss briefly broke protocol and nodded with a toothy smile. "You look much more at home in your own chair than in Pulgey's big one."

"I feel more at home in mine, too," Fox shot back. "It fits, for one thing. I never claimed to have Pul's stature."

Suud and Entiyti both let out snorts of amusement.

"How are you, Pulgey?" Echo asked. "Looks like you're in your own bedroom, at least."

"I am, Echo, I am," Entiyti said, and offered them a tired smile. "It is good to be out of the hospital section and in my own bed. I am still rather weak yet, and fortunately Suud's spouse does not mind that he is over here a good bit, helping me out. Sigrund is still on sick leave while he gets physical therapy for the regenerated shoulder, then he is taking an extended holiday, so Suud is kindly functioning as my temporary chief bodyguard once more, you see. And young Duuniiss is now officially part of my bodyguard corps and doing excellently. But I am here, and that is more than could be said, were it not for Suud, his friends, Division Five, and the men and women I see before me. And for that, I thank you all."

"You know better than that," Echo noted. "I think everybody just did what they had to do."

"What he said," Fox agreed. "There's no need to thank us, Pul. We had general chaos on our hands. And being who we all are, we could do no less. I'm only thankful we managed to avert a galactic disaster."

"I think that makes all of us, boss-man," Romeo averred. "Man, 'at 'uz some weird shit we all went through."

"Ain't THAT the truth," Omega declared. "I'm really glad we ALL came out of it more or less...intact. Sort of."

"Sort of," Entiyti sighed. "On several levels, eh, Echo?"

"Yeah, Pulgey. Wings and reputations notwithstanding, I suppose," Echo said quietly.

"It's all right, zun," Fox murmured. "I know it hasn't resolved quite as well as we'd hoped so far, but we aren't done yet. Several of us in a position to do so are still working on that. I've been singing your praises to quite a few others at my level and above, and the Ennead is fighting to undo their little gaffe, and what it has caused you."

"I heard about that," Entiyti grumbled. "I had a little chat with Teela and Ari about it, too. What the geessht were they thinking?"

"Don't blame 'em too much, Pul," Fox said. "I had a talk with Teela about it, too, and I strongly suspect the fake Adita influenced that, to then take advantage of it. Besides, they really were pretty confused about Earth's conjugal relations."

"'Though why that would confuse 'em, I have no idea," India complained. "It isn't like there aren't several dozen species out there who are WAY the hell more complicated."

"I don't think it's so much the, um, mechanics an' stuff," Omega said thoughtfully. "Some of us have really deeply held feelings and beliefs, and it's THOSE that get complicated. And since what we're asking has to be able to accommodate those beliefs, they gotta make sure, when the amendment gets made, it does that without tromping on anybody else's toes with respect to THEIR beliefs."

"Well, th' best way ta do that is prob'ly just to make the marriage thing more of a legal deal, then allow for th' legal deal t' get executed by a minister or a priest or rabbi...or whatever," Romeo said. "Includin' maybe th' Director or a department chief, or somethin' like that, f'r those who ain't got a belief system, or whose belief system don't have a deity. Maybe even designate a specific kinda 'legal chaplain' sorta thing."

"Which is what I had been going to suggest, before I nearly got blown to ttthhssiiss asssshh hiiisss geessht," Entiyti said. "At any rate, we ARE all here, if...not quite the way certain of us entered this hiigiissht mess." He sighed.

Omega, watching, bit her lip in sympathy, then tucked her head. Echo eased an arm around her, squeezing gently, offering subtle comfort.

"Ah, I saw that," Entiyti noted then. "I am sorry, Omega. I did not mean to upset you; you have been through enough of late without empathizing with me, dear girl. Zebra told me you would likely feel for me as least as much, if not more, than anyone else among you humans, because of your personal background and love of flying. But it is all right. I seldom have—had—opportunity to fly any more anyway, so I will simply have to get used to it."

"Aw," Omega managed to get out, but didn't dare say more.

Suud leaned over and murmured something to Entiyti.

"Yes, I think that is an excellent idea, old friend," Entiyti agreed. "Omega, you have never been to Emdali, have you?"

"No sir, I haven't."

"Perhaps you and Echo would like to visit sometime soon? Maybe Fox can send you on an errand to Emdali, and you can spend a few days here in my house and 'guard me' while I get some fresh air and sunshine and begin to walk on my own again. It should help that damaged reputation, as well, for people to see that Echo is trusted to guard the galactic president, I would think. And Suud has offered to take you both to one of the less touristy offworlder glide parks," he suggested. "You can learn what it feels like to be a Draconan, with wing devices of your own. They will not work for me, because I am too large, but for humans, they will be delightful."

Omega and Echo exchanged one glance, grinned broadly, then turned to Fox, who threw up his hands.

"All right, all right, let me see what I can come up with,"

the Director agreed. "Pul has a point about it boosting Echo's reputation, so I think it's a plan sometime soon."

"That invitation goes for all of you, if you wish it and can find time," Suud noted. "I see Echo's mother sitting in the corner, being very quiet and looking uncomfortable. You need have no fear, I assure you, madam. I know you have never actually seen us before, but we have seen you and remember you, and we knew a very good boy, now become an excellent man, that you reared."

"Indeed," Entiyti said, with almost his old energy. "I should very much like to meet you, if it would not unduly upset you. I know we are the ones who took your boy from you. But he came back to you a fine man, as Suud said."

"He came back to me an Apache warrior," Dihl averred. "I am very proud of him, never more so than now I know he has done such an honorable thing, despite the consequences. And yes, I think I should like to meet a friendly dragon and his bodyguard, as Omega once explained you to me."

"Then perhaps I can see the lot of you sometime soon?" Entiyti said, hopeful. "I know how schedules are, and I do not expect you all to come at once, though it would be delightful."

"It's going to be a few weeks before you're up for houseguests, Pulgcy," Zebra chastised. "Let us look at things, and get you a little more back to normal, then we'll look at who can go where, when."

"Very well, then," Entiyti declared, cheerful. "But when this is all behind us, I want to have a big family gathering here at the house! I want my brothers Franz and Suud, and Suud's family, and all of Franz' family sitting there, and Lydhuu! We will have a huge...what is the word, Franz?"

"I think family reunion is the term you want, Pul," Fox decided, "though for some, it'll be the first meeting. And damn, will we need security on it, with the lot of us."

"Reunion!" Entiyti roared, and laughed happily, then choked, coughed, and panted for a bit. "A family reunion! Yes, yes, let us do it, by all means! Something to look forward to!"

"You need to rest now, Pulgey," Suud said, keeping his voice quiet. "You know Dr. Eretigen told you not to overdo this tonight."

"Ah well, time for a nap, I suppose," Entiyti said, still cheerful. "It is so good to see you all again. It is so good to be seen again! Thank you...all of you...for everything."

And the screen went dark.

"I think 'e's got a plan," Romeo declared into the quiet.

"Me too," Omega agreed.

* * *

"...And Agent Echo will be attending the meeting with me next week," Fox noted, as he reported in the division chiefs' meeting a few days later from his office in Headquarters, overlooking the Core. "I want to ensure he gets familiar with that, and has the protocols down, before he needs to do it himself."

"Oh, Fox, surely not," the Xemlon director of Division Eight protested. "You cannot want that untrustworthy agent as your successor! Pick another protégé and have the Ennead approve it."

"No," Fox declared, "I will not. Echo is entirely trustworthy, as you would see if you read the release from Lady Teela."

"Bosssht," the director from Eriki, in Division Two, said with a shrug. "All political claptrap. Face facts, Fox; Echo grew arrogant and presumptuous. He thought he could do as he pleased. We cannot have agents like him running about who disobey direct orders."

"Even when those orders have been subverted?" Fox pointed out. "And the agent in question is intelligent and moral enough to realize it? Would you have had him participate in what amounted to illegal sex-slave trafficking of his own partner and colleagues? Especially to a species so sexually incompatible with humans that intercourse would have been tantamount to internal butchery?"

"Wh-what?" several voices said, dumbfounded.

"Gentlebeings," a patient Fox explained, stifling a sigh, "firstly, the orders presented to Echo were intended to place him in a no-win situation. The Ennead was attempting to determine specific information related to a petition that I and several of my Agents submitted to them recently, regarding an amendment to the Agency charter."

"What kind of amendment?" Division Five Director Taassass Siisshiiss deliberately gave Fox the opening he wanted... as they had planned, prior to the meeting.

"Well, as you know, neither the Agency nor the Coalition are public knowledge on Earth," Fox reminded them. "This means we must remain secretive and cannot therefore have identities outside the Agency. This also means our relationships, when we have any, must also remain within the Agency. Unfortunately, when our charter was set up, no one thought that far ahead, and there is no provision—at all—for anything approximating marriage or espousal between agents. Not even I have that ability. We have designated and defined what we term 'life partnerships,' but many of us, upon finding our mates, have felt it was...insufficient. The petition was supported by quite a few couples in our Agency, but the names at the top of the petition comprise myself and my mate Zebra, who is assistant chief of Medical; Alpha Two, who have been life partners since around the first of the Earth year; and most recently Alpha One, Omega and Echo. Please note the Agents set up by this no-win situation were Alpha One and Two."

"Mm," Siisshiiss hummed, thoughtful.

"Meanwhile, a breakaway faction of a foreign power—notably the Persan Federation of what Earth knows as the Andromeda Galaxy—that was trying to wrest control of BOTH galaxies, had infiltrated the Ennead and took advantage of their fact-finding attempt—and most likely manipulated it, into the bargain. The orders as delivered to Echo—already a deliberate no-win scenario—were thus modified by the infiltrator to be even MORE stringent, and were not the orders the Ennead sent, as verified by Ennead members Teela Krimnet of Kor and Ari N'Do of Celro. More, the person who delivered those orders to Echo was not who he claimed—he was himself the usurper. He was responsible for the cabal that nearly killed En-tiyti, he implanted a sleeper assassin in Lady Teela's security, and had every intention of using the fact-finding 'mission' to set up Echo's partner, Agent Omega, to appear to have killed Persan Premier Hsrs."

"What?! How could Agent Omega have been set up so?" one asked.

"One member of General Aggum's coup attempt was aboard his flagship," Fox continued. "Well, there were more, but one was tasked with killing Hsrs and framing Omega while killing her—a Trachytoid concubine in the harem. Trachytoids are hermaphroditic, one of the molluscal races of the Persan Federation, so the concubine would kill Hsrs, then rape Ome-ga, thus killing her as well. It would then have positioned Hsrs and Omega to appear that HSRS raped her, and she killed him for it, as she herself was dying...or vice versa, that she attacked him, and he overpowered and forced her before dying himself, depending upon who viewed it, and with what perspective."

"Oh, great Maker," someone whispered on the vidcomm, sounding horrified.

"By the gods," another swore. "This is what the orders de-manded?"

"In effect, yes, especially by the time Aggum was finished with matters. And Aggum took full advantage of it. Having already engineered the attack on Pulgey, he usurped the Divi-sion One directorship from Echo and sent him on the 'mission,' knowing both he and I would thereby be off Earth. He then pro-ceeded to counter standing orders and established procedures, not merely on Earth but ACROSS THE DIVISION, resulting in increasing chaos in operations, and failure of rule of law—we have had turmoil here, straightening matters in the aftermath. More, as some of you will be aware, this was already starting to cause problems between Division One and the other divi-sions, which would have fomented unrest—made worse once Pulgey died, and worse still when Lady Teela was likewise murdered. If I correctly understood the report I read from the

Deltiri who located and interrogated the sleeper agents among Teela's guards, another anti-personnel bomb was intended to be used...against the entire Ennead, while in session. It would not have been merely Teela we lost, but The Nine—the entire core of the Council at large."

The vidcomm erupted in a babel of outraged, stunned voices.

"But that would have unsettled the entire Coalition!" Yaacrun Elyryqoli from Ryynqitsk, the Division Seven director, declared.

"Precisely!" Fox said. "That was exactly what he wanted. Then Aggum, in disguise as Ordik Adita, 'the only surviving Ennead member' by dint of being on Earth usurping my office when the Ennead was assassinated en masse, would have stepped in as Coalition leader. Meanwhile, his forces on the Persan flagship would have declared General Aggum in charge, by dint of declaring war on the Coalition for 'sending an agent to kill the Premier,' and the false Adita, really Aggum, would then remotely 'surrender' to himself. Adita would disappear, and General Aggum would declare himself the new ruler of essentially the entire Local Group."

"Argdun," Elyryqoli cursed. "We have had a near escape."

"We have," Fox agreed. "And that, because Agent Echo saw fit to disobey orders he perceived as unjust and immoral."

The vidcomm fell silent, as the various directors pondered that.

"Fox," Siisshiiss declared, "I would like it known that I fully support you, Agents Echo and Omega, and Division One. It sounds like you have a good successor in that Agent."

"I think I have a truly excellent successor in that Agent," Fox averred, "and his partner is apt to follow him as Alpha Line chief, and be just as good. And she survived because he took action."

"I believe perhaps what you just explained to us—which was not in the initial report..." Elyryqoli began.

"Only because we hadn't worked out all the details at that

point," Fox noted. "We were still sussing out all the embedded henchmen, and the full measure of the plot."

"...Perhaps it should be an addendum to that report," Siisshiiss added, for Elyryqoli.

"Exactly," Elyryqoli confirmed.

"I'll get on that as soon as we end our meeting," Fox agreed. "Now, do I hear any more problems regarding my duly approved successor?"

The vidcomm remained silent.

"Excellent. Thank you, gentlebeings, for your understanding and astuteness," Fox murmured. "Might I make one more request?"

"Go ahead, friend Fox," Siisshiiss said softly. "You have served the Coalition valiantly through many octads, most recently by helping us save Lord Entiyti, and in determining this hiigiissht plot, let alone helping identify the ssllitthhssshhtt who tried to kill him. I—we—owe you. What do you need?"

"I think Echo and Omega would appreciate it if you could see fit to inform your personnel of all this, to help clear his name," Fox said. "There have been...some issues...arising from it. I don't expect matters to settle overnight, but I hate to see his excellent and hard-won reputation in the galactic community sullied so. All because a kind of test was nearly turned into an alien conquest."

To Fox's relief, there was a unanimous affirmation.

* * *

"And here she is, back at last," Zz'r'p said, as Omega entered his private office once more. "Are you recovered from your immune system flare?"

"According to Zebra and India, I am," Omega agreed, "though I'm not sure if I'll be able to use the implant y'all developed especially for me, on account o' that. And I'm sorry about it; I think, if you'd trained me how to use it, and it worked the way y'all originally DESIGNED it, it woulda been a good tool. I know Echo liked being able to communicate with me so privately...though you didn't hear that from me."

"No, indeed!" Zz'r'p gave the Deltiri equivalent of a chuckle. "The notion that our very private and reclusive Agent actually LIKES sharing his thoughts directly with his beloved is inconceivable! Nor will any other soul hear it from my mouth or mind."

They laughed.

"Let me add, however," Zz'r'p noted, "that our scientists and engineers are more than ninety-nine percent certain the immune response was induced by the modifications made to the implant. In other words, when the Ennead's technicians deliberately 'broke' it to induce difficulty in your mission, that is what caused your immune system to react, because it was designed to work with your especial bodily system, and when the technicians changed it, it was no longer compatible with your system. We do not believe, once it is reconfigured to its original settings, it will cause you any problems. That said, we do understand if you—or Echo—are reluctant to try again."

"Mm," Omega hummed, considering. "Let me think about it, all right? I might, if you're really that sure...if I can get past the squick factor of having a chip in my brain, that is. 'Cause I'm not lying when I say it really WOULD be useful, in my line of work. Never mind being able to discuss things with Echo, no matter where we were, together or not."

"Especially once he becomes your mate," Zz'r'p agreed. "It has been my experience that spouses need a private means of communication from time to time, and I must admit I have never quite understood how non-telepathic species manage such."

"Wait—but, but I thought you weren't married," Omega said, startled.

"I am not now," Zz'r'p said, voice quiet. "I was, once. My wife's name was Aa'n'a. She died in an occupational accident on Deltir, many years ago. I was not there and did not know anything was wrong, and the shock of sensing her sudden death was..." He drew a long breath. "I think there are not words in your tongue, my young friend. And the dissolution of her nd't'lq, after so long and close a marriage as we had, very nearly incapacitated me. After that, I volunteered for the diplomatic corps, to escape painful memories." He shrugged. "And of course, I have my experience as a counselor, which has sometimes included couples with marital issues, so I have seen this, too. But these are all reasons why I have been able to mentor you as I have, in the matters which I have."

"Aw, Zz'r'p, I'm so sorry," Omega murmured, eyes moist.

"Hush, child," he said, seeing and sensing her emotion. "I know you are relating to me now, placing yourself in my position and Echo in the position of my late wife. Do not torture yourself so needlessly, nor think of matters which may not occur in YOUR life. Yes, it still causes pain when I think of her, even as you still miss your parents, but it also reminds me of the great love we shared. And it was many of your decades ago, and the grief has eased, as such things are wont to do, given enough time."

"Can I ask how old you are?"

"You can, and I would not mind telling you, but I have never reckoned it in your years," Zz'r'p said. "I do know I am considerably older than Fox, though not as old as Teela."

"Fox and Teela used to be an item, didn't they?"

"Yes, they were," Zz'r'p confirmed. "Though I have never told Fox this, so you must not either: Teela is several of your centuries old, but Fox is not even one century old yet, and was much younger when they met. So Teela—she does not even know that I know this—Teela considered Fox, as you or Romeo might put it, 'her boy-toy.' She was very fond of him. Eventually, however, he outgrew being someone's 'boy-toy.' The parting was amicable, as you saw, and they moved into a long, trusting friendship."

Omega stifled a giggle.

"Exactly," Zz'r'p grinned. "And that is why I have never told Fox...though he is astute and may suspect it. Now, on to business! How are you feeling?" He tapped his temple.

"Ashamed," Omega said, hanging her head. "I messed up

again, and I know it. Big time."

"How?"

"I keep assuming that Echo can't possibly love me the way I love him. Because...because of what I am."

"When you know he does."

"Yeah. It's just..." Omega broke off, searching for a way to explain.

"You know you can show me." Zz'r'p tapped his temple again.

"I know, but I sorta think I need to figure out the words for myself, because I don't even really know, really understand it, my own self..."

"I comprehend. Continue, then."

"There's a part of me that's just...it's like I'm waiting for the other shoe to drop," Omega tried. "Have you heard that expression?"

"I have, for there is a similar concept and expression in Deltiri culture. The anxiety-producing suspense of waiting for the upstairs neighbor to remove the second shoe and drop it to the floor, after lying in bed and hearing the first one bang on the ceiling above you."

"Exactly! And, and, when I was aboard the Persan ship an' all that shit went down...I thought it had."

"Has it occurred to you that you are projecting your own feelings onto Echo?"

"Sorta, yeah," Omega admitted. "I can't...I just, just can't wrap my head around what was done to me. Even after all this time."

"Oh please, youngling," Zz'r'p said tolerantly, "there is no 'all this time'—it has only been around an Earth year since you found out what was done to you. A little bit more, as I recollect. But it is still so new that the ramifications and effects are continuing to crop up. This is one reason why you are struggling; you have not had time to establish an equilibrium for everything being thrown at you."

"So...that's not...not long enough? Am I expecting too

much?"

"A great deal too much, I should say. Give yourself time; cut yourself some slack, as you and Echo might say. I have several things I want us to do today, and they are all related to this."

"Okay, shoot."

"First of all, I want you to start focusing on seeing Echo's reactions to things without imposing your own personal filters on his reactions. That is to say, I want you to see what he is actually doing, what he is saying, what he truly feels and thinks, without relating it to your own reactions to yourself. It will mean you will need to slow down in YOUR responses and pay closer attention, but as much as you love him, this should not be a hardship."

"Nah, I can watch him all day," Omega said with a grin. "Yeah, I started realizing on this mission that I was doing that really bad. Or at least, once we got to Aleancë, I could. I kinda had to get out of the clamor of the Persan ship, first."

"Yes, I can see that...both conceptually, and in your mind, your recollections. If it helps, you should know that were I in that situation, and if my innate telepathy had been altered as your implant was, I should have had very similar difficulties."

"REALLY?!" Omega practically shouted. "OH, that makes me feel SO much better!"

"Good. Now, do you think you can do as I ask?"

"Yeah, I think I can, though it might haveta sorta...grow, if you get me. It'll take a while to get the hang of it."

"Yes, and that is fine; I would expect it to. Now, the second thing I would like you to do, is to begin to face your fears in this respect. You love Echo and you fear losing him, as you lost your parents, as you fear losing the adoptive family you have constructed here. And that is understandable, but you must overcome that fear to have a happy life, else it will haunt you, make you miserable. And in the end, could drive the others away, becoming a self-fulfilling prophecy that did not have to be. And the beginning of overcoming it is facing it."

"But...how do I do that?"

"I have always found that to face a fear, I must first confront the possibility inherent in the fear, face-on. What is the worst possible thing that could happen in your relationship with Echo?"

"He'd find me disgusting, and walk away," Omega said immediately, in a low voice.

"Very good. You have already recognized it and can consciously verbalize and define it. Now let us analyze the matter calmly and logically. Echo observed you when your programming initiated, did he not?"

"Yes."

"How did he react at the time?"

"Mm. Surprised."

"Fearful? Disgusted?"

"...No."

"Was he not waiting for you when you emerged from the room where I deprogrammed you?"

"Yeah..."

"And how did he react? What did he say to you?"

"The first words out of his mouth were, 'Are you okay, baby?'" Omega told Zz'r'p.

"Concern for you."

"Yes."

"Fear? Disgust? Distrust?"

"...No."

"What about when you decided to leave the Agency shortly thereafter, on what everyone now calls your 'sabbatical'? How did he feel?"

"He did about everything he could think of, to keep me from going," Omega said, chewing her lower lip in thought. "He wasn't happy about it at all."

"No, he was not, and Fox asked me to verify he was all right and ready to resume duty, though you did not hear that, and Echo does not know I did so," Zz'r'p said. "Are you aware he kept track of you the entire time you were gone?"

"What?!" Omega exclaimed, startled. "But...didn't he know I wouldn't betray...?"

"Of course he did. That is not why he kept track of you, and Fox did not order him, and may not have even known he was doing it. He did it, Omega, because he cared. You deliberately cut yourself loose from the last living ties you had; you were alone, by choice. He was worried about you, and wanted to make sure that, if you needed a friend, one would be there for you within moments. HE would be there. That is why he was so close when the spacecraft crashed in Nevada."

* * *

A sudden lump filled Omega's throat. She tried to swallow, but could not. The tears which had begun threatening a few moments before chose that instant to overflow.

"A-and he st-stuck with me like, like glue, through the whole, whole mess with Wright," she whispered, hiccupping through her tears. "D-doing whatev-ever it took to get me through it."

"Yes. And was he disgusted with you?"

"N-no. Mad at Slug, hell yeah. But not me. Hurt, 'cause I was struggling, and, and afraid I'd embarrass myself AND him, so I kept him a-at a distance a li'l bit, but...but then he went and, and talked to India an' Bet...so he could UNDER-STAND!"

"I am not surprised." Zz'r'p nodded. "Have you told him the last of it?"

"You mean the, the animal DNA?" she clarified. "An' the, the degradation at-attempt?"

"Yes."

"With help from Fox, yeah." She nodded.

"And?"

"He was GOOD WITH IT!" Omega said, choking and crying. Zz'r'p reached behind his chair and produced a box of tissues, setting it gently in Omega's lap. She promptly grabbed a wad and mopped her face. "He...it didn't matter, he said. He loved me anyway. He was willing t-to work with wh-whatever comes, just to b-be beside me.”

“So tell me, my dear child, why would you ever think he would desert you? Find you disgusting? He is willing to stick by you ‘through hell or high water,’ as he says. And he has, and is.” He smiled. “Now, sit there and let it all out, for you have been keeping far too much pent up for far too long.”

Omega buried her face in a double handful of tissues and wept in sheer relief, even greater than what she had felt when Fox had revealed her secret for her.

* * *

“There now. Are you better?” Zz’r’p asked, having patiently sat for a quarter-hour while Omega vented.

“I...I think so.” She mopped her face again with fresh tissues, discarding the soggy ones in the waste can Zz’r’p held for her. “I’m gonna be all stuffy, but India has some things that’ll fix it.”

“Good. Then we have one last thing to consider today, and I want you to wait three days before coming back, to allow your conscious and subconscious to process all this,” he said.

“Hokay. Fire when ready.”

He reached over to his desk and produced a hand mirror, hidden under several psychological journals. “Here,” he said, handing it to her. “Look at yourself. Ignore the signs of tears, and truly look at yourself. And let me read what you see.”

Omega studied her image in the mirror, trying to get past the red nose and bloodshot eyes, truly seeing her own features for the first time in more than a year: the pale blonde hair, the high forehead; vivid blue eyes—seeming a brighter blue because they were bloodshot; wide cheekbones, pert nose; full, almost sensual lips...and then she remembered what had been done to her, and wondered how much of the attractive woman in the mirror was original, and how much was ‘tinkered.’

Nonsense, came the mental response from her counselor. *Did you know Echo, India, and Romeo found one of your family albums at your farmhouse? And they decided you looked so much like your mother did at your age that it was amazing? Or that you had your father's smile?*

I do? she wondered. *I mean, I remember them saying I looked like Mom, but...that much?*

Yes you do, and they all saw it. They thought it was delightful, seeing your parents in you.

She smiled, remembering the 'family chat' on the back porch at sunset.

THERE, Zz'r'p said. *Look in the mirror. Right now.*

Omega obeyed the mental command without thinking about it, and saw a mature young woman with a soft, warm gaze, a relaxed face, and a happy, gentle smile. Twin sparks of intellect and memory lit her eyes, and the overall expression was one of love, joy, and quiet contentment.

You see it, Zz'r'p noted. *You see the true you, shining out. Not an animal. Not a beast. Not a monster or a killing machine. A woman in love, who loves her family dearly. THAT is who you are, Omega, not what you fear you are.*

She lifted her gaze to meet the Deltiri's, and saw the smile on his face, even as she remembered something Echo had said in the moments after Fox had revealed her deepest secret.

I'm a who, not a what, she thought back at him.

YES! PRECISELY! Zz'r'p mentally exclaimed, delighted. *That is what we have all been trying to tell you! Echo, perhaps, most of all.*

Omega nodded, dropping her gaze to the carpet, then redirecting it at the mirror. "I'm a who, not a what," she reiterated aloud to her own image reflected at her.

"And that shall be your mantra for the time," Zz'r'p averred. "Each day that you can—I understand if a mission does not allow for it—I want you to look into a mirror at least once and repeat the exercise we just did. Then I want you to tell yourself, 'I'm a who, not a what.' Can you do that?"

Omega met his eyes again, still ruminating over what just happened. Finally she replied.

"Yeah, Zz'r'p. Yeah, I think I can."

* * *

"Cheerio, Omega, old girl," Madrid said, standing to meet her as she entered his office. "How are you after...everything?"

"Decent, considering," Omega decided, as they gave each other friendly hugs. "That whole mess with the fake Adita, and the apparent confusion on the Persan ship, then Echo getting arrested, seeing him in force cuffs...damn. I coulda done without alla that."

"Which makes me think, congratulations on your engagement! The two of you make a bloody brilliant couple. But I expect you ARE glad to see the back of that shambles." He waved her at the visitor chair, then sat back down behind his desk. "I gather you're here on semi-official business, to judge by your actually scheduling an appointment to meet with me. What do you need, mate?"

"Well, it's not so much what I need, as what a friend needs," Omega said thoughtfully. "And while I have a few ideas, you're a lot better with the overall design and execution, because it's what you DO."

"It better not be another bloody emergency personal force field," Madrid muttered darkly.

"No, no," Omega laughed. "Nothing so serious as all that. No, but you'll know about the assassination attempt on Pulgey Entiyti."

"Oh, of course."

"Did you know he lost a wing, as a result?"

"I...didn't know he HAD wings," Madrid said blankly. "I've not had occasion to meet him personally. I'm afraid I was out of pocket when he came through with Fox last spring."

"He's basically a bipedal dragon, except he doesn't breathe fire," Omega said with a fond smile. "Well, metaphorically, I guess, if you get him mad! But no, one of the wings got pretty much shredded in the bomb blast, and I gather the docs had to amputate it, else it could have gone nasty septic and killed him anyway. And they were FUNCTIONAL wings."

"Ah. I think I see where this is going," Madrid said, a spark of interest lighting his eyes as he grinned slightly. "Yes, you and I could probably gin up a pretty damn decent mechanical prosthesis with electronic controls, and maybe even tie it into his nervous system, if I can get some specs on the original wing. For starters, bird or bat?"

"Bat," Omega determined, fetching an electronic tablet from a warp pocket. "And I delicately picked Fox's brain by way of getting him to reminisce a bit and by being my general curious self, so I have length, width, and a couple digital images. Heck, Fox even had a video of him unfurling his wings and taking a short flight, from back in the day! So we have motion, overall structure, the whole bit."

Omega opened the pertinent files, then handed the tablet to Madrid, and the two of them leaned together over it, pointing and brainstorming.

* * *

Echo and Omega were up on the roof of the Headquarters building, stretched out on a blanket, stargazing. Nearby lay a discarded sketch pad; it lay open to a rough draft of a large, single-bedroom apartment blueprint, complete with furniture arrangements.

"It's beautiful, isn't it?" Omega murmured, staring up into the diamond-spangled blackness.

"Mm-hm," Echo agreed. "Wanna know a secret?"

"Sure. From you? Always." Omega glanced at him with a grin.

"I really like stargazing—as long as it's with my favorite astronomer."

Omega's face lit with happiness at his statement. Then she sobered. *Well, at least that's one thing I know is all mine,* she thought. *I'm trying hard to face my fears like Zz'r'p says I should, but damn. And while we handled the number one fear, and I'm feeling better about that, we haven't got to the number two fear. But this conversation is trampling all over it.*

* * *

Echo saw the expression change.

"Meg," he asked perceptively, "what are you afraid is the

real reason I want to marry you?"

Omega twisted on the blanket to stare at him with wide eyes.

"Meg?"

* * *

Omega averted her face and closed her eyes, unable to vocalize that particular fear despite her best efforts; she could barely stand to think it.

I'm afraid I'm just a substitute for... she began, but couldn't even complete the thought.

* * *

Echo blinked in shock.

Holy shit, he thought in stunned amazement. *Did I just hear what she was thinking through the nd't'lq, or do I simply know her that well?* He decided to test the matter and see. "Meg?"

"Hm?"

"It's Chase, isn't it?"

Omega remained silent.

"If you've been believing you aren't lovable 'cause of the 'tinkering,' and now you know that doesn't matter to me, then the only reason you have left is the notion that you're just a substitute for Chase," Echo hazarded. Omega sat up suddenly, bowing her head.

"Well, Ace," she whispered huskily, "my guess is, the nd't'lq is still working. You even nailed the words."

Bingo, he thought. *I DID hear her.* "So that's it?" Echo sat up, slipping an arm around her; she nodded. "You know it's not so, don't you?"

"I...I think so. But..."

"But you're still not sure."

"I know how you feel." Omega sighed. "Just...not why. I keep trying to tell myself it's because I'm me, but there's a part of my head that thinks I'm only telling myself what I want to hear."

Aw, Echo thought, sympathetic. *I get that feeling. Like, when it sounds like good news, but they don't say it straight out, so then you're left wondering, well is it, or isn't it?*

"Let's try this," Echo suggested after a moment. "Why would I choose you as a substitute? Tell me."

"I don't know," Omega said in a low voice. "Maybe I look kind of like her. Maybe I smile like her. Or move like her. Or...or even kiss like her. Or something. Or maybe I'm just... around."

"Meg, you're nothing like Chase. Chase was a very unusual woman. And so are you. You know what Fox told me yesterday?"

"What?"

"That I was a lucky man." Echo turned his gaze upward.

"Why?" Omega asked.

"Because I'd had two special women in my life." He shrugged. "Even if one of 'em wound up choosing somebody else in the end, I guess. Chase was still special, in her own unique way. And I learned things about myself from being with her, so that was a plus, even if she did go with the other guy. But you know something?"

"What?"

"If the Big Guy Upstairs brought her back and stood her next to you, and asked me to choose? Knowing what I know now? I'd pick you, baby. In a heartbeat. Every time."

"Oh..."

"As for being around...well, isn't that the point of getting married?" Echo proposed.

"What do you mean?" Omega asked, studying the dark, starlit eyes of her partner.

"As a general rule," Echo remarked, straight-faced, "when a man tells a woman he wants to marry her, it's because he wants her to be around him all the time. And vice versa."

"But I am around all the time."

"Well...not quite," Echo said, raising one eyebrow suggestively. "Not...ALL the time."

"Oh."

They fell silent again, gazing upward together, arm in arm.

Then Omega spoke one word.

"Why?"

"Why what?"

"Why did you pick me? Why WOULD you pick me?"

"Why did you pick me?" Echo replied in a Socratic fashion. "You've told me you dated other guys, when you worked for NASA. Okay, maybe you never 'went there' with 'em, never let it get to the point of a true romance, because of the whole fear of intimacy thing Slug's damn torture created. But there WERE other men. Even other Division One agents. Mu, for one. You had other options."

"Yeah, but...they weren't...right," Omega tried to explain. "You and I have the same sense of humor. Pretty much the same likes and dislikes. The same hobbies. We even think alike," she observed. "I just...like being with you, Echo." Omega paused, and Echo watched as she blushed. "I like...looking at you, too," she admitted with a grin.

"What about—" Echo began, with a mischievous twinkle in his eyes.

"That, too," Omega interrupted, grin growing wider. Then she sobered. "The truth is, Echo, I...can't imagine you not being here, beside me, with me." She lightly patted his thigh, half-tentatively, half-possessively. "And I'd rather not try."

"You answered my question, and your own, too," Echo said softly, pulling her against his side and looking out across the city.

"I did?"

"Yep."

"So you picked me because..."

"You're you," Echo said simply. "Not Chase, not an alien, not some 'thing.' You. Meg. MY Meg. And I don't even want to try to imagine you not beside me." He paused, and the corner of his mouth twitched in mischief. "Besides, I think the monograms will be interesting, with one Roman letter and one Greek letter."

"Oh, you—!" Omega exclaimed, twisting around and grappling him to the blanket. Echo fought back good-naturedly, until she had him where he wanted her.

"Come here," he murmured then, pulling her down into his arms. "We need to practice our communication some more."

"Do we get paid for it?" Omega replied impishly, settling into his embrace as she felt his warm breath on her face.

"I'll ask Fox," Echo replied against Omega's lips, "but don't hold your breath..."

Author Notes

My thanks for this little tome you hold goes to beta reader Evelyn Zinn and editor Courtney Galloway, without whose perusal these stories would make a lot less sense, I think. As always, the bangin' cover art is the work of my husband Darrell Osborn. And thanks go to my parents, as well, Steve and Colene Gannaway, for their staunch and loving support, even through their own medical crisis. At this writing, Mom is home again after her two strokes; the cardiac procedure to help prevent a-fib-caused thrown clots from the atrial pocket was a success, and she is now off all medication for same except a low-dose aspirin. She's feeling better, and while she's still undergoing various rehab therapies, we're all delighted with her progress. Many thanks to those of you who sent up prayers for her recovery; I can't tell you how much it meant to all of us.

Additional thanks goes to one James Resoldier (whose real name shall remain anonymous) for his help in working out the military history of Kappa and Nun, early in the story! Also to Robert Bicknell for the idea about certain indigestible foods for Draconans...

And yes, I do know that the proper term for a larval salamander is 'eft,' but most people aren't familiar with that word, so I used one from a different amphibian that more people would be apt to recognize.

This story is a little bit different, I suppose. It's really two stories in one; I've done that in other series before, but not to this degree in *Division One*. There are antecedents to one of the story's plotlines that some of you may recognize, and which Fox certainly would, if he were there for it. I had the idea when observing Purim with some friends...which probably tells you all you need to know about the antecedents, if you're familiar with that holiday. And possibly it adds a certain enlightenment to that particular subplot. Except for the ending, I suppose.

Never mind throwing a Nazi zombie apocalypse into the

mix. When that idea hit, I couldn't resist. And it gave a tie-in to later events, as well as a chance to bring Kappa and Nun into the mix early in the game, ready for end-game events.

I wanted the Persans to be strange, and yet vaguely familiar; something which the Agents could recognize, but to which they could not readily relate. The Persans are, after all, from a completely different galaxy, and according to the most recent astronomical data, the Andromeda Galaxy is roughly the same size and mass as our own Milky Way, which is no slouch of a giant spiral galaxy. AND it's over two and a half million light years away!

Yeah, yeah, I know — serious fudge factors to travel these distances in anything like timeframes useful to an adventure story, even assuming advanced drives. Still and all, I went with an Alcubierre drive for the standard interstellar drive in this universe, and that works by basically being a wave function. And a wave function is not limited by lightspeed; if you can figure out how to generate and propagate it, and supply the energy to maintain it (ah, there's the rub! or half of it, at least, but SCIENCE FICTION!), then there's really no reason you can't travel great distances at stoopid-ridiculous speeds.

The Persis Federation is, like the Coalition, comprised of many races of beings, found throughout the Andromeda Galaxy—I think I 'documented' at least four just in this tome. Unlike the Coalition, it is a monarchic commonwealth, not a representative republic. And so most of the beings in control are variants on Cephalopoda. To that end, I tried to decide what English might sound like, if spoken by an octopus underwater. More, said octopus is not possessed of a beak, but a soft, somewhat unstructured mouth—so the language really isn't at all like Klack's. And since Hsrs hasn't had long to learn English, even with the assistance of a BLT, he tends to accidentally swap around some consonants in his pronunciation. So think of it as a kind of bubbly, underwater pronunciation with a certain amount of dyslexic/dysphonic confusion thrown into the mix.

Anyway, this story has one plotline that is pretty much

pure mystery/political intrigue, and the other one is political intrigue/court intrigue/a touch of romance/I dunno what, but it was interesting to write, especially given the fact there's a symbolic antecedent to one of 'em. I hope you enjoy it.

~Stephanie Osborn
July/August 2018
Huntsville, AL

About the Author

Stephanie Osborn is a former payload flight controller, a veteran of over twenty years of working in the civilian space program, as well as various military space defense programs. She has worked on numerous Space Shuttle flights and the International Space Station, and counts the training of astronauts on her resumé. Of those astronauts she trained, one was Kalpana Chawla, a member of the crew lost in the *Columbia* disaster.

She holds graduate and undergraduate degrees in four sciences: Astronomy, Physics, Chemistry, and Mathematics, and she is "fluent" in several more, including Geology and Anatomy. She obtained her various degrees from Austin Peay State University in Clarksville, TN and Vanderbilt University in Nashville, TN.

Stephanie is currently retired from space work. She now happily "passes it forward," teaching math and science via numerous media including radio, podcasting, and public speaking, as well as working with SIGMA, the science fiction think tank, while writing science fiction mysteries based on her knowledge, experience, and travels.

For more, go to http://www.stephanie-osborn.com/.

Don't miss any of these highly entertaining SF/F books by Stephanie Osborn!

The *Division One* series by Stephanie Osborn:
Alpha and Omega
A Small Medium At Large
A Very UnCONventional Christmas
Tour de Force
Trojan Horse
Texas Rangers
Definition and Alignment
Phantoms
Coming soon:
Head Games
Break, Break, Houston
And more!

* * *

The *Burnout* series by Stephanie Osborn:
The Fetish
Burnout: The mystery of Space Shuttle STS-281
Coming soon:
Escape Velocity

* * *

Sherlock Holmes: Gentleman Aegis series by Stephanie Osborn:
Sherlock Holmes and the Mummy's Curse
Coming soon:
Sherlock Holmes in the Wild Hunt
Sherlock Holmes and the Tournament of Shadows

* * *

The *Displaced Detective* series by Stephanie Osborn
[being re-released by Enigma House Press, an imprint of Hydra Publications]:

The Case of the Displaced Detective: The Arrival
The Case of the Displaced Detective: At Speed
The Case of the Cosmological Killer: The Rendlesham Incident
The Case of the Cosmological Killer: Endings and Beginnings
A Case of Spontaneous Combustion
Fear in the French Quarter
Coming soon:
A Little Matter of Earthquakes
The Adventure of Shining Mountain Lodge
And more!